SECRETS

THE COMPLETE COLLECTION
VOLUMES 1-5

H.M. Ward

www.SexyAwesomeBooks.com

Laree Bailey Press

COPYRIGHT

This book is a work of fiction. Names, characters, places, and incidents are either the product of the author's imagination or are used fictitiously, and any resemblance to actual persons, living or dead, events, or locales is entirely coincidental.

Laree Bailey Press
First Edition: Dec 2013
ISBN: 978-1-63035-009-3

SECRETS

Volume 1

PROLOGUE

Everyone has a secret.
Some people will do anything to protect it.

I'm practically giddy with excitement as that dream is within grasp. I'm sitting across from Sophia Sottero. She's an amazing wedding photographer for the affluent families of New York. In a nutshell, she is everything I want to be, and meeting her in the flesh is so overwhelming I can barely contain myself. I try not to squirm in my seat as her gaze slides over my resume.

Sophia is in her early forties with jet-black hair that is smoothed into a neat chignon at the base of her neck. A slender, black suit showcases her figure perfectly and makes her look regal at the same time. I hold my hands in my lap, trying hard not to fidget. The smile that lines my lips is making my face hurt, but I can't stop. A tiny voice inside my mind squeals with excitement.

Sophia glances up at me, "Tell me, Miss Lamore, why do you want to work at Sottero?"

Beaming, I reply, "Sottero is the most prestigious photography studio in New York City. The style your shooters attain is breathtaking." My hand clutches my racing heart. It's true. And with every fiber of my being I want to learn what she knows. "Everything about your studio makes me want to be a part of it. It's not only the soaring reputation, but also what you do for each and every bride who comes here."

"And what is that?"

"You make them feel like the most beautiful woman alive. For that entire day, each bride knows she's flawless. You don't just give them photographs, Ms. Sottero, you capture their dreams and freeze them in time. It takes heart and skill to do something like that, which is why I would love to have my internship here."

Sophia's gaze lowers to my resume as I'm speaking. When I'm done talking, her dark eyes lift to meet mine, "May I ask where else you applied?"

Normally I would figure out a way to dodge that question, but I want this job so much. I smile calmly and tell the truth, "Couture and Le Femme."

A dark brow lifts when I say Le Femme. She places my papers on her desk and leans forward, "Le Femme? Really? What on earth made you apply there?"

"The University requires a minimum of three interviews, and we are supposed to diversify the positions we are looking at. They think it gives us a better footing post-graduation." I practiced this response before I came. Anyone who finds out that I have an interview at Le Femme won't take me seriously. It's a blight on a pristine resume and an excellent grade point average.

Sophia tilts her head, like that is the most ridiculous thing she's ever heard. She points a perfectly manicured nail on the shiny desktop. "Listen, Anna. Let me do you a favor. I realize the kind of hoops you have to jump through to get your diploma, and the interview at Le Femme is just a waste of time. Cole Stevens is blight on the industry.

His work is trash, and any aspiring young photographer should steer clear of him. I know it's a necessary evil, so I'll tell you how to end the interview quick and easy. Go in there and act confident to the point of cocky. Wear something that you should never wear to an interview and they'll show you the door before you even sit down… Unless?" She lets the question hang in the air.

"Unless what?"

"Unless you want to work for Cole Stevens," Sophia says with distaste, as she leans back in her chair. Although she's trying to hide it, Sophia's become tense since we started talking about Le Femme. I can't tell if she just hates what the studio does, or if it's more personal than that. She watches me for a moment, taking in my reaction.

I visibly shudder when she suggests such a thing. "I have no intention of working for Cole Stevens, Ms. Sottero. That interview is a means to an end. I want the internship here with Sottero. I'll be the best intern you've ever had because I want to be here."

"It's a dream?"

"It's more than a dream," I say leaning forward in my chair. "Sottero is the place where dreams and reality collide. And somehow you figured out how to capture those moments in photographs that are too stunning for words. Forgive me for being blunt, Ms. Sottero, but I admire your work, your studio, and everything you stand for. If I was given the opportunity to learn from you I know it would give me a secure footing in a difficult industry."

We speak for a little longer. I don't fumble anything. Sophia appears to genuinely like me. As she walks me out, the older woman shakes my hand and says, "I think you'll do well here, Miss Lamore. Contact me after your interview with Le Femme and we'll see what we can work out."

A grin spreads across my face. I shake her hand too long and too hard, but I don't care. My dream job is sitting in the palm of my hand. The only thing left to do is finish up with Le Femme to satisfy the University's requirements and then I'll have an internship at Sottero!

CHAPTER 1

Sunlight pours through the slats in the blinds, forming narrow bars of light. I blink once, clearing the sleep from my eyes. Nerves don't slither through my body the way they had yesterday. Today is different. Butterflies don't erupt in my stomach and threaten to fly out my nose. My tongue isn't dry and tangled. There is no frantic pounding in my chest. Not today. A slow grin spreads across my face as I stretch. Today is a means to an end.

After showering quickly, I slap on the outfit I selected the night before. Without glancing in the mirror, I head into the kitchen. The apartment is quiet. It's Saturday and Emma is still asleep. At least I thought she was.

"Anna, what the hell are you wearing?" she asks groggily. My roommate is in the hallway, halfway into the bathroom. She stops and stares at me. A tattered robe clings to her narrow figure. Black hair is frizzed around her face, completely flat on one side. In a few hours, she'll look like a model. It's been like that since we started college. Emma is the hot one, and I'm "the hot girl's friend." Emma blinks several times, like her big blue eyes are broken. "Don't you have an interview?"

I nod, grabbing an apple from the kitchen counter. As I sling my bag over my shoulder, I grab my keys and head toward the door, "All part of the plan."

She doesn't have time to respond before I'm out the front door, which is good because I would have lost my nerve. The entire time I've known Emma she has never let me escape unquestioned. I know she'll pelt me with questions as soon as I get home. It makes sense that she's a mass communication major. When she gets a job as a reporter, I know she'll be good at it. Questioning people is in her DNA, and my outfit was sure to raise questions.

Sophia mentioned that she worked with Cole Stevens at one point and divulged some pet-peeves of his that will promptly end my interview. After the third interview is complete, only then can I get hired. University requirements.

I run down the stairs toward the street. Our apartment is a fourth floor walk-up, standard shoe-box-sized so that no one in their right mind would want to stay any longer than necessary. Emma and I rented it two years ago when we started graduate school.

Breakfast on the go isn't a part of my ideal morning. Actually, getting up at the crack of dawn on a Saturday isn't even sane, but this is the time slot I needed, the one where the interviewer is so tired that she needs to prop her head up with coffee mugs. Besides, who puts business meetings on Saturday morning at 7:00am? That makes this the worst interview time possible.

It's just a formality, Anna, I tell myself. The past week has made me a jittery mess. The internship matters. The placements can mean getting a good job after college, and I need to be the best in my field to get anywhere in this field. Choosing the arts was insane enough, but being a photographer was even crazier. Everyone and their dog own a camera and claim to be awesome. Botching the internships could mean I'll have to be some schlep trying to find work on Craig's List, and I have sworn that won't be me. Photography is art and I'm an artist.

Ambition got me this far. The rest of was guts.

My position with Sottero is cinched. I just have to finish this last task before I can take it. I stare straight ahead as I round the corner and descend underground to the subway. The air smells like burnt pretzels and blows my hair gently. I breathe deeply, relaxed—confident. When I went to my interview with Sophia Sottero, I was a mess. My palms were sweaty and I could barely stand still as the train clunked along the tracks. The same scenario occurred for my interview with Couture. Both are outstanding studios run by women that I admire. I want the internship with Sottero so badly. Couture is my fallback, and Le Femme—I can't imagine the person who wants an internship at Le Femme. Probably some perv-with-a-camera like the infamous owner, Cole Stevens. Now, that isn't totally accurate. The man has to have some talent to shoot high-end lingerie on nearly naked models. One of those barely-there panties costs more than my grocery bill. It isn't my thing, but like I said—three is the magic number and this is my third interview—the one I don't care about.

Glancing around, I notice that the subway is relatively empty, which is normal for New York on a Saturday morning. That's the only bonus to the early interview time—I didn't have to get up at 5:00am. I switch trains a few times and walk up into the sunlight. Structures of glass and steel tower above my head, but I don't look up. New Yorkers never look up.

Checking my watch, I hasten my pace. Although I don't want this job, the University still checks to make sure I apply myself, which means at least showing up on time. I find the building and exit the elevator onto the seventieth floor. A silver plaque hangs on a dark door: LE FEMME STUDIOS.

CHAPTER 2

I push through the door and step into a quiet office. I stop in my tracks. There is no one here. No receptionist. No employees. Turning, I look around the room slowly. Large portraits of Stevens' work line the pale blue walls. All the surfaces—the desk and coffee tables—are pale blue glass. A to-die-for view of the Manhattan skyline fills the windows that line one wall. It's a sight that costs a fortune, a clear status symbol to anyone who walks through the door.

I step further into the room, "Hello?" My voice doesn't really come out. Why am I whispering? "Is anyone here?" I pad across to the window after looking over my shoulder. Convinced I am alone for the moment, I scan the city far below, and rest my fingers against the pane. "This must look amazing at night," I mumble to myself.

"It does." Startled by the male voice, I jump. My heart ratchets up a notch when I see that Cole Stevens is the one standing behind me, looking over my shoulder. He smiles down at me like my reaction was funny. He is older, close to forty, but you'd never think it by looking at him. Everything from his bone structure to his stance screams model. He has the kind of confidence that comes from a lifetime supply of money, and the designer clothes to match. Dark jeans cling to his narrow hips, topped by a white linen shirt that's rolled up to his elbows. The top button is undone. Cole's dark hair has that carefully messy look.

The man is famous, sexy, powerful—he's also everything I detest. He spent the last fifteen years of his life making his name, but he did it on the back of his father's fortune. I pay for college myself. There is a permanent rift between me and people like him, people who have had everything handed to them. That's part of the reason I don't want to work for Le Femme. Aspirations of being a wedding photographer for the affluent have been running through my veins for years. The idea of capturing a woman on the most important day of her life appeals to me much more than this fettishography kind of stuff that Cole shoots.

Cole's hands are in his pockets, his blue eyes assessing me and my outfit. He seems like he's been up for hours. He must be a morning person. That would make working with him even worse. People who thrive at 5:00am are freaks. Unlike me, dressed to impress.

Pressing my lips together, I peel my hand off my blouse and act like I was just brushing off a speck of lint. Confused, I look past him. I thought his assistant was doing the interviews. People like Cole don't bother with college interns. Shaking off the shock of seeing him in the flesh, I introduce myself. "I'm Anna Lamore. I have an internship interview at seven."

He pulls a hand out of his pocket, extending it to me. His shake is confident, his hand warm. "Cole Stevens. No one is here this early since its Saturday."

His smile is kind, and it isn't until now that I really look at his face. There are tiny wrinkles that line the corners of his mouth, like he smiles often. Taking his hand, I shake it and nod. His grip is gentle, but firm. Something about him sets me off kilter. Butterflies erupt in my stomach and I don't know why. When he ends the handshake, Cole glances at me once more and turns away—gesturing for me to follow. I take in the posh offices as we walk down a long hall.

"Welcome to Le Femme," he says. The casual tone of his voice makes me think his head isn't as big as the media says. "As you know we are the world's premiere boudoir studio, predominately shooting lingerie accounts for swank designers. We do everything in-house, from selecting models to make-up and postproduction. Nothing is out-sourced," he stops and holds open a glass door. His hand flicks on the lights and we sit at a huge wooden conference table. This room has a much warmer feel than the waiting area at the front. Walking past him, I catch his scent. It's a light clean fragrance. His eyes are on me as I pass, no doubt studying my absurd outfit.

I slide into a seat and lean back, steepling my fingers like I'm plotting to take over the world and smile at him. Cole tells me more about the company he created as I tap my fingertips together, trying to muster the guts to finish doing the things Sophia suggested so I can put this interview to rest quickly.

"The internship is a prestigious position, Miss Lamore. Many students compete to get it, and there is only one position. An internship here gives you access to employment with the company when you're done. Correct me if I'm wrong, but you're at the top of your class."

His fingers tap the top of the table as he stops speaking. Cole's gaze slides over my face, the slouch of my shoulders, and then drifts to my jeans that are rolled up to my knees, showcasing striped rainbow knee-highs. Sparkling yellow Chucks are on my feet. They match the tutu around my waist. His eyebrows creep up his face before he looks back up at me. I'm not certain if he's questioning the data or stating that he can't believe it from the sight of me. I should have been dressed in a suit. If I was brave and wanted this internship, I would have worn some fashionable business attire with a snazzy flare. But I'm dressed like a bedazzled circus clown. I had to make sure I don't have any chance of getting this job, and showing up dressed like this would ensure it even if I did take Sophia's suggestion a little too far.

Smiling, I nod, "Yeah," my fingers tap on the table top, strumming like his. He notices the mirrored movement, and his eyes flick to my hand before returning to my face. "I'm the top in my class." Silence fills the air before Cole finally speaks again. My manners are intentionally horrible. He notices my lack of proper decorum, my utter indifference. It's screaming through my body language even when I'm not speaking.

Cole's gaze narrows. The look he gives me is irritating. It's smug, like he knows what I'm up to. Leaning back in his chair, he folds his arms over his chest. For an old guy, he's pretty chiseled. "Let's cut to the chase, Miss Lamore. I don't normally do the intern interviews. Your resume looks the same as a hundred others. Your work demonstrates potential, but it's nothing phenomenal." He pauses, taking in my reaction.

I'm surprised at his candor, but don't react. I don't want this job, I remind myself. I have nothing to prove to him. I don't care if he thinks I suck. I know better. I know Sophia Sottero was excited when she met me.

I know I want that internship and not this one.

Cole leans forward, "The reason I wanted to meet you, the reason you caught my attention, was because you chose the worst interview time we offer... " He grins at me, and leans back into his chair again. "It implies that you wanted this position very much."

I shrug, folding my arms, mirroring him again, "It was the only slot left." The lie slips easily off my tongue.

"No, it wasn't," he replies, leaning forward, calling me on the lie. There's a gleam in his eye that wasn't there before, like hot curiosity igniting a match-tip. His gaze is intense, and I can't help but squirm when he looks at me like that. "You were the first person to sign up. So tell me something, Anna, if you would—" he looks down at the ring on his index finger and then back up at me, "why did you wake up at the crack of dawn to come to see me? Why do you want to work for Le Femme?"

His words say one thing, but his tone says something else. It's a dare, a challenge almost, to continue with my plan. My pulse is racing. I march ahead with my idea, muttering things that Sophia assured would get me tossed out. Ignoring that gaze of his, I lower my eyes and pick at my nail polish while I speak, "Well, Le Femme has been around for a while. I mean, the company itself was formed nearly two decades ago. I mean, you're not a fly-by-night studio, so that's appealing. But, you're not ridiculously old, either." I flick my nail and a piece of red polish flutters to the carpet. I continue speaking, watching it fall, "It's not like you've never seen a digital camera and insist on using an ancient Brownie or something crazy like that." Immediately, I want to laugh and shirk off the nerves that are spilling down my spine like ice water, but I can't.

"Thanks," he says, smirking at me, his eyes shifting to my fingers as I pick and flick. When the piece of polish lands on the carpet, we look up at the same time. "I'm thirty-eight by the way

I'm not old, he means, *I have a lot I could teach you.*

"Yeah," I clear my throat and lean forward. I'm tactless, crass, and rude. Everything he wouldn't want, yet he is looking at me like there is nothing he wants more. That gleam in his eye tells me that something is off. I redirect, trying to offend him, "Like I said, not that old." I pat his knee like he's a geriatric patient who got lost in the mall parking lot and lean closer, speaking a little too loudly, "I know things are changing fast and that's why interns are good—they're young and can help older people in our industry with shifting trends." I wink at him and lean back in my seat. My heart is pounding in my chest. It's the most brazen thing I've ever said to someone's face. I slammed his age, ability, and company in one breath.

"Really?" his expression is hard to read. Leaning back, he steeples his fingers and taps them one at a time, his eyes never leaving mine. The room fades away and the only thing I can see are his eyes, dark as sapphires, and glinting like he's amused—or pissed—I can't tell which one. Damn it. Why does he hide his reactions so well? It's obvious that I don't belong here, and yet, he's still talking to me.

"Yeah, of course." I shrug and lean back, draping my arm over the back of the chair. In the back of my mind I'm thinking that he should have ended this already and shown me the door, but he prods me to talk. And the more I talk, the more insane I sound. Pretentious brat doesn't even come close to some of the trash coming out of my mouth.

"Coming here would be a risk for me though," I say. "People say you're losing your edge—that it's only a matter of time before Le Femme is replaced by someone else."

"And what do you think?" he taps his index fingers together once and waits for me to answer.

I've been flying by the seat of my pants, making up passive-aggressive insults for over twenty minutes. I decide to give him the shove he needs to show me the door. Glancing at my arm draped over the back of the chair, I pause and then look back up into his face. Maintaining a calm exterior is getting harder and harder. I'm lying, blurting out anything I can think of to get him to dismiss me as some arrogant twit.

Looking him square in the face, I answer, "I think you're already past your prime. I mean, come on. Let's be honest. Your work's been slipping for years." I feel bad saying such a thing. I may not like his subject-matter, but Cole is a good photographer. Saying anything else is a lie, but I need to get him to show me the door and he hasn't.

When I finish, no one speaks. His expression is neutral even as I verbally bitch-slapped his company, and then him personally. It's clear that I think he's a has-been. At least I think it's clear. Cole just stares at me from behind his palms, occasionally tapping his pointer fingers together.

I stare back.

We watch each other in silence for a few moments. When Cole speaks, he's looking at the table. Suddenly he moves and pulls a cell out of his pocket and rests it in front of him. The light stubble on his cheeks is distracting me a little. He is easy on the eyes, even if he is nearly twice my age.

Cole's voice is deep and rich, "You know what I think?" He glances up at me from beneath his brow. He takes his phone and taps it on the table, then continues, "I think that you're trying to blow this interview—that you don't want this job."

CHAPTER 3

I start to say something, but Cole talks over me. Holding up his hand to silence me, he says, “And for the life of me, I can’t understand why. What would make you so incredibly cocky that you would walk in here and tell me to my face that I’m just another old man with a camera?” He’s grinning at me now, like he knows something I don’t. He taps the phone again.

Before I realize I’m doing it, I’m wringing my hands, my gaze lingering on his cell. I have no idea how he figured that out. Arrogant and crazy must look the same in his brain. I didn’t tip my hand. I didn’t blow my cover. At least I don’t think I did, but I’m a big girl. I can admit it when I’m busted.

“I’m sorry,” I say, utterly embarrassed. I can’t look at him. “I didn’t mean to waste your time,” I say softly. I start to stand, but he leans forward, stopping me. I feel the light touch of his hand on my wrist.

"Wait," he says. I look up at him and our eyes lock. My stomach tingles at his touch before he slides his fingers away. There's a slight pause before he leans back, saying, "Tell me where else you applied and why you want to work there more."

"Are you serious?" I blink at him, thinking I've already wasted enough of his time.

He nods, "Yes. If you have no desire to work here, then I'm obviously doing something wrong." He tilts his head back, the corners of his lips seem like they want to pull into a smile, but they don't.

Since I don't see the harm, I sit back down. Hesitantly, I say, "I applied at Sottero, Couture, and here. I thought they'd be better suited to teaching me what I want to pursue. Both are wedding photographers. The University requires diversification during the interview process. This was my third interview." He nods as I speak, his eyes flicking up from the table to my face as he tilts his head and leans back listening to why I didn't chose Le Femme. "Both Sottero and

Couture are self-made. They pulled themselves up by their bootstraps and became two of the best studios in Manhattan and—"

"Both are women," he interrupts. He says it like it's a bad thing.

My brows pinch together. I'm not sure where he's going with this—if he wants to help me or if this is payback for wasting his time. Cole Stevens makes me uneasy. I nod my head slowly, replying, "Exactly. And I think that's an asset."

"Not to you," he says, shaking his head. "You said on your resume that you wanted to be a wedding photographer for the rich," he lifts the paper and looks at it, before looking back up at me, "Was that true or did you lie about everything?"

My cheeks flame and I squirm in my seat. Regret washes over me. I wish I didn't listen to Sophia. I should have come in and said what I usually say and leave. Instead I'm sitting here with my stomaching twisting and doing my best not to wring my fingers and dive under the table. Mortification doesn't look good on me.

I press my lips together and look up at him. At least I try to. I feel foolish for getting caught. My voice is soft and steady, "I didn't lie. My resume is real. My accomplishments are true. I just felt like I'd do better somewhere that was more..."

"More like what you already do. Anna," he pushes away my resume and looks straight at me, "internships are to learn. While you might admire Sophia Sottero, her work is lacking. She's a single medium artist."

"And Couture? You think her studio is substandard, too?" I ask calmly. Those two studios are owned by women in a man's industry. I respect them with every fiber of my being. They made something from nothing. They do exactly what I want to do. And this guy is slamming them. Tension lines my arms and trickles down my spine. People like Cole Stevens have no idea how hard it is to go it alone. Everything was handed to him.

I smile, shaking my head softly, and say what I'm thinking, "How can you be so arrogant? How can you dismiss them so quickly? Their work is beautiful." He starts to answer, but I talk over him, "That is what I want to do—and Couture or Sottero can offer me the training I need to accomplish that dream. I want to show women what they look like on the most important day of their lives. I want them to see how stunning they really are." My face pinches together, "I don't want to learn how to turn them into a wet dream."

He laughs, one short laugh, "You think that's what I do? Make fantasy girls?"

"Yes," I say. I don't know where this streak of confidence is coming from, but he thought he was right and he isn't. He doesn't understand and I want him to. "You don't get what I want to do. Women are more than some fantasy. They have brains, and hearts, and bodies that they never think are good enough. I want to show them they are good enough, just the way they are. I want beauty to be defined by the woman, not society. I want a woman to feel powerful and beautiful when she looks at a shot I've taken. It's art, Mr. Stevens.

"Work like yours blindsides everything I want to do—everything I want to be. It's not about heart with you, it's about seeing how far can you push the line and still be able to shoot your ads to turn a profit." I'm practically breathless when I suddenly stop speaking. My jaw dangles open, and I'm shocked that I've spoken to him like that. Everything that I hold against him came pouring out of my mouth. I sit frozen and pull my jaw shut.

Cole's glaring at me now. His eyes flick to his phone. Before I know what's happening, he flips it on and the screen flares to life. He presses a number and says to me, "This has been a very informative meeting. I had no idea feminists hate me so much," he says playfully.

I smile and say, "Yes, you did." Leaning back into my chair, I fold my arms across my chest. I have no idea what made me say it. I meant to be playful, but it came out wrong, "You just didn't know regular women don't like you, either." For a hideous moment, I can feel a flirtatious smile slip across my lips. Cole stops whatever call he's about to make and stares at me. God, his eyes are so blue.

He blinks once, hard, like he can't believe I just said that. Neither can I. What the hell is wrong with me?

After a moment, he says, "Actually, you're one of the only applicants who spoke frankly with me this week. I may not have conducted their interviews, but I did speak to each of them briefly. It's been a blinding array of endless flattery. Your apparent distaste is refreshing." I smirk at him, but don't reply. I don't trust my mouth anymore. My head is spinning and there is nothing I want more than to get out of there. Cole's eyes drift over me, lowering to my shoulders and quickly sweeping to my shoes before he looks me in the eye and asks, "So, tell me. The clothes—do you usually dress like that? Or was that just for me?"

A lopsided grin spreads across my lips. My voice is soft, and I can't look at him when I say it. In hindsight, listening to Sophia was definitely a mistake.

"No, the deranged clown look was just for you. It'll give you something to talk about for a while..." my voice trails off. Cole doesn't seem amused. I feel bad and stand to leave, holding out my hand. The phone is next to his ear and I can tell he's on hold. "No hard feelings, I hope."

Cole stands, presses the phone to his ear with his shoulder, and takes hold of my hand, "None."

A smile lights up his face. I glance at our hands. He hasn't released me. Something feels strange, surreal, like this moment matters more than any other. His pink lips are parted slightly, and Cole breathes slowly, gazing into my eyes. I pull away, and my hand slips from between his fingers. A shiver runs through my shoulders and into my chest, stealing my breath.

Cole watches me, like he's completely aware of my reaction to his touch. His eyes pin me in place. For that moment, I don't want to move…I don't want to breathe. I don't know what I want, but something is pulling inside of me, demanding that I don't walk away from this man. Cole stands close enough to me that I can feel his breath on my cheek. When I drop his hand, he steps toward me. Every inch of my body reacts.

A voice rings in his ear breaking the moment. Startled by the draw to Cole Stevens, I ignore whatever happened. I don't even want to think about it. Goosebumps cover my skin and I rub my hands over my arms quickly to smooth them down.

Nodding at Cole, I turn and start walking toward the door, taking it as a sign that I've been dismissed and that there are hard feelings. Damn. I didn't want that. As I lift my hand to the knob, I look over my shoulder. Cole doesn't look at me. He doesn't say good-bye. Inwardly, I cringe. This is one of the biggest mistakes I've made. I can feel it and yet I have no idea what kind of impact this one event will have on my life. I twist the knob and pull the door open.

Talking to the person on the phone, Cole says, "Finally. What were you, sleeping? Yeah, well, I've been here chatting with Anna Lamore."

My eyes go wide and I nearly trip over my sparkling feet as I come to a stop, and look back at his broad shoulders. He turned away from me, but I can see the grin on his face when he turns his head. "What are you doing?" I whisper, panicked, and walk in front of him. An insane thought crosses my mind—I could jump on his back and take the phone—but I can't. Whatever he's doing is already done. He already said my name, told someone I was here. My stomach sinks and my hands shake. This feels bad. Whatever he's doing throws me into a full blown anxiety attack.

Cole covers the phone with his hand, "Talking to your dean." He uncovers the phone, "Yes, she is."

Terror courses through me as my eyes go wide. If he tells the dean what I did, the university will be pissed. Attending this interview and making sure Cole didn't want me still counted as an interview, right?

A thought takes hold and makes me feel sick—this could mess up my chances with Sottero.

For a moment, I wonder if Sophia did this to me on purpose. It could have been a cruel trick on her part, but for the life of me I can't see why. If she intended on offering me the internship, why would she encourage me to do something to Cole that would warrant this kind of reaction? She knew him. They worked together. She told me these things, the clothes, the kid in need of a serious attitude adjustment, would make his people show me the door faster than I could blink. Instead, Cole grabbed the phone and called my dean.

My stomach twists when his eyes lock with mine. A mischievous grin spreads across Cole's lips, he looks sweet and playful, but

I'm too on edge to notice, "She told me that I'm a washed-up, sexist, has-been and that she has absolutely no intention of working for me. Yeah," he laughs, "she really did. So I wanted to make sure that I got hold of you first." His voice turns serious. The smile fades from his face, "Tell Sottero and Couture that they're too late. I hired Anna this morning."

CHAPTER 4

I stand there like I've been sucker-punched. My ears are ringing with his words, but I can't believe Cole did it. For a few moments after he hangs up, I just stare at him wide-eyed. My mind is reeling, trying to determine why he did that.

I'm near tears. "How could you?" I gasp, and fold my arms across my body. I fall back into the chair, completely deflated.

My shot with Sophia Sottero is gone. In one phone call Cole changed my future. Instead of being the elegant wedding photographer to the famous, I am going to be something else, something that will ruin my career before it starts. Shocked, I glare up at him. Cole is leaning against the side of the table. His gaze rests on my face, waiting for me to react. I try to hold everything in check, but I don't understand. Why did he do that? Rage floods through my tiny body.

Rising to my feet, I step toward him. My hands are balled into fists at my sides, shaking, "How could you do that? You had no right!"

Cole remains relaxed, like he pisses women off all the time, like my temper-tantrum is theatrics, but it isn't. He folds his arms across his chest, "I did you a favor, Lamore. The last thing the world needs is another wedding photographer—"

I cut him off, shoving my finger into his chest. "That wasn't your decision to make!"

"The hell it was," his eyes are cold, his expression rigid. He grabs my finger and flings my hand away. "Who's the arrogant ass here, Anna? Who walked in here looking like a side-show act? That was you. Remember?"

I try to control my temper and force back tears that are building behind my eyes. "It's not the same thing," I say coolly. "I had no intention of working here. Ever. You know what the University puts us through. You've had interns before! Maybe I didn't approach it right, but I didn't deserve this. And just because you made one call, doesn't mean I'll work here." Glaring up at him with barely contained fury I continue, "I'll call

Sophia myself and tell her that I'm still on the market—that your claim with the dean was an attempt to steal me away from her."

A cold dark expression crosses his face. His brow rises slightly, and his arms unfold. He leans toward me, making my heart race faster, "I wouldn't do that if I were you."

"Is that a veiled threat?"

He leans closer to my face, his warm breath flowing across my lips, "No, it's a plain old overt threat. If you don't work here, you won't work anywhere. New York moves in social circles that you aren't a part of. One word from me will keep you on the outside." He pulls away, the tension in his jaw easing slightly.

Fury rages in my eyes. Every dream I had was just ripped apart. I make a false start and then press my lips together and shake my head. When I steady my voice, I say, "So this is what I get for screwing with you and wasting your time? This is my punishment for messing with the famous Cole Stevens?"

"Something like that," he replies before pushing off the table and standing in front of me. "Don't screw with things that you can't control." The fire in his eyes softens.

Rage flows through me, engulfing every muscle, every fiber of my body. The floodgates behind my eyes are ready to overflow, but I try to hold them back as I stare him down, shaking. A tear escapes from the corner of my eye and streaks down my cheek. His gaze shifts, watching it fall. Wiping it away with the back of my hand, I steady my voice. It is deep and dangerous, my rage barely in check, "I'll never forgive you for this."

CHAPTER 5

Fumbling the dish, it slips between my hands and lands hard on the counter. Emma is here, locked in her room. I try to be quiet. I don't want her to know I am home. I don't want to talk about Cole or what he did, or the threat he made. I'd go at him if I could, but I am a nobody. There are no socialites in my circles, no way to do any damage, no way to bend his arm to let me go.

The dish clangs on the counter. As I reach for it, the noise echoes loudly through the tiny apartment. Every emotion that surged through me that morning comes rushing back. Taking the bowl in my hands, I swing my arm, and send it sailing into the wall. It shatters into a million pieces, shards flying everywhere. Tears sting my eyes, and I finally give in and let them come. Burying my head in my arms, I lay it down on the counter, sobbing.

The music in Emma's room shuts off and she opens her door. "Anna?" she asks, hanging her head out. Her eyes drift to the broken dish and then to me. I hate crying. I never cry and I'm near hysterical. "Oh my god. What happened?" She rushes toward me, not knowing what's wrong. "Anna, are you all right? Did you cut your hand?"

"No," my voice bleats between sobs. Raising my head, I look at her. I'm still wearing my tee shirt and jeans. I've taken off the tutu, socks, and sneakers. Tearstains chill my cheeks. "That dick screwed me. I... I tried to... And he..."

Emma starts looking me over like she thinks some jerk grabbed me on the subway. "No, Em! The interview. It was the interview! Cole Stevens screwed me over." I finally get enough control over myself to tell her what happened. Emma listens to the entire story.

When I finish, she pushes a long lock of dark hair behind my ear, "So, he was mad? He did this to get back at you for wasting his time? Anna, that doesn't make any sense. It seems too cruel." I shoot a look at her, shocked that she doesn't believe me. She smiles at me, knowing what I'm thinking, "Of course I believe you, but it just seems a bit drastic. You didn't do something else to him, did you? Something that he'd want payback for?"

"Em, think about it," I lean my head back against the wall, wiping away the tears that soak my cheeks. "I'm going to have to see him every day for three months. There were better ways to screw with me, right? I don't understand what happened. One moment everything seemed fine—he was acting like he thought it was funny. Then he had the dean on the phone, and the whole thing fell apart." I get up, grab the kitchen towel, and run cold water over it, before pressing it to my face.

Emma leans back against the counter, her dark hair falling over her shoulder when she looks at me. "He ruined your shot at Sottero?"

Clutching the damp towel, I nod. "What do I do? I have to do the internship to graduate. I need the experience to get a job. And without that internship referral from a prestigious studio, I'm screwed. There's no way I'll make it." My lip starts to quiver again.

Emma takes me by the shoulders, and shakes me once. "Snap out of it, Anna. You have to suck this up. Here's what you do: Hate his guts, do your internship, and then get the hell out of there. You probably won't even see him. Interns are like Labradors—they fetch crap—and if you're really good they'll throw you a bone that'll look good on your resume. Piss on his pants when he's not looking, and chew up his shoes. Okay? You can do this. You've dealt with worse than this pampered ass. You can do this."

Her pep talk floods through me and suddenly I feel really tired. I nod at her, mute. There is nothing left to say. I have to go through with the internship at the slut factory, but I'll do more than be a nuisance, like Em suggested. I'll find dirt on Cole Stevens that will destroy him.

CHAPTER 6

"I thought you wanted to intern with Sottero? How'd you do a one-eighty and end up at Le Femme?" Edward holds up his hands and grins, "Not that I blame you. Having a girlfriend who shoots at Le Femme is sexy as hell." He looks me over like he's never seen me before and waggles his dark eyebrows.

I elbow him in the ribs, and he laughs, nearly dropping his popcorn on the movie theatre floor. "Yeah, that's why I did it. So you can fantasize about me shooting half-naked chicks all day." I reached into my purse, fish out a tissue, and hand it to him. "Wipe the drool off your face," I say holding the tissue out between my fingers. It dangles there between us for a second. I can't keep my tone serious and I snort by mistake.

Edward pushes his hair out of his eyes and slouches back in his seat. His long lean legs are extended in front of him. There's a soda between us in the cup-holder that's built into the armrest. I reach over and grab some popcorn. Edward throws a few kernels at me and they get stuck in my hair. I stick my tongue out at him, and he lunges in for a kiss.

"Awh, gross," Emma says and looks away. She's sitting on the other side of me. Although she knows the whole story, she says nothing to Edward. I didn't want to deal with his temper and if Edward knew what Cole did, well—I just didn't want to deal with it—so I said I chose to work with Cole.

Emma says, "It's bad enough you have to date my brother, but do you have to suck his face off in front of me too?" Em's elbow bumps into my ribs and I choke. She effectively removed her brother's lips from mine.

He grins at me, and throws popcorn at his twin sister. It sticks to her hair and she shoots him a look.

"Real mature, Edward." She picks out the kernels and throws them on the floor.

We got to the theatre too early. Edward is like that. He wants to be in his seat fifteen minutes before the movie begins. Em and I would have walked in five minutes before, and as long as it wasn't opening weekend, that works fine. There are only three of us, but Edward is a little bit of a control freak.

It's funny, although I have known him for years, we didn't get together until a few months ago. I took my one and only business class. It was about marketing. I thought that would come in handy one day when I had my own studio. The class had all business people in it, people who spent their entire undergrad time sitting in classes and absorbing the vernacular. Meanwhile, I was learning about shadows and shading in the art department. From the first class, I felt like I was drowning in a sea of words and concepts that I didn't understand. Edward sat next to me and helped me figure it out. During midterms, we were studying and it was late. One thing led to another and his lips met mine. Since then, I haven't been able to stop thinking about what I want him to do to me with those sexy lips.

We lean our foreheads together and I smile at him for a second, thinking naughty thoughts. "I'm glad you're here," I whisper so Emma can't hear. He wraps his arms around my shoulder and I lean my head against him.

Emma slumps down in her seat and rests her feet on the empty chair in front of her. It's after ten and the theatre isn't full. The lights fade and the coming attractions begin. A Le Femme ad is lumped in with some others. Edward and Emma are staring at the screen, no doubt seeing perfection that doesn't exist. Rage floods through me when I see the ad. Cole's perception of beauty doesn't exist. It's an ad produced for men, with a product aimed at women. It makes no sense and pisses me off.

Edward seems to sense the tension building in my shoulders. He mistakes it for something else, "Nervous?" he whispers in my ear.

I shake my head as the ad ends. Monday morning I start an internship that I don't want, with a man that threatened to destroy my career. Nervous is the wrong word. Enraged is more like it. My mind swims with ideas, ways to get back at Cole for doing this to me. Come the end of summer, he's going to wish he never met me.

CHAPTER 7

My legs are draped over the side of the bed. Edward has his hands on my shoulders, applying gentle pressure, massaging my tension away. The movie was good, but my mind was elsewhere. We came back to the apartment, and quickly ducked behind my bedroom door before Emma could comment on her brother being in my room so late.

Edward leans closer, his warm breath tickling in my ear, "I had fun tonight." I smile absently, the hairs on the back of my neck prickle as his breath lingers.

We haven't been together yet. The time never seemed right. Or maybe I just keep putting it off because I'm not sure that I want to have sex with my best-friend's brother. That is a lifetime of awkward moments if things don't work out. He'll be picturing me naked in his mind, doing all the naughty things I like to do—things no one knows about—with that adorable grin on his face every time he sees me. I don't know if I'm up for that.

Edward's hands slide along my shoulders, his fingers slipping under my collar, tracing my neck with his fingertips. I close my eyes and shudder at his touch. He's beautiful and funny, witty and smart. He's everything that makes my heart race, but I still feel nervous about being with him. He doesn't pressure me, not really, but he doesn't stop trying to seduce me either. Eventually, I'll give in. He knows it and so do I. It's only a matter of time until I can't resist him any longer.

"So did I," my voice is weak, like I've been sleeping. I clear my throat, trying to bat away the butterflies forming in my stomach.

As I turn toward him, Edward reaches for my face and pulls us together. His lips are soft and hot. Gently, he kisses me, over and over. The kisses are so soft and sweet that I gasp. My heart is pounding. It feels like my head is spinning and I want nothing more than to feel my body sliding against his. I want to forget this day, escape it—with him.

I slip my fingers beneath his shirt and trail my hands up his hard stomach. Our kiss deepens as I do so, and he moans softly. I pull him tighter for a moment. His bare skin is scorching under my palms. I want to lose myself in him. I want to stop thinking, stop freaking out over what happened earlier. I was so upset and scared—terrified—that my future had been ripped out of my hands. I never saw it coming.

Edward's hand cups my breast, his lips kissing me, making me hotter and hotter. He squeezes me hard and I gasp, wishing he'd do it again. As he lowers me onto my bed, his blue eyes lock on mine. Edward's hands slide under my shirt and he pulls it over my head before my back hits the comforter. I lay in front of him with my hair splayed around me in long dark curls. I'm wearing a lacy black bra and jeans that sit just below my waist.

He sits above me, his eyes taking me in like he could never get enough. "You're so sexy, Anna," he says, and lowers himself on top of me. Edward kisses my cheek, then my ear, and starts moving down my neck. The heat of his mouth leaves a hot trail in his wake.

My body is strung tight—my back arches into his touch—into his kiss. My pulse pounds faster and faster. I'm so hot. The pit of my stomach has no floor. It's fallen away with his kisses, and the heat between my thighs is completely unbearable. He feels my body shift beneath him, notices my legs opening for him. Edward's fingers reach for the button my jeans and he slips it through the hole, then lowers the zipper. His hand slides into my pants, slowly pressing into my panties until I feel him hesitate.

Gasping, I say, "I want you. I want to feel you. Please, Edward. Touch me."

He smiles that beautiful smile that I love and his fingers press against the bare skin between my legs. I slide against his hand, my jeans pulling tighter as his hand moves. Edward dips his lips to my breast and he nips me gently, tugging my nipple with his teeth. A moan escapes my lips. I'm burning up inside. I want him. I want to feel him. I want to ride him and be with him.

His fingers circle the tender flesh between my legs, gently rubbing and stroking until I can't stand it. The heat flashes through my stomach as I arch my back, begging him to touch me. He slides a finger into me and I moan, pushing back against his hand. Teeth nip my breasts, and his tongue teases me through the lace bra. I gasp, saying his name. With one hand he continues to stroke me, making me wetter and wetter. My body moves against his hand, craving more. His other hand finds the closure on my bra and flicks it open. The lace loosens and he pulls it away. His lips kiss me gently at first and then harder, drawing my tender flesh into his mouth, sucking. Writhing, I come against his hand. He pushes into me hard as he feels me pulsate, his lips still on my breast. Every time his hand pushes into me, I moan.

Edward kisses me gently and pulls away. He jumps up and walks toward the door, "Be right back." He grins at me.

Breathing deeply I watch him, wondering what he's doing. I never let him touch me like that before and I didn't expect him to get me so riled up and then stop. I thought this was foreplay, but he's left me alone. Sweat is covering my body. The air feels too cold with him gone. When I look up, he's standing in the doorway with a towel in his hands.

It takes me a minute. I'm dazed with a lust-induced stupor, but I figure it out and ask, "You washed your hands?"

He nods and tosses the towel aside, closing the door behind him. "Yeah. Why? Does that bother you? Most girls like that I want to be clean."

I arch an eyebrow at him. My pulse is slowing, my senses returning. He just said several things that bothered me, but getting up and leaving me there to wash his hands was the worst. I can't even process what he just did so I latch onto the obvious, "Girls? How many have you been with?"

Leaning on the bed, he drapes his arm over my waist, "Enough to know what I like. Enough to know I want you." His eyes rove over my body like he's still filled with desire, but the way he washed me off his fingers broke whatever spell he wove. The illusion is shattered. Maybe getting up and washing in the middle of having sex didn't bother other girls, but it bothers me. I pictured my dream guy loving my scent, burying his face between my legs like he couldn't get enough, licking me off his fingers and then begging for more. That isn't going to be Edward. He ran to the bathroom before we were even done.

Edward eyes me lazily and leans forward, sliding his hand into my waistband. Placing my hand over his, I stop him. He looks up into my eyes. I can't let it go. I have to know what I am dealing with. Is he mental or was this just a precaution since we haven't been together very long?

I ask, "If you found the right girl, the one you wanted in every way possible, would it be different? Would you want the scent and the feel of her on your hands?" *Would you want to taste her? Would you swallow?* I wonder, too afraid to ask . The questions rush out. Suddenly, this conversation feels very awkward.

Edward sits up and withdraws his hand from my waist. He looks confused. I pull my shirt over my head so my breasts aren't just out there.

He watches me carefully, knowing he blew his chances with me tonight. He runs his fingers through his hair, "It bothered you." He breathes deeply, shaking his head like he's annoyed with himself. "I'm sorry,

Anna. I didn't mean to hurt your feelings, it's just that—"

I waive my hands at him, shaking my head, "You didn't hurt my feelings," the words are falling out of my mouth before I can stop them. It did bother me. It seemed like he couldn't get me off his skin fast enough. I was offended, but my mouth is saying I wasn't. What the hell is wrong with me? Why can't I just tell him what I want? I've only been with two guys and neither of them did what I was hoping for either. I am barely twenty-two, but I know what I want. At some point I started to think that the things I want are strange. And I can't talk sex with Emma—not when it's sex with her brother.

Looking relieved, he touches my cheek gently. "Good, I'm glad. I don't know what it is, but the idea of having someone else's fluids on me just makes me feel like I need to wash it off." He shivers like it's gross—like I'm gross—and my heart sinks.

I can't look at him. The bedspread is twirling between my fingers, my voice soft, "So, you probably don't like the idea of tasting me. There." The question is in my voice. I sound frail, like his words could hurt me. Maybe they could. I want him to say yes. I want him to want me.

Edward notices my tone, but he misreads my question. "I'd taste you there. I could do that." He doesn't sound eager. "Honestly, the idea of you doing that to me is more appealing." He fumbles his words, laughing nervously.

I blink hard. What a dick. Did he really just say that?

Another question bashes me in the brain before I can think—why didn't I notice this before?

Carefully, I ask, "So, I could go down on you and swallow, and you'd like that?" He nods at me, like he's ready to do it now.

This is what I was afraid of, he doesn't want to touch or taste me like that. It's one-sided. We can't do the things I want to do. Sex with him will be very limited if he doesn't like sweat and other slippery substances. The pit of my stomach drops. This relationship wasn't going to work. Damn. I'd asked him if he had any sexual preferences I should know about. Clean-freak didn't come up. I lean my head back against the headboard and stare at the ceiling. I know there's no future for us, but I can't admit it. Things can't be this way. Not again.

"Anna?" he asks, his hand sliding over my knee.

"Hmmm?" I can't look at him. It feels like my insides have been carved out. I feel the loss of things I thought I'd have with him, things that will never be.

"I love you," he whispers. My neck snaps and I blink rapidly, staring at him. My heart rate shoots up to stroke territory. A boyish smile forms on his lips. He doesn't realize the effect of his words. "Just because that doesn't appeal to me doesn't mean that I don't want you."

My eyes are glassy. I feel like I'm going to cry. He loves me? But he's too grossed out to show me the way I need. The way I want. I smile softly at him and he takes me in his arms, stroking my hair.

"I know I said it too early," he says into my hair. His breath warms my throat. "But, I couldn't let you think—"

I pull back and look him in the eye. Smiling, I say, "I love you, too." My words are sincere. I care about him. I think about it and realize that I do love him. I want things to work out between us, so I say it. But I say it too soon after he drops a bomb on us and the consequence is disastrous.

CHAPTER 8

The next morning I find Emma sitting in the kitchen shoveling Cheerios into her mouth. "I can't believe you're dating my brother. That's so gross." Milk drools a little from the corner of her lips and she snort-laughs, wiping it away.

I roll my eyes. We've had this conversation already. "I know. Ick. Yuck. Don't tell you about sleeping with him. I know the rules, Em. I won't make it weirder that it has to be."

She points her spoon at me, "I never called them rules—"

"Same difference," I shrug. It was a condition of going out with her sibling. She didn't want to know details, didn't want to hear anything.

Memories of the night before play through my mind. I told him I loved him. That feels like the stupidest thing to have said. It will drag out the relationship when it should have been shot in the head. I need to talk to someone about it. I don't know what to do. Edward is great. This was his worst trait, and it doesn't seem that major in the light of day. But then again, it does. He made me feel like I was undesirable. The expression on his face when he left to wash his hands was burned behind my eyes. If he did that after we have sex, I wouldn't be able to take it. It was like he couldn't wait to get to the soap. I sighed, throwing my head back in an exaggerated whine.

"Don't even," Emma says, "You're the one who wanted to date him. And I heard you last night—which wasn't ideal by the way—if you tell me what happened, I'll cut my ears off."

"Well, then you'll look really dumb. And I'm not telling you a thing," I snap and walk away.

It's Sunday. I head to my room and pull on a pair of ratty shorts and a tank top. Screw this. I'm not sitting at home, moping. I'm not that kind of girl. When things get messed up, I can sit around and sulk or try to figure out how to fix them. There has to be a way to fix this. I don't want to put my sexual fantasies to rest yet, although the last two guys had similar reactions. From what I've read on the internet, the things I want aren't that weird.

My feet pound the pavement until I make it to the park. I have an earbud in one ear and the other is tucked into my sports bra strap. I want to be able to hear if someone is coming up behind me. I find my pace and jog the familiar trails beneath the leafy green canopy. The sunlight forms patches of lace on the ground. The splattering of light is a photographer's nightmare, and a nature-lover's dream. I'm both. I love the feel sunlight on my skin.

My mind goes back to last night. If I can get through this with Edward, everything will be all right. It's always a little bumpy in the beginning, right? I think back to the other two men. Honestly, I 'm not even sure if they count. We did stuff, but my first boyfriend wasn't exactly skilled. And the second guy turned out to be an ass. I huff a steady stream of breaths. The music soon diverts my thoughts and I sing softly to myself, going faster—trying to outrun problems that would crush me.

I don't realize how zoned out I am. Normally, I make sure I pay attention while I'm running, but today I'm out of it. As I pass the clearing toward the swank end of the park, I see someone on a bench stand up. My mind makes a mental note, but I don't notice that it's him until it is too late.

Suddenly, a strong hand touches my shoulder. Without hesitation, my elbow flies back and my fist comes up. I twist out of his grip and pivot, my knee rising to kick him in the crotch, when I see it is Cole Stevens. He is dressed in a suit like he's been at church. My knee nearly connects. When I realize who it is, I try to stop. It throws off my momentum and my knee kind of brushes his pants and I lose my balance.

Before I can fall back, his hand shoots out and grips my arm. He steadies me, "I didn't mean to startle you. I'm sorry, Anna."

Crap. Can this day get any worse? I just brushed my boss's nuts with my knee. I pull out of his grip, and bend at the waist breathing hard. Sweat drips down my spine. I sputter, "What the hell, Stevens?" Tiny beads slip over my neck and when I look up, they slip down between my breasts.

He holds up his hands, palms facing me like he means no harm. "Again, sorry. It's a mistake I won't repeat. You nearly took my balls off." His voice is light and he seems off balance.

I nod, admitting that's exactly what I would have done. He says nothing. After a moment, I ask "What do you want? Did you stop me to throw more threats in my face?" I shouldn't mention it again, but I had to.

"No. Nothing like that," he twitches slightly, like my words surprised him. "Actually, I wasn't sure it was you, until you attacked me—"

My jaw drops, "You scared the hell out of me! I thought you—"

He's smiling, laughing at me, "I know. I'm teasing. Listen, I'm sorry for the way things went yesterday."

Straightening, I wipe the sweat off my temples with the back of my hand, "Yeah, me too. I shouldn't have shown up dressed like a circus freak and you shouldn't have been a prick. Does that sum it up?" I push the damp hair out of my face. "Let's cut through the crap, Stevens." The smile melts off his lips. My voice is cold and curt, "I don't like you and an apology isn't going to fix it. You fucked up my life, and I'm not letting it go, so deal with it."

I stare into his eyes and wonder if he's a sociopath, but when our gazes lock my body reacts to something else. My heart skips a beat and my stomach twists. Annoyed, I turn on my heel, ready to jog away. His hand shoots out and clasps my wrist. The movement slows me. My body is covered in sweat. His hand pulls away damp, and he makes no effort to wipe me away—no movement to show how repulsed he is by my appearance. I can't help but notice his reaction is different than Edward's.

Cole's jaw tenses, like he's trying not to fight with me, "I plan on it. In the meantime, I wanted to tell you that I'm willing to start over whenever you are—with everything." His gaze is intense; his dark lashes lower after a moment. He looks past me, then back at my face.

"Then let me go." My voice is soft, and askance. It doesn't sound like me.

Unblinking, I look into his face. His eyes are an intense shade of blue with black and silver flecks. They are locked on mine.

His lips form a thin line and he shakes his head, "It isn't what you want."

I look both ways, making sure no one is within ear shot, "Fuck you, Stevens! You have no idea what I want." My voice is low, threatening. He took away the thing I wanted most. In one move he out played me and I'd pay for it for the rest of my life. I jab my finger into his chest, poking his ironed shirt. "No, wait. Actually, you do know what I want, because I told you. I was stupid enough to trust you and I told you exactly what I wanted."

"The internship with Sottero."

I nod, dropping my hand. "And you made sure I'd never have it."

"Fine," he says pulling a phone out of his jacket pocket. The way the suit clings to his lean body makes me notice his figure. That suit fits him like it was made for him. It probably was. Fucking rich people think they own everyone. I don't want to stand there. I don't want to talk to him, but that phone makes me nervous. It feels like he's doing a replay of yesterday.

"One call puts things back the way you wanted," he says. "I'll call Sophia right now. We swap interns. It's your choice." He arches a brow and glances at me, the phone cradled in his hand.

Shocked, I glance at his palm and then back at his face. I don't buy it, "You're lying. I don't know why, buy you've decided—"

"Lamore, you're trying my patience." He shifts his weight to the other foot, like he's been standing there too long. "You pissed me off yesterday, and there were better ways to deal with you. I apologize. I'm not saying it again, and I won't offer this again. You blamed me for fucking up your life, so fix it. Have me call Sottero and you'll start there tomorrow."

I blink. It feels like I'm falling off a cliff. There are no bearings and I can't tell which way is up. "Why are you doing this to me?" My breath hitches in my throat and I want to punch him. "Why are you batting me around like my life doesn't matter? I don't come from a pampered-ass home like you did. Everything wasn't handed to me on a silver platter with a side of gold doubloons. I carved my own path, and you decided to crush it on a whim!" My hands ball at my sides. No one pays any attention to us. They walk on by, ignoring my tirade.

"Doubloons?" his lips pull into a smirk. My eyes widen, shocked that he decides to tease me when I'm ready to rip his head off in the middle of a very public park. Every inch of me is vibrating with anger and I know he can see it.

The smile fades from his face, "Fine." He presses a number on his phone. It dials and I hear a woman's voice, but I can't make out what she's saying. "Sophia," he says curtly. "Cole. Yes, I'd like to exchange interns with you. I know you wanted Miss Lamore." He pauses, then nods. "Yes, a trade. Mine for yours. That's my offer. I'm handing the phone to her. It's her call." Cole extends his arm, shoving the phone at me.

Time slows to a crawl. Light-years pass as I reach out to take it. Sophia's voice echoes in my ear. It's her. It's Sophia Sottero. She wanted me to be her intern. Yesterday could be erased. All I have to do is say yes.

"Anna, darling let's put this whole mess behind us." She laughs, but it sounds bitter, "You know, for a moment I actually believed that you choose to work for Cole. As if you would sink to his level…" she continues to criticize Cole, undermining his ability and reputation.

I stare at Cole wondering if he has any idea how much Sophia Sottero hates him. I missed it during the interview, but now it's completely clear. He's put his hands in his pants pockets and is looking at his shoe. The action makes him seem younger than he is. Why did he do this? He chased after me through the park, risked getting maced, and clipped in the groin by my knee—for what? To say sorry? To set things right?

Something keeps me from speaking. I can't find my voice even though Sophia is excitedly chattering in my ear about the internship and the things I'll learn—skills that I can use toward my own business one day. Skills that will help me get a kick-ass job at the end of the summer. Skills that I don't have and desperately need.

Skills that Cole can't give me.

Cole pushes a rock with his shiny black shoe. He doesn't look at me until it's obvious Sophia has grown quiet and I'm not speaking. It feels like the air is fluid. I hear nothing. Sophia's words float away from me as she asks if I'm still on the line.

Cole looks up at me. There's something there—I can see it within him in that moment—something that is better than I am. I would have never tried to fix a mistake of this magnitude like this. He is offering me everything I want, I just have to take it. He apologized. He fixed his mistake. I didn't.

Without a word to Sophia, I hand him back his phone wondering if I'm insane. He takes it, but doesn't end the call. Glaring at him I say, "Last time I trusted you, you screwed me."

"Likewise," his expression is hard.

"So, what?" my eyes shift over his face, taking in the stance of his body, the tension in his shoulders. "We just start over?"

He nods, "Yes. Or say yes to Sottero and good-bye to me."

I eye him, my gaze sliding over his suit. My mouth hangs open and I shake my head, not believing what I'm doing.

Reaching out, I take the phone from him and press it to my ear. "Good-bye Sophia. Enjoy your afternoon. I'll be interning at Le Femme." I press end call and hand him back the phone. "Prove to me that I didn't just make the biggest mistake of my life."

He seems surprised, but takes the phone back and slides it into his pocket. "There's no reason to. You'll see it for yourself soon enough."

CHAPTER 9

Stupid men. One won't touch me. The other won't stop screwing with me. My head is spinning. The past twenty-four hours have left me in emotional overload. Edward is sitting next to me while I eat chocolate ice cream out of the carton. My hands are getting sticky. I can tell it's bothering him, but he says nothing. I consider taking his face in my hands and smearing the ice cream over his cheeks, and pressing my lips to his. Getting covered in ice cream and licking it off his skin sounds wonderful, but I don't do it. Edward would freak out. No sticky sex.

The TV flickers with some show neither of us is watching. Glancing at the carton, Edward says, "You don't have to be nervous about tomorrow. Le Femme has a sterling reputation. I'm sure you'll do fine."

Edward thinks I'm nervous. He thinks it's because tomorrow is my first day and I have new-job-jitters. I didn't tell him what happened in the park. Without meaning to, I bypassed an important part of my life. I just didn't want him to freak out about Cole, and now I can't backtrack and add what happened today.

I nod and shove another scoop in my mouth. "Thanks." I put the carton down and push it away. Grabbing the napkin, I wipe my hand off. When I go to hold Edward's hand, he takes it, but makes sure that he doesn't the touch the spot I cleaned with the napkin. "I've known you for what, two years and I had no idea you were such a germ-a-phobe."

He glances at me out of the corner of his eye, "I'm not. I just don't do sticky."

I snort, "Then what do you do?"

"What's the matter?" his voice is soft and comforting. He wraps his arms around me and my anger deflates. "You seem bent out of shape. Like something's wrong. You can tell me, baby. If it's the ice cream, cover me in it. I'd do sticky for you. I'd do everything for you."

Those are the words I wanted to hear. I melt in his arms. The tension flows out of my body. I feel better. He made things better. "I know you would." I lean into his chest and blink at the TV, not seeing the picture on the screen. "Can you stay a little longer?"

He nods, "As long as you need." His hands pull my hair away from my face. "Summer sessions don't start for another week. I can stay overnight, if you'd like. On the couch," he adds quickly.

I smile, "When you stay overnight, it won't be on the couch." I feel him smile against my head. He's happy. "What'd I say?"

"You said when... not if." Turning me toward him, he tips my head back and lowers his lips to mine. His kiss heats my body and makes me feel better. When he releases me, he kisses my temple, and whispers into my ear, "Just let me know when. I'll be there for you in every way you want."

They are nice words, words that I wanted to hear—words that I needed to hear. But even as he says them, I know they are like the early morning mist that burns away in full heat of the sun.

CHAPTER 10

The skinny girl looks like a model, not a receptionist. "Yes?" she asks as I push through the door on Monday morning. "Can I help you?"

I'm dressed normally now, a dark suit clings to my body. It's not as nice as hers, but interns aren't paid much and I'm next to broke. "Anna Lamore. I'm the new intern."

"Ah, yes," she presses her manicured finger to a button on her desk phone. It looks like a sleek piece of glass. Figures. Cole has a designer phone, and a designer receptionist. The piece of plastic beeps and I hear his voice.

"Yes," Cole's voice sounds relaxed.

"Miss Lamore is here. Should I send her back?" I stand there in shock. Why is she telling him? Cole can't be the one training the intern. That doesn't make any sense.

"Yes," he replies.

She stands and smooths her outfit. She's wearing a silk skirt with a vibrant floral pattern. Her blouse is sheer and I can see a lacy cami underneath. Her arms are bare. The heels make her nearly a foot taller than me. "This way Miss Lamore. I'm Vanessa Todd..." she speaks as she takes me through the building toward Cole.

I trail behind the woman, feeling like an ogre in comparison. I try to remember everything she's saying but feel a little bit overwhelmed. When we stop in front of the mahogany doors, she places a hand on my shoulder. I glance up at her.

"If you need anything, have any questions, I'm happy to help you get on your feet here."

Dazed, I nod and smile, "Thank you." She walks away leaving me alone. The studio is quiet and I can't help but wonder where everyone is. This is a huge company. There should be graphic designers, photographers, and assistants—but there's no one in the halls. The offices we passed are empty.

I look at the silver plaque on the door. It's Cole's office. His name is scrawled across the plaque in an elegant script. I push the door open and step through.

I don't feel nervous, but I'm not confident either. Yesterday knocked me off kilter. The day before that blindsided me. Since I met Cole Stevens, nothing has gone according to plan. The thought of hanging up on Sophia Sottero made me feel sick. There's no way to know if I've made the right decision, not until it'll be too late, but I refuse to second guess myself. Something burned through me yesterday in the park. It was like a spark of fate ignited within me indicating my future was somehow tied to Cole. I don't believe in destiny, but the surge of—whatever it was—was too powerful to ignore. It made me confidently end the call with Sophia Sottero and walk into Cole Steven's office today.

Cole's sitting on his desk wearing designer jeans that hug his beautiful body perfectly. I wish I could afford jeans like that. After the thought passes, I realize that I'm over-dressed. He swings his legs once, dangling his feet. The desk is made from dark, carved wood. It must have cost a fortune.

Cole looks up at me from a manila file folder on his lap. “Miss Lamore. Good to see you.” His gaze slips over my body, taking in my formal attire. “For future reference, casual clothing works best here. Crawling around during shoots in a pencil skirt isn’t ideal. I would have mentioned it the other day, but your outfit kind of shocked the hell out of me.”

The corner of my lips pull up and I laugh. I didn’t know what to expect today, but this surprises me. “That was my intention.”

“Ah, well. It worked. I’ve never seen anyone show up to an interview dressed like a giant Skittle.” He looks me square in the face and grins. “I was hoping you weren’t insane. Good to see you can dress yourself.” He’s teasing me. It makes me smile and relax a little bit.

I step closer to the desk, half listening while looking at the books that line the walls. “Har. Har. Very funny. So tell me. Why is this place empty?” I can’t address him with revere, not after the way we met.

He looks up from the papers in his hands. They look like bills. There are numbers across the sheets, dates, and dollar signs. "What do you mean?"

"No one is here, except for Amazon Barbie at the front desk. Where is everyone? I would have thought Le Femme had at least twenty employees on any given day, running around half clothed—or half naked, depending on how you look at it." Was I joking? Where'd the light teasing tone come from? What the hell is wrong with me?

I blink hard, trying to find my brain and make it work while I scan the spines on the bookcase. It's filled with art books about Romanticism. My mind tries to make sense of that. The Romantics are known for their somber sublime works. Looking at those pieces of art make the viewer feel a sense of loss and uncertainty. Cole's work makes people want the girl in the shot, or her underwear. I don't turn to look at him as I ask. I don't want him to notice my shock.

I feel his eyes on my back when he answers, "Miss Todd is the receptionist. She's here weekdays. Everyone else is already out on the Island. We're keeping a skeleton crew here for the week. Guess who's on skeleton staff?"

I whip my head around, and my hair flies over my shoulders. What? Is he serious? I'm alone with him here for a week? "There's no one else here? For a week? Why?" My mouth is hanging open. It won't close and I have no idea why.

He chuckles and puts the papers next to him. Leaning forward on the desk, he puts a hand on either side of his hips. The effect makes his arms look perfect.

"Is that a problem, Miss Lamore?"

I shake my head. It feels like it's full of rocks. "No, it's just—"

"Just what?"

I shrug, "I thought that someone else would be in charge of me, I mean my internship."

He looks me over once and says, "Well, like it or not, I'm the boss of you this week. We have a shoot later today, and then three more later in the week. I want you to assist, and then I want you to second shoot on Friday's session."

I can't swallow. My mouth goes dry. I don't think I heard him right. Did he say shoot? I cock my head and stare at him like he's crazy, "Excuse me? Did you say you want me to shoot a real session in less than a week? I've never done this before!"

He blows off my high-pitched protest with a wave of his hand, "You'll be fine." He slides off his desk, shoves the papers in his drawer and it finally sinks in. What he said about everyone else being out on Long Island finally sinks in.

"Why is the staff out East? Is there something going on?" Truth be told, I had no idea what was going on. For all I knew it was a company retreat.

He shakes his head, "Not really. Just an expansion."

My mouth forms an O but I don't say anything else. Damn. A second studio on Long Island. Unless he stuck the new studio in the 'hood, Cole was paying more in rent each month than I could earn in a year.

He looks up at me. His dark hair curls slightly as it hangs over his forehead. He pushes it back. "Ready?"

I answer straight-faced, totally dead pan, "Ready as I'll ever be. Show me to the naked girls."

Cole nearly chokes, and then laughingly scoffs at me, "Why do all you feminists think I shoot naked women?"

I follow him down the hallway. We are headed towards a million dollar shooting room. Curiosity alone makes me want to see it. "Because you do," I answer bluntly.

Cole turns and looks at me over his shoulder, "They're wearing more clothes than most women wear at the beach. That's hardly fair."

"Life's not fair, dude. Get over it."

He stops in his tracks and turns in slow motion. His dark brows are lifting into his hairline. "Dude? Seriously? You called me dude?" He looks shocked and can't hide the smile that's running across his lips.

Not realizing that I said it, I try to cover my tracks, "No, I—"

"Said dude. You called me dude." His eyes are so blue. The way he looks at me makes my heart race. The grin on his face makes the corners of his eyes crinkle a little bit. The expression he's making is cute and confused. I should be embarrassed, but I'm not.

I shrug, like it doesn't matter, "Would you prefer something else?" My lips twist into a smile. I can't help it. It doesn't matter that I wanted to torment him yesterday. This side of him makes me want to tease him more.

His eyes sweep over me before returning to my face. He laughs, "You're so young. You have no idea—"

I nod once, the smile fading from my lips. Completely serious, I look him in the eyes and say, "I'm sorry. I didn't mean to be disrespectful. From now on, I'll refrain from calling you dude." He looks at me. I nod, and after a moment, I add in my most respectful voice, "Old dude or geezer would be way better." Our eyes remain locked. My lips twitch as I try not to laugh. I have no idea why I'm teasing him again.

He huffs, rolling his eyes, "You're such a child." Running his fingers through his hair he mutters, "I'm getting too old for this crap."

"Mmmm," I answer, "Then you shouldn't have hired the chick dressed like a circus clown."

CHAPTER 11

The studio is the coolest thing I've ever seen. It has everything I want in my own shooting room and more. Cole shows me around quickly and tells me to ditch my jacket and heels. We're shooting for the rest of the afternoon. A model is due in at any moment. While we are waiting for her, I slip off my shoes and kick them under a table. That leaves me barefoot in a black pencil skirt with a sleeveless blouse.

I feel underdressed now, but barely process it because I'm too captivated by the shooting room, especially the sets. The walls are lined with them. There are four total—one white, one black, one pink, and one gray. Each set has its own feel and different items. They are all posh feeling with lots of different textures. The white set's easily my favorite. White flocked wall paper surrounds a white velvet chaise that has a fuzzy white throw over the arm. Bleached wood floors give it just a little bit of warmth so it doesn't feel sterile.

Cole speaks as he moves about the room, explaining how the shoot will go and what to expect. "Never touch the model without asking. Never say anything inappropriate," Cole glances at me like he isn't sure if I can control my mouth. "Those are the only two rules that you need to know for today."

I nod, "What am I going to do? I thought that I'd be getting coffee or something."

My gaze is on a rack of wardrobe, if you could call panty and bra sets wardrobe. They are the things we're shooting today. Honestly, they're cute. And one is insanely sexy. It is a white shelf bra with a matching lace G-string. It is the kind of thing I would want to wear, but it wouldn't look good on me. I have too many curves for that kind of skimpy thing. I rub the lace with my thumb, feeling how soft it is.

Cole stops moving, watching me for a moment before saying, "Maybe if you were at Sottero. At Le Femme, you work. If you don't work, you don't get paid."

Dropping the bra, I turn sharply. "I get paid?"

He nods and looks at me surprised, "What'd you think, you were working for free?"

"Well," my eyes are wide and I'm still shocked, thinking he's dicking with me, "yeah. Internships aren't paid."

He shrugs, "This one is. You get about $2200 per week, take home, after taxes. Miss Todd can give you the exact amount."

"Holy shit!" the words fly out of my mouth. My jaw is hanging open. I quickly slap my palms over my face and shut the gaping hole to keep anything else from flying out.

Cole looks at me like I'm crazy. He shakes his head and lifts his camera off a shelf. Selecting a lens, he puts it on and adjusts the settings. "How did you not know it was paid?" He shakes his head. "You're going to learn so much more here than you would anywhere else.

"Lesson 1: Never work for free. Some new photographers think you have to, that you can build your client list by offering free sessions. Don't do it."

"Why not?" I ask, still shocked that I'm getting paid and really happy about it.

He looks over his shoulder at me, "Because free is never free. It always costs something. Money. Time. Reputation. Those are things that you need to work hard to control. Giving them away for free screws with perceived value, and your worth as an artist."

I'm staring at the side of his face, shocked. Cole shoots girls in their underwear. What does he know about marketing and business practices? He sells sex, and sex sells itself. Cole notices me staring at him. He glances up and opens his mouth to say something, but the intercom buzzes. The model is in the building and on her way back. Whatever he was going to say died on his lips.

CHAPTER 12

For the next three hours Cole is serious. He tells me what to do and I do it. I'm standing, bending, kneeling and doing the assistant's job. At one point I have to reset the model's hair. She moved and it's no longer in place. It's when she's wearing that shelf bra. Her perfectly man-made boobs fill the thing up. To make the ad compliant with the company's guidelines, there can't be any nipples showing. Cole was right. Most of the shoot hasn't felt weird, not once I realized that she is covered. The only thing that's awkward is this.

"I'm sorry, Cole," Angela says, her sultry voice matches her curvaceous body. I'm slightly envious, but she's too tall. In real life it must be hard to find someone to kiss without bending down. That sucks for a girl.

"It's not a problem," he says. "Miss Lamore will reset your hair. Don't move.

Everything else is still perfect." Cole gestures for me. I step onto the set of the white room, and he says, "Take that strand of curls and drape it over her breast. Ask her before you touch her. Company policy."

I feel stupid. She's leaning backward over the chase. Her hair is spilling all around her and I'm asking to move a strand over her boob. I ask, and do as I'm told. She smiles at me and grants permission. I take the lock and drape it across her flesh, but I can't see if it covered her properly from the angle Cole is shooting.

"Is that okay?" I ask and step back.

"No, I can still see her. Use more strands," he replies. He's looking at his camera and adjusting settings. "Make sure I can't see anything through the center of the curl."

I ask the model if I can touch her again and move more curls. Her hair doesn't want to stay. It slides off her breast and I'm starting to make it frizz. The hairstylist is standing in the corner with her arms folded over her chest. The make-up artist is watching from her chair on the other side of the room. No doubt they both think I'm going to screw this up. How hard can it be to get some hair to stay? She has enough of it and it's insanely long. I try again, but the curls slide off. I'm starting to get bent out of shape. I'm blushing horribly, touching some girl's breast and I still can't do it. I refuse to ask Cole for help, but he's already next to me.

From over my shoulder, he says, "Hook the edge of the curl on her nipple. The one curl will hold and then you can place another over it."

I freeze when I hear him speak, and shiver. The way he says it, like he uses the word nipple frequently, shoots up warning flags in my mind. His proximity puts me off kilter. I feel his eyes on my back, waiting for me to do it. Suddenly I wonder if I can do this job, and everything it entails. Being comfortable around bodies changing in the gym is one thing, touching to make the poses right is another.

I swallow hard, my fingers hovering above the curl. Cole seems annoyed—or disappointed—and says, "Come on, Anna. This is the last set for today. Once we shoot this, we're done." He hoovers, waiting for me.

My hand is shaking for some reason. It might have something to do with Cole being so close. It might have to do with paying such careful attention to someone else's nipples. Irritated with myself, I blow out a huff of air between my lips and take the curl.

I chose this. I passed up Sottero. This was my choice.

I do as he says and the curl stays. I beam like an idiot, and then quickly drape the other locks in place. They all hold. I step back into Cole, smashing his toes with my bare feet. He's not wearing shoes either. Cole steadies me, his warm hands on my elbows.

From behind my shoulders, he says, "Don't be shy when you're shooting. It makes your job harder. You could have used fashion tape to hold the hair in place, but we don't want to do anything we don't have to. Tape in hair sucks. The temperature in the room is warm, but it's still chilly enough—for obvious reasons. I thought you'd be okay with this kind of stuff." His hands slip away from my elbows and he passes in front of me. The sound of the shutter snapping fills my ears. He's so at ease, moving, speaking, and acting like this woman is anyone else and not a nearly-naked super-model.

I don't answer.

I didn't want this job, but I chose it. This wasn't my career goal, but here I am. I'm perplexed because this shoot isn't what I thought it would be. I moved at ease through the room, right up until this last part. And the only reason I hesitated was because of Cole. It wasn't like I didn't notice the half nude person in the room, it's that I wasn't as uncomfortable as I thought I'd be.

And Cole, he was nothing like I thought he'd be. I expected him to be sleazy, touchy, and filled with innuendo. As the shoot progressed, I don't know if he even realized the woman he was shooting wasn't clothed. This was second nature to him. It's like he is a fish and this scandalous world of his is water. He doesn't notice it, and he moves through it with ease.

Today I learned that Cole Stevens isn't the photographer I thought he was, and neither am I.

CHAPTER 13

Edward's arm is draped across my shoulder. We are walking down the street to the steady hum of car engines. The buildings glow against the inky sky. The diner was packed after work. We met there, shared a meal, and are walking back to my place. By the time I finished with work, I was starving.

Edward squeezes my shoulder, and grins down at me, "So, tell me how today went. What do you do all day? How's working with your boss?" We didn't talk about work at dinner, instead I put it off. He lifts his chin and we stop at a corner, waiting for the light to change. A car horn blares behind us. When the light changes, we walk in the mass of people.

I say, "Well, it turns out my boss is Cole Stevens."

Edward gasps, "No way." He knows who Cole is. Everyone knows who Cole is, so that isn't surprising. But, like me, Edward assumed someone else would be overseeing the internship.

Nodding, I say, "Yeah. It turns out that he's in charge of my internship. I stay here with him to do some shoots in the city this week, and then the rest of the summer, I'll be out East on Long Island somewhere. I probably should have asked where." My voice trails off.

I grew up out there. In the back of my mind, I'm hoping that the new studio is near enough to my parent's house to commute. Housing arrangements would be an issue, paid or not. Renting something short term on Long Island was expensive.

His shoulders sag and Edward stops walking, "No. The whole summer? Are you serious?"

"I'm sorry. I didn't realize exactly what this internship included until today, but it's only a few weeks." He still looks crestfallen. I add, "And it's not like I'm that far away. I'm sure we can get together a few times a week."

He's smiling at me again. Pulling me close, we stop on the sidewalk. People walk past us, some bumping into me, but I don't care. In the moment, there is only Edward and me. He lowers his lips to mine and that familiar light feeling floats through my stomach. Gently, he pushes my hair away from my cheek.

He breaks the kiss, and breathes deeply. A rush of warm breath flows from his lips as he breathes, "Oh God, I want you. When you kiss me like that, I can't think. You're amazing." His fingers tangle in my hair. I look up into his cool eyes. The way he looks at me makes me squirm. Someone bumps my elbow. It brings attention back to where we are.

"We'd better get home so I can make you think even less," I try not to giggle. I try to be sexy, but I laugh softly anyway. Taking his hand in mine, we walk faster down the street.

By the time we plow through the apartment door, his hands are all over me. One is pushing up my skirt, my leg is hiked up and wrapped around his hips, while he cups the curve of my ass. We don't break the kiss. I'm so hot. It feels like every inch of me is on fire. I want him. I need him. The place between my legs is throbbing. Feeling his lips there is what I want, but I'm too afraid to ask. I want him to do it, I want him to take me—and not ask permission—to have me how he wants. But Edward won't do that. He's too cautious, that carnal part of him seems buried too deep. I wonder if I'll ever get at the part of him that's wild and dauntless. The part of Edward that's more animal than man, the part that wants me in every way. I tell myself that every relationship has problems and that we can learn to deal with them.

My hand slides down between us and below his waistband. I stroke his hard length, hoping he'll ravish me the way I want him to. His breath hitches and before I can do anything, his fingers are around my wrist. "Slow down, babe." He's breathing hard in my ear, his face is flushed.

Disappointed I say, "Don't you ever just want to tear my clothes off and take me?"

Between kisses down my neck, he says, "Of course."

My heart is pounding. Pulling his face back, I hold his cheeks between my palms.

Breathing hard I say, "Then do it. Anything you want, anyway you want. Right now."

His eyes are wide and dark. They look into mine with an expression that makes me afraid. Edward doesn't move. His eyes drift lower, watching the deep breaths making my chest rise and fall. After a moment, he steps back and releases me. A rush of cold fills the void. Ice drips down my spine. He's going to reject me. That look on his face says what I already know.

He pushes his hair out of his eyes and looks up at me, "I—" he starts to say, but a noise stops him from speaking. The telltale sound of metal scraping lets us know the door is being unlocked. Emma will step into the room any second. His eyes are apologetic, like he can't be the man I want.

I don't understand.

We blink at each other as Emma pushes the door open and turns to yank her key out of the lock. She sees us, but doesn't sense the tension right away, "Hey guys. Anna, you gotta tell me how today went. I can't wait—" she turns and realizes she walked in on something. It's probably not what she thinks it is.

I act like nothing happened, and turn toward the kitchen. I pull open the fridge door and bend over, peering inside. "It was interesting. That's for sure." I need a drink. Where's the wine?

I hear plastic bags being set on the counter. Emma says, "I bought your favorite." She holds up a bottle of White Merlot. I could die. Smiling at me, she holds the bottle by the neck. "You guys can celebrate without me. I totally didn't mean to..."

I cut her off, "You didn't. And we already celebrated, didn't we Edward?"

He nods, "Yup. Dinner and stuff." He's staring at me. I can't tell what he wants from me. I wish he'd just take me in his arms and say he wanted me. But he says nothing. He stands there with his arms folded like he's an awkward kid.

Emma pulls out two glasses and looks at her brother, "Well, I want to hear about it. Sorry if it's old news to you. So are you staying or going?" She has her fingers on a third glass, but he shakes his head.

"Nah, I'll head home. Things to think about." His eyes are on me, but I can't look at him. “Congratulations, Anna.” He steps toward me, and kisses my temple. I smile at him, but it’s one of those smiles that feels wrong, like the lines of my face are filled with cement. “See you tomorrow?”

I nod, “Sure,” my voice is too soft.

He knows our relationship is broken. He likes slow and steady. I like everything else. Slow makes me fall into a coma. Steady isn’t my idea of romantic. But I don’t want to lose him. In every other way, we’re perfect together. He steps toward the door and lets himself out. I watch him go. Part of me wants to call him back and be with him his way, but I don’t move.

Emma watches me. She can tell I’m out of sorts, but she doesn’t mention it. Instead we talk about Cole and work and half-naked models. I tell her that I hold reflectors, move lights, and adjust things on set. I leave out that adjustments include things of a more sensual nature.

“So, Cole was with you today?” she asks, knowing it’s weird. “Anna, interns are treated like dirt, and you have the owner doing yours. You ever wonder why?”

For a second the only response I have is a half open mouth. "I have. And I don't know. For some reason he didn't want Sottero to have me. That much, I'm sure of."

She nods at me. Although she hasn't said it, the question—the reason she's thinking—has crossed my mind as well. Maybe it was more than he didn't want Sottero to have me. Maybe he actually wanted me. But that doesn't make sense. I have next to no reputation, and the one I do have says I'm a pain in the ass, stubborn to a fault.

"So, next week you'll be out East somewhere. How'd Edward take that?" she asks, and then adds. "You don't have to say anything, if you don't want to, but when I walked through the door, you looked like someone hit you in the head with a frying pan. I'd be a shitty friend if I didn't ask."

I snort, and pull my knees into my chest. We're sitting on the living room floor. Half the bottle of wine is gone. Tucking a stray hair behind my ear, I stare at my glass, "He was okay with it. That's not the problem. He's always supportive, exactly the kind of guy a girl hopes for."

She watches me. After a moment she asks, "But not you?"

Shrugging, I say, "It gets into things I can't discuss with you." I stare at my toes. Sighing, I finally just ask her, "You know I've only had two serious relationships. One was a stoner, and the other was—" I try to find the right words, but Emma choses them for me.

"A dick." She throws back the rest of her wine.

I nod, "Yeah, so I don't really know what to expect. I mean, if a guy was great in every single way but your bedroom preferences didn't exactly line up, what would you do?" I stumble over the words as I say them.

She blinks once and stares at me. "If you asked me that before my third glass of wine, I think I would have puked on you. And I might now, anyway."

I roll my eyes at her, "Stop it. Be serious for once. I need you. I'm not talking about your brother. I'm talking about me. I'm a freak, Emma. Guys seem to think that I'm this little goodie-two-shoes kinda girl, and

I'm not. I want things... things that they seem to think are weird. What do I do?"

Emma seems intrigued. "What kind of things do you want that no one will do?"

I shrug, "I don't know. Things." I can't say it. I don't want to. But I know what I want, and if I'm with Edward, I'll be three for zero, in terms of guys that make me melt.

"Okay, you're a bad liar. But I understand if you don't want to tell me. I've done some things that I wouldn't tell anyone about either." I glance up at her surprised. She shrugs, "The right guy makes just about anything sound sexy. But that's not your problem." She pushes her dark hair out of her face. "I wouldn't throw away an entire relationship based on the sex, but staying in a relationship where you both want different things, I don't know..." Her tone is leading, but she's saying what I already know.

"It's settling, isn't it?"

"Seems that way," she nods and reaches for my glass. She refills both our cups and the bottle is empty. She glances at her glass, "After I drink this, I won't have any recollection of our conversation, so if you have to ask me funky sex stuff that involves my twin, you'd better do it now." She makes a face and I laugh.

I hold onto her shoulder, "I can't do that to you. Telling you that I want more than he's willing to give is enough."

"And that's the problem that you'll face with every guy," she lifts her glass and taps it against mine. The crystal rings. "Cheers, Anna. May your future be filled with someone who can give you everything you need."

CHAPTER 14

"That's not what I need," Cole says in a huff.

He pushes past me and grabs a different white cloth from the prop closet. There are so many props. I have no idea how he decides which to use. He steps in front of me, takes the prop, and walks toward the set.

A model is sitting on a chaise with her back toward us. She's wearing a tiny panty made of strings. It connects below her hips with a snake wrapped around a red crystal apple, the symbol of Evil Eve. Like Eve was in on it with the serpent in the Garden of Eden. I keep my feminist statements to myself, and follow Cole.

"The set is too smooth," Cole explains. "Adding something like this will visually add texture and softness. You want the viewer's eye to rest on the curve of her back, right where that apple is. The snake is the leading line that creates the flow of the composition.

If you don't put something in the bottom quadrant of the image, it won't work as well." Cole tosses down a fuzzy white rug. He bends at his knees, barefoot, and plays with it until it lies haphazardly, like was thrown there.

I watch him place the rug, but I am having trouble. Shaking my head, I say, "I don't see it."

He doesn't turn toward me. Instead he lifts his camera to his eye and shoots. His fingers curve over the lens and the shutter snaps. Over his shoulder, he says, "You will."

I don't reply.

Cole shows me settings on the cameras and lights. He has me move things on set. Basically, I'm his beckon girl. He asks for something and I do it. As the day progresses, I'm starting to see what he's doing. It comes together with the shoot from the other day. He works his way through the four sets, always shooting to show the model's best assets while complimenting the teeny tiny lingerie she's wearing. The trademark Le Femme sexy poses aren't by accident. Every bit of them is Cole. It's the way he sees a scene and makes it come together.

—

At the end of the day, I'm backing up the shoot onto his computer along the back wall of the studio. Cole walks up behind me after shutting off the lights in the massive room behind us. The crew and model have left. It's later than usual. I want to leave, but the shoot ran late.

I watch the data transfer. As each thumbnail shows up on the screen, I look at it. I kind of like that panty after seeing it all day. It's sexy, or at least I think it is.

I wonder how many things are sexy because someone told me they are.

Cole reaches past me, his finger pressing the screen. A thumbnail just appeared. He's pointing at it, "That's the shot before the rug. This is the shot after." He leans in, not paying attention to how close he is, "See how this image makes you glance and look away?" I nod. It does do that, but I didn't know why. "It's because the composition is messed up. The flow is broken. There's nowhere for the eye to rest or reenter the image. But this one," he points at the picture with the rug, "is better. Since it's white on white, the texture doesn't detract from the focal point, but it lends to the overall image." He turns to look at me. He's in my circle of space, but I don't feel the need to force him out. Although I haven't been around Cole very long, I've already noticed that he isn't a touchy person. He doesn't seem to linger this close to anyone else. I wonder if he's doing it on purpose.

"This shoot was more risqué than the one we did the other day."

I nod slowly, "Yeah, I suppose it was." He's still too close. I arch a brow at him, wondering what he's doing.

He grins, "You didn't notice, did you? That she was wearing a piece of string all day?"

Thinking about it, I lean back in my chair. Cole steps in front of me and sits down on the desk. "I suppose not. Actually, I hated that piece of clothing this morning... but it grew on me during the day."

His eyebrow rose, surprised, "Did it?"

"When I first saw it, I thought it was saying women are evil, you know the temptress bitch scenario." He laughs even though I'm being serious. "Shut up. It's real. Look it up," I say, grinning. "Anyway, as the day passed, I thought it was sexy. I think that's kind of amazing about this place—you get to define what's sexy."

His arms fold over his toned chest while I speak. There's a gleam in his eye that I can't ignore. It makes my stomach flip-flop when he looks at me like that. "That's why I wanted you to work here. I knew you'd see it. Le Femme isn't about making women into sex objects. You missed that before. When you first spoke to me, that was all you thought we were. But now you see it. Don't you?"

I nod. Cautiously, I say, "It's more about defining femininity and power. You showcase your ideals, putting them into pictures."

I'd only been here for a few days, but there is a reason why I am the best in my class. I see things no one else does. When I find something I don't understand, I want to know everything about it until I understand it fully. Right now, I feel that way about Cole. He confuses the hell out of me.

I tilt my head, looking up at him, "Was that your intention when you started shooting?"

He laughs, "You didn't ask if you were right. Most people would have waited for confirmation of their claim, and then asked the next question." He has a dimple on his cheek when he smiles hard.

"Dude, we both know I'm right and that I'm slightly arrogant—kind of like you—so let's just call it what it is so you can answer my question." He laughs. "When you started Le Femme, did you set out to showcase femininity and power?" Sometime while I was speaking, I sat up. By the time I finish, the tips of my fingers are on his knee, and I am looking up at him. I smile noncommittally, and lean back into my chair, slouching, not sure why I did that.

His lips press together into a straight line, almost disappearing. His hands rest on either side of his hips on the desk. He leans forward when I lean back, "You're dangerous, you know that? Not only do you see things clearly—well, when you actually take the time to look at them—but you also call people on it. You demand honesty."

"I'm scary as hell," I joke.

"More than you know," he says seriously. His eyes rove over my face like he's considering something. He looks to the side, careful to avoid my eyes. Rubbing an imaginary spot on his jeans, he says, "I started Le Femme as a fly-by-night artist. I wanted to be a painter, but that didn't pay the bills. Someone took pity on me and handed me a camera. I was able to cut my own path from there.

"When I was on my own, I didn't like what I saw. Women were portrayed as weak. They were cast into a mold that no longer fits," he looks up at me and continues, "if it ever did. The pieces that dominated the market only show a certain type of woman—a specific type of beauty. I want to show what I think is beautiful. I want the world to see things through my eyes. And I can do that Anna, I can make you see my perspective through this lens." He taps at the glass on the end of his camera and looks up at me. "It tilts the world on its side. It has the potential to change everything, every concept you have, every belief you hold..." he places the camera down and shakes his head, running his fingers through his hair. "God, if you saw my earlier work, you wouldn't believe it. Le Femme pays the bills. Le Femme is the tame version of me and that's the Cole Stevens the world knows.

"So, yeah, my ideals leaked into my work. I've found that it's impossible to keep them out, no matter how hard I try."

While he speaks, I'm glued in place, mesmerized. His blue eyes pierce me and hold me still. I forget to breathe. Stunned, I wonder, who the hell is this? Who is this man? Do I know him at all? Was every assumption I made, every educated guess about him completely wrong?

I drool at him, lost in the shy passion barely contained in his voice, until he says he was on his own. Liar. I know that's not true. I know he comes from money. Everyone knows that, so I wonder why he says it—why he tries to tell such a blatant lie. Does he think I'm a moron? Maybe. Instead of calling him on it, I listen to the rest of his story. His passion is addictive.

As soon as he stops speaking, I want to hear more, even if it is lies. No one talks like that anymore. No one says what they actually think, what they believe. I find myself staring at his dark eyes wondering how I could be so drawn to him when we are so different. It's a question that I smash away with a mental broom as soon as it surfaces. Thinking about Cole Stevens is not the pastime of a prudent person.

My inner-self reminds me that I am not a prudent person.

Damn.

CHAPTER 15

The week creeps slowly by. The days are long and every minute of it spent with Cole. Work is more fun than I expected. I still wonder if I made the right decision. I have no idea what to do later in life with the things Cole is teaching me. I'm not going to shoot this kind of stuff, although I start to see more of him. He seems to trust me, and speaks more freely. It's strange how often I have a smile on my face lately.

I am seeing double by the time we stop after lunch. Cole stays in order to keep working, getting ready for a meeting later, but he sends me home. The halo that's burned into my retinas from editing images all day on the computer has started to dull and fade. I don't know how he stares at a screen all day.

The changes he makes to the photos during editing are so minute. It's like shifting a grain of sand on the beach. The one tiny movement seems to pull the whole thing together. I'm still uncertain of myself, of what he expects from me. But I show up and I'm trying. I feel like there's more to learn from him, but I'm not sure what. The speech he made the other night is still fresh in my mind.

I avoid Edward. I don't know what to do with him. He said he loves me. I owe him an honest explanation about what I'm thinking, I know I do, but I can't do it. Not yet. Mainly because I have no clue what I'm thinking.

I pull my hair into a pony tail and slip on a pair of cotton shorts and a tank top. My plan is to lounge in front of the TV while Emma is out, and let my subconscious deal with Edward.

As soon as I kick my feet up, my phone rings. I tilt the screen so I can see the name. SUFFOLK COUNTY POLICE is across the screen. Sitting up, I answer it. "Hello," I say, wondering who is on the other end of the line.

"Anna, good you're there."

"Cole?" I ask, shocked. "Are you okay?"

"Yeah, I can't talk. I only have a minute. I hate to ask you this, but I need a huge favor. I'm in jail. Please go to the studio, take cash out of the safe. The combination is scratched onto the back of my main camera body. Take ten grand and come get me out. Please."

I'm trying so hard to remember everything he says, but I just blink at the phone like it's a joke. "You're serious? You've been arrested and you're all the way out in Riverhead?"

"Yes," he says. "If you don't get here by six, I'm going to be stuck in a cell overnight. It's four now. Do you think you can make it?"

I glance at the clock. There are a million questions I want to ask. Emma walks through the door, but I ignore her. "Fine, but you owe me huge."

"Fine, anything you want. Just don't tell anyone. That's why I asked you."

I scoff at that. Walking away from Emma and into my room, I close the door and hiss, "You trust me? Are you insane? How the hell am I supposed to keep this a secret? You're a frickin' socialite! The papers will be all over this!" I rub the heel of my hand over my eyes. I have no idea why he called me. Me, out of all people!

Cole says, "I have a pretty good idea of what kind of person you are. You won't tell the press. I know you won't. And you keep your promises." It's a statement, a true cold hard fact that he picked up from working with me for hours on end. In that moment I understand why he called me and not someone else. I won't draw attention, no one knows who I am, and no one would ever expect the intern to go bail out her boss.

He trusts me. And he's shrewd.

"Gah," I sigh like a melodramatic teenager and laughingly say, "You suck. You know that." But I've already made up my mind. Cole was right. I won't tell anyone he's in jail and I won't tell him no. I can't turn my back on someone who asks me for help. Call it a code of ethics, or maybe it's just a desire to be a better person, but somehow Cole sniffed it out. And that made him call me and not Miss Todd.

Shaking my head, I say, "Riverhead. Fine. I'll be there in a couple of hours."

He's quiet for a moment then says, "Thanks, Anna."

"Sure," I reply. I press END CALL and he's gone.

CHAPTER 16

When I hang up the phone Emma is lurking in the kitchen. She's a bit of a busy body, always wanting to know what's going on. I suppose that fits her personality. "Hey," she says smiling at me. "You're home early."

I tug on my boots quickly and lace them up. When I come out of my room, I've already pulled on jeans and my leather jacket. "Yeah, well, it was short-lived. I have to go out to the Island. Something came up. I'll probably just stay out there tonight."

My parents live out there; I could crash at their house after I free Cole. I wonder what he did. I walk to the closet and pull out a black full face helmet and a second larger helmet. It's white like a giant ping pong ball. Emma's eyes drift to the white helmet.

"Riding out there with someone?" she asks. Emma is leaning her hip against the counter. Her arms are folded over her chest. She seems relaxed, but I know she's not. I'm moving too quickly for her to think everything is all right.

I shake my head. “No.” I hold up the white helmet on my fist, “I prefer this one at night, if I ride back later.”

She arches her eyebrow, “Since when?”

“Since it’s summer and I’m taking Ocean Parkway. Geeze, what’s with the third degree?” I’m a little defensive. I strap my backpack on. This is insane. I’m going to be riding with ten grand in cash on my back.

She shrugs and uncrosses her arms, “Sorry, I didn’t mean anything by it. I just wanted to make sure you were okay.” She walks into the kitchen and grabs a loaf of bread. “You want some food to take with you? I can toss you a PowerBar or something.”

I shake my head and grab the keys to my bike. “Nah, I’ll eat once I get there. Talk to you later.” And I’m out the door.

I fly down the stairs and run across the street into the parking garage. My bike is right where I left it. Grays and blacks cover the frame. There isn’t a spec of chrome or plastic on it. A pink stripe goes down the gas tank and explodes into a splash of color.

Swinging my leg over the side, I kick start the thing—mostly because the time constraint is making me nervous—and pull out.

I zip in and out of traffic like I don't value my life. It's too close to rush hour. If I don't get to the Tunnel fast enough, I'll be trapped. I'm lucky. I manage to get downtown quickly and park on the sidewalk in front of Le Femme.

I rush past Miss Todd, saying that Cole forgot something. She eyes me suspiciously, but doesn't follow. I find his camera body and flip it over. No scratches. No safe combination. Damn it. Where'd he put it? I turn it over twice in my hands, looking for the markings, but don't find any.

I'm wasting time. I reach for the other camera bodies, but those are all clean too. I go back to the first body—the one he always uses—and take off the lens. I look at the housing between the body and the lens, tilting it to try to see hidden markings, but nothing's there. I reattach the lens and flip the camera over in my palms. Opening the battery door, I slide the battery out and still see nothing but black plastic.

My heart is pounding. This is taking too long. Pressing the lever for the memory cards, the little door on the side of the camera swings open. Three numbers are scratched into the curve of the casing on the inside of the door. I exhale a rush of air.

Taking the camera, I run to Cole's office, and open the safe. There are several things that catch my eye, including a small Tiffany's ring box. It's pale blue with the famous logo printed in silver letter across the case. Normally I wouldn't snoop, but the box looks like it's been crushed, stomped under foot. The blue leather is gashed and scuffed. The lid no longer closes correctly. It pains me to look at it. Something happened involving this piece of jewelry. I reach for the tiny box and lift it out. The lid falls off in my hands to reveal a solitaire engagement ring. The stone is huge and perfect. I lift it from its padding for a moment, staring at it, wondering who it was meant for and what happened when he gave it to her. From the look of the box, it didn't end well. My heart sinks as I hold the ring. Cole acts pulled together, but at the moment I'm not so sure. It's like he puts his best foot forward and hides the rest. Things like lost loves and battered Tiffany's boxes aren't visible on his face. I breathe slowly and realize I'm holding a piece of Cole's past, something he locked away from the world. I return the ring to the box and put it back. Ignoring it, I reach toward the back of the safe where cash is piled in neat little bundles. I grab enough stacks and shove them into my backpack. Miss Todd is going to think I'm a thief if she sees me. I move faster.

Before I slam the safe closed, a piece of paper falls. I reach out and catch it. It's an old photograph. I can't ignore it. It's out an old picture of Cole wearing army clothes. STEVENS is across his chest, some medals line the other side. His eyes are cold and hard. He looks so young, younger than I've ever seen him. I flip the piece of paper over, looking for a date, wondering if it's real. Was Cole a solider? Why would he enlist?

Before I have another moment to consider it, I hear Miss Todd's heels clicking down the hallway toward me. Her slow steady sashay gives me time to put the photo back where it was, close the safe, and zip up my backpack.

When she walks through the door, I held up his camera like I've found it. She cocks her head at me, like she can't believe it. "He forgot his camera?" she asks, her narrow arms folding over her chest.

I nod and stuff that into my bag too. "Yeah, well, these things are expected. I think Cole's getting a little senile," I smile as I say it, half joking and not offering any other explanation. I have to get out of here.

She doesn't laugh at my joke. "But he went to a business meeting. At least, I thought—"

Nodding, I pass her and head toward the door. Speaking over my shoulder, as she follows me out, I say "He was. Then he said he wanted it. I don't know. Cole said he usually has one on him, and asked me to grab it. He'll be back later tonight. Tease him then. I sure will." Smiling at her, I wave and run through the door, leaving Miss Todd standing there with a response on her lips.

The cash on my back is making me nervous. If I get pulled over for driving like a crazy person, they'll instantly add my name to the terrorist watch list. That would suck.

Checking the time, I see that I'm cutting it really close.

After pulling into traffic, I open the throttle and punch it. The bike takes off, humming like a bee. I bob and weave through cars and trucks trapped in rush hour traffic. As soon as I'm back on Long Island, the wave of panic recedes. An hour and a half later I'm in Riverhead and my butt is vibrating like I'm still on the bike.

I leave my helmet with the motorcycle and walk into the jail. After a few wrong turns, I'm sent to the right person.

An old lady with face-saddlebags looks up at me, "Who are you here for, hun?"

I'm out of breath, and sweat makes my hair stick to my face. I push it back and say, "Cole Stevens."

She looks up at me from her metal desk. The eyebrow drawn on her face doesn't move. "The bail bondsmen closed at five. You'll have to wait until tomorrow. Next."

The guy behind me tries to push me out of the way, buy I hold out my arm like I'm going to close-line him if he tries to push in front of me. "Wait. I don't need a bond. I have cash." I say to her, reaching around for my bag. Suddenly I feel like saying that out loud was a stupid idea.

The look on her face confirms my stupidity. She sniffs and raises her bloodshot eyes back up at me, "You have ten grand on you? In cash?"

I nod. The tension in the room jumps about ten slots. She waves a pudgy hand at the guard. He steps closer. "We need a secure desk for this one." She jabs her thumb at me. "She walked in with ten grand in cash." They both roll their eyes like I'm an enormous pain in the ass. It's just after five, but by the time they get a secure desk, which was me and another civil service employee and a cop, it was nearly 6:00pm.

They are talking to each other after the amount is counted, and acting like I'm not even there. Finally, the woman hands me the bail slip and spews a bunch of stuff about how to get the bail money back.

"What do I do now?" I ask.

"Nothing," the cop says from behind me. "They'll show the judge the bail, and he approves it. If he gets the slip in the next ten minutes, your friend is out today. Otherwise, come back first thing tomorrow."

I nod and go to the waiting area. It's half empty. A pregnant woman sits across from me on a wooden bench from the fifties. No one looks at anyone else. I wonder what Cole did to get tossed in here. Part of me is nervous about that. I don't want to ask. It will conflict with the new image of him that's floating through my mind.

I think about the picture in the safe, that younger version of Cole in the uniform. I realize that I have no idea who he is. It's strange because after the past few days, I felt like I did know him. Cole seemed more at ease. He didn't hold back when he was teaching me. Passion filled his voice when he spoke about photography and art.

But this? This is insane. I hardly know him and yet I'm the one he trusted with his safe combination and bail money.

The metal security doors open and a cop walks through with Cole. He's dressed in a black suit. The jacket is hanging over his arm, his shirtsleeves are rolled up. Cole looks like he fell asleep in his suit. The cop tells Cole to get his things from the cashier's window, and then turns and walks back behind the doors.

The few people in the room look up when Cole walks out and quickly avert their eyes. Cole straightens his shoulders like he doesn't belong here. His cool blue eyes scan the room. He sees me and nods. I walk over to him. Part of me hesitates, like he could be dangerous, but my feet keep moving. I stop next to him.

Cole turns toward the cashier's window and takes a yellow envelope from the woman. He puts a ring back on his finger, his watch, and stuffs his wallet into his back pocket. He hands the envelope back to the woman and she throws it in the trash.

Cole turns and I follow him to the doors. When we step outside, there are no reporters. He smiles at me, "You did good, kid. Thanks." He sounds relieved. His posture changes and his shoulders relax a little. He takes a deep breath and runs his fingers through his hair.

I want to roll my eyes when he calls me kid, but I tease him instead, "No prob old dude," but I'm tense and I know he can hear it in my voice. Cole looks around, breathing the air like he was inside too long. I can't keep quiet. I have to know. "So, what'd you do?" He eyes me, startled, almost. He seems surprised that I ask. Tilting my head, I fold my arms across my chest saying, "You can't ask me to drive all the way out here and not tell me. What'd you do?"

He sighs and rubs his hands through his hair again. He does that when he's upset. I've seen him do that at work when he can't get a pose to work right. "It was nothing. Really—"

I can't let it slide. It would be the height of stupidity to do this and not insist on knowing what happened. I lean my face a little closer to his. Catching his gaze I say, "Ten grand worth of nothing? By the way, that was insane. You have a mini bank in your office. Who needs that much cash? Is that why they picked you up?"

He shushes me, and puts his hand on my back, leading me toward the parking lot. "Oh my god, Anna. Stop talking. Really. They're still criminals around. Do you want my office to be tossed before we even get back?"

Turning to look up at him, I ask one more time—one last time, "Listen, I think you're..." I'm so upset that I want to cry. I like working with him. I like my internship and whatever he just did shot it all to hell. There is no way I can finish now, and the craziest part is that I want to. When did that happen? I push away the thought. I'll deal with it later.

A knot forms in my throat. "Why'd you have to go do something horrible, Stevens? I actually liked going to work, and now you messed it up." I rub my face with the heel of my hand.

"What?" Shock is in his voice.

We're standing on a cement island between the police station and the parking lot. I'm so disappointed with him that I can't hide it. "I can't work for a felon, and I think it'd be better for both of us..."

His laughter cuts me off. His face lights up like I said the funniest thing ever, "What are you talking about, Lamore? You think I did something? What do you think I did!"

"I don't know. Something bad, since you won't tell me. I can't work for someone who might knock me into the East River one night." I'm only half joking. He worries me now. I thought about it on the way out here and unless he was tossed in the slammer because of unpaid parking tickets—which he should have been able to tell me—then I can't work for him anymore.

"You watch too much TV, Anna. Seriously." He scans the parking lot. "Where's my car?"

I look at him like he's crazy, "Not here. I took my ride. And I'm leaving." I wait half a beat and when he says nothing, I say, "Have a nice life, Cole" and walk away.

Cole reaches out and grabs my arm. A shiver shoots through my body from his touch. I jerk my arm away. He holds his hands up, like he doesn't want to fight, "Sorry. I didn't mean to..." he closes his eyes. When he opens them again, he says, "Anna, I didn't do anything. I was headed out here for a meeting and got ID'ed. Apparently some tranny slugged a cop today. I—" he swears and shakes his head "I can't believe you're making me say this. I got picked up because I look like him. They took me in because I matched his description. Then, I called you. Nothing happened. I swear."

I stare at him as he speaks. My lips part and my jaw drops. "You were arrested for looking like someone else?" He nods. "Someone who assaulted a cop?" He nods again. "A transvestite?" my voice squeaks the question as my lips quiver into a smile.

"Yes," his hisses, obviously still mad. "Now you see why I didn't want to tell you, and why I don't want anyone else to know. It's the kind of mistake that smears people and it doesn't matter if it's not true." The strain flows out of his voice and I feel his hand on my shoulder. I'm shaking from trying not to laugh. "Miss Lamore?"

I don't trust myself to answer; I nod, "Hmmm?"

Both his hands rest on my shoulders and I avoid his gaze. The giggles lick my stomach and toes, causing convulsions to rake through me as I try to hold myself still. Cole lifts my chin to meet his eyes. When a smile forms on his lips, I'm doomed. Before I know what's happening, we're both laughing. I double over, clutching my stomach, barely able to stand. Cole is leaning on me, laughing just as hard.

Wiping a tear from the corner of my eye, I straighten and look at him. "Your secret's safe with me."

"There is no secret, Miss Lamore. I don't wear women's clothes. I don't punch police officers." He's still smiling, his voice lighter. He shakes his head at me, like he can't believe he's laughing. He must have sat inside stewing for hours. "So where's this car of yours?"

Looking him in the eye, I grin, "I never said it was a car. Come on, old dude. I'll take you home." He follows me through the parking lot. When we stop before the bike, he tenses. I shove the golf ball helmet into his hands and tell him to put it on.

"You're kidding?" he asks, his voice too high. "You drove here on that?"

I nod, fastening my chin strap. Swinging my leg over the seat, I say, "Yup, I rode here on this. And this is your ride home. Get on." I start the bike, but Cole just stands there. I glance back at him. "What?"

"They just accused me of being..." he sputters, blinking hard like he's in a nightmare, "I can't ride two-up on the back of a pink bike with a girl helmet."

Grinning, I pat the seat, "Come on, Cole. Suck it up. Be my bitch for a few miles and we can call you a cab. There's a diner a few miles away. We can stop there, I can eat—you can grab a cab from there, that way no one knows where you were." His lips are in a soft smile, like he's in shock, and I wonder if he is.

Finally he slams the helmet on, fastens it, and gets on the bike behind me. "You've done this before? Driven with two people on this thing?"

"Yeah, just keep your feet up and don't grab my boobs if you freak out." He laughs. I feel his hands slide around my waist. His weight shifts behind me when he puts his feet on the back pegs. "Hold on tight," I say, and we're off.

CHAPTER 17

The diner was one of those circa 1950 deals, complete with shiny façade. Cole and I walk inside. Before we even have a chance to sit down, a guy walks in behind us with a girl on his arm. Her hair is teased out to Mars, and her implants bounce around under a tiny tank top. She's snapping her gum and I instantly hate her.

A middle-aged waitress sees us and holds up her pointer finger—the universal signal that she'll be right back. I glance through the place. There are about five tables filled, all in the same section. Great. That means she's waiting tables alone, so gum-smacker would end up right next to us. I try not to roll my eyes.

I don't really notice the guy she came in with until he speaks. He has that fake Brooklyn accent that Italian guys think is so macho. He's wearing a bowling shirt with a once-white undershirt peeking out. His hair looks like a skunk crawled onto his cranium and died. There's a peppering of dark hair all over his body. He looks like a Sasquatch with gold medals hanging around its neck. When he walked in, he had his hand in the girl's back pocket. They were laughing like something was hysterical.

It doesn't happen until the waitress walks away. The tension didn't balloon into anything until the ape-man tapped Cole's shoulder, "Hey buddy, you lose your balls or what? Who the fuck lets the dame drive?" He snort-laughs like he's hysterical.

As he's speaking, I turn and glance over my shoulder at him. My mouth starts to open with some snappy retort, but Cole's already acting. His fist flies into the man's face and connects with his nose in a loud crack. The hairy guy grips his face and blood streaks between his fingers. Before he can say a word, Cole is tugging my hand and pulling me out the door.

I'm stumbling through the parking lot toward the bike. Ape-man's girlfriend follows us out, but she doesn't approach. Instead she stays by the door screaming profanities at us, saying she's calling the cops.

"Cole, what the hell was that?" I finally manage, looking back over my shoulder. He sucker punched a guy in the face. Every muscle in Cole's body is tense. His fingers release my wrist when we get to the bike. He thrusts my helmet at me, an obvious sign that he wants to leave.

"Are you insane?" I scold. "You just made bail and now you punched some schmuck in the face?" I'm yelling and shaking as I start the bike.

Cole says nothing. We pull away and I don't know where to go. If they called the police, Cole's screwed. He doesn't tell me where to go or where to drop him off. He just sits on the back of the bike with his hands around my waist, rigid and fuming.

Since we are already out on Long Island, I decide to head toward my parent's house. They aren't too far away, and with the way Cole's fingers are digging into my sides, we can't get there fast enough. His reaction seems unwarranted, but he had his masculinity questioned too many times today. Apparently he was at his limit.

Cole doesn't complain, but I can tell the bike isn't his thing. Instead of wrapping his arms around my waist, he's been trying to keep a respectable distance between us, which makes it harder for me to keep a respectable distance from the asphalt. Cole didn't do corners when we started, but after the diner, he holds me tighter and leans farther as the bike winds down the ramps and turns corners. It makes it a hell of a lot easier to drive. I can't really blame him for not adapting to the motorcycle at first. Trust fund babies don't ride Harleys, not unless they are taunting some distant relative into disowning them. Me on the other hand, I was on my own and could do whatever I damn-well pleased.

The bike slows to a crawl and I stop a few houses down from my parents. Cole's grip on my waist loosens. Lifting my visor, I speak to Cole over my shoulder, "My parent's house is right here." He looks surprised, so I explain, "A guy and girl on a bike with a pink splotch is kind of easy to pick out. If that guy at the diner called the cops—"

He cut me off, "I know. I'm out on bail, even though I didn't punch the cop earlier."

I nod. "I know and it looks like you're punching your way to the Jersey shore." My lips pull into a smile. Cole's grimace doesn't crack. I get serious, "Hey, stay here for the night. It'll give you a few hours until your lawyer is back, and then you won't have to worry about being thrown in jail. From what I've heard, if you get tossed in after six, you stay there for the night." I cringe, and look at my parent's house muttering, "Although I'm not really sure if this'll be much better."

Cool blue eyes examine my face. They move from my left eye to my right, then down. It is such a sweet expression. I can tell that he doesn't understand why I'm being so nice to him. Looking at his hands, he asks, "Why are you helping me? I mean, I know you're altruistic, but I kind of deserve whatever I get after today."

Glancing at the side of his face I notice a dusting of stubble lining his jaw, and the tension lines between his eyes. "Yeah, well…" I debate telling him how much he's grown on me, how much I like him. "Let's just say that I wanted to punch the girl in the face, but I didn't have the guts to do it. We're a little more alike than I would have thought."

"Well spoken," the corner of his lips twitches like he wants to smile.

I grin, "Well, one of us has to be. We can't all turn into thugs and just smash people."

"Assholes," he corrects. His hands rest on my thighs just below my hips. The weight of his palm feels good. The crinkles at the corners of his eyes make me smile.

I laugh, "Fine, assholes. But I gotta tell you, my dad will probably mess with you, call you a girl, tell you that your way too old to be his daughter's boyfriend—and if you punch him—he will shoot you in the face. He's crazy like that."

I pull my visor down and drive down the street with Cole sputtering, "Boyfriend?"

CHAPTER 18

We're standing on the front porch. I've rung the bell and we're waiting. I can hear my Mom upstairs in the kitchen. They live in a spilt-ranch, so the house is broken up into several levels. The clatter of kitchen noises carries out onto the porch. The screen door is open to cool the house. The sun has set and the street lights just came on.

It's a balmy night. I pull my hair into a ponytail to keep it from frizzing, while we wait.

Cole follows me and stands there watching me before saying, "Boyfriend?"

I nod with a plastic smile on my face, my eyes looking straight ahead, knowing exactly what we are in for. "Yup. Wait and see. It doesn't matter what you say. I could tell them that you're a gynecologist making house calls and they'll still say that's nice." I glance over at him, "They're insane."

An older woman emerges on the landing. We can see her through the door. She's wearing a swimsuit cover-up. Her dark hair is frizzed at the temples. When she looks up, she walks toward the door with her arms extended, like she's planning on hugging me through the screen, "Anna, honey!" She's beaming, all five feet of her. Turning, she calls up the stairs, "Anna's here! Set another plate!"

I pull open the screen, and say, "Hey Ma," when she leans into hug me, her eyes shift to Cole who is standing behind me in the shadows. She stops, mid-hug.

"And who's this? You seeing someone without telling us?"

I shake my head. I don't know why I bother to talk, "No, Ma. This is Cole. We aren't dating." I give her a hug and step inside. Cole follows behind me, his expression a little concerned.

Ma steps toward Cole. He extends his hand, buy she swats it. I hear the slap. His eyes grow wider when she takes him in her arms for a hug, "Pish! You're practically family!" She's laughing and calls up the stairs,

"Better make that two plates! Anna brought her boyfriend!"

Suddenly my dad is standing on the landing. He's a stout guy with a beer belly and orange shorts that are a size too small. The neon color doesn't do anything for him either. There's a sausage impaled on his fork, "Anna's boyfriend? How'd you know she had a boyfriend?" Dad looks at me, shaking his head, smiling, "You never tell me nothing. Anna, why you holding things back from your old man?"

He waves his hands as he's speaking, shaking the fork. The impaled meat bobs on his utensil until the sausage flies off, and slaps me in the face. It stings before it falls. Cole reaches out and catches the meat before it hits the floor.

Cole leans in close to my ear so they can't hear, obviously terrified, "Oh my God—"

I don't bother muffling my voice, "Yeah, this is nothing. Wait for dinner."

I wipe the grease stain off my cheek, and follow my dad into the kitchen. Cole trails behind me trying to tell my mom the truth—that he's my boss—but she won't hear it. My dad just smiles and nods like a deranged hood ornament. It's like they hit fifty years old, and their brains entered I-need-a-grand-baby-now mode. It never turns off. Needless to say, they are perfect for scaring the crap out of guys I want to ditch. Since I was hoping things would have worked out with Edward, I didn't mention him, yet. As for Cole, it was the perfect alibi, assuming he didn't run from the house screaming after dinner.

CHAPTER 19

Ma hands Cole a plate and dumps a mound of anti-pasta on it. Tonight must be meat night. Dad stabs another sausage and puts it on his plate before over-loading mine. He pinches my cheek and says, "You're too skinny," while I stare directly at Cole, who's sitting across from me. He's trying hard not to laugh.

Cole lifts his glass to take a sip when my mom says, "It's not good for a pregnant woman to be so skinny. You remember that Cole. Fatten her up before you knock her up." She raises her glass to my dad and they clink them together, laughing. They think they're hysterical.

Cole chokes on his drink. Before he can recover, they've started talking about conception superstitions. I'm staring straight ahead with a blank look on my face, counting. If I leave the table before seventeen minutes, they'll pester us for the rest of the night. But I don't know if we can do it. About ten minutes have passed, and Cole looks like he's going to die. I lean back in my chair, and shove another piece of pork in my mouth.

Ma's saying, "It's a spoon under the bed, not a shoe!" She's yelling at my father who smiles sheepishly.

"A shoe seemed right," Dad mutters.

Cole's eyes meet mine. I can't tell if he's trying not to laugh or cry. The fact that my mom was a debutant makes this even more amusing, but he doesn't know that.

Two minutes left. Just two. We can do this. I count backwards from 120. My counting increases in speed as the conversation enters ground zero.

My mom ignores Dad, saying, "If you put a spoon under the bed while you have sex, you'll make a boy." She's pointing her fork at Cole while talking. She stops for a second and taps the empty utensil to her upper lip, "What's it for a girl? Frankie, do you remember?"

Dad grins, "A red ribbon. That's what your mother put under her mattress when we made you."

Ma slaps her hands together and points at Dad, "That's right!" They share a look that makes me sick. Then she gazes at me, saying, "And it worked, Anna!" She turns to Cole, and is talking to him like he's across the room. She's so loud, "We wanted a baby girl, and see—the red ribbon brought Anna."

She's still talking, saying things that make me cringe. I pick at dinner and notice that Cole hardly eats. I make a mental note to sneak into the kitchen after they've gone to bed. I also note to never wear a red ribbon ever again.

I tune back in when my mom is starting to talk positions, "Missionary is God's preference for boys, but girls, Cole you have to—"

Three. Two. One. I jump up. Cole mirrors me and finds his feet. I say, "Thanks for dinner. Since we're living in sin and trying to fornicate a set of twin grandbabies for you, do you mind if we share the den tonight?"

Ma and Dad are speechless. They say nothing as I take Cole's hand and pull him out the backdoor. We sit in the yard talking until my parents go up to bed. They watch us out the window like we're celebrities while they do the dishes. Periodically they wave through the window.

My parents are a little crazy, and I understand why. I just can't tell anyone about it. They're alone. I'm their only child. It was hard when my mom was disowned. Every single relative cut her off, and all because her evil mother didn't like my dad. Frankie the Dock Dude wasn't classy enough for her daughter. Grandmother forbade the relationship. My mother responded by eloping. Grandmother disowned them, and threw her daughter out like she was trash. They've never spoken again.

My parents had been dirt poor. There were times when we had no food, no medicine. I still remember in vivid detail how hard they tried to give me things that the other girls had, but I usually went without. I learned from them that life isn't about the stuff—it's about the relationships—and some relationships are worth fighting for.

I want that. I want to be so insanely in love with someone that I'd walk away from everything I knew, just to be with him.

CHAPTER 20

I feel restless, like I won't ever be satisfied. Cole's hands are warm. His smooth skin slides over my bare waist as he kisses me harder. My lips burn, they throb as I pull him closer to me. His thick hair is tangled in my fingers, his strong arms around my waist, pulling us closer—tighter together. Heat fills me. A burning desire to feel him inside consumes every thought I have.

There is nothing but him and me.

My nails claw his back as his kisses leave a hot trail down my neck. Our clothes are gone. It's just his slick body against mine, but he won't take me. He won't push inside of me. I cry out, saying his name, begging him to take me. The third time I plead, he answers me. Without a word, he flips me over. I land on the sheets, and look up at him. My legs are splayed before him, completely exposed.

Cole doesn't hesitate. His hard body meets mine and he pushes into me, rapidly, over and over again. I can't stop calling his name. I want him, I want him to fill me with come.

I want things I shouldn't want. I feel things I shouldn't feel.

There is no hesitation, no holding back. We move together like we were made for each other.

"Cole," I say softly.

A hand shakes my shoulder. The dream shatters, and fades, but the emotions are still flooding my body. The spot between my legs is pulsating like he was really there, even though he wasn't. Slowly, I realize I was dreaming and open my eyes.

Horrified, I'm looking up into Cole's face, "Anna, you okay?" His eyes are concerned, searching my face for answers that I can't say.

Pushing up, I shake the sleep from my eyes, "I'm fine." My voice catches in my throat.

Cole nods and sits on the coffee table across from the couch. He's still watching me. I feel his sapphire eyes on the side of my face, though I don't look at him.

After that dream, I don't think I can ever look at him again. Heat sears my cheeks and I wish I could hide, but there is nowhere to go. I know my mind was only replaying the lies I told my parents, but it felt real and that's what scares me.

SECRETS

Volume 2

CHAPTER 1

"I wasn't really sleeping well either," Cole says sympathetically. He has no idea what he's doing to me. I'm breathless, embarrassed by things he can't possibly know, but it still makes my cheeks burn.

My emotions are jumbled. I look up at him. He's too old. I'm too young. He's from money. I hate money. I glance at Cole again. Damn. I still want him. That stirring, whatever put the idea into my head didn't leave when I woke up, and having him that close is like setting a magnet on a compass. My emotions are spinning like a top.

It's after 2:00am, but I feel wound tight. Pushing off, the couch I tell him, "I'm getting a drink. You want one?"

Smiling, he teases, "Sure, but are you legal?"

My cotton shorts cling to my hips as I walk away. I laugh over my shoulder, "Legal to do things you couldn't imagine, old man."

I have no idea why I said that, but it makes me feel better. Cole remains in the den, but by the time I come back with drinks, he's sitting on my bed, also known as the couch.

He was sleeping on the floor next to me. The den doors were closed and my parents left us alone to make babies all night.

I hand him a glass with whiskey at the bottom and a can of Coke. I have a glass of wine. When he takes his glass, I clink them together, "Cheers."

He nods, pours the Coke into his glass, and puts his feet up on the table and looks at me, "What are we drinking to?"

I say the first thing that flies into my head, "To your appreciation for women, but not women's clothes. Unless you count Le Femme's panties. You don't wear those, do you?" I laugh and sip my wine.

"Only on my head. That one with the apple makes a really cool mask," he laughs and I spew a sip of wine, trying to stifle a laugh. "That's second grade underpants humor, Lamore. Seriously, underpants jokes make you laugh?"

I'm covering my mouth so I don't spew again and try to swallow the wine left in my mouth. Nearly choking, I laugh, "Combined with the image of you dressed as a super hero, sporting tights, with a panty-mask on your face, yes."

Cole grins at me.

I rest my head against the back of the couch. Cole sits next to me, his bare chest is distracting. He's wearing his jeans, and is barefoot. I watch his chest rise and fall out of the corner of my eye. Damn dream. I shrug like he doesn't affect me. I don't want him to.

Changing topics I say, "I'd like to see your paintings, the ones you told me about the other day."

"Oh," and then he's quite. His eyes look into his glass like it has answers that he doesn't.

"I take it that you don't show that stuff to people too often?"

He shakes his head, "No, not really." He's silent for a moment, then says, "If you really want to see them, I'll show you. I owe it to you for tonight."

"Psh," I say swatting him in the shoulder, "You owe me nothing. It's not like I would have left you sitting there." I stare at the ceiling, not thinking. Well, not wanting to.

"You're a rare breed, Lamore." He finishes his drink, sets it down, and threads his fingers behind his head.

"You have no idea," I glance at my wine glass and set it down. I rub my eyes with my hands.

He watches me before saying, "You say that like it's a bad thing."

"That's because most of the time it is." I look at him.

Cole's sitting next to me, stretched out, completely at ease. At least he appears that way. Everything about him says he's comfortable in his own skin, that he likes who he is and what he's become. He glances at me out of the corner of his eye, "How? How is that bad?"

"It just is. I'm a moron magnet. Being me attracts every loser in a twenty mile radius. The guy seems nice at first, but each and every one of them is totally messed up. Or maybe it's me. Maybe I'm the one who's messed up." These were thoughts that had been banging around in my brain. Without Emma to talk to, they stayed there. Cole rattled me and has made me feel ten times more alive in the past day than anyone else ever has.

Cole laughs initially, but when he realizes I was serious, he says, “Anna, you can’t be serious. It’s not you.”

I pull a pillow across my chest, “How would you know? You just met me. And it’s not like you know me that way. You can’t be sure it’s not me.” My voice softens as I speak.

“It’s not you,” he repeats. Tension lines his shoulders. It wasn’t there a moment ago, but it seems hard to miss now.

“Sorry,” I say. “I’m making you uncomfortable. I didn’t mean to—”

When he turns to face me, my breath catches in my throat. His eyes are so soft, so sincere, that I can’t look away. He takes the pillow that I crushed against my chest and I feel exposed.

He says certainly, “You’re not making me uncomfortable.” He places the pillow on the floor. When he turns back to me, he asks, “Do you know how I can tell that it’s not you?” I shake my head. My heart races faster. His eyes search my face like he can’t believe that I don't see that I'm not the reason morons flock to my side. "You're naturally inquisitive. You question everything, to the point of exasperation," he smiles at me like it's an endearing trait. "Anna, people who question things usually know themselves pretty well. They want to know why things work and they try to fix them when they don't. If he was doing that—if he was trying to take care of you—you wouldn't be asking me this right now, you'd be asking him."

Blinking hard, I look away. I pull my knees into my chest, and wrap my hands around my ankles. "He's tried to do what I want." I realize where this conversation is going. I'm not sure if I want to talk about it with him. I barely know Cole, but after today, things have changed. The fact that he blindly trusts me wasn't missed. And it's so easy to talk to him.

"And?" Cole prompts.

"And he offered to do what I want, but it's not the same. It's like the difference between really wanting a cookie and just thinking it's so-so." I'm staring at my feet. When he doesn't' answer, I look up at him.

He's smiling at me with a strange expression on his face. "What?"

"Cookies? Really? We're using a cookie metaphor in a sex conversation?" he smiles at me, and nudges my shoulder with his. "Come on. Talk to me. You know my darkest secret. You can tell me yours."

I smile softly, "How'd you know it was about sex?" I cringe as I say it, my cheeks growing hotter.

"Why else would you be beat-red right now? And I'm onto your diversions. Cookies, Skittles—do you always chose food when you're trying to skip over something important?" I smile shyly at him, but don't respond. I can't say it. I want to, the question is sitting on my tongue, but I can't. "Come on Lamore," he urges, bumping my shoulder again

"Fine," I say nervously. "I'll just ask, but don't laugh at me. This is a girl question, and you're not a girl."

"Obviously," he grins.

I bump his shoulder back and then say, "Do you think a relationship has a chance if one partner is too bland for the other?"

"Bland?" he asks like he doesn't know what I mean.

I nod, "Yeah, like he likes things kinky and I like things vanilla." I have no idea why I switched our roles. Edward was vanilla, and I wanted to be the kink goddess. I didn't realize I was wringing my fingers until Cole patted my hand.

"Stop," he releases my fingers when I look up at him. "It doesn't mean it can't work out, but there will also be a rift there for him. You won't feel it, but he's not going to feel satisfied as frequently. That's an issue in any relationship. And it's not something that's your fault. It's just the way it is."

"You don't think he'd change? That he could be more… vanilla?" There is desperation in my voice, like I know the answer before he even says it. Somewhere in the back of my mind, I already know that things are destined to fail with Edward. I just don't want to write off a good man for something that seems so selfish, especially if he is satisfied. At the same time, dealing with bland sex for a lifetime is something that doesn't hold much appeal.

Cole looks aside, and shakes his head. "Sorry, but no. People like that tend to be passionate and they want to show it. It surfaces in other areas of their lives, too. A person who speaks, acts, and breathes passionately isn't going to become a subdued lover. It's not who they are... "

Staring at his eyes, I speak without thinking, "A person like you."

Cole is passionate. He knows what I'm talking about. While he was telling me what he thought, I realized that he's talking about himself. My face flushes when I realize what I've said. His eyes fixate on my lips until I look away.

He grins at me, "A person exactly like me. Listen, Anna—" he reaches for my hand. When he brushes his fingers against it, I look up at him. He doesn't touch me for long. It's little things here and there. I look up at him, and he says, "I think I'm just telling you what you already know."

His voice is soft, his eyes don't quite meet mine. Cole rubs his thumb against the back of my hand. I can't stop staring at it. My heart is pounding. I can't control how he makes me feel.

"Don't change for anyone. In the end, it's not worth it," he says and then grins again. "Besides, depriving the world of Anna Lamore would be a sin. I'd have to seriously punch this dude in the face."

His words are so unexpected that I snort-laugh. It is one big honk. My hands fly to my mouth to hide it, but my face turns beet red anyway. Cole laughs, his eyes bright blue and shining. The warmth in his voice fills me up inside. The rich tones flow so easily, so confidently. I want what he has. I want to feel comfortable in my own skin.

When our eyes lock, I wonder what he's thinking, what he sees when he looks at me. Previously, he's said I was a child, but his gaze now says otherwise. The intensity of his eyes makes me hot. A current runs through the center of my body. I can't look away. Cole leans closer until I feel his breath wash across my lips. Every inch of me is vibrating. I want him to touch me, to feel his palm against my face and taste his beautiful lips.

My gaze drifts to his mouth. He blinks slowly, once, and I know he's going to pull away. Before he has the chance, I pretend that nothing happened, that I don't feel the attraction. I lean into his chest before he can say anything and rest my head against his shoulder.

Surprise fills me when Cole's arms wrap around me, pulling me tight. We stay like that for a long time, each of us too afraid to move. This is the first time I know how much of an effect Cole Stevens has on me. It shakes me to my core. The dream blindsided me, and there's no stopping it.

My body has reacted to him from day one, but I refused to acknowledge it.

After a few moments, we pull apart. Cole lowers himself to the floor and I close my eyes and lean back on my pillow. I twist the blankets between my fingers. My heart thumps in my chest like I'm startled. I am startled. I like him. I have a thing for Cole. Every muscle inside me cords tightly, while my fingers tug at the afghan in near panic.

CHAPTER 2

The next morning, I wake up ready to pretend nothing happened, not that anything really did happen. It just feels like it did. Cole isn't next to me on the floor when I sit up. His blankets are folded on a chair. He let me sleep and is enduring my parents alone. Quickly, I pull on my jeans and tank top, and run a brush through my hair. As I approach the stairs, I hear my mother's voice. She's laughing, along with my dad and Cole.

When I get to the top of the stairs, I hesitate. Cole is sitting with my parents and it appears that they are having a somewhat normal conversation. I stand still, listening.

Ma says to Cole, "So what about this one? Was this airbrushed?" She pushes the paper toward him. Cole reaches out and slides it closer while sipping his coffee.

He nods, "Yes, the models in the ads are Photoshopped—that's like airbrushing, but it's more than that. All of these are manipulated to some extent. Real thighs don't look like that."

Ma tugs the paper away and looks at it closer, "How do you know? I can't see it. And this girl is so skinny. Her thighs could really look like that."

Cole shakes his head and pulls the paper back. "It's my job. We do this all day long. So does Anna, and she's very good at it. But, sometimes on the cheaper product lines you can see artifacts, like—" he's turning pages. After flipping three times, he stops and smooths the newsprint, "here. See this?"

Ma tugs the paper back, and her jaw drops. She thrusts the pages at Dad, who is smiling like he already knows all this stuff. "Frankie, did you see this? Did you know they could do that?"

"Yeah. They've been doing that for years. I told you real women don't look like that. You're beautiful and always have been. Those twigs got nothing on you, baby," he takes her hand while he's talking. He's always adored her. They gaze at each other.

Cole smiles and looks up, seeing me in the doorway. He stands and crosses the room, "Good morning, lover. Can I get you some breakfast?" He kisses me on the cheek and I nearly fall over. A voice inside my head giggles hysterically and instructs me to never wash my face again. I stare at Cole as he takes a plate and fills it with pancakes and sausages. He hands it to me and grabs me a cup of coffee. "Come on. Sit. Eat. We have time."

I make my way to the table. We sit together and eat. The conversation doesn't drift to loins or babies. A smile spreads across my face and I can't hide it.

———

It's Saturday. By the time I get back to the apartment, Emma is gone. I get in the shower, and crank up the hot water. I stand there letting it wash over me until my skin is numb. There are so many things that I want to do, but I don't know where to start. Cole left my parent's house right after breakfast. His driver picked him up in a shiny black car. He offered to take me home, but I didn't want to leave my bike behind. I thanked him and told him I'd be in later.

This week has been so strange. If someone told me that the man who shattered my dreams last weekend would be spending the night with me and starring in my naughty fantasies, I wouldn't have believed them.

Before I leave for work, I call Edward and tell him that I want to meet up with him later. Breaking up is going to suck, but it's inevitable. There's no future for us. This is more humane, even if he does love me. I just hope that he'll understand. I can't change for him, and he shouldn't have to change for me. Somewhere out there, there's a girl that's perfect for him, and I know that it's not me.

I tug on a pair of shorts and a cami. I'm not really dressed for work, but there are no clients today and it's insanely hot. I leave my motorcycle in the garage across the street and make my way to Le Femme via the subway, then trek the last stretch on foot. By the time I arrive, my cute outfit is soaked in sweat and my hair is deflated. I look horrible. After I push through the door, I walk to the mirror, trying to salvage my appearance, at least a little bit. Snatching a tissue, I blot the sweat off my face. Most of my make-up floated away a few blocks back. Sun-freckles and rosy cheeks peek back at me. The sheen on my face refuses to be tamed. I stand there for a second and look at the tissue, wondering if I should even bother.

"Hey," Cole walks up behind me. His voice sounds soft at first, almost timid. "You're here. And… um, wow… You look…"

I huff, "Like a mess. Tell me there are no clients today. Please. I can't fix this." I gesture to my face which is glowing again in an I-just-worked-out kind of way.

Cole leans back on Miss Todd's empty desk. The muscles in his arms bulge. His shirt clings to his body and I realize that I haven't seen him dressed like this before. He looks like he's headed for the beach, wearing shorts and a tee shirt. The office is warmer than usual. There's a sheen of sweat on his skin. He grins, "There are no clients. We're editing all day. And you look great, so don't worry about it."

I laugh, "Yeah. Nice try, but I saw the way I rendered you silent a few seconds ago." The way he looks at me makes my stomach flip. It's like seeing me in a disheveled mess makes him like me more. I stop fussing in front of the mirror and toss the tissue.

He slides off the desk and walks toward me, "The air conditioner is having issues. We'll be lucky if it doesn't totally die. The repair guys will be here later to work on it. Come on. Let's get to editing." He tilts his head and turns. Cole shoves his hands in his pockets and I follow him back to the studio.

A few hours later, sweat is pouring off of me. The air conditioner totally died and the repair guy hasn't shown up. Cole calls them and is assured that we are next on the list, so we sit and wait. I stop editing and lay down on the cool concrete floor. Sweat was dripping into my computer keyboard; it's so insanely hot up here. The cement feels nice on the back of my neck and legs. I sigh and fold my hands behind my head.

When Cole notices, he walks over and stands above me, his hands on his hips, "Get up, Lamore. There's more work to be done, and we'll be here until tomorrow at this rate." He holds out a hand to me.

I don't take it. "It's got to be 20 degrees cooler down here. We should move the computer to the floor. This is way better."

When I don't take his hand, Cole cocks his head and places his hands on his hips. I laugh. He looks ridiculous, "What? Are you gonna yell at me? It's like a hundred degrees in here. Besides, you'd be sitting on the floor if you could get up again. Ya know, without using that button around your neck." I change my voice to mimic the old lady on the TV, "Help! I've fallen and I can't get up!" My laughter obscures my words by the time I finish teasing him.

Cole moves fast. He falls to his knees and lands by my side before starting a tickle fight that brings tears to my eyes. His fingers move over my slick skin. I'm laughing so hard that I can't breathe.

"If I could get up again," he mutters with a smile on his face. "I'm not that much older than you, Lamore. In fact, you're going to be the one who begs for help getting up." He tickles me more. My legs kick as I try to roll out of reach. I manage to flop onto my stomach, but he grabs my ankle and pulls me back. I squeal as my cami hikes up. Frantically, my hands shift from the tickle fight, trying to keep my shirt from revealing too much skin.

Cole is laughing, "Surrender, Lamore. Beg me for help." He bats his eyes and says in a girlie voice, "I've fallen and I can't get up." His fingers wiggle against the bare skin at my waist, as I laugh hysterically.

Kicking at him, my foot connects with the side of his face by accident. The impact is audible. I didn't mean to do that. Startled, we both pause for a moment. His jaw drops, so does mine. No one laughs. No one breathes until he grins, saying, "You're gonna pay for that."

Before he grabs for me, I try to crab crawl away, but Cole yanks my leg and I fall on my back. Suddenly he's over me, his hands trying to still my wrists. We roll around on the floor for a minute, both of us much hotter than a few minutes ago. Sweat trickles down my face. The little beads roll down my neck and into my cleavage. Cole's eyes trace the movement. I try to knock him off his knees, but when he goes down, he pins my body to the floor, clutching my wrists.

We're both breathing hard when he yanks my hands and slams them down over my head, stretching me. As he does it, our gazes lock, and now my shirt has crawled up, revealing more than I'd normally show. I feel the bare skin on my stomach against his shirt. It makes me feel like I'm falling. I don't want it to stop. There's no laughter, just ragged breathing as we stare at each other. He remains on top of me and I can't move.

I feel lost. My head is swimming, stuck in the haze that comes with being high from laughter. The way he looks at me sends a shiver through my body. He feels it move through me, but he doesn't release me. I don't want him to. I want to know what this passionate man will do, how he treats his lovers. I can't ignore the dream I had last night at my parents' house.

I close my eyes slowly, and look back into his beautiful face, "Do I really have to beg, Cole?" My voice is too deep, too sensual. I meant to be playful, but can't manage it. My voice betrays me and my innocent question sounds anything but innocent. Heat rushes to my cheeks, and it feels like every bit of my dream is painted across my face. I don't breathe as I watch him, waiting for him to react, but he doesn't.

Cole's expression doesn't change—his intense gaze darkens, his lips part. There is no smile on his face. Not anymore. Something changed, a moment of flirtation that crossed a line. We both know it. Cole's grip on my wrists tightens; his eyes are still locked on mine. His taller frame allows him to pull me slightly, stretching my body. My breasts push into his chest harder. I gasp, wishing, wanting something that I can't quite comprehend. Every inch of my skin feels cold and hot at the same time. Cole's lips are just above mine. I want him to pull us together, and nip me, taste my kiss, and then do it all again.

Cole's body is tense, every muscle perfectly formed. His ribs expand as he tries to steady his breath. I can feel his heart pounding when he tugs me. The movement makes him lay flat against my chest. His eyes are so dark.

He whispers, "Hell, yes. Beg for it, Anna. Beg me…" His lips are so close to mine, but he won't kiss me. I wriggle beneath him, trying to close the distance, but he won't let me.

Before either of us can say another word the chime from the front door sounds. We split apart. Cole springs to his feet, rubbing his hands through his hair. His back is to me as he leaves the room to let the repair guy in. I can't read the expression on his face, but the way he moves, the way his broad shoulders slant as he walks away—it looks like regret.

My stomach falls. I wonder if he regrets not kissing me, or regrets being in that position with me at all. I'll never ask him.

CHAPTER 3

When Cole returns, I'm working at my desk. I glance at him out of the corner of my eye. He doesn't notice. When he sits down he acts the way he did before our roll on the floor. My stomach is twisting in knots. Looking at him makes me want to touch him, his beautiful face, his silky hair, so I turn back to my computer. The screen glows in front of me. I edit pictures until I can't see anymore. The world has turned blurry, and my eyes sting. Cole tells me to leave several times, but I won't. The work isn't done yet, and in truth, I don't want to leave him. I want to see if there's more there. If he'll take me in his arms when the last photo is edited, and the computers are shut off. But, he doesn't.

We speak to each other like good friends and nothing more. I've become accustomed to his voice, the intensity of his gaze. Passion burns within him in a way that I couldn't have imagined. When we finally get through with work, we ride the elevator down to the lobby together. It's past midnight. I cancelled my break-up dinner with Edward to finish working. That was the only good that came out of staying late.

Cole is leaning against the metal rail in the elevator. His eyes are on the side of my face. I have my head tipped back against the wall, tilted up, eyes closed. Every muscle in my body aches. Between the heat and the number of hours I've been awake, I can barely stand. The thought of walking and then taking multiple trains home clouds my thoughts.

Finally he breaks the silence, "You shouldn't go home tonight." His words sink into me. I wonder if I'm hallucinating when I open my eyes and look at him. He's staring straight at me, acting like he just said something completely reasonable.

I know what he means, but I smile and say faintly, "Yeah Cole? Where should I go?" I shift my weight to the other foot. I can't look at him. I don't want any of the hope that's filling my chest. It's telling me that he wants me, that he likes me, that he'll act on it.

I beat it down, and stuff it into a closet at the back of my mind.

He leans an arm above me. Tilting my face up to see his, he says, “Come home with me. I can tell you’re exhausted—”

I stare at him. My heart is pounding. I can’t tell what he’s thinking, what he’s offering. I play it safe. Shaking my head, I say, “It’s okay. The subway isn’t too far and I’ll be home in less than an hour—“

His hand cups my cheek, “My place is less than ten minutes from here. Think about it. In fifteen minutes you could be in a hot shower, in thirty you could be relaxing with your feet up.” He reaches for a strand of hair and tucks it behind my ear. “Come on, Lamore. I can’t turn you loose on the streets. What if someone molests you?”

Lamore. He put that distance there, like we’re buds—but he’s tucking hair behind my ear and standing too close for that. I don’t understand what he’s doing. It’s like he wants me, but hasn’t committed to the idea yet.

My voice is light, “Oh, and you won’t?” I laugh, but it sounds hollow. I tell myself it’s because I’m tired. It has nothing to do with making bad decisions based on libido in an elevator.

He leans closer, his lips nearly brushing mine. When he speaks, his warm breath slips across my mouth, "Not unless you want me to—"

Our eyes lock. It's the first time either of us has said anything, made any indication that… that what, Anna? My inner nun is beating me over the head with a ruler. He's too old. He's too wild. He's nothing I want, nothing I need. Cole Stevens is chocolate-covered sin and I need someone steady, like fiber. My mind flashes to Edward, to vanilla, good old reliable Edward.

I smile softly at him and lean my head back against the wall. "I can't," I hear myself say. "I have to get home and pack. We're supposed to leave for Long Island tomorrow and I haven't packed a thing. And there's something else I have to do. It's important." I'm biting my lower lip. His eyes fixate on the movement.

Cole nods, saying, "I see." Stepping back, he slides his hands into his pockets.

I realize that it sounds like I'm blowing him off. I reach out and touch his shoulder.

He looks down at me more cautiously than before, "Cole, I really have to do something. I need to break up with my boyfriend. I can't leave for three months and lead him on. I was supposed to do it tonight." I'm staring into his eyes, thinking *but I want to stay with you and here you are offering and I'm saying no. What the hell is wrong with me?*

"I was just offering you a bed for the night," he says, like he meant nothing—like I mean nothing. The elevator chimes that we are on the ground floor. The doors slide open and save Cole from getting slapped. I want to scream at him. I want him to stop playing and tell me what he thinks, but he strides away. When we exit the building I grab his arm. He stops and looks at me.

"Tell me what you want." There. I said it. Point blank. My heart is slamming into my ribs and I feel like I can't breathe.

He nods, smiling, and continues to walk toward a black car parked at the curb. I follow. Emotions are flowing through me in a maddening rush. I don't know exactly what I want from him or what I expect him to say, and when he responds I can hear the darkness in his voice warning me away, "Miss

Vanilla, you shouldn't say things like that to me. You won't like where they lead you."

By the time he pulls the car door open, he's back to being carefree happy Cole. He looks apathetic, like he doesn't care about me one way or another, but his eyes tell another story. His eyes are nearly twenty years older than mine, and have seen things mine will never see. It's like the speck of soul that shines through has been snuffed out and replaced with a Cole that knows the world and knows there's no future for us. My stomach falls into my shoes. I don't like that world.

Before he slides into the car, he looks at me and says, "Last chance." The way he looks at me makes it clear that this is an invitation to his bed, not his home.

Something about the way he says it sounds like a one-night-stand. While Cole might be insanely hot, I'm not that kind of girl. I shake my head. My voice is soft, "I don't do one-nighters. Sorry." Before he can say anything else, I turn on my heel and walk away.

CHAPTER 4

The sun spills into the room. I cover my face with a pillow. I want to go back to sleep, but I can't stop thinking about Cole. Miss Vanilla. Ha! If he only knew. I breathe deeply and finally decide to get up. It's a little after six in the morning. I hear Emma in the kitchen. When I emerge I see her dressed in work clothes, sipping a cup of coffee.

"Hey," I say rather groggily.

"Well, look who's home. Edward was looking for you."

I nod, "Yeah, I had to work late last night." She glances at me over the rim of her cup. "I told him to come by in a couple of hours."

"So, the new boss is a pain in the ass?"

I shrug, "Maybe a little." I take a cup and fill it with coffee. I feel her eyes on my back while I do it and I start to wonder what she's thinking. "Why do you ask?"

"Oh, I don't know." She tears a piece of toast in half and offers me a piece of her breakfast. I take it. "He has you working odd hours, is dragging you out to the Island again, and I'm not going to see you for the rest of the summer. He's a pain in the ass, Anna." She's laughing, as she turns and puts her empty mug in the sink. Glancing in the mirror, she checks her make-up and heads for the door. She shouts, "Check in once in a while so I know you're safe. Your boss gives me the creeps."

"Sure," I reply and the door slams shut. I'm staring at her toast. Something bothers me, something she said, but I don't know what.

Ignoring the sensation, I jump in the shower. I take my time getting dressed and then pack. When I pull open my negligée drawer, I wonder if I should take anything. What Cole suggested last night killed me. A one-night stand. I slam the drawer shut. There is no way I'm sleeping with him. Whatever I thought happened, didn't. It is that simple. He sees me as a tryst and nothing more.

The doorbell rings, and breaks my thoughts. I walk toward the door telling myself that this is necessary, but when I yank open the door, Edward is standing there with a huge bouquet of yellow roses. My mouth opens into a little O and I can't talk. I feel like scum. He hands me the flowers. I smile at him sadly, but he mistakes my emotion as something good.

"Hey, baby," he kisses my cheek and pushes past me into the apartment. "I remember you saying you love yellow roses, and well, I thought since you were going away for a while, that you could take them with you to remember me by."

Gazing at the flowers, I say, "Edward… these are lovely. Thank you, but—"

He turns and looks back at me. Taking the flowers from my hands, he places them on top of my suitcase in the hallway, before reaching for me. He slides his arms around my waist and pulls me to him. I feel like I'm hugging an eel. I can't muster the strength to pretend anymore. This relationship has run its course and I want out.

He smiles huge, and turns, saying, "Emma has a vase here. She said you could take it with you…"

"Edward, stop." But he doesn't. He's smiling like he's happy, totally ignoring that my mood doesn't match his. I push away from him, but he's walking away from me to get the vase. I follow him into the kitchen. "Please stop. I need to tell you something," my voice is too loud, too curt.

He straightens and turns to look at me. His eyes sweep over me and he shakes his head like he's missed something, "Oh, I'm sorry babe. I didn't see it before. You're all shaken up because you're going to miss me." Reaching for me, he takes my hands in his and says, "I love you, babe. It won't be that long. We can—"

I cut him off, "This isn't working out." I blurt it out while tugging my hands away. The way he came through the door and continues to speak makes it very hard for me to say anything. I realize that he keeps doing this to me—when I try to talk, he talks over me. It's like he's trying to control the relationship and keep it from ending. But after I've yelled at him, I think I'm wrong. Edward looks like I've hit him with a frying pan.

I sound apologetic, "I really like you, but I just think we're a mismatch. We're too alike in some ways, and not enough in others. In the long run, we'll both be sorry for it. I can't do that to you. I think we need to take some time to—"

"See other people. Sure, why not?" He shrugs, sounding angry. His fingers ball into fists and he turns like he wants to punch the wall, but he doesn't. Instead he takes a deep breath and tries to shake off the rage building inside of him. I've never seen him so angry. I never thought he had it in him.

Holding his head high, he turns back to me, "Just tell me why."

"I did," I say. I feel nervous now and I don't know why. Something about him makes me step away, "We won't make each other happy. You're vanilla, Edward, and I'm sticky. You said so yourself—"

He steps toward me, hands out, "Baby, I said I could change that for you. I could—"

"No, you can't. You can't change who you are, what you want, what turns you on. We're not the same, Edward. We never will be. It just wasn't meant to be." He stands there silently, looking completely shocked. "I'm sorry," I say.

Edward nods, but says nothing as he heads toward the door. I feel horrible. The tightness in my throat is making it impossible to swallow. I want to say something to him, comfort him, but that will only make it worse.

Before he pulls the door open, he turns and looks at me, "We could have been great, you know. You could have learned to like the way I love you."

I stare at him for a moment, and then say, "But I want more that…"

He glances up at me, "So, there's someone else?"

Hell no, there is not someone else. I feel the retort bubbling inside of me, but I shake my head and say, "No. I'm not seeing anyone else. I'm not sleeping with anyone else. It's been me and you this whole time and we haven't had sex once. Every time I'm with you, I feel like you don't want me, that I'm not good enough for you." I am scared to tell him how much more I want, how much more I need. He doesn't know, but I think he suspects. "I can't do it anymore. I've had this relationship before. It doesn't end well."

He blinks slowly. The sadness fades from his eyes. His gaze meets mine and he says, "I love you, Anna. I always will."

"Then let me go."

CHAPTER 5

By the time I'm driving East on my bike, I'm in a horrible mood. Edward wouldn't take no for an answer. He is convinced that we belong together, that destiny will reunite us. I ended up being harsher than I wanted. I took his beautiful roses, shoved them back into his arms, and pushed him out the door. I literally threw him out. He gave me his love and I tossed him out like trash.

I wish there was traffic, something to distract me during the drive, but the roads are fairly empty. When I hit the end of the highway it turns into rural roads and barrenness. There isn't another vehicle in sight.

I follow Cole's directions and stop at a beach-front home that has been converted into his studio. Outside there is the Le Femme sign, but the colors are different—hot pink and black. His New York City studio is pale blue and gray. I wonder why this one is different, but don't pay it much attention. Different locations can have different colors. Besides, what do I know? Le Femme is his business, not mine, and if he thinks it makes sense to rebrand his studio, that has nothing to do with me.

Parking the bike on the side of the house, I get off and stretch. The air is balmy and warm. The sound of the ocean fills my ears. Seeing Cole after this morning's event with Edward is too much. My emotions are in overdrive and I can't contain them. It feels like my eyes will betray me and gush tears at any moment.

No, I can't see Cole. Not yet. So, I set my helmet on the bike and walk toward the water. The sound of the ocean lapping into the shore calms me. Cole is so lucky to have this place. I'd live here year-round if I had a place like this. It is isolated, but part of a smaller town outside of the Hamptons hamlet, or whatever you call them. Townships? Anyway, it is perfect. The town itself feels like a piece of Americana New England. It is picturesque. Add in the house and it's a dream. I sit down on the sand, and watch the waves crash into the shore. The wind whips my hair, separating tiny strands that float on their own. My mind clears after a few moments and I feel a little better.

"It's beautiful, isn't it?" his voice flows over my shoulder, sending a chill down my spine. I turn, sucking in a deep breath. Cole's staring at the surf like there might be mermaids in there.

"Sublimely so," I answer softly. I wonder how Cole can act like nothing happened last night, but he does. It makes me wonder if I misread him, if he was really just offering me a guest room.

"Ah, and that's the most bewitching kind of beauty. Isn't it?" Cole is standing barefoot a few paces from me.

He offers his hand, but I don't take it. "Come on, Lamore. Let me show you around." He puts his hands back in his pockets and gazes at the ocean once more before turning back toward the house. He walks away from me before I can get up. I jump up and follow him inside.

The exterior of the studio looks like a little a Cape Cod style house complete with gray shingles and white trim. It's perfect. We pass through glass sliding doors that lead to the beach.

Cole says, "The studio has several rooms. There is a guest section with full bedding. Each room has a private bath." And it does. As we peek in the empty rooms, Cole shows me the upscale finishes with marble tiles and white fixtures. It's so soft and feminine. I wish I had a bathroom like this. It's completely perfect. Cole forgot nothing.

He looks down at me and says, "The staff gets these two rooms, and the others are for clients who need to stay overnight. Some will want to fly in or need the session in the evening. The assistant will oversee all this, so you don't have to worry about it." Before I can ask anything, he's walking again. I stop gazing at the room and follow him.

Cole leads me into a room that still smells of paint, "This is the shooting room. The electricians fell behind, so it isn't ready yet. That slows things down a little bit. The lights will be there and there. Additional units can be placed at these intervals." He shows me the room, and is talking layout, but I don't understand what he's shooting.

The set-up is similar to his city studio, but it's different—smaller and more posh. The sets have more details, more color. One set is solid pink like strawberry soda. It has a lightness, and feels girlie and seductive at the same time.

I walk through it, and touch the velvet blankets, and then the flocked paper on the walls. It makes my jaw drop. I notice things as we walk around. After seeing the shooting room, Cole shows me the office where I'll be working and which computer is mine. Everything is pink and black. The décor doesn't match his other studio. His branding is glaringly different, like he's trying to do something different out here, but for the life of me, I can't tell what.

Finally, I ask, "So what is this place, Stevens? It has your studio's name, but none of your branding. What gives?"

He leans on the reception desk and folds his arms across his chest, "It's a new division of Le Femme, a division that I'm putting you in charge of." He watches me from under dark lashes, waiting for my reaction.

"What?" I breathe, turning to him. Is he serious? He can't be. I'm an intern, which makes his suggestion insane.

"I'm trying something new. This was the reason I wanted you to take the internship with me and not Sottero. I've been keeping track of you for a while, watching you turn into the perfect artist to work here."

My eyebrow creeps up my face as he speaks. I don't ignore the fact that he's been watching me, but I can't get over the obvious. "But, I'm an intern," I sputter.

He looks at me like I'm insane. "So?" he shrugs. "And that's bad because—?"

"Because I'm too young to be entrusted with something like this."

A dark brow lifts. He shakes his head, "Says who? You? You're telling me that you wouldn't want this? That you couldn't do it?"

My eyes narrow. I wonder what game he's playing, if this has something to do with last night or if he just wants to make me cry. I feel too emotional today. I can't handle his teasing, not after everything that's happened. "Don't jerk me around just because you can. We weren't all born with a silver spoon in our mouths. A job like this would matter to me--"

He cuts me off, "You don't even know what the job is." He's smug, "So don't go pulling the silver spoon crap. And for your information, this studio came from my own blood, sweat, and tears and no one else's. Both studios did."

I laugh. My arms fold over my chest defensively. "Yeah, right. The trust fund baby must have had a hard time getting everything set up." There's a bite to my voice when I speak again. It says don't screw with me and I know Cole senses it. "Every single thing you have was handed to you because of your name or your fortune. Don't tell me about blood, sweat, and tears. Those are things that you don't understand. The rich are cold conniving snakes, playing games for eternity, trying to outwit everyone around them, but in the end they lose—they always lose—because they find out they never had anyone who didn't love them for their money." By the time I'm done, my body is close to shaking. For some reason this feels incredibly personal. Steadying myself, I realize that it's because of my Grandmother and the effect she's had on my family.

Cole's brow inches higher and higher as I speak. "So, you think you have me all figured out?"

"I didn't say that." I want to tell him that I have him figured out, that he's just like the rest of them, but I know it's not true. There's a piece that doesn't fit. Trying to figure out Cole is like having a puzzle with several pieces missing. I have an idea of what's there, but without those pieces, I'll never see the whole picture.

He's silent, watching me fume. Finally, he says, "What do you want, Anna?"

I want you to want me. I want your arms around my waist, your hand on my cheek. I want to feel you against me. I want you… I don't say any of it.

I breathe hard, and look away. "Just tell me what you want from me. I've been jerked around enough for one lifetime."

He watches me like he's assessing something. His expression is unreadable. He glances down and says, "Fair enough." Our gazes meet when he looks up. "I want you to run this studio. My intention is to spend the summer with you, teaching you how. In the fall, I'll return to the city and we'll catch up a few times a year when we go over fiscal information. Like I said, I've been keeping tabs on you for a while. You have the skills needed to do this."

I eye him. He keeps skipping something, a pertinent detail. I still don't know what he's shooting out here, so I ask, "What type of studio is this?"

"Boudoir."

"Cole!" I'm yelling and I don't know why. It's my dream job, but instead of shooting brides, I'll be shooting naked women. Tears sting my eyes, but I blink them back. I turn toward him and he slides off the desk. I slam my hands into his chest. "How could you do this to me? You offered everything I want and everything I said I'd never do!" It isn't something that should leave me in tears, but I am balling. Tears race down my cheeks and I can't stop them.

Cole's fingers wrap around my hands, keeping my palms from shoving him again, "Why are you crying? I thought you'd be happy. You like it out here. Your family is nearby. You won't be alone. And the studio…"

I try to yank my hands away, but he doesn't let me. I feel the rhythm of his heart beating in his chest. I look up at him, "The studio is perfect. It's beautiful, but I want to shoot brides, not boobs. I can't do this! I can't!"

I threw everything away. Ditching Sottero screwed me. I can see the beginning and end of my career in this building. Although I don't mind shooting models, I don't want to do this forever. Le Femme is supposed to be a stepping stone. Cole is supposed to teach me. I know he has skills that Sottero doesn't.

"Listen," he snaps at me, tightening his grip on my hands. It makes my panic throttle down. "I don't think I was wrong. You can do this. You have the skills. You just have your head stuck in this fantasy of being a wedding photographer. Why? Why does it matter so much that you shoot brides?"

"Because it's the most romantic moment of their lives. It's the most important."

"And this isn't?"

"No! It's not! These are please fuck me pictures. These aren't even art. Cole, the fact that you—"

He drops my hands like I've burnt him and shakes his head. He turns away from me and runs his hands through his hair. "Anna!" His voice booms. When he turns back his blue eyes are livid. I've insulted him. His jaw twitches like he wants to say things that he bites back. Finally he says, "If you can see this is art—if you see that this is romantic and important—will you do it? Will you try?"

"There is no way that I'll ever say that."

He laughs and shakes his head, "You are such a pain in the ass. Just say yes or no. If you can see that it's art will you do it?"

His laughter disarms me a little bit. I nod and fold my arms over my chest. "Yes. Now please prove to me that you haven't fucked up my life beyond repair. Show me the artistic boobies so I can go beg Sottero for a second chance next year."

Cole growls, leaning close to my face, "The only person you'll ever beg for anything will be me."

My heart is pounding. I can't breathe. I want to punch him. I want to kiss him. This arrogant bastard thinks that I'll believe anything he says, and he says he made this place for me. I can't let him get under my skin like this, but he's already there.

I lean closer to him and breathe, "I'll never beg you for a single thing."

CHAPTER 6

Cole avoids me for the rest of the day. He probably doesn't have any ideas on how to prove to me that this studio is artistic. I'm sitting in my new room, on my bed, with my head against the wall. It's a little guest room off the main hall.

A girl wraps her knuckles on my door and pushes it open. "Hello?" she says. A massive amount of red hair peers around the door with a strikingly pretty pale face at the center. Impossibly green eyes blink at me. "Are you Anna?"

I nod and scoot the edge of my bed. "Yes. Can I help you?"

She walks into the room. "I'm Regina Davenport. I'm Mr. Stevens' assistant. I heard you're the new intern, well, the only intern."

Confused, I ask, "What do you mean?"

She laughs, "I'm sorry. I thought it was common knowledge. Every year Le Femme takes in one intern, and every year that intern quits before it's over. Sottero usually scoops them up and it pisses Mr. Stevens off to no end. We've never seen him on speaking terms with someone interning after this long."

My mouth is hanging open, "It's only been a week."

Her eyebrows lift, "Yeah, like I said, a long time in internland." She hesitates and then asks shyly, "Is it true? Do you really get to run this if you finish the internship? I mean, it seems like a sweet deal, assuming you can tolerate Stevens…"

I nod slowly. "He chases off the other interns? How?"

Regina looks back toward the door like she shouldn't be talking, but she's the only person I've seen today that is within a few years of me. I know we'll be working together if I stay here and so does she. She grins, "He's just difficult to get along with. He's got his own ideas about things and if yours don't line up, well, there's no future for you here. But he offered you this, so he must respect you an awful lot."

I don't know what to say, so I nod. She says, "He's looking for you. He said something about some artwork to show you. I told him I'd check, that I thought you were sleeping. What would you like me to tell him?"

She's protecting me from him. I don't really understand why. I don't even know her. A thought occurs to me and I blurt out, "You're trying to make sure that I don't burn out?"

She smiles like she's guilty and nods. "A girl's gotta make a living, Miss Lamore. And it's so much prettier out here than in Manhattan. No commuting. Can you imagine?"

I finally understand, "You'd be the assistant who stays out here, with me?"

She nods, smiling, hope flowing from her eyes. "That's the plan, Ma'am. So, what should I say?"

"Tell him I'll be right there. And Regina…"

"Yes?"

"Don't call me, Ma'am. I'm younger than you. And if you talk to me like I'm an old person, I'll truly lose my mind."

CHAPTER 7

Cole downshifts the car and accelerates hard as we enter highway traffic. Narrow headlights shoot beams into the darkness as we navigate the back roads. The drive to civilization makes me uneasy. There is nothing around for miles. It looks like an alien abduction road. Cole's gaze keeps shifting to me, and makes me extra nervous. I can't tell what he is thinking. The sick part of my mind wonders if he is taking me into the strawberry fields to kill me. My pinky lifts for the door handle as we slow.

Shaking his head, he grins, "Dear God. Miss Lamore, just jump. If you really think I'm going to kill you, please jump now before I really do."

I scowl, "I'm not—"

"You are so. Your entire body is wound so tight that I could… well, never mind what I could do. I can tell you don't trust me." His voice is cold like I've offended him. After a moment he asks, "Do you care to tell me why? What have I done to warrant this reaction from you?"

Biting my bottom lip, I'm not sure if I want to answer. I'm still upset with him, but I find myself saying, "I don't really know you and I don't know where I am."

He glances at me out of the corner of his eye. His grip tightens on the steering wheel of his Porsche. "You're north of the studio, nearing the highway, with a man who values his reputation and wouldn't waste it on dumping your body in a farmer's field, no matter how much you irritate him."

"*I* irritate *you*?" I laugh. I fold my arms over my chest to make sure I don't flinch and reach for the door again. I mutter something about farmers and pitchforks.

He smiles, glancing at me out of the corner of his eye. After a moment he says, "So, Miss Vanilla," my stomach drops when he calls me that. It brings back the dream and every sensation that lit my body on fire, begging for his touch. I stiffen. Cole glances at me and continues, "tell me why you so abhorrently object to fine art nudes. I find that ironic, being that you claim to be an artist and all."

He's baiting me. I know it, but I answer anyway, "I'm not Miss Vanilla, smart ass, so stop calling me that." I'm quiet for a moment, trying to put it into words. "As for the nudes, I think they belong in paintings, not photography. Nudes in photography usually equal pornography."

He laughs, a deep belly laugh in one short burst, "You actually believe that?" I nod with a serious expression on my face. "Then you're a hypocrite, Lamore. You can't be an artist and only value one medium and disregard the others."

"I am not," I say calmly. I'm holding my hands in my lap, watching the world zoom by. Cole's foot is heavy when he's irritated. I appear to have easy access to his crazy buttons and seem to be punching them like a typewriter tonight. "It's not the medium. It's the content."

"But the same content is okay in a painting?"

I nod, "Yes. Botticelli was an artist. Heffner is a pornographer. No one jerks off looking at Venus on a half shell."

His voice is charged with emotion, "Guys jerk off to all sorts of things, so that shouldn't be your criteria for anything. As for your identifying factors of what's art and what isn't, tell me—what makes something art? Can you define that?"

I think about it for a moment. In my gut I know. I know it when I see it. My lips part and I'm telling him, "It's art when it's evocative, when it can convey emotions and feelings to the viewer. An idea—or ideal."

"And sensuality doesn't count?"

"No. Well," I think about it. Sensuality isn't my issue. I'm not sure what is. I shake my head, not looking at him I say, "Yes, it counts." Cole is silent with a surprised expression on his face. I stare out the window as lights blaze by in the darkness. We're on the highway now, zooming closer and closer to his apartment. I'm nervous. Nervous of what I'll say. What I'll do.

His voice is soft, "Why? Why does it count?"

He's no longer challenging me, but sounds like he genuinely wants to know what I think. This entire conversation is way outside of my comfort zone, but I don't back down. I want him to see that I'm right and not just some crazy prude. Leaning my head back in the seat, I think. "Because it's an emotion. Sensuality isn't what I object to… it's more the fact that nude photos are degrading to women."

Cole laughs, "Oh my god! How many crazy women are living inside your brain? How do you manage with all of them in there telling you what to say? Does one tie the others up and randomly take over?"

"You're such an ass," I sigh, shaking my head at him. "You asked my opinion. Don't ask if you don't want to hear…"

"No, that was not your opinion. It was what you've heard, what you've learned. It isn't what you think. Last week I saw it on your face during those shoots. This kind of photography—this kind of work—isn't what you thought it was."

I shake my head, "No it isn't. None of this is what I thought it would be."

"That makes two of us."

CHAPTER 8

When we arrive at a tall building, it's late. He pulls up in front, gets out and walks around to my door. Before I can move, he has it open and pulls me up to my feet. Cole tosses the keys to a valet and we walk inside.

The doorman nods, "Mr. Stevens." Cole nods and passes him, his hand in mine tugging me along.

The elevator door opens before I know it and Cole leads me inside. When the doors close, my heart is pounding. I stare at him, remembering his hands on me… remembering the dream. I swallow hard.

Cole keeps his distance. I know where we're going even though he doesn't tell me. I figured it out somewhere on the highway back into the city. He is taking me to see those paintings, the ones he mentioned before. My stomach twists as he gazes at me. The elevator stops and the doors open. We're in the penthouse. His home.

Cole steps through, but I can't move. Fear snakes up my legs and binds me to the floor. Everything from the scent to the colors has my heart racing faster. It's Cole. This place is his haven, his security blanket. I don't belong here.

Before I can do something stupid, he sighs and walks back toward me. He holds out his hand, "Come on, Anna. I won't bite."

My eyes slide over his face and I put my hand in his. I don't like this. Being in his home is demolishing the remaining ill conceptions I have of him like a buffalo in a china shop. Everything just shatters. There is no cold sterile modern furniture. Everything is plush and warm, decorated in deep blues, browns, and blacks. It's not one of the museum homes of the wealthy, it's Cole's home and he lives here.

He flips on lights as we walk through. They illuminate the walls creating a subtle golden glow. Cole stops in the kitchen and goes to the cabinets, pulling out wine glasses. I don't say anything. I feel nervous and I don't know why. Part of me is scared that I'll agree with him and change my mind. The other part senses something about him, about Cole, that makes me nervous.

He hands me a glass of wine. "I don't know about you, but this is unusual for me." I know what he means. This situation makes him nervous. Since I feel the same way, I take the glass.

I follow him into a room at the back of the apartment. When I see the bed, I realize it's his bedroom and stop. It feels like I'm being strangled. My grip on the glass is so tight it could shatter. I raise the wine to my lips and sip, hoping it will calm whatever has me on edge. I enter the room behind Cole, but I don't see the art he wants to show me. The walls are barren like he hasn't decorated this part of the apartment. A large poster bed made from dark wood is in the center of the room. I look at it, thinking things about Cole that I shouldn't. Tearing my gaze away from the bed, I look down at the dark wood floor and glance around. There is a row of windows and a balcony that overlooks a perfect skyline.

I'm not sure where he's going, but Cole continues walking in front of me and crosses the room. My heart rate steadies, but there's still something intimate about this. I inhale a little too deeply and notice it's Cole's cologne that I like after I've already done it. Guilt flames my cheeks and I pretend that I didn't do it.

Cole passes straight through the room without comment, and pulls open the closet doors. A light pops on. It's a huge walk-in with clothing lining both walls and a chair. Oak drawers and shelves line the lower part of the walls. The room smells like Cole. I don't cross the threshold. I stop and watch him.

Cole crosses the wardrobe in three strides, and reaches for a knob at the back of the closet and pulls open a door. There's a tiny darkened closet back there filled with large rectangle-shaped sheets. Those must be the paintings. I don't understand why they are hidden in his closet if he values them.

He looks back at me. As if reading my mind, he says, "They're hidden for a reason. What I'm showing you is rarely seen. I'm curious what you think—and terrified." He swallows hard, his sapphire eyes on my face. He stands there for a moment, suspended like he can't decide if he wants to show me or not.

My voice is small. I step toward him asking, "Why would it matter what I think? I'm nobody." Condensation is beading on my glass. I wipe a trail through it with my thumb. I don't look up at him. I don't want to see his face when he answers.

There's a pause before he says, "That's where you're entirely wrong."

I lift my eyes and see him watching me. Cole's blue gaze makes my stomach feel like it's in a free fall. His lips part like he's going to say more, but he doesn't. I wish he would. I wish he felt comfortable saying his secrets to me, but I suppose this is a secret. The paintings are something he doesn't show people and I'm standing here waiting to see them. A warm glow spreads through me until I remember the circumstances of my being here. It was to prove a point, and nothing more. I clutch my glass harder.

Instead of saying more, Cole reaches into the shadows and pulls out a large painting that's draped with a white sheet. Moving closer, I walk into his dressing room holding my breath. Goosebumps line my arms. The hairs on the back of my neck stand on end. I'm nervous. My stomach is twisting and I don't know why.

Cole's voice is too soft. He hands me the painting and says, "Here." I take it from him.

"Cole," I stand there frozen. For some reason this doesn't feel like he's just trying to prove a point. I can't pull the sheet off. It feels like I'm seeing something forbidden.

After a moment, Cole glances at me, "Just look at it, Anna."

I swallow hard and pull the sheet. The drape falls to the floor and I don't understand what I'm seeing. I feel Cole behind me, but he's silent. My eyes take in the piece of art in my hands. The stretched canvas is too big to hold for long, so I set it down. It has no frame, just a black edge. My gaze follows the blue lines across the painting. It's the curves of a woman's body, her neck, her arms, her waist, her breasts, but I can't see her. She's lost in shadow. It's a sensual showcasing of her curves in shadow and light. I'm mute, staring at it. While the piece is stunning, that isn't what rendered me speechless. I can't admit why I'm drawn to it.

I swallow the lump in my throat as I stare. I move closer, trying to understand how it was created. It looks like a photograph printed on canvas that was painted, but the light is so unusual. It almost looks like watercolors, soft and pure.

I find my voice and ask, "How was this done? Why does your light source look like that?"

"I promise I'll tell you," Cole says, "But tell me what you think."

I swallow hard. I feel the longing in this piece. I can't stop staring at it. "It's beautiful," I breathe. "I've never seen anything like it. The light is so pale it looks like she's been painted, but it's not a painting—is it? It's a photograph, or at least it started that way." I reach out to touch it and stop myself.

"Go ahead," he says, allowing me to commit a cardinal sin. My fingers slide across the smooth canvas. I can't fathom how he made it. "What else?" I feel his gaze on the side of my face. Every time my heart beats, I feel it. I feel everything. It's like I'm inside Cole's body, touching his soul. It makes me shiver. I don't have words for it.

Finally I say something. "She's different from your Le Femme models. This woman is unedited, imperfect." I notice that first. The majority of my time at Le Femme has been spent editing away cellulite and smoothing skin. I stare at the unedited piece. "But that imperfection makes her real. It makes me wonder who she is and why she feels so lost. The way the light falls across her naked body, the way she was moving, reminds me of—" I bite my tongue. It was a silly thought, a memory from an old story.

"Reminds you of what?" his voice is too sweet, too fragile, to not answer. I look over my shoulder at him and then lower my lashes, not able to look him in the eye when I say it.

"It reminds me of Bathsheba bathing on the roof in the moonlight, unaware of her effect on the king. She has no idea how beautiful she is, what she does to him, how she makes him feel… It's beautiful and tragic. Like this…" I turn and look up at him. Stubble lines his cheeks making his eyes appear bluer than this morning. I repress a shiver and turn back to the piece. "When did you make this?"

"A lifetime ago."

I press my lips together when I realize this piece fits my description of art. I don't want to admit it, but he's right. It is evocative. I close my eyes, realizing what I said, that I just proved his point for him. When I open my eyes I whisper, "I'm not a hypocrite. They can't all be like this. Every image can't portray emotions like that, Cole. It's not possible."

As I start speaking, he turns away and takes the next painting from the closet. He pulls the drape off and I gasp and turn away from it when I realize what I'm looking at. He sets the painting down and says, "You promised you'd look. Anna, this isn't something you've never seen before. Look at it and tell me what you see… why you looked away."

"Cole, she's! That's!" I'm sputtering like an idiot. The image was beautiful, but I feel my face growing hotter and hotter. I can't look at it.

"It's what? I don't understand you," he says, baffled. Cole steps in front of me and looks at the piece and back at my face. "How can you look at the first one and not this one?"

Suddenly, I don't know. They should be the same. But they're not. This one shows a woman with her back arched, her breasts thrust upward, her hand just below her navel. It's sexy, all lines, and curves, and shadows. A pale light source defines her curves in a creamy violet. The rest of her body is lost in inky shadows.

Nervously, I look at it again, "Because they're not the same."

"They are. I made them the same way. How are they different? I don't understand you. Is it evocative? Can you feel a strong emotion when you look at it?" His voice is soft. I remember that he doesn't show these to anyone, but I still can't hide my shock.

"That's not the point," my face is flushed and his eyes on me make it worse. Suddenly I feel like the room is too small and Cole is too close. I want to back out, but I can't.

"Anna?" he asks, almost pleading with me.

Looking at him, my voice catches in my throat. He looks so vulnerable, like a single word could crush him. The expression in his eyes makes me answer, "The first one was beautiful and sensual. This one is too graphic, too bold. You can't do that. You can't take pictures of women doing that. It's not right."

He glances at the painting and back at me, "Doing what?" He's serious. I look past him at the painting and blush. "Anna," he says, "Is it possible that your mind is much dirtier than the images you're seeing? Is there any chance that you think things happened there that didn't?"

Maybe. I hesitate. "She's not… touching herself?" I ask timidly. That's what I thought when I looked at it. The arch of her back, the way her breasts are thrust upward, and I can't see her other hand.

He laughs, "No. She was laying on a cold floor. It made her arch her back like that." He's watching me, his eyes study my face. He's not arrogant now. Uncertainty sits well on him, if anything it makes him sexier. Seeing this confident man care about what I think makes me wonder why.

He interrupts my thoughts, "Anna, I wish you could see what I see." The tone of Cole's voice is soft, wistful.

I can't be quiet. I glance at him out of the corner of my eye. "What do you see in that piece?" Now I want to know. If it's not what I thought, then I want to know what he thinks it is. I force myself to look at the piece of art again. It makes my stomach twist. The way her body is laying, the arch of her back, the tension in her arms—she looks like she's in ecstasy. I can't ignore it. The evocative nature of the image is too powerful.

Shaking my head, I breathe, "No one has ever touched me so that my body moved like that." Once the words are out, I wish they weren't.

Cole steps closer to me. His eyes are on the side of my face, drinking it in like he can't get enough. I can tell that he wants to say something—that he wants to answer me—but he doesn't. My heart races as he watches me. I can't breathe. He's too close. This is too intimate. It feels like I'm coming unglued and I don't know what to do, what to say. The effect he has on me is powerful, and I'm having trouble hiding it. If my heart pounds any harder, I swear to God, he'll hear it.

Cole tucks his chin. He puts his glass of wine down somewhere. His arms fold over his chest. That beautiful dark shiny hair falls over his eyes, making it impossible to see them in the dim glow. I wish I could read his face, his eyes, the same way he reads mine. I wish I was inside his head when he made this painting. Did he really see something else? Was it really not a depiction of ecstasy? And if it was, was it wrong? Was it pornographic? At this very moment, I don't feel like it is. It feels like sublime beauty, like the last canvas he showed me.

Finally, he answers my previous question and turns from me. His voice is deep, seductive, "I see shadows and light, curves and lines. Beauty mingled with power. Femininity and softness. I see desire. I see someone who doesn't know if her body is good enough. The position of her hand makes me think that. It sits on her stomach as if she's hiding something. As if she has secrets I'll never know…"

Silence engulfs us and we both stare at his work, neither of us brave enough to speak. My body is covered in goose-bumps. I don't know what to think. I'm caught in the middle. My mind registers things like this as trash, or they are supposed to be, but after seeing it—after hearing Cole speak about it—how can I think that? It was my mouth that said the requirement for something to be art was the ability to evoke emotion, and here I am stunned into silence by something I wouldn't have considered art yesterday.

Damn. I'm a hypocrite. I don't like it. It feels like I've been blindsided, but Cole doesn't stop. He doesn't let me catch my breath.

Instead, he takes another canvas from its resting place and pulls the sheet off. When the drape hits the floor my toes curl inside my shoes. I can't breathe. It's another nude, another woman bathed in golden light. Long dark hair falls to her hips in curls. Her arms are stretched over her head, thrusting her chest out. The light catches the curve of the bottom of her breast, the softness of her jaw, the fullness of her hips—and there are glittering jewels hanging from her nipples.

Staring at it, I'm hyperaware of every inch of my body. My eyes fixate on her breasts, on those dangling jewels. It feels like someone sucked all the air out of the room. Heat engulfs me. I shouldn't be looking, but I can't stop. This kind of thing is too sensual, and it's too beautiful. I can't look away. I can't understand why I don't feel offended, and realize that it's because this is art that reflects Cole's heart. I'm seeing part of him when I look at these pieces. This woman meant something to him. She had to.

Glancing at him, I wonder who she is—this faceless woman who is concealed in shadows and hidden at the back of his closet—locked away from the world. It's part of a life he hides, a part of Cole Stevens that remains a secret.

"Who is she?" I ask finally.

Cole shakes his head once. Dark hair sways over downcast eyes. He doesn't look up. He doesn't answer. I don't know if he won't or he can't. This isn't a random model. The images feel too intense for that.

Trying to be less personal, I ask, "How did you make these? The light is so soft. So stunning. I can't figure out how you did it—"

Cole unfolds his arms, resuming the role of teacher. "It's painting with light. It uses the camera, but the exposure is much longer. The model sits in a pitch black room. I set the camera on the tripod and release the shutter. Then I literally paint the model with a colored light. I move the light over her and it's kind of like a paintbrush, highlighting the areas I want and leaving the rest in darkness. It makes a soft color-wash over her skin."

I blink twice and turn my head back toward the print. "But I don't see you in these." For that to happen, the exposure had to be pretty long—like minutes, not seconds. I'm astounded that he thought to do this. I've never seen it before. At least, I've never seen this concept with boudoir portraits. Cole is watching me as my mind races with questions. He knows I'll latch onto the technical aspect and appears eager to discuss it with me.

"How long is the exposure?"

"Several minutes," the toe of his shoe picks a spot on the floor. Arms folded over his chest, he says, "You won't see me unless I stand still for a moment, but I'm there—moving through the shadows, spilling light across her body like rain pouring from the sky."

Something occurs to me while he speaks. Turning to Cole, I say, "This is the kind of work you want me shooting, isn't it? The Le Femme studio you're putting out East isn't like the one in the city. You want it to be something else—something like this." I already know the answer, but it doesn't stop the shock from spreading across my face. When he asked me to run the Long Island studio and said it was boudoir photography, I totally freaked out thinking he wanted something else.

But this. This intimidates the crap out of me. I don't know how to do this. I don't know how to make powerful images like these.

"Yes," he nods. "Or something similar. I want you shooting art. I want your images to be evocative and powerful; seductive and feminine."

I look at the canvas and don't turn my face back toward him. For a moment, I say nothing. A crazy thought is bouncing around in my mind and it won't shut up. Seeing these, seeing this part of Cole, is shocking. I don't know why, but I assumed he wasn't capable of this. I just stand there, mute until he asks again and this time I nod. At this moment, I recognize that my perception has changed. I can feel it shattering, cracking apart like shards of ice, and falling away.

His art has changed me—Cole changed me.

My mind resists accepting it. My body feels like I'm being strangled. I can't do this. I don't know how. Cole's passion spills across the canvas more powerfully than anything I've ever seen. It's feminine and beautiful and powerful. It's everything I want to do, everything I want to be. Wedding photography is something that most women will need at some point. It is a single chance to show them that they are beautiful, but this—what Cole is offering gives me the chance to do that but even more so. I see it. It's crystal clear. And I realize that I want to learn how. My mind is at war with itself. The prudent side is assaulting my rationale trying to poke holes in it. I can't tell who's winning, but my mouth shocks the hell out of both of them when I speak and say the crazy idea that's forming in my head.

Glancing at Cole, I say with complete certainty, "I want one."

"What?" Cole turns toward me. He blinks and opens his eyes wider like that might disprove what he heard me say.

That was the thought that was trapped inside my mind. As soon as I felt my previous conceptualizations crack, I knew that I'd want to learn everything about this. I'm intrigued and terrified.

My heart thumps when I say it and my palms grow hotter. "I need to know what it feels like on the other end of the lens. I can learn the practical part with models, but this—" I shake my head, "it's not about knowledge, it's about feeling. It captures the client's beauty in a powerful way. The only way for me to know how the client feels is to actually be the woman in the portrait." My gaze locks on his. His sapphire eyes search mine, his brow pinched with shock. "Shoot me, Cole."

He seems shy, like the idea hadn't crossed his mind. He doesn't look away when he says, "I don't think that's a good idea." His lips part like he wants to say more, but he doesn't.

"Cole," I don't know what I'm going to say. I just know that this is important. I can't understand this wholly if I don't. "Please. It's a shoot. We're both grown-ups here. We can manage this." Well, I was hoping we could. I shrug like it's no big deal, "Besides, you said you only do one-nighters and I'm not that kind of girl."

He works his jaw and looks up at me from under his brow. "I never said I only do one-nighters. I offered you a one-nighter."

"And I said no," I reply absently, no longer looking at him. "So there's nothing to worry about."

I'm staring at the paintings. The thought of a shoot like this has butterflies swirling in my stomach. I walk past Cole and pull out more canvases, looking at more of Cole's work. He watches me, silently. The paintings aren't what I thought they'd be. If light could be liquefied and poured into a paint can, that is what Cole made—something sensual, beautiful, and completely sexy.

"I can admit I was wrong," I say turning toward him. "This is art. I see it now. You showed me something I didn't think was possible and there's no way in hell I can shoot this kind of stuff without submerging myself in it.

"There's a reason why Sottero wanted me, Cole. There's a reason why I'm at the top of my class. I don't do things half way. If I see something I want to do, I learn everything about it, and I'm taking you up on your offer. I'll run the Long Island branch of Le Femme. I'll shoot this kind of stuff, but you have to shoot me first. It's nonnegotiable."

He blinks at me and shakes his head, "God, Anna. I—" He runs his hands through his hair and sighs. I know I've won. I know he'll do it.

CHAPTER 9

We stay in his apartment for the night. I sleep rather restlessly in his guest room. The place smells like Cole. I can't stop thinking about him, but I finally pass out not wanting to consider what I offered earlier in the evening. He lets me sleep late and I emerge from the shower around noon. We go into the Manhattan office and work until sunset, editing the remaining images from last week's shoot.

Neither of us says much. When we leave, he holds the door to his Porsche open and I slide in.

I feel his eyes on the side of my face as we drive back to the new studio. Cole is silent. His fingers are wrapped around the steering wheel tightly. It's like nothing happened last night, like he didn't agree to do something completely sexy with me. I lean my head back and stare out the window. I don't turn to look at him.

It's late by the time we hit the open stretch of highway back to the beach house. I wonder about him. I wonder who he really is, what he really sees. He does such a good job of hiding everything that I realize I have no clue. There's a passionate side to Cole, but there's something softer and more vulnerable, too.

"What are you thinking?" he finally asks, glancing between me and the road.

I shrug, like I'm not thinking anything, like I'm not obsessing about him and wondering about his past. "Just wondering about stuff," I mutter the half-truth to cover the lie, then add, "Nothing really."

"You have that far off look in your eyes. I've been around you long enough to figure out what that means, so spill Lamore. What has your brain in a knot?" He smiles softly at me.

I glance over at him wondering if I'm so transparent all the time, or if he just reads me better than others. I sigh and shake my head, "It's none of my business, but I saw something I wasn't supposed to see when I grabbed your bail money." I shrug like it's no big deal, and glance at him out of the corner of my eye. "It was a picture of you in an army uniform and a beat up Tiffany's box. It looked like it'd been run over." He says nothing and stares at the empty road, concentrating as if it were rush hour. I'm looking at my hands, running my thumb over the thumbnail on my other hand.

My voice is soft, "You looked so young and afraid. And the ring, I guess there's a heartbreaking story there?" His shoulders tense. Cole works his jaw and swallows hard as I finish speaking. I think he's angry, but I can't tell. "I didn't mean to look. I'm sorry. I shouldn't have said anything."

He doesn't glance at me anymore. His eyes take on a vacant stare like he's remembering something he wants to forget. "It's fine. I'd forgotten it was in there. The rest of those pictures were burned." He doesn't acknowledge the Tiffany ring.

Burned? There's a story there, a part of him that I want to know. I can't *not* ask. Carefully, I say, "Why'd you enlist? I mean, most families would have disowned a kid over something like that."

Now he glances at me. His eyes are cold as stone and I visibly flinch. "What makes you think mine didn't?" His words are filled with scorn for someone else, but some of it drips onto me.

I falter. My mouth hangs open. "But, you're the only heir—" I sputter, shocked, not believing what he's implying. A sole heir wouldn't be disowned. That's extraordinarily bad. I can't even imagine what he'd done. Enlisting doesn't seem big enough to warrant such a reaction, but as I look at him, I know I can't ask. I seriously doubt my mother would have been disowned if there were no cousins, if there were no one else to claim my mother's birthright.

Hedging, he says, "You seem to know some things, for a girl who hates rich people so much."

I laugh, but there's no joy in it, "Yeah, well, let's just say life wasn't kind to my parents. I saw things from the wrong side and it took its toll on me." Suddenly I stop talking. That's my darkest secret. It fills me with anger and shame to even bring it up—anger at my Grandmother for treating her daughter so cruelly, shame that I'm not more like my mom. She has backbone that I'll never possess. I look out the window, but I still see Cole out of the corner of my eye, watching me.

"I understand," he says and glances at me again. "Things struck a little closer to home for me and it didn't matter that I was the sole heir. I enlisted to prove a point. They disowned me to prove a point." He's staring out the windshield. His voice is cold. He doesn't look at me. Gripping the steering wheel of the Porsche, his knuckles turn white. I feel like I've picked open old wounds for both of us and desperately wish I could take it back. The pain in his eyes floods me and I want to take it away. That distant look, the feeling that he's not good enough—that he'll never be good enough—is plastered across his face.

Turning, I stare at him with my jaw hanging open. There's a word that's lodged itself in my throat, something I was going to say—but I've forgotten what it was.

It can't be true. He couldn't have been disinherited. Cole Stevens didn't have his family's millions? But, he's said it all along—he made Le Femme, it was his blood, sweat, and tears.

Oh my God. Staring, mouth still agape, I don't know what to say. I want to tell him that I understand, but I don't get it the way my mother does. I don't know what it feels like to have everything one day and nothing the next. His parents blindsided him. They chose money over love. They rejected their only child.

I finally say, "I'm sorry. I didn't know."

Shrugging, he says, "It's not your fault, so there's no reason to apologize. And no one knows. It was part of our agreement." He laughs and shakes his head like it's some cruel joke. "I was allowed to keep my name—my fucking name—if I didn't tell anyone that I'd lost my inheritance. Even that wasn't mine. Anyway, it's a long story, but the short version is that you should never piss off a Stevens'. They have long memories and will tear you apart when you least expect it."

The savageness in his voice startles me. "But," I say softly, "you're a Stevens." *You're not like them. You can't be*, I think.

His eyes are on the road, staring into the inky night. "I know."

CHAPTER 10

When we arrive at the studio, I'm exhausted. I stumble out of the car and follow Cole inside. The other two people staying here are already asleep. Before Cole leaves me to find my room, he says, "That shoot will be first thing tomorrow. If you have body jewelry, wear it." He doesn't look at me as he speaks. Instead, he walks over to the front desk and picks up a pile of mail, and sifts through it. My heart hammers. I nod and silently walk off to my room with my heart in my throat.

Sleep finally comes, but my dreams make me restless. I dream about Cole as a young man. I see the haunted expression in his eyes—the fact that he knows there is no such thing as forgiveness. He learned that lesson too well. There is no way he will ever forget.

The dream fades to Edward. His eyes are a void of black. Bleeding twin trails of ink spill down his pale cheeks. He says, "You destroyed me." He reaches for my throat, his fingers moving toward my eye with a black nail in his fist. I know that will make my eyes bleed black like his, that my heart will never heal. I know I'm dreaming, but I scream anyway.

I wake, frightened, and trembling. The sun is barely over the horizon. I swing my legs over the side of my bed and rub my eyes. I breathe deeply trying to push away the nightmare.

There's a knock on my door. "Come in," I say. When I look up, Cole is standing in the doorway. I'm wearing cotton shorts and a thin cami. They're dorm pajamas, which means they're guy safe. At least that's what Emma and I used to say.

Stubble lines his cheeks. A white tee shirt clings to his torso. Dark jeans hug his narrow hips, and he's barefoot. Cole seems to have something against shoes. His eyes are red like he hasn't slept. "You all right? I heard you scream."

"Yeah. Fine." I don't elaborate. I look up at him and push the rat's nest that is my hair out of my face. "What time are we shooting? Tell me it's not in fifteen minutes." I'm only half joking. Cole's a morning person. Apparently that's still true even though he's only had a few hours of sleep.

He smiles, "No, not in fifteen." He looks at his watch and back up at me. "Why don't we try for nine? You can get a few more hours rest."

I laugh and push off the bed, shaking my head. "It'll take me that long to get ready. And I have to tell you that I didn't bring anything with me that might be even a little suitable for this shoot. Do you have props or something I could look at?"

"No nudes, Miss Lamore?" he asks leaning against the door frame, and folds his arms over his chest. A dark brow rises on his face. His eyes lock on mine.

My stomach flutters. A soft smile lines my lips and I shake my head, "I thought I should see what my options are. I hear lace photographs well," I tease, knowing it will annoy him. Anything about wedding photography seems to get under his skin.

"Damn wedding photographers and their lace," he laughs softly. The sound is stunning. I wish he were like this all the time, but it's the Cole that vanishes like smoke. I think that's the real Cole, the one he hides from everyone at all cost. He pushes off the door frame, and shakes his head, "Come on. I'll show you where the wardrobe is located. Use whatever you want. They literally finished the sets last night and installed the lights. We'll christen the new studio and then get back to work."

An hour later Cole is gone and I'm still looking through boxes. I find some jeweled dangling earrings that I can use. They have a hook, but I grab some wire and wire cutters. I plan on modifying their intended use, slightly, if I have to. Other than that, I don't see anything else.

Regina walks in and flips on the lights, "Hey boss. Can I help you find something?"

Quickly, I decide to tell her what we're doing. It makes it seem less risqué, even though telling her about the shoot makes me blush.

Regina is very professional. She doesn't react. Instead she helps. She digs through a few boxes, showing me more necklaces and outfits from Le Femme.

She hands me a panty and I press the thin lace between my fingers, "This is beautiful, but I wanted something different."

"How different?" she asks.

I shrug at her and put the panties back. I laugh nervously and look at her. "I have no idea what I'm looking for. Or what I want. I just need it to be sultry, cover me a little bit, and be something that screams, Anna." I shake my head. "None of this stuff seems to do all that."

Regina nods, listening. Grinning at me, she says, "I have something." She looks over her shoulder like she's doing something that she shouldn't and reaches for a box on the top shelf. I look inside when she pulls it down. It's filled with tiny crystals. Many are clear, like tiny diamonds, but some are vibrant colors. She pulls a paper from the plastic sleeve on the top of the box. "I got these thinking we could use them—to do this."

"What is it?" I ask and unfold the paper. My cheeks flush when I see it, but I can't look away. My jaw drops.

"Vajazzling. At least that's what the article calls it." She shrugs. "I guess you can do anything from pouring the crystals over your body, to applying them in a pattern." She points at the paper to a woman bared from the waist down. The patch of hair between her legs is gone and in its place there is an intricate design of a butterfly. The sparkles disappear between her legs. "That one is really pretty," she says pointing to the butterfly. "Of course, that only works if you already have a Brazilian."

I scan the paper, reading it. A smile creeps slowly across my face. As a matter of fact, I do. "This is perfect. Thanks Regina."

CHAPTER 11

The moment I see Cole, my confidence fades. The box of crystals is in my hand and my stomach is twisting so violently that I nearly drop them. I feel hot and cold at the same time. My heart is pounding.

Cole doesn't notice. He strides toward me, lost in his own thoughts with his camera around his neck and a small light in his other hand. He places them on a table in the back of the shooting room. It still smells new, like paint and sawdust. Regina lit a candle to help ease the paint fumes from the room.

I'm standing on the other side of the table with my box of crystals. When Cole looks up, I decide to can Regina's original idea. I'm not that brave, and I wasn't able to apply the jewels myself. There wasn't enough time and I couldn't see what I was doing. When his eyes slide up my body from the box to my face, I realize that I'm in over my head. I can't do this. But I can't back out.

Cole says, "Nice bathrobe. Tell me we're not shooting you in that?"

I shake my head, and put the box on the table. My hands quiver slightly. Trying to hide it, I shove the box and it slides at him. "I thought we could pour these over me." That seems like a tamer version of my original plan. I have no idea how wrong I am until we get started.

He peeks in the box and his brow furrows. Looking up at me, I can see he doesn't understand. "I'm not seeing it, Lamore. Walk me through it. What else are you wearing? Are these just accent pieces?" He dips his hand into the box and when he lifts it, crystals pour between his fingers.

When I don't answer, he looks up at me. My face is flushed. Cole shakes his head and smiles softly, looking down at the crystals. "How are you so shy? You're twenty-two for Godsakes. How do you still blush like that?"

His words make my cheeks flame hotter. My eyes grow wider as he speaks, and I can't hide it. "Shut up, Stevens." I smack his arm. He glances up at me from across the table, a boyish look on his face. I laugh, "My brain's just wired wrong, okay? And you out of all people should have known that."

He presses his fingers to his chest, "Me?" he laughs.

"Yes, you," I say, smiling like an idiot, feeling the blush still burning my cheeks, "You've been around me enough to know that I do everything wrong and backwards."

Laughing, he says, "Yeah, maybe." He grins at me. "Sorry, Anna. I didn't mean to make it worse. I know that this isn't easy for you." He clears his throat, and tries to be serious again. "Okay, so you want to use crystals?"

I nod, "I thought we could pour them across me so there are tons of them in a line—like a ribbon draped across here," I gesture to my breasts, and then across my hips, "and across here." He's nodding, like he understands what I'm thinking. His blue eyes are sliding over the robe, then they flick up to me.

"What else will you be wearing?" he asks.

"Nothing," I breathe. I hurry on before I have time to notice the flush spreading across my body, "I liked the art you showed me. I thought I wanted something similar, but not so revealing. The crystals will cover me enough."

He's smiling, watching me as I speak. When I finish he looks down at the box in his hands, "Okay, I see what you want to do, but I have to tell you that I lied the other night. I can't shoot the exact same thing. I'm not the same person anymore. And you're—" he glances up at me grinning, "different. So the question is, do you trust me to make something new, something equally alluring and beautiful?"

His question takes me by surprise, "Trust you?" Smiling, I shake my head, surprised that he has to ask. My heart pounds harder when I reply, "Yeah, of course I trust you. I wouldn't be here if I didn't. I'd be hiding out in the strawberry fields, jumping from moving cars, and that sort of thing, remember?" I laugh nervously.

"Anna Lamore, artist, action hero, and a little bit crazy." His voice mimics that deep voice in movie trailers right up until the last word and he laughs.

"Mmmm," I say nodding. "That's right. Better watch your back, jack." I waggle my eyebrows at him and he shakes his head.

Cole glances at me, grinning, and strides around the table, stopping in front of me. "Okay, from here on out, this is my shoot. You'll do as I ask quickly, without question, and hopefully, you'll learn whatever it is you need to so you can do this." I nod once. My nerves are twisting me into insanity.

Cole leans against the table, and clasps his hands in his lap. Explaining the shoot he says, "This will take a few hours. I'll be searching for the perfect shot. It's easier for me to find it if I take my time. The lights will be out, so it'll be totally dark. I'll take some test shots to figure out what pose I'd like you in before we shut off the light. Once I chose the pose, we'll get started. I'll use the lights, so you'll see those and you may see me a little bit, but I won't be in the finished product. Remember, you can't move. Even breathing deeply can mess up the image, so no matter what—don't move once the shutter clicks open."

I'm nodding as he's speaking, trying to resist the urge to twist my fingers like a nervous child. I've done enough shoots with him to know how he is, that Cole will be beyond professional, but my heart is still pounding wildly.

His eyes are sweeping over me as he speaks. When Cole stands and walks behind me, I don't move. His voice is behind my ear, "I'll take your robe so we can get started." Cole's out-stretched hand is next to me, waiting.

Slowly, I turn toward him. My eyes meet his. I knew this would happen, but it seemed much more sensible in my head. Breathing too hard, I reach for the bow at my waist and pull. The knot releases and the belt falls to the floor, revealing bare skin from my neck down. My fingers slip under the shoulders of the robe and it slides off and lands on the floor next to the belt.

I'm completely bare and standing in front of him. I resist the urge to cover my body with my hands and ask, "Where do I go?"

A blank expression fills his eyes as I slip out of the robe. When I drop the robe to the floor instead of into his hand, Cole swallows hard. Instead of answering, he points to a white backdrop on the other side of the room. I turn and walk to the place he directs me to, feeling uncertain.

Cole softens, his tone is sweet and uncertain. He asks me to stand here, to pose there. I lay my wrists on top of my head, putting my weight on one foot. The pose forces the curve of my hips, the soft slope of my back, and thrusts my breasts forward. My nipples perked up as soon as I dropped the robe. I try not to be horrified.

Cole circles me, his eyes sliding over every inch of my body, examining me. Butterflies flitter through my stomach. He stops behind me and rubs his hands through his hair. He's already put me in several poses and taken test shots, but he seems dissatisfied. He shakes his head, "This isn't going to work. The crystals aren't going to stay put. There's no way to drape them over you, Lamore. You're too curvy for that. Every pose I've put you in shows those curves off perfectly, but that means the crystals will roll right off of you." He pauses, stroking his chin. I feel his gaze on the side of my face, but I don't turn toward him.

My heart sinks into my stomach as he speaks, "So you can't do it?"

Shaking his head, he runs his fingers through his hair, "I didn't say that." He stops in front of me, and looks into my eyes. My heartbeat accelerates. "I can do it; it's just more complicated than you originally thought."

I gaze into his eyes, and when I feel every inch of my skin burning, yearning for his touch, I look away. "Just do it, Cole. I know this is your way of telling me that my idea was good, but flawed. Just make it right and do what you want." My voice sounds curt, but I didn't mean to be. I'm beyond nervous and I don't know what he wants to do.

Cole nods and leaves the room for a moment. The tension drains from me as soon as he walks away. I sit down on a chair, cross my legs, and scold myself; Focus, Anna. When Cole returns, he has an arm full of plastic bottles and a few paint brushes.

Confused, I ask, "What are those for?"

He takes one bottle and pours clear contents into another container, "To make the crystals stick."

I watch him as he mixes three clear liquids and then shakes the bottle hard. The muscles in his arms bulge slightly as he does it. My eyes are on his arms and my brain isn't working. He stops, pours the contents into a cup, grabs a brush and says, "Up." He passes me and walks to the other side of the room. He points to a stool and says, "Sit."

I have no idea what he's doing. It isn't until the brush is dipped in the clear liquid and the brush is coming at me that I pull back and ask, "What are you doing?"

He glances up at me. Cole is in work mode. His eyes have glossed over, but he snaps out of it when he hears my voice, "Applying the crystals. I'll paint on the adhesive and place them by hand. Then we can pour on more so that they still look loose and flowing." He's staring at me, absorbing my confused expression. He laughs, and rubs his face with the heel of his hand. "I forgot the box of crystals on the table. No wonder you were confused." As he hurries off to grab the box, I sit there with my jaw hanging open.

When Cole returns, he dips the brush again, and dots the cold viscous contents three times on my throat. Then he turns to the box and selects three different sized crystals, all white, and applies them. They stick. A smile spreads across his lips and his brush dips into the mixture again, moving lower this time.

I sit on the stool with my hands on the seat, fingers crushing the wood. Every time his brush touches me, I try not to flinch. It's so cold. And then he presses the crystals to my skin. His warm fingers brush against me as he does it. I can't breathe. My arms start to shake as his brush caresses the top of my breast. Cole stops what he's doing and looks up at my face. His attention had been concentrated on the curve of my breast and which stones to put where, but when I start shaking, he blinks twice and looks up at me.

"What's wrong?" he asks. His voice is too soft. I don't notice because I'm ready to crawl out of my skin. His little touches are driving me insane. His fingers have already seared a path across my chest and the closer he gets to my nipple, the more I can't stand it. That sexy blue gaze meets mine.

I want to say that I can't do this. I want to throw myself at him, but I don't. My nails dig into the wood, "Nothing," I say. "I just… well, this is kind of a bit much." I know I'm rambling, but I can't stop myself. For some reason it doesn't matter how many nude paintings I've seen, it's entirely different when I'm the naked girl being painted. Literally. With glue. And then getting bedazzled by Cole's perfect fingers. My brain snaps as I'm speaking. I can feel it happening, but can't stop the rush of words. "And the glue, and the crystals—Cole—it's just…"

He stills me with a firm hand on my shoulder. I look into his eyes, at those dark lashes, "It's a little more personal than you thought it'd be?" I nod once, and he averts his gaze. Cole's hand releases my shoulder and I shiver. "Yeah, it's that way for me, too." He clears his throat and looks back up at me. "Do you want to stop?"

Sadness pours through me and I shake my head. "I wanted to do this. I wanted…" my voice is strained.

Cole pushes the hair out of his eyes, and says, "I know. And this is a great idea. I know exactly what I want to do… " he breathes hard, "but it's strange because it's you. I know you." He looks at me for a moment and realizes how silly he sounds. A smile lines his lips and he sits down on the table. "So, we both want this, but it's—"

"Awkward. Awkward as hell," I slouch on my stool. While we were talking, my arms have tried to fold over my breasts three times. Each time I had to stop myself or I'd shift the crystals. The glue hasn't dried yet.

"Yeah, it is." He glances up at me. Cole seems more relaxed than me. My gaze locks with his, my lips part. I know I'm gazing too long, staring at him, willing him to walk over to me and do unspeakable things to his intern, but I know he won't.

Cole lets the gaze linger. His voice pins me in place, "We need something to break the tension, to help you relax."

"Yeah," I reply, nodding, not taking my eyes off his. As he steps closer, my stomach flutters and my skin tingles. Cole stops before me. His hands are in his pockets. His shoulders are slumped forward slightly, like he's uncertain about something. And his gaze doesn't leave my face. The look in his eye makes my pulse pound harder.

Cole is standing so close that I can feel his breath on my skin. He leans closer to my face, and doesn't stop until we're nose to nose. I fight for control of my breath, trying to still my racing heart. He breaks the gaze, and looks down at my breasts covered in crystals, then lifts his eyes to my lips. When he speaks, I melt, "This shouldn't be like this… but it is. I want to have an excuse to touch you, anything… and now that I have one, I can't do it."

"Do what?" I'm gazing at his face, unable to look away. Is he saying what I think he's saying? My heart pounds harder, threatening to crack my ribs. I can't look away. I can't move. My lips tingle, as if they know what Cole is saying before the rest of me realizes it.

He leans closer and I feel his hot breath slide across my lips. I watch as he lowers his lashes, and moves toward my mouth. When his lips brush against mine, he barely kisses me. I stop breathing. My head rushes with sensations that make me feel giddy and light. My lips tingle, wanting more. Cole hesitates as I sit in front of him, naked. I feel his fingers on my cheek, slowly sliding across my face, pushing back my hair. I feel him fighting it, trying to deny the attraction that's pulling us together harder and harder. His hand slips down my cheek until his thumb brushes my bottom lip. He rocks it slowly, feeling the softness of my mouth against his finger, tracing my lower lip. His mouth is right there, close enough to kiss me, but he doesn't. His other hand doesn't touch me. He keeps a space between his body and mine. I tremble as he touches me, as he watches my reaction to him.

"This," he says, answering my question. His voice is filled with deep rich currents that pierce me through to my core. When he slides his thumb away, he moves slowly, like before. His lower lip touches mine, gently testing to see what I'll do. My hands lift on their own, finding the thick hair at the nape of his neck. I pull him down, so his lips press firmly against my mouth.

Every inch of Cole's body is corded tight, like mine, and when I touch him, he melts. His lips press into mine, softly. His teases me, kissing me softly before his tongue slips between my lips. His hands cup my face, his fingers sliding across my cheeks and into my dark hair. One hand slips down my neck, inching painfully slow toward my breast. Every inch of my body feels like it's on fire. I press my chest against him, thrusting my breast into his hand. The crystals are dry. I feel them under his hands as he slides his fingers over my taut nipple, rolling it gently between his fingers. I moan into his mouth, and he kisses me harder. My entire body has melted in his arms. I'm leaning into him, and sliding off the chair when a voice blasts us apart.

"Hey boss. Just checking…" Regina looks up, mortified. Her words die in her mouth as she averts her eyes, "Just seeing if you need anything." She stands there, not knowing what to do or where to look.

Cole pushes away from me, his hands slip off my body. He turns to her saying, "No. We're fine." Regina nods, and scurries for the door without a backward glance.

My heart is pounding in my chest, every inch of me is flushed bright red. Cole looks over his shoulder at me with an expression that I can't read. I'm wondering if he's going to deny the attraction again, but he doesn't say anything. Instead, he walks back toward the cup and the paint brush. I slide back onto the stool and he paints me in tiny strokes, placing crystals over me as he goes.

Neither of us says a word. We act like nothing happened, even though I wish more had. His brush moves over my nipples, and Cole's fingers press against my tender skin, pressing the stones in place one at a time. His hands pass over my body and I enjoy every second of it, but a suspicion starts to take hold in the back of my mind. What if he kissed me to get rid of the tension? What if it didn't mean anything? I sit, waiting for him to say something, but Cole is silent. I wish I knew what he was thinking.

When he finishes placing stones on my side, he says, "Stand."

Without a word, I do as he says. Cole runs his thumb over the smooth skin that disappears between my legs and I gasp. "The crystals should trail across your hips and across here, correct?" His finger draws the curved line he intends to cover with crystals. It feels like he drew on my skin with fire.

I try to hide my emotions, and do the same thing he's doing, but I utterly suck at it. My voice quivers when I speak, "Yes." That one short word betrays me. Cole is on his knees in front of me. He reaches for the crystals and the cup of adhesive and puts them on the floor.

"Spread your legs, Lamore," there's no teasing nature in his tone. He sounds hard again, cold. He waits, but I don't move. He looks up at me and starts to explain. "Part your—"

I cut him off, "What's with you? Did you kiss me because you wanted to? Or was there some other demented logic behind it?" I sound angry. I don't like the way he is talking to me. His tone implies that I am nothing to him.

He doesn't look at me, "Demented logic, Lamore. What other reason would there be? Now, let's just get through this. Please separate your ankles so I can finish?" he looks up at me, exhausted. I don't say anything else. I spread my legs slightly and he strokes my sensitive skin with his brush. When his fingers press against my smooth flesh, I remain rigid, like he is doing nothing to me. As though the thought of his lips, his breath, that close to the spot between my legs isn't intoxicating.

When he's done, there are a million sparkling crystals glued to my body. He stops us in front of a full length mirror so that I can see. But, I don't bother looking up and begin to walk to the set he wants to use.

Before I can walk away Cole snatches my wrist, and pulls me back, "Look at yourself."

"I know what I look like, Cole. Let me go." I pull out of his grip. I don't want to see what I look like. It will sear the memories made today deeper into my mind. With Cole acting hot and cold, I don't want to risk it.

He doesn't reach for me again. Instead, he sets me up in a pose on the white set. I lay naked on the floor. Cole moves around me searching for angles, and I stare past him, my gaze getting lost somewhere on the ceiling.

"You're frowning," Cole removes the camera from his face, and looks down at me. I try to stop, but I'm too irritated with him. Cole watches me for a moment, and then tethers his camera directly over me on a boom that swings out from the wall. He pulls a square black remote from his pocket and turns it on. Cole tests it, and I hear the shutter snap shut.

As he sets things up for the pose he wants, he says, "Why do you always offer an escape clause?" The sneer slides off my face and I look at him. His broad shoulders are reaching above his head as he moves the lights back away from the set.

"What are you talking about?"

Cole doesn't look at me when he replies. He continues moving around the set, putting things in place. "You ask these jarring, emotionally loaded questions that demand an honest answer, but you tack on these clauses that allow the person you're asking to back out and not answer."

"Again, what are you talking about? I'm tired of your games and you're PMS is giving me whiplash."

Cole stops and looks down at me. His eyes are glinting, brilliant blue. "It's amazing that you're that blind—that you can't see what you do to me. I swear, Anna…" his hands clench and he forces them open. His eyes shut tight and when he reopens them, he looks down at me shaking his head, "Deranged logic? Really? That's easier to believe than the truth?"

"Oh, please," I say, feeling too exposed. "Like you'd tell me the truth anyway." I avert my gaze, too upset to look at him, but Cole stands over me. He falls to his knees with the remote in his hand.

"I've told you things that I never told anyone. I'd tell you anything you have the guts to ask without adding those ridiculous clauses to at the end." He flicks the light and the room goes black.

My heart is racing and I twitch when I hear the camera shutter. It's a prolonged exposure and I know that I can't move or I'll mess up the image. A blue light appears and he starts to move around me, running the light up and down my sides quickly.

His voice fills the shadows, "If you asked, I'd tell you that you inspire me. Your passion ignited something within me, something that I thought was gone a long time ago. I'd tell you that I think you're too young for me. That I'll only hurt you if I act and do the things I want to do with you." The light is over my lips and they part. My gaze is on his face. He's close to me, kneeling, crawling around my naked body on the floor. "Stay like that. That's perfect, Anna."

The question I want to ask burns in my mind, but I don't move. Cole grows quiet as he crawls around me, covering my body in light, inch by inch. When the shutter clicks again, I know I can speak.

I start to sit up, but his hands are on my shoulders holding me down. "Don't move. Everything is perfect. I don't want to reset the pose." I still under his hands, and he releases me, saying, "Ask your question, Lamore."

"How do you feel about me?" Before I can say anything else, the shutter on the camera snaps open and I'm still again. Cole doesn't respond right away. His light is next to my hair, moving in rapid sweeps over the right side of my body.

Finally he says, "Too many things. I feel like I know you, but I'm not entirely sure I do." Moving to my breast, he waves the light close to my skin. I fight the urge to move, to speak. He continues, "I feel like I want to know you more. There is nothing about you that doesn't captivate me. You're addicting, and I can't help myself, Anna. I want things from you, things I can't have. I feel things I shouldn't feel." His voice trails off as he moves around me.

My body reacts to his words and it becomes harder and harder to stay still. He's so close. That light sweeping over my body puts his hand just above my skin. As it passes over, I wish he was really touching me. My mind is racing with thoughts. While I know the age difference is large, I don't know why he holds back.

When the shudder snaps, I ask him, "What do you feel, Cole?"

He presses the button almost immediately. I barely had time to ask. He speaks as he works. A dim blue glow outlines his face. He looks haunted, pained almost. His voice is a breath, barely a whisper. He doesn't move this time. The light doesn't flash, outlining my body. He just sits there next to me on his knees, staring into the darkness, "I feel like I'm falling in love with you Anna. And it doesn't matter what I do, I can't stop." He's breathing hard, looking down at me.

When he answers this time, I reach for him. I thread my fingers behind his neck and pull his lips down on mine. Cole tries to pull away, but I don't let him. I can feel him warring with himself. The tension in his back and the strength of his arms says he's trying to resist, but I hold him to me, gently stroking his lips with my tongue. When I push inside his mouth, when the kiss deepens, he melts into me. His body relaxes and Cole kisses me back, softly at first. His hands find my face and I hear the remote fall to the floor. His body lines up with mine, and I can feel his erection through his jeans. He presses against me and I moan, wanting to feel him inside of me. My hands drift down his sides, feeling the curve of his body beneath my hands.

Cole's fingers tangle in my hair. As his hands slide down my face, he touches my neck, skimming my breasts until they land on my hips. He pulls me tighter to his body and kisses me harder, sweeping the inside of my mouth with his tongue. Every kiss grows hotter, making my heart pound harder. His hands on my bare skin are sending currents through my body and I can't ignore them. I realize that I don't want to. The room is so hot that Cole's body slides against me.

Running my hands under his shirt, I place my palms on his back. When Cole holds me tighter I feel safe and wanted. His fingers find my nipples and he teases me, holding them between his fingers, kissing me gently.

I gasp as he does it and arch my back to thrust my breast toward his mouth. I want him to kiss me, to taste me. There's nothing in this moment besides me and him. The longing I've felt fades away, as I feel my body growing hotter in Cole's arms. I want to feel his body moving with mine. I want to know every inch of him. I want to slide my tongue over his beautiful body and make him scream my name. Cole's kisses explode with passion. He moves like this isn't real, like I'll suddenly tell him to get off of me. His warm kisses trail my neck as his breathing increases. Another hard breath rushes from my lungs. Every muscle in my body is tense, crying out for release.

Cole shifts his weight so that one of his legs is between mine, and the other is off to the side. The muscles in his arms are corded tight as he holds himself up to keep from crushing me. I take his hand in mine and lower it slowly. His fingers are beneath mine.

As I move his hand, I feel his palm slide over my stomach and down to my thigh. Cole lifts his lips from my neck. He breathes hard, watching me, feeling my skin. His palm is hot as his hand moves lower and lower.

Our eyes lock. This is more than kisses, more than lust. I feel it. I know he feels it. As his hand slides over the crystals on my lower lips, I look into his eyes. He doesn't breathe. My mouth is parted, waiting for him to reach his fingers between my legs and stroke me. My knees part and as I move his hand there, but he stops. The sound of my pulse roars in my ears. Cole breathes slowly, stilling his hand. It rests just a little too high. His thumb rubs one of the stones on my skin, hesitating.

Breathless, Cole pulls his hand away and sits up. "I'm sorry, Anna."

I don't know what happened. Sitting up, I try to take his arm, but he's already pushing off the floor. I can see him in the dim blue glow of the light he was using. I roll onto my side and grab his wrist before he can walk away. Just as I grab him, the blue light flickers once and dies. There is nothing but touch and shadows.

We are disembodied voices in the dark. I can't see him. I can only sense where he is. I swear that I can hear his heart pounding in his chest. My hands search for his face. I find his cheeks and slide my hands across his strong jaw, feeling the stubble beneath my fingers. "Cole, stop. I want this as much as you do..." He's quiet. The tension grows between us. I lean forward until I can feel his breath on my lips. "Cole?"

"Anna, I—"

I breathe, "Do you want me?"

He says nothing, but he doesn't pull away. Every inch of my skin is prickling. I can't release him. Not until he says it'll never happen. The longer the silence stretches, the more my heart sinks. I finally add, "If you don't, I'll never mention this again, but if you do... if you really think you're falling in love with me—"

He pulls away and rips my heart out of my chest. I'm shaking, and I can't stop. I hear his footfalls cross the room. The light flips on. He tosses me my robe. It falls on the floor next to me. He doesn't turn back.

Facing away from me like I'm too difficult to look at, Cole says, "Get dressed. I got what I needed."

The way his voice carries across the room makes me shudder. It's like part of him is locked away and I'll never get it. As he hurries away from me, I'm shocked into silence. I don't understand what's happening, why Cole shuts downs like this. Sitting naked on the floor, I realize that the only time Cole behaves like this is when he acts on his feelings.

CHAPTER 12

By the time I pull on my robe, Cole is nowhere to be found. I walk to my room and shower, washing off the rest of the adhesive that clings to my skin. I want to know why Cole ran. How could he say he's falling in love with me, and then refuse to touch me? For a moment, I feel sick, like maybe he didn't want me, that he just said those things to touch me—but that isn't like him. I've seen him shoot other women. Cole isn't that guy. He doesn't give or take affection lightly. The water pelts me in the face and I realize that I can't rationalize what happened. I can't make it go away.

By the time I get dressed, it's midafternoon. I pull my hair into a high ponytail and go to search for Regina. As mortifying as it is, I have to smooth things over with her. When I find her, she's in the storage area sorting through old backdrops. Her red hair is draped over her shoulders as she hunches over boxes, unpacking them one by one. Regina glances up at me as I enter the doorway and quickly averts her eyes.

Before I can say anything she straightens and blurts out, "I had no idea you two were intimate. I thought it was a shoot." She drops the fabric that was clutched between her fingers. The look on her face tells me that she's equally as horrified.

I lift my hand to silence her, "It was a shoot, but—" I shrug like I don't know what happened "things took an interesting turn. I would have told you, you know. If we were…" I trail off. The knot in my throat is strangling me. If we were what, Anna? There's nothing between me and Cole, save a few kisses. In the back of my mind, I hear his voice—that hushed tone confessing that he's falling in love with me. I can't ignore it.

Regina watches me for a moment. She doesn't seem to know what to say. "It's not my place to ask or know about anything like that. You don't need to tell me anything, Miss Lamore. I just hope that I didn't make you so uncomfortable that I lose my job." Regina's face flushes as she says it. The woman could have avoided me for days and never asked, but she's too blunt for that.

I smile. I like her straight-forwardness. Shaking my head I say, “Your job isn’t affected by my stupidity. I promise.” She smiles at me and I nod.

When I turn to leave, she says, “For what it’s worth, I haven’t seen Mr. Stevens with anyone for some time. You must have really turned his head.”

I stop and look back at her, “What do you mean?”

She hunches over the box and goes back to work. I can tell she doesn’t want to say more, but she does, “Let’s just say that his playboy ways are something of an illusion.”

I don’t know what to say, so I nod. Regina goes back to work. I walk away feeling more confused than before. I wander out of the studio, planning on going for a ride on my motorcycle to clear my head when I notice Cole’s car is gone. No Porsche. I close my eyes and shake my head. What did I do? Sighing deeply, I walk over to the bike and lean against it.

It has to be me, right? I mean, Cole was in the moment and then something made him run. It was like he was sprayed with ice water. He didn’t even stick around to give me an explanation. I can't figure him out and its driving me nuts. I wonder if that little shoot just destroyed our relationship. I wish I could take it back. I wish I hadn't done it. Tears sting my eyes, but I refuse to cry. I rub my eye with the back of my hand when a voice makes me jump.

"It's beach time baby! I figured why wait until you invite me. I mean, how hard could it be to find this place?" Emma is standing there with her head tilted to the side and a wry smile on her face.

"Emma," I turn toward her and feel the tears break free.

"Whoa!" she says when I wrap my arms around her and start sobbing in her ear. She pats my back, "What's wrong? What happened?"

I shake my head, too upset to talk. Sniffling I say, "Let's just get out of here. Tell me you drove, because I can't see straight to drive us."

She nods, taking me to her car on the other side of the house. When we're inside, I bite back the sobs that want to keep coming as tears stream down my cheeks.

“What the hell happened?” she asks, looking over at me.

“I thought everything happened, but it turned out to be nothing. Emma, take me away from here.”

CHAPTER 13

We drive along the parkway. The scent of the ocean fills my head as I tell Emma what happened with Cole. She listens and doesn't say anything for a long time.

When she finally speaks, she seems confused, "Edward seems to think you guys are still together."

I slam my head back onto the seat and look up at the ceiling. "No, Em. We broke up a while ago. He took it really hard." Silence fills the air as the little car bobs and weaves through traffic. After a few moments I ask, "I guess he's not doing too well?"

She shakes her head, "Apparently not. He said you needed space, but that you guys were fine. He's always been a bit of an idealist, but this is a little weird—even for him." She tilts her head to the side as she changes lanes, saying, "Then again, it's not like I'm usually friends with his girlfriends. You know how people can act one way with one person and totally different around another. It seems like my brother's got a little of that going on.

"But he's not what's bothering you. Why are you so bent out of shape? I mean, did anything happen with Cole before now?"

I shake my head, staring out the window. "Not really. I don't know why it's bothering me so much. It's not like Cole promised me anything. I just hoped that—" I swallow my words. I don't know what happened, but I intend to find out. Things can't stay like this between us. I don't want to push Cole, and I don't want to take something he isn't willing to give. I just wish I knew why. There's something between us, something preventing him from acting on his feelings. I feel it stuck there like a chasm that will swallow us whole.

Silence fills the car. Emma finally says, "You really like him, don't you?" I nod. She laughs, "When you first met him, I thought you hated his guts. You did a 180 pretty fast, Anna. Even for you."

"Even for me? What's that supposed to mean?"

"Nothing bad," Emma says. "Don't take it like that. There are two types of people that flip that fast. The first group is the flakes, the people who don't know what the hell they want. That's not you. You're in the second group—the people who know exactly what they want, but they can't find it."

"The thing is, I think I have found it. Cole isn't like anyone I've ever known." He's passionate, driven, powerful.

"He's kind of old for you, isn't he?"

"Thanks for stating the obvious, Em." I snap. "Sorry," I say pushing my hair out of my face. I look over at her. "Do you think that's why he's acting the way he is? Because I'm too young?"

"Anna, if I ever have a clue why a guy does anything I'll die of shock." She darts between cars as we drive toward the city. She glances at me before jerking the wheel back, "One thing is certain—he thinks you're hot and is too chicken to act on it. You can either forget the whole thing happened or corner him and get your answer."

That sounded like a bad idea. Cornering Cole. I shiver thinking about it. We drive in silence when it finally dawns on me that Emma drove two hours to see me and didn't call first. I glance at her, just noticing that she seems happy, but is trying to hide it. A lopsided smile spreads across my lips, "You're awesome, you know that?"

She laughs, "Yup! But what'd I do?"

"Something major had to happen for you to come all the way out, without a phone call..." I smile at her, waiting for her to tell me. When she grins, I know I'm right.

"I got a job! It's mine, Anna."

"That's great! Is it the one you wanted, over at the paper?"

Emma's giddy now. She nods, "Yup! All I have to do is finish the internship, graduate, and it's onto the lowest branch of the newspaper totem pole." She squeals and I can't help but feel excited for her. "It's perfect, Anna. And oh my God! You should have seen me at the interview. I nailed it! Like, totally nailed it! I'll be working alongside Stacy James—"

"No way," I say leaning forward.

Nodding enthusiastically, she slaps her hands on the steering wheel and squeals, "I know, right? He'll oversee the internship and I'll start getting my own stories in a few months. It's totally perfect!"

"I'm so happy for you, Em. I know how much you wanted this. You're gonna rock it.

Just imagine, your own newspaper article with a little square picture of your head. It'll be retweeted worldwide and you'll become an overnight sensation."

She snorts, "That's why I was coming to get you! I knew you'd be the perfect person to celebrate with!" She glances at me, "I have a beach bag filled with towels, bikinis, and trashy romance books. My original plan was to lounge on your beach, but I think some time away from Cole will help your brain work better. We need a Cole-free zone. Why don't we detour to Jones Beach and hang out for a while? You can relax and I can celebrate."

Leaning my head back against the seat, I say, "That sounds completely perfect."

Emma cuts across six lanes of traffic and I think I'm going to die. We make it onto the exit ramp for the beach and we both start laughing.

CHAPTER 14

The beach is one of my favorite places—when it's empty. Today it's overflowing with people. Emma parks in a distant field and we pick a spot on the sand between several other sun-seekers. I lift my face and breathe in deeply. The sound of the ocean fills my ears, as the salty breeze lifts my hair. Emma throws down the towels and smooths them out. While Em runs off to change, I lay down on the towels in my tank and cutoff jeans, adjusting my sunglasses so they're in the right place. As I lace my fingers behind my neck, I close my eyes.

This is perfect. It'll give me time to think, to decide what I want to do before I see Cole again. Part of me wants to ignore the whole thing and not deal with the drama, because since I met Cole I've noticed that is the one thing he promises—lots of drama. I'm not sure if I'm up for that. Especially with the way my life is. I have plenty of drama on my own. Kicking it up a notch with Cole might make my head implode.

You're a coward, Anna, a voice whispers in the back of my mind. Maybe I am. Maybe Cole's not the right guy, but as soon as I think it, I know that's wrong. Cole feels right.

The sound of his voice makes me jump, "Anna," Edward says. His shadow falls over me. I squint up at him, wondering how he spotted me. I'm packed between tons of people and after what Emma said, I really don't want to talk to him right now.

I push myself up onto my elbows, "Hey. Em just ran to change. She'll be right back."

Edward stands there frozen, hands on his hips, wearing a blue swimming suit that shows off his body. He has a deep tan that suggests he's already been here for hours. I wonder if Emma knows he's here, if she's trying to make our paths cross. My stomach twists. That can't be right. She planned on staying out in the Hamptons, not coming here.

"I know," he says, running his hands through his hair. "Actually, I came to see how you were doing. It's been a while."

Actually, it hasn't, but he seems sweet enough.

Making my hand into a visor, I press it to my forehead so I can see him. The sun is behind his back. "I'm good. Working a lot, but good." I pause and try to look at his face again. Something about the way he's standing makes me uncomfortable. I can't decide why. I clear my throat and ask, "How's school? Staying out of trouble?"

Raising his hand to his face, he grins down at me. I can see his eyes now. "School's fine. Good. I heard you were staying out in the Hamptons for the summer?"

"Yeah, for the internship, remember?" He nods. I don't understand why he acts like I never told him about it. I did. I remember the conversation. "I thought I already told you that?"

He smiles sheepishly, "You did. I just panicked and didn't want to walk away, yet. Anna…" his tone is too soft, beseeching. It kills me to hear it.

Before I can say anything, Emma walks up behind me and seems surprised to see her twin, "Hey, Eddy. What are you doing here?"

She turns her head both ways, looking for the rest of his friends, but turns back to her brother with a raised brow.

"Just hanging out."

"Cutting class, no doubt," Em retorts. She grabs a huge pair of black plastic sunglasses from her bag and slides them on. Her black bikini makes her look like a super model. As I look around, I see many male eyes on Emma, no doubt wondering if they should try and talk to her.

My phone rings. I pick it up and look at the screen. Cole. I send it to voicemail. I can't talk to him now. Edward is watching me as the conversation with his sister commences.

"As are you, unless the paper fired you already—" He knew how to press her buttons. His words make Emma puff up, ready to fight.

"For your information, I got the job and Anna and I are out celebrating. So go dig a hole or something and leave us alone." She makes a face at him and points, indicating he should leave.

Edward smiles, "Is that so? Well, good for you, Sis. Good for you." He looks over at me and nods, "See you around, Anna."

I nod back, watching him leave. Part of me wonders if I made a mistake, if Edward was the right guy. It seems like a minor thing, after all, a relationship isn't just about sex. Most of the time a relationship is spent doing other stuff, stuff that I enjoyed with him. Internally, I groan. I sound like an eighty-year old.

Emma is leaning back on her hands, people watching. "There are a lot of hot guys here, Anna." Her gaze is locked on a group of young men a few towels down.

"Then go get them, Em. I'm not in the mood."

"Psh," she says, swatting me. "You're never in the mood. It just means you haven't found the right guy yet—one who lights a fire in your panties and makes your heart bounce around in your chest until it feels like you'll keel over and die."

I stare at her blankly. I do feel like that about one guy. That is the problem. I laugh and shake my head, "Do me a favor and just take the guy you're picking out for me, too. I seriously doubt he'll mind." I'm joking, but Emma has a devilish smile on her face.

"We'll see about that." She stands up and brushes the sand off her lean legs. Without another word she strides toward the group of guys playing volleyball. Her sights are set on a man that is clearly my type and not hers. I straighten and watch her in horror as she stops behind him. The guy turns and looks at Emma and then back at me. He nods, listening to her and then smiles at me. I return his smile, but feel foolish. Emma is a dead girl as soon as she comes back.

They talk for a few minutes. The guy is forced out of the game when his friends resume it without him. He follows Emma back toward our spot and says, "You're friend here invited me to join you for a little bit."

"Mmm," I eye Emma and mouth, *I'm gonna kill you*, when the hot guy turns to look at his friends, but she just swats her hand at me.

"I'm Jesse. Jesse Oden."

"Anna Lamore," I reply feeling silly. Jesse looks like he's in his early twenties. It's clear that Emma is telling me to stick with guys my own age. I hate it when she does stuff like this. I decide to curtail the whole thing, "Listen, Jesse—I don't know what she told you, but—"

He smiles down at me. "She didn't tell me much of anything. Just that you were her friend and I was your type. So I thought I'd come over, say hi, and see if we hit it off. If not," he shrugs, "no harm. Right?"

I'm shooting daggers at Emma, who's standing behind him and nod slowly. Why does everyone need to prove a point with me lately? Am I that thick? Internally, I moan, but he's too nice. I smile at him and nod, "Sure. Why not?"

As it turns out, we have a lot in common and soon I find I'm laughing and talking to him because I want to, and not for any other reason. Emma runs off into the surf after a few minutes and leaves us alone on the towel. Jesse sits down next to me. He is totally my type—dark hair, blue eyes, and completely breathtaking. His smile is so perfect he could be on a toothpaste commercial.

Goosebumps pop up on the back of my neck. For some reason I feel uneasy, but it has nothing to do with Jesse. I shiver, and brush them away. Turning, I look around through the mass of people. It feels like someone is watching me, but I don't see anyone staring. There are people everywhere. It's stupid to get spooked like this, but I can't help it. I ignore the sensation and go back to talking with Jesse. He makes me smile.

"No way," I say, shocked, pulling my feet closer to my bottom, "when did you graduate?" I wrap my arms around my knees as I talk.

"Last year. Oh, I know where it was! I sat in front of you in art history with Peters. I thought you looked familiar." He is convinced he saw me on campus, but I can't place him. That isn't abnormal since the university is huge. So are the classes. However, in this case, I am just obtuse.

"Oh my god! That was you? That was you!" I laugh, shaking my head. "Small world, huh?"

"Apparently so. Good thing for us, right? I mean, what are the odds? Out of all the places to park and then set your towel, what are the odds it'd be by mine?" He flashes me that movie star smile. Jesse is so sweet.

"Well, it must be fate, because I have no luck."

"I think you might have a little," he leans closer to my face and brushes a kiss against my lips. I'm stunned, but I don't move. A thousand thoughts rush through my mind and each one stems from Cole. I feel caught in the middle. Jesse is the kind of guy that I would go for. Emma did well, but I don't want to give up on Cole.

I don't kiss him back.

Jesse hovers for a moment, his warm lips waiting for me. When I don't kiss him, he pulls back. Jesse smiles and runs his hand through his hair, looking at the waves in the distance, he says softly, "Guess it's not the right time for us, is it?" Through lowered lashes I glance up at him and shake my head. "Well, whoever he is, he's lucky. I hope he knows it." He pushes off the towel and stands. "I really liked meeting you. If my luck changes, let me know."

He hands me his number, and I take it.

I watch Jesse walk away and wonder what I'm doing. I just turned down an awesome guy after Cole made it clear he doesn't want to be with me. Staring at the waves, I decide that I have to find out why. There has to be a reason. It makes no sense for Cole to have that little moment of truth scene and then douse it with outright rejection. There has to be an explanation. Part of me shies away and doesn't want to hear it, but I can't leave it alone. I can't leave Cole alone. There's something about him that captivates me, something worth fighting for.

CHAPTER 15

Emma drops me off at the new studio, and as I walk in a blue uniform catches my eye. The mailman is standing by the desk with a large envelope, alone. "Can I help you?" I ask.

He nods, "Thank God. Where is everyone?" Shaking his head, he thrusts the parcel at me and hands me a pen. "I was about to leave, but this needs a signature."

"Thanks for waiting for me. I know you didn't have to and I really appreciate it." I smile at him and his gruff curtness seems to melt despite my appearance. I'm sure I look like I'm crazy—windblown hair frizzed out along with a cherry glow across the bridge of my nose—but he doesn't seem to notice. It must be part of having a mail route in the Hamptons.

He nods once and says, "Sure thing. Have a good day." He leaves me standing alone in the lobby with a fat envelope.

I've been wondering why there only seems to be three people working here. I've been assuming that I just keep missing the others, especially since Cole said the NYC crew was sent out here, but aside from the first few days, they seem to have disappeared.

I glance down at the letter in my hands. It is from J. H. Hashre, esq., and stamped TIME SENSITIVE MATERIALS ENCLOSED with an "open by" date of today. What is this? Looking at the envelope, I think about opening it, but it is addressed to Cole, not the studio.

As I walk through the building, I flip on lights looking for him. Regina isn't around. She must have finished her work and went to dinner. I stop in the shooting room and look around. Memories of earlier in the day flood my mind. His hands on me, his lips. I want more of that—more of him.

"Miss Lamore," Cole's deep voice echoes through the space. He stands across the way on the other side of the shooting room in an adjoining hallway.

"This came for you. It looks important. Thought you'd want it." I cross the room and place it in his hand. When he looks down at it, he stiffens.

"Thank you." He turns to leave, but I grab his arm. Cole stops and looks down at my hand on his skin.

"Tell me," I demand, my voice firm. I fold my arms over my chest and look at the side of his face. "Tell me how you could do those things, say those things, and then walk away like it meant nothing?"

His eyes meet mine, "Because we don't belong together, Miss Lamore. Because it would be a horrible mistake to do more, to say more, than I already foolishly said. There's no future here," he gestures between us, "nothing to pursue. I apologize for not controlling my tongue. There's no excuse for it."

Each word feels like a barb in my heart. "I see." My voice quivers slightly. I don't understand. How is it a mistake? I have no idea, but from the look in Cole's eyes I can tell there is no way to convince him otherwise. I lower my head and look at the floor, at his bare feet. Cole seems like he can't wait to get away from me. He shifts his weight from foot to foot, looking anywhere—everywhere—but at me.

Finally, I say, "Maybe I should work somewhere else?"

That catches his attention. His brow pinches together, "Did Sottero talk to you?"

"No, Cole. She didn't. I just thought that maybe it would be too awkward to stay here, that I should—"

He shakes his head, "Anna, I won't be here much longer. It's only a few more weeks." He taps the envelope against his thigh and I glance down at it. "I promise that it won't happen again. Regina can show you a lot of what you need to know, and as for your skills—I think you'll be perfect for this position. I really hope you'll stay." As he speaks his voice softens.

"Cole, I don't understand why you want me to work here. There are more qualified people, honestly. And the staff…"

He looks up at me confused, "What about the staff?"

"Where are they? I thought you had more people. When we were in the city, you said they were out here, but now that we're out here, there's just Regina."

His gaze falls to the floor and he breathes in deeply. Shaking his head he says, "There are some things going on, some things that require me to make changes. I made them. And I only kept the best."

"Cole," I whisper his name and see him respond to my voice. I want to touch him, to push his hair back and open the letter that hangs in his hand like a lump of lead. That has something to do with this, I can sense it. But, before I can say anything else, he turns away.

"There's a shoot in the morning," he says. "Better get some rest."

CHAPTER 16

The shoot the next morning feels tense. Cole's out of sorts and silent. I speak for him, and take over the shoot without him asking me to. At one point he hands me the camera. "Time to show off, Lamore. Do your best. I have what I need." Cole moves to the back of the room and presses a button. Regina shows up and he disappears into the back, out of sight.

The client is patient. She knows of Cole and his work, and she trusts him. She doesn't bat an eye at Cole handing the shoot over to me, which makes me even more nervous. Why does everyone think I can do this but me? After a few poses I feel less nervous. I start to see what I want to shoot and I forget that I haven't shot on my own yet. I don't worry about Cole yelling at me for messing up the session. He trusts me, maybe too much. I glance around wondering where he went.

The client and I chat about lots of things until she asks, "Has Cole shot you?"

Her question takes me by surprise. I nod shyly, my cheeks flaming, "As a matter of fact, he has. Although I haven't seen the results yet."

She grins, "I hope you show off his work. There's something about the mind of an artist like Cole. I don't know. It's like he's broken and it just makes me want to fix him. At the same time, if he weren't so messed up, he couldn't create such beautiful work."

She laughs lightly and I stare at her. Is that what draws me to him? Cole's broken. He was abandoned by his parents, leading life totally alone—a life that no one knows about. Cole has been on his own since he was eighteen, since that picture of him in the army uniform. And now something else is happening to him, something that is weighing on him. She is right. I want to fix it. I want to let Cole know he's not alone.

The session continues and I steer the conversation away from Cole. Although I don't know where he's gone, I'm not sure if he can hear us. And a level of protectiveness washes over me when she talks about him like that. I don't know what's tormenting Cole, but I can't make light of it the way she does.

When she leaves, I try to find Cole, but I only see Regina. After the client leaves, Regina moves to the front desk to answer the phone and return calls.

"Where the hell did Cole go?" I ask.

She looks up at me, "I tried to ask, but he took off without a word. He looked pissed, Anna. What happened?"

Wide-eyed, I say, "Nothing. We were shooting, and then he shoved the camera in my hands and walked out. I didn't do anything."

Irritated, I push through the front door and walk outside into the afternoon air. The salty smell of the ocean fills my lungs as I walk down the path behind the studio. My heart falls into my shoes when I see him. He's sitting on a bench between two massive pines with his head in his hands, shoulders hunched toward the ground like he's utterly defeated.

I'm certain he knows I'm there by the time I step next to him, but he doesn't move. To see him like this consumes me with grief.

It feels like there are two hands on my throat, pressing away the air. I slip onto the bench next to him. Looking at the scattered pines that stand between us and the ocean, I ask, "How long did it take you to pick this property for the studio? You wanted it for a while, didn't you?"

He doesn't move. After a minute, he turns his face slowly toward me, "How'd you know?"

I shrug, "It just seems like you're familiar with this place in a way that someone who's been here before would be. Maybe more than once." He smiles but it fades too fast. He rubs his hands through his hair and sits up.

"I came here a few times when I was younger. I told myself that if it went up for sale, that I'd get it. Everything about this place reminds me of things I love." He shrugs. "I didn't think I was that transparent."

"You're not," I reply. He arches a brow at me like he doesn't believe me. "That's the only thing that I figured out and I wasn't even sure I was right. "So, do you want to tell me why you walked out of the shoot?" He blinks once at me and returns his gaze to the ground. The expression clearly says NO. "Okay," I say, "Well, at least tell me you're leaving next time."

"There won't be a next time," he says and glances over at me, "I'm going back to the city. You can do this. I don't need me to be here anymore. Besides, there's something that came up and it would be easier to deal with if I were at Le Femme and not here."

My mouth hangs open and I try to snap it shut, but shock washes over me too quickly. After one solo shoot out here, he's leaving? Cole says nothing else. I don't know what to say. It feels like I should be excited, but I'm not. Everything feels wrong.

"So, it's just me and Regina?" He nods and doesn't look up. His gaze is on the ground, on the pebble path beneath his feet. "Cole," he lifts his head and looks at me. I want to take him in my arms and hold him. "You don't have to be alone." He laughs when I say it, but it sounds so tormented that I want to cry. "I'm serious."

"It's not an option for some people, Anna."

"Fine," I say and his dark laughter gets cut short. "Let's accept it. You and I are alone. We rely on no one. We sleep alone, if we sleep at all."

"What are you getting at?" he asks.

"Just that life doesn't have to be so damn lonely." My eyes meet his and I can't look away. Those endless pools of blue pin me in place. Inside my mind I'm pleading with him, begging him to let me in, but I say nothing. There's nothing more to say. Standing, I turn to him and rest my hand on his shoulder, and pause. There are so many things I want to say. I feel the words in my mouth, but I say none of them. My hand slips off his shoulder. I walk away and Cole lets me.

CHAPTER 17

Weeks pass. I shoot at the studio and the only person to keep me company is Regina. I try to work, to take care of the clients as best I can, but my mind keeps returning to Cole. I can't get him out of my head. Picking up my phone, I walk back into my room, and pull up his number. I've done this so many times, but I never press the button. As I sit down on my bed, I hold my thumb over his name. One touch and it will call him. I'll hear his voice again. Sitting perfectly still, I know I can't do it. There are too many things with him, things that can't be said over the phone. I have to be there to convey them in person. Why I let weeks go by is beyond me. Maybe I am a coward. Annoyed with myself, I throw the phone on my bed and pull on a pair of jeans and a tank top. I yank my hair into a ponytail and head toward the garage for my motorcycle.

The ride into the city passes in a blur as I think about what I'll say, what excuse I'll give for showing up on his doorstep unannounced, but I can't ignore it anymore. The closer I get to Manhattan, the darker and cooler it becomes until tiny droplets of water fall from the sky. The streets become slick as glass. The little sunlight that was left is gone and the street lights turn on. By the time I pull up in front of Cole's building, the sky has opened up and I'm totally soaked. My black tank clings to me like a second skin. My jeans are holding an extra ten pounds of water, making them feel stiff and heavy. I park the bike and slosh to the door. Before I can step inside the doorman stops me.

"Cole Stevens," I say and try to walk past him.

He's standing under the portico, perfectly dry, and doesn't let me pass. He glances at me once and says, "I'm sorry, but Mr. Stevens isn't expecting anyone tonight."

"I know," I reply, pushing my sopping wet hair out of my face. The guy looks at me like I'm nuts. "I didn't tell him that I was coming. Can you just tell him that I'm here?"

He shakes his head, "I'm sorry Miss. Better be on your way."

I'm about to protest when I see the valet pull up in Cole's black car. I turn toward the doors with a slow smile spreading across my lips. Finally, something is going to work in my favor. Cole will step outside and see me. We'll talk and everything will be better.

But that isn't what happens. Cole walks through the door dressed in a black tux. He looks stunning. My lips part as my jaw drops and it's all I can do to keep breathing. The way its cut, like it was made just for him, showcasing every angle of his perfect body. His dark hair is smoothed back, away from his blue eyes. He extends his elbow and a woman in a red gown follows him out.

Just as reality slams into me, just as I realize her couture dress and shoes, her status—Cole sees me. The expression on his face falters as our eyes meet. I feel the desire in that gaze, the pull on an imaginary line that runs between us. That same line that's been tugging me back to him ever since he left. But Cole doesn't say anything. He keeps walking, and helps the beautiful woman into his car. When her door closes he looks up at me.

Our eyes meet and I feel like I'm going to be sick. In every single way possible, I don't compare to her. Her elegance, her grace, her fluid movements scream of refinement that is the prideful trademark of the wealthy.

Before I can walk away, Cole says to the doorman, "Show her in. I'll be back shortly."

The doorman nods, surprised, "Yes, Mr. Stevens."

I'm deposited on the doorstep of Cole's apartment and walk inside. It's vacant.

Shivering, I wait in the kitchen, dripping on the floor, thinking he'll be right back. But Cole doesn't come right back. I wait in my sopping wet clothes, overemotional and tired. After grabbing a few towels, I set them beneath me and sit on his couch.

Before I realize what's happened, Cole's voice is in my ear. "Anna, wake up. We need to get these clothes off you. You're freezing."

Bleary-eyed, I looked up at him. He's still wearing that tux. I feel horrible and completely frozen. My arms are plastered close to my body and I can't stop shivering. I let him pull me to my feet and turn on a hot shower for me. By the time I finish, it is well after one in the morning. I wrap the towel around my body and walk out into his room.

Cole has removed his jacket and tie. The crisp white shirt is open at the collar. Cole is sitting in a blue leather chair in the corner of the room, his fingers pressed to his temples.

When I step into the room, he looks up. His eyes soften, "Feel better?" I nod, clutching the towel to my chest. "Good. You want tell me why you were riding your motorcycle in the rain?" he says, and anger vibrates in his voice.

"It wasn't raining when I left."

"It was stupid, Anna." His voice is clipped, tension lines his shoulders.

I mutter, "I do stupid things, Cole." Like continuing to think about you when you obviously have better things to do. I want to fight. I feel it inside of me, the tension waiting to explode.

He glances up at me. His expression is soft, serious, "You're staying here tonight." It's a statement. A fact.

"I am?" I don't want to leave, but something about the way he says it grates.

"You are. Let me get out of this and we can talk." He rises and goes to his closet. He grabs some clothes and tosses me a white tee shirt. "You can sleep in that."

I put it on while he's in the shower and climb onto his chair. I'm so cold, I can't stop shaking. Cole takes forever in the shower. At least it feels like forever. Between being an emotional lunatic, the long ride into the city, and the rain, I can barely keep my head up. Resting my head on the arm of the chair, I fall asleep again.

Cole's voice rouses me, but I don't fully awake until I feel his hands slide under my cold skin. "I can't let you freeze in a chair." He deposits me in his massive bed and buries me beneath blankets, but I still shiver. After a moment, I feel him sit next to me. His hands move down my sides, tucking me into the blankets so tightly that I can't move.

He looks down at me, "Better?"

I nod. "Thanks." I don't know how I feel. I don't know what I want. Part of me wants to just lay here and see what happens.

My heart flutters when his hands tuck the blankets. Did he really put me in his bed? The last time I was here, Cole gave me a guest room. This time he is sitting next to me and we are in his room. In his bed.

"I hope I didn't mess up your evening. She was very pretty, Cole. I'm really sorry."

He glances away and says, "You didn't mess up anything." His voice is soft, like he wants to say more about it, but he doesn't. "So, what was so important that you drove here in the rain?"

I try to shrug but I'm cocooned in blankets. Drowsiness is pulling at me hard. My eyelids feel like lead. "I had a bad feeling that something was wrong. It just felt like you needed help. I can't explain it. It makes no sense. So I jumped on my bike and came to make sure you were okay."

He's looking straight ahead when he answers, "You have impeccable timing… keeping me from making hideous mistakes." He grins down at me, dark hair falling into his eyes.

"Mmmm, maybe—but she looked way less than hideous to me."

Cole laughs. His entire face lights up. "God, I missed you, Lamore."

And I know he means it. I don't press him on who the woman was, because I'm the one who is in his bed.

Cole lays on his side next to me and I can feel the change in him as we lay there and talk. The tightly wound muscles in his neck seem to relax as minutes turn into hours. Sleep pulls at me, but I don't surrender.

After a while, I roll onto my side and we're facing each other. Cole's head is on his pillow, his bright blue eyes blink slowly like he's exhausted. "You're right," he says.

"About what?"

Smiling, he lowers his dark lashes and replies, "Everything, Anna."

There's a pang of pain in my heart when he says it. They are the words I'd hoped to hear, but not the right tone. His voice says he can admit it, but I know he's still holding me at arms-length, in the safe zone.

There is no way to get closer to Cole, and I know that's where I want to be.

CHAPTER 18

Stretching, I blink a few times as my heart pounds in my chest. I gasp and sit up quickly.

"Forget where you were?" Cole asks from the leather chair. He's already dressed, sitting with an e-reader on his lap.

Breathing hard, I smile sheepishly and relax. "Maybe," I grin. He's smiling now, watching me.

"I never thought I'd get you in my bed, Lamore," he jokes, shaking his head. That soft smile makes his eyes shine like he's happy.

"Yeah, well, even you have to get lucky once in a while," I laugh. My fingers caress the silky sheets. The thread count has to be close to a zillion. They feel like butter, soft and supple under my palm. I fall back onto the pillows and look at the ceiling. "I'd better get going. My boss is going to be pissed. I didn't call in sick today and I'm going to be close to three hours late by the time I get there." I stare at the ceiling, noticing it has a pearlescence that makes the room have a soft glow.

"Yeah, I heard he can be a dick. You might want to hurry up and get out here, take care of your clients, and maybe he won't chain you up in the basement for being so damn late…well, not for more than a few nights anyway." The corner of Cole's lips pull up. It's a sexy smirk that makes my stomach flip. His fingers tap the e-reader, and he lifts it, his eyes scanning the lines, but I saw the screensaver and know it's not even on.

When he looks up, our eyes meet. My heart shudders like I'm being electrocuted. Our gazes lock and heat sears through my stomach and between my legs. The room suddenly feels overly warm. I want to push back the blankets and walk away. I don't want him to have this effect on me, especially because it seems to be mostly one-sided. I can't hold him like that. Hell, I can't even get him to kiss me. These thoughts run through my mind as his blue eyes bore into mine.

It feels like he can see every inch of me. I realize I'm not breathing and suck in a shaky gasp. My entire body is tingling. I break the gaze and throw my feet over the side of the bed and stare at my toes. What am I doing? Why am I chasing this guy? He's too screwed up to ever be with, and yet—I can't walk away.

"Lamore?" he says my name and I glance over at him. He's leaning back in that chair like nothing happened, like he doesn't feel anything.

"Yeah, boss?" I pull my lips into a smile, but it feels hollow. I glance at him from behind a wall of frizzy dark hair.

"What time is your last shoot today?"

I think about it for a second and say, "Six. Mrs. Patterson wants me to shoot something sexy with her Pomeranian. You knew how bat-shit crazy they are out there, didn't you? Sexy pictures with a dog. There must be something in the water..." I'm talking to myself now, shocked at the strange requests people have. It's like no two people can agree on what's sexy. "What the hell am I supposed to do with a dog?"

Cole ignores my bewilderment, "I'll come by at eight and you can show me your work. I'll help keep you on track when stuff like this comes up. The best way is to shoot it the best you can and then talk about what to do next time. And since I failed to feed you breakfast, I'm taking you to dinner." He sets the e-reader down as he's speaking and stands. As he finishes the last word, he's standing in front of me. "Assuming you eat dinner and don't have other plans?"

The spot between my brows pinches and I look up at him. He's holding a white slip of paper between his fingers. It has ten black digits and the name JESSE OWDEN, slightly crumpled and linty from a spin through the washer and dryer. I glance past him, annoyed that he went through my clothes, but I can tell he washed them for me. My clothes are folded neatly on Cole's dresser. The paper was left in my pocket and got soaked, but any idiot can tell what it was.

"Not tonight," I hedge, not wanting to say anything. I stand and realize that he's much taller than I am. I pluck the slip from between his fingers.

"Want to tell me who he is?" he asks, his arms folding over his chest, his head tilting to the side like I've done something wrong.

I mirror his pose. Folding my arms, I tilt my head, and say, "Want to tell me about the hot chick in the red gown?" We stare at each other, each of us driven to hide our secrets. The tension in the air is thick, coating us until my hairs are standing on end.

Cole folds first, "Well played, Lamore." His arms unfold and he looks into my eyes. The gaze is so vulnerable, so sweet that I can't believe it belongs to Cole. "I'll see you at eight." With that, he turns and walks away, leaving me alone in his room to get dressed.

CHAPTER 19

During the shoot my brain is all over the place. I can't focus. The little dog yips every time I go to fix the pose. Posing dogs is like trying to teach a Frisbee to walk.

"Regina, please reset the dog," I say, pressing my temples with my fingers. For a split second I imagine myself fanning a brides train and the happy couple smiling back at me. Then I look down at Mitsy who thinks biting constitutes talking. She nips at Regina as she repositions the dog by her master's hand.

The pose is perfect. I chose the white set and have the client laying face-down on satin sheets. She's propped up on one elbow slightly. The pose shows off her curves without being too revealing. It's the kind of pose that looks seductive. It works perfectly for her. Everything is white on white, with layered textures. Linens, lace, throws and silk pillows are strewn through the set. It's completely perfect. Even the little dog helps pull the shot together. His snow white fur adds just the right about softness, but the little beast won't sit still.

Regina picks up Mitsy. The little dog bares her tiny teeth and is very unhappy to be placed back on the bed. Regina runs off the set and I shoot. Working fast is new to me. Normally, I take all the time I need. When I think I have the shot, we move on. The final piece is going to be a high key black and white. Everything is pale from the client's skin to the dog's fur. She wears nothing but a white thong. Her implants make her look like she is twenty, even though those years of her life are at least a decade behind her. She holds the dog in her arms, its fur helping to conceal her breasts. The dog is happy in her arms and the owner looks straight back into the camera, staring at the lens. The finished product will be striking.

Later that night, Cole arrives and thumbs through the unprocessed shots with me. When he gets to the end of the shoot he stops and looks at the poses with the dog in her arms more carefully. He leans in close to the screen with me sitting in front of the computer.

He taps a pen to his lips, "Open it." I double click the image and it opens in an editing program. "Show me what you plan to do."

My hand moves on the tablet, clicking settings and altering the image to black and white. I adjust a few settings, run a few of Cole's actions to smooth her skin, and then pump up the contrast. "What do you think? The dog threw me for a loop. I didn't know what to do with it, and the stupid thing wouldn't sit still."

He leans over my shoulder, his gaze on the screen. He puts a hand on my shoulder. It feels warm and strong. His scent fills my head and I think back to last night, to laying in his bed and sleeping right next to him.

"I think this is amazing. I mean, people ask us to do and shoot all sorts of things, but this—damn Anna…" he strokes his chin, staring at the screen. "You even made the dog look sexy." He laughs and looks down at me.

I beam, "Thanks, Cole. That means a lot to me." The weight of his hand suddenly feels like something more. My skin tingles and I want him to touch me, to stroke my face with his hand. Cole watches me with that expression that I can't read.

He pats my shoulder before stepping away, "No problem. I knew you had a talent for this before I even met you. Some people just have it. You're one of them. You're lucky, Lamore."

"Yeah, well, not so much. Actually, me and luck are strangers. Maybe even enemies," I joke. I put things away for the night and shut down the editing program, the screen glows dimly before its light goes out as the computer powers down. I reach for the scattered pens and papers on my desk, and shove them into a drawer. "If I saw Luck on the subway, she'd probably mug me. Nothing lucky has ever happened to me."

Cole has that smirk on his face as he listens. He slides his hands into his pockets and tilts his head, "Oh, I don't know if I'd say that. Luck's the kind of thing most people notice in hindsight. It's hard to see it in the moment."

I stop what I'm doing and turn to look at him. He's oozing with boyish charm. Everything from the way he stands to the curve of his mouth makes my heart race. I shake my head, trying to evade his charms. Why am I tormenting myself by hanging around him?

"And at this moment, am I lucky? Is there something happening that I can't see?" I pull a folder to my chest and wait for him to answer.

"Maybe," he says, voice soft and sensual.

My eyebrow lifts. I stand there for a moment at a loss for what to say. I hug the folder tighter. His eyes drift toward my hands before he turns away, nodding his head toward the door. "Come on, Lamore. Dinner. Now."

I place the folder down and follow him out. As my hand flips off the lights, I wonder when I became so obedient and discover that I don't care. If it means being around Cole, and seeing him happy, I'll jump when he snaps his fingers. At least a little. It goes against every fiber of my being to let someone else be in charge, but with Cole, it feels comfortable.

CHAPTER 20

Somehow a routine develops. I work out East, Cole works in the city. We have dinner together and then head back to his place where we talk until one of us passes out. I've woken up in his bed more times in the past three weeks than I've slept in my own. I wonder what this is, what he's doing, but I'm too afraid to ask. I'm just glad to have him in any capacity at all.

One night after dinner, I'm laying on his bed staring at the ceiling. I feel Cole's eyes on me—they are always on me—but I don't turn to look at him. His gaze lingers, sliding over my breasts, watching me breathe as my chest slowly rises and falls. His fingers slip the buttons through the holes on his shirt. I let him look. I like it and wish he'd do more. The man has self-control like nothing I've ever seen.

"Cole," I ask, still looking at the ceiling.

"Mmmm?" he says, his eyes still searing into my body as he peels the shirt off his chest and tosses it in the hamper. He stands there bare skinned, in nothing but jeans. I'm dying to look at him, but I don't. He hesitates like he knows I want to look before grabbing a tee shirt from the dresser.

I want to ask him how he does it, how he can lay next to me night after night and not touch me. My fingers twist the sheets. "Are you seeing anyone?" Maybe that was it. Maybe he has a sex friend and I'm his other friend. The one that he sleeps with. Jealousy flames through me at the thought. I want to be the sex friend. Hell, I want to be his only friend.

"Why would you ask that?" he stops and looks at me bewildered.

I shrug, "I don't know. It's just… " Suddenly he's much closer. He's standing next to the bed looking down at me. I keep my gaze on the ceiling.

"Just what?" he asks, like this is normal. I lower my gaze and look at my hands. The question is caught in my throat. I don't look at him. "You want more?"

I feel his eyes on my face, but I can't look up. My heart is pounding, wondering if I just ruined whatever we had.

"There isn't more than this. This is the best of what I can offer you. The rest is too...," he shakes his head, "It's just not possible."

SECRETS

Volume 3

CHAPTER 1

I don't understand. I stare at him with my mouth hanging open. "What's not possible? At least tell me."

Cole leans close enough to kiss me, but he doesn't. My heart jumps. Those blue eyes are on me and my brain melts. His perfect lips form words and I can't take my eyes off of them.

"Us. We're not possible." He licks his lips as he speaks. My eyes fixate on the movement. I think he's going to say more, but he doesn't.

Disappointment leaks across my face. My heart is pounding and I don't even know why. The way he looks at me, the soft touches—that kiss—all of it says we're out of the friend-zone, but this utterly confuses me.

Cole sees it in my eyes, I know he does. But instead of putting my confusion to rest, he leaves it there. I feel hollow, like fragile glass, like I might shatter.

I want him to say it. I think about forcing the issue, but I can't. Blowing the relationship apart, banishing the pieces I have for the pieces I want, seems foolish.

The disappointment slides off my face. Cole crosses the room and sits in the blue chair. His dark hair falls forward, obscuring his eyes. Tension lines his shoulders and creases his brow. This relationship will break if I push him. Something is there, something hidden that I can't see. It holds him back. It makes him act like this.

I shift my weight in the bed and pull my knees into my chest. I don't take my eyes off of him. Cole feels my gaze and looks up. I manage to say, "Then give me something else." My heart is pounding. "You hold me at arm's length with some things and then with other things, well—" I point both hands at the bed I'm sitting in, "Just give me something. Anything." The plea in my voice makes my stomach twist.

Cole gazes at me from the chair, "What do you want, Anna? No one is as close to me as you are. No one else shares my bed. Ever. It's been years since another woman walked through that door every night," he points toward the front of the house as he says it. Cole doesn't sound mean, but he does sound like I'm asking for something he can't give.

My voice is soft, "I'm not asking for everything. I actually like this, even though it sounds insane." I wish it was more, but if it's this or nothing, I choose this. I lick my lips, watching him shift his weight in the supple chair. "Tell me something, something about you. We can trade secrets. Tit for tat."

Cole's gaze narrows and a dark brow lifts, "Really? You'd be willing to answer anything I asked you? A complete revelation? No holding back? No areas off limits?" He leans forward, placing his elbows on his knees. Cole shakes his head, but he smiles softly as he does it, "I hardly think that's wise, Miss Lamore."

"Half the things I do aren't wise, Mr. Stevens. As an act of good faith, you go first." My hands are pulling the sheet over my lap. My bottoms are nothing more than a lacy boy short.

Cole is bare-chested. Soft flannel pants hang from his hips showing off his toned body. His tanned skin is smooth and completely lickable. Cole wiggles in the chair as a smirk lines his lips. "This isn't a good idea, but..."

"It's too tempting to refuse?"

He nods, "Like so many things about you, it has the same seductive allure." The corners of my mouth lift and I look away. His gaze is too intense. Cole straightens and leans back in the chair, "Very well, I'll play along, but it's only because I have a few questions that you aren't forthcoming with, and your logic is baffling at best—"

"Just ask, Cole."

He takes a breath, "The day you came to the internship interview, it was obvious that you didn't hold me in the highest regard—"

I laugh, "I didn't like you, dude. You can say it." I lower my voice and bob my head as I imitate him, "Anna detested me."

"Is that what you think I sound like?" he grins and shakes his head. Smiling,

I lift a brow at him and say, "Is that your question?"

"No," he becomes serious again. "I am however wondering if I want to know the answer. It seemed like I disgusted you. I want to know why." Cole's voice becomes a whisper as he speaks.

I fidget in the bed. Swallowing hard, I look him in the eye, "The reasons seem stupid now. I didn't know you, then. I thought I did, and I was wrong."

"That was hardly a personal answer, Miss Lamore. Care to elaborate?" His voice is teasing, but I can hear the genuine curiosity there as well.

I press my lips together gathering my thoughts. "I thought you were a sleaze, running a sleazy studio, groping girls in their underwear. Add to that your money and you didn't have a chance."

"The money made it worse?" he asks, his fingers steepeled at his lips. Those blue eyes gaze at me, unblinking, waiting for an answer.

I nod slowly, feeling more exposed than I thought I would. "Yes, the money made it much worse. It would have been better knowing you were disowned." I straighten and kick the sheets off. Moving to the end of the bed, I flip onto my stomach and pull my feet up behind me, twisting my ankles together. I can tell he wants to ask more, but he doesn't.

"Now it's my turn."

Cole seems nervous, but he doesn't look away. He leans to the side, resting his head on his hand. "Ask me, Anna."

"Who's the chick in the red dress?" I nervously tuck some of my loose curls behind my ear. Ever since first seeing her, I've wanted to learn who she was and what she means to him.

"My lawyer. She's been helping me prepare for something... unpleasant." His voice is cool and even as he says it. This wasn't the answer I expected. It's revealed more questions I don't have the answers to. But, whatever is going on, whatever Cole is dealing with, must be crushing him. The things that make him sound like that—voice level to the point of apathy—are the things that are the worst. Something bad is happening to him, something that requires legal advice.

"And?" I prompt.

"And nothing more. I believe you were inquiring as to our relationship status. It is professional and always has been. The formality of our attire was for appearances only, part of a public display to help cushion what's coming." As he speaks, Cole's eyes take on a distant expression. The muscles in his arms tighten as his fingers fist. He tries to hide it, but he can't. Something's going to happen to him, something that I can't stop.

"I'm sorry," I say. "I had no idea." I want to fix it, I want to take away his burdens, but I don't know how. I don't even know what's wrong. Attempting to lighten the mood I say, "Ask me about Vanilla."

Cole's eyes dart up and meet mine. He holds my gaze and finally says, "Tell me why you prefer vanilla, Miss Lamore."

"Anna. Call me Anna, Cole."

His chest expands as he takes a deep breath and I openly admire him, my eyes drifting and lingering on his smooth skin. "Why do you prefer vanilla, Anna," he breathes my name and sends shivers down my spine.

A wicked grin twists my lips. "I don't." The words roll of my lips and I'm suddenly very aware of my tongue.

Cole's eyes darken. The stubble lining his cheeks accentuates the strong lines of his jaw. He's gazing at me with a predatory look. "Explain."

"My ex liked things plain and simple. I don't. I like things he didn't think were sexy. I like sticky, sweaty, slippery sex. I'm not Miss Vanilla, Cole. I'm the opposite."

Cole works his jaw as I speak; his eyes riveted to my face. He stares at my eyes, then my mouth. He sucks in air and tilts his head back as I speak. "The opposite?" I nod slowly. My hair slides forward and I reach around and pull it to one side. Cole's eyes drift to my chest and the cleavage that becomes visible as I do it. Something changed, but I don't notice it yet.

"Yes," I say looking back up at him. Shrugging I add, "I'd just met you and was thinking I was a bit of a freak for even wanting what I want. It seemed like a strange thing to tell you, so I hid it and switched things around."

Cole's tension sky-rockets as I speak, but when I say that I think I'm a freak, he drops his hands and stares at me slack-jawed. "How could you possibly think that?"

"You don't know what I wanted to do," my face flames as I choke out the words. Cole opens his mouth to ask more, but I shake my head. "Just so you know, we're crossing my hell-no line, and whatever I ask you next has to be comparably horrifying. So tread lightly, Mr. Stevens."

Cole nods slowly as his lips pull into the sexiest smile I've ever seen. Shaking his head, he says, "I understand. And I promise I'll answer whatever you ask, even if it crosses my hell-no line, as you call it." I grin at him and waggle my eyebrows. Taking a deep breath, I pull up the sheet. I can feel the question building before he even says it. I want to hide behind the sheet. Cole's voice cuts through me and makes me melt. "What do you want most that he wouldn't do?"

A high-pitched moan travels up my throat. I don't want to tell him. I want to tell him. I clutch the sheet and cover my face. It sizzles as he asks; it burns because I know the answer. Cole stands, crosses the room, and pulls the sheet from my face as he kneels on the floor in front of me. We're nose to nose. I feel his breath on my lips as his gaze pins me in place. I can't look away. My pulse pounds in my ears and I shiver.

"Tell me," he says gently, taking my shoulders in his hands. His fingers swirl little circles on my smooth skin. He swallows hard, waiting.

Butterflies fill my body, making me giddy. His hands are strong and warm. I feel them pressing against my skin and I wish they were on my face, cupping my cheeks. As if he heard me, Cole lifts his hands and splays them on the sides of my face. His thumbs stroke my skin as his fingers slide back into my hair.

"It sounds silly, like nothing." My voice is light as a caress, barely audible. I watch Cole's lips as I say it. I can't look him in the eye and take the full on heat of his gaze. "I wanted him to kiss me between my legs where no one has, taste me, swallow, and ask for more." Fear twists my stomach, sending a series of shivers cascading over my skin. I'm clutching the sheet, strangling it. Whenever I brought up oral sex with my previous boyfriends they were ecstatic that I wanted to do that with them, but they felt no desire to reciprocate. It made me feel like wanting them to want it was dirty.

Cole releases my face a beat after I say it. He remains in front of me, but looks away. "There's nothing freaky about that, Anna. It's a normal sexual act and I'm sorry he deprived you, but that doesn't necessarily mean you're into kinky things." He looks up at me, his expression soft and kind.

"Ah, that's just an example, Cole. The thing I wanted most that he wouldn't do. I didn't say it was the kinkiest. That's the tip of the unfulfilled, sexually frustrated iceberg." My voice is husky and I can't look away.

Cole stares at me like he's never seen me before. The rosy glow that was limited to my cheeks now sears my entire body and he grins. "So, you're telling me—let me make sure I got this right—that a kinky sex goddess has been laying in my bed every night for the past few weeks?"

Smiling, I nod once. The way Cole looks at me makes me think it's okay, that things will be all right. He lowers his dark lashes and releases a breath slowly. His hands run through his hair tousling it even more. When he looks up at me, I can't breathe. Everything about him tempts me beyond control. I want to tangle my fingers in his hair and pull his mouth down on mine.

Cole shakes his head like he can't believe it and then sits back in the chair. It's my turn to ask a question. Internally, I'm fighting over what to ask—about the ring in the safe or why he won't touch me. Every inch of my skin prickles as I think about his hands on me. I wish he were close. I wish so much that he'd tell me. While I want to know about the ring, I want to know this more.

"Why won't you touch me?" My voice is a whisper. I don't look at him. I expect his answer to punch me in the gut. I expect to hear, because he doesn't think of me that way, that I'm too young, too inexperienced to be with him like that.

"Anna," he breathes my name like it haunts him. When I steal a glance, his eyes are closed and his face is in his hands. I turn away before he says it. I don't want to hear the reason. I'm sorry I asked. As Cole opens his mouth to speak, I cut him off.

Raising a hand, I reach it out in front of me, holding up my hand and say, "Stop. Wait." Breathing hard, I look into his face. Remorse consumes him. I wish I could fix it. I wish he'd let me hold him and take away whatever sins haunt his memory. Cole's lips remain parted, but he doesn't speak. He waits for me to finish. I sit up in the bed and pull my feet under me. "I don't want know."

It's quiet for a moment and the only sounds I hear are my racing heart and my ragged breaths. Then Cole says, "The answer isn't just one thing. I can't dismiss you Anna, but I can't make this more than it already is."

"What is it, Cole? Are we friends? This feels like more to me, but I can't wrap my mind around it. I don't understand how you can lay next to me at night without touching me." I feel the panic in my voice and try to shove it back down, but it won't recede. "Don't lead me on. Don't make me think one thing and then do another. I—"

Cole crosses the room in two steps and scoops me up in his arms. He sits down on the bed with me in his lap and I rest my head against his bare chest. His heart is racing. His arms tighten around me before he kisses my hair gently. "It wasn't my intention to lead you on."

"Then what is your intention?"

"To protect you. To keep you from getting hurt. I thought that this was better, but it's not. I should have kept my distance, but I didn't. I can't reverse this Anna. I can't undo weeks of you sleeping in my bed and seeing your face every morning."

I glance up at him. Fear pinches my throat tight. "Do you want to?"

His blue eyes are crystal clear and lock onto mine. I start to look away, but Cole gently pulls my chin back to meet his gaze. "No. Every memory of you, every moment was—" he presses his lips together and stops speaking for a minute. Finally, he breathes deeply and sets me down on the bed. "I have to maintain my original boundaries, otherwise this won't work and I'm not ready to say good-bye yet. It's utterly selfish, but it's the best I can offer."

I don't understand, but I don't say so. Dejected, I slide back into the bed away from him. What is this? Why won't he let me get closer? I lay my head back onto my pillow and stare at the ceiling.

There's nothing more to say.

CHAPTER 2

Early the next morning, I slip away to the parking garage across the street to get my bike. It's safe, well, as safe as a parking garage can be. It's well lit and has a guard booth at the front, but it still makes Cole uneasy. If I park in one of his slots, below his building, he knows nothing will happen to me or my bike. After last night, though, I don't want to bring up anything that might torch our already precarious relationship.

Pressing my eyes closed as I reach the bike I sigh and press my fingers to my eyes. What relationship, Anna? There is no relationship. Correction, there is no sexual relationship. Somehow I've ended up in the same goddamn boat I had been in with Edward. With that thought, the skin on the back of my neck begins to prickle, making me glance around, but I can't see anything except parked cars.

I reach for my helmet and unlock it, pocketing the keys as I slip it onto my head. I fish a ponytail holder from my other pocket and work my hair back to the base of my neck and twist the piece of elastic in place. As I'm fastening my helmet, I feel like someone is watching me. My skin prickles all over and my heart starts to race. I turn and look around, but I still don't see anyone. A car drives by and heads toward the exit. I can see the street from where I stand. The early morning traffic catches my attention with glittering red taillights and raucous horns blaring. Then I see him on the sidewalk. Edward. He sees me, waves and approaches me from the street.

Jogging over, he says, "Anna, good to see you." Edward looks perfect. His jeans hug his slender hips and his long-sleeved pale-blue shirt brings out his eyes. But something puts me on edge. I can't say what, I just feel uneasy around him and want to get away as quickly as possible. But I can't seem to get my helmet strap tightened. Apparently, it twisted when I pulled it through the metal loops. I try to fix it without taking it off. I want to leave.

I nod and smile even though I don't feel like it. "Good morning, Edward." I can be civil. There's nothing wrong. The fluttering in my heart and the panicked feeling telling me something isn't right is insane. This is Edward. "What are you doing over here so early in the morning?" I glance up, wondering where the security guard is. His booth is empty, and a car that's waiting for him decides to bypass payment and darts out into the street. It's quiet again. No car engines rumbling inside the sunken cement, no exhaust fumes clinging to the ceiling.

He shrugs and slips his hands into his pockets, "On my way to an interview up the street."

I arch a brow at him, "Who's over here? I thought all these buildings were residential?" The helmet isn't cooperating. I can't seem to get it untwisted. I undo the chin strap completely, pull it, and start over.

Edward's eyes fixate on my hands fumbling the helmet strap. "It is, but there's a—" he stops talking and steps toward me. He reaches for the black straps and says, "Here, let me do that. You seem shaken up."

I want to jerk my head back, but I don't. Instead I stand there like an idiot and let him strap my helmet on. His fingers push the black strap through the metal loops and he pulls, tightening it. I grip my hands in front of my waist and try to slow my pulse.

When he finishes, he grins at me. When I don't smile back, he asks, "What's wrong? You seem out of sorts."

I want to say *only around you*, but I don't want him to think that he affects me. Besides, this doesn't make sense, any of it. Why is he here? What are the odds that he'd walk in front of this garage at this time? Is he following me? I think I'm being paranoid, but the feeling doesn't fade.

I turn away from him, smiling nervously and reach for the bike. "Nothing's wrong. I'm just jacked up on caffeine. You know me." I lie and swing my leg over the motorcycle.

"I do know you, Anna. And I'm here if you need me." He glances at me on the bike for half a beat and adds, "Be careful with this guy, Anna." He says it like he knows something I don't, like it's more than a general warning.

I wonder how he knows anything about me and Cole. It must have been Emma. She must have told him I was with Cole.

Irritation shoots through me. I didn't think it was necessary to tell her not to discuss my love life with her brother, but apparently I was wrong.

I start the bike and say, "I can take care of myself, Edward. And you better get to your interview or you'll be late."

He laughs, "I'm never late. I'm still early actually." That was probably true. He is always early. It irritated me when we were dating. Everywhere we went, he had to arrive half an hour early. Edward looks from his watch to me and steps in front of the bike. He rests his fingers on the handlebars and looks up at me. "Just be careful, okay?"

I nod at him, wanting this conversation over. "I gotta go." Edward steps aside and I rev the engine and pull away from him. I can feel his eyes on my back until I'm out of the garage and on the street zipping through early morning traffic.

I stop on the side of the Long Island Expressway and grab a cup of coffee. The morning air is cooler than usual. I breathe deeply, admiring the white fluffy clouds strewn across the sky. If I was still in high school, I'd be drawing clouds today. I had one art teacher who was always excited when those fluffy white ones appeared. I didn't understand why until I tried to draw one. It turns out that drawing clouds is hard. Mine looked like floating bricks. There was nothing light and fluffy about them.

I pull out my phone and rest the coffee on my thigh. I won't have time to see Emma until this weekend, but I have to know if she told her brother about me and Cole.

I text her as I sip my coffee.

Me: Hey Em. Saw your bro. Did you tell him anything about Cole?

A few minutes pass. Emma is in class. I don't expect anything back right away, but my phone dings.

Emma: No. That'd be worse than talking to u about him. What happened?

Me: Saw him in the garage this morning. He warned me away from Cole. Wondered how he knew.

Emma: idk. I swear I didn't say anything.

Me: OK. Just asking. Will u b around tonight?

Emma: Yup. Catch up then?

Me: Hell yeah. Lots to tell u.

For a second I just stared at the screen. How did he know about Cole? And did Edward really know something about Cole, or was he just screwing with me? I wasn't sure, but it left me feeling very uneasy.

I poured the rest of the coffee down my throat and tossed the cup before pulling back into the traffic. Why I took the LIE is beyond me. It's always crammed with traffic this far west. Once I got out onto the Island a little ways, it would clear up. In the meantime, I bobbed and weaved between cars and trucks, passing the occasional driver who was horrified of motorcycles. One woman nearly drove into the wall trying to get away from me. I zip past her and feel the rush of early morning air on my face.

I refuse to let my mind play games with me. Edward's not a stalker. I dismiss my lingering apprehension from this morning and push it out of my mind, giving the situation with Cole full access to my entire brain.

Last night didn't go the way I planned. I want more from Cole, but I don't want to risk losing him. Finding out the woman in the red dress was his attorney doesn't make me feel better. At first it did, then I realized that if she's around that much something must be very wrong. I wish he'd ask me for help or at least lean on me a little, but Cole is so closed off. He keeps his emotions close to his chest and it's hard to tell what he's thinking. But after last night, I did learn one thing—I do mean something to him—I just have no idea what.

CHAPTER 3

"Regina, we have a full calendar today so I need you to fix the sets as we rotate through. That way as soon as the next client is here, we can start."

Regina looks up at me. Her copper hair dangles over her shoulders. The green top she wears makes the color more awesome and her crop pants are so cute. Like all Le Femme employees, she's barefoot. She nods, "No problem. Oh, there was a message from your school. They said they hadn't received your internship papers yet and they need them back by the end of the week."

"By tomorrow?" My brows pinch together as I straighten and look at her. I drop the rug I'm holding and stare at her. That's not right. The internship papers weren't due until two weeks after the internship was over. That is four weeks away.

"Yup," Regina says. She looks up at me when she sees my expression. "I wouldn't worry about it. Cole probably lost the papers or something."

I nod slowly and go back to what I'm doing, "Or something," I say under my breath, trying to figure out what it is.

By the time I get to the campus, it's nearly 5:00pm. They'll close before I get to talk to someone. I glance at my watch. The line at the registrar's office is moving at snail speed. When I finally get to the front, I'm really anxious and not looking forward to talking to some kid about the lost papers or why the university wants them back early.

I step up, ready to ask what the hell is wrong with them, when Jesse Oden looks up at me from the desk. "Can I help—" he smiles when he sees me, his expression completely changing. "Anna."

"Jesse? What are you doing here? I thought you graduated?" The girl behind me audibly sighs and folds her arms.

He ignores her, "I did. I'm doing some grad work over the summer. Student job. So what do you need? Enrollment forms? Application for graduation?" he guesses.

"No, I've done all that stuff already. I got a phone call today that said my internship papers weren't turned in. I thought they were due after the internship was over. I have two weeks left. Could you check my account and see what they want?"

"Sure," he smiles tapping the keyboard. After I tell him my student number, he's into my files. He grins, "Impressive GPA."

"Snoop," I laugh. He looks up at me and winks.

"Let's see," he says, his finger tracing lines on the screen, scanning it quickly. His expression changes as he does so. He glances up at me and I can tell something's very wrong, but he says, "Yes, they want your papers early. There's a note here for me to hand them to you when you come in, and schedule you an appointment with the dean."

"The dean? What for?" Everyone is watching me now. This isn't typical. Something is wrong, I just don't know what.

Jesse nods as he collects the papers I need from the slots on his desk. Taking the stack, he taps them once on his desk and shoves them under the stapler, then hands them to me. "Get these back to me by tomorrow. And I'm scheduling you for an appointment with the dean for tomorrow at 4:00pm." He hands me an appointment card. I'm annoyed and worried. I just take it and don't look at it.

"Thanks," I say and head out the door.

If I blow this internship, I don't graduate. I want to pull my hair out. I exit the building and find a bench. Sunlight pours through the leaves forming a lacy pattern on the ground. Taking my phone, I enter the appointment time for tomorrow and notice Jesse wrote a note on the back of the card.

Wait for me.

I sit under a tree and watch the students as they head toward their evening activities. About ten minutes later, Jesse walks out of the building and sees me. He smiles initially, but it fades quickly. He sits next to me on the bench.

"So, what's new?" he asks teasingly.

"Oh, my God! Is it that bad? I saw your face. Just tell me."

Jesse looks up at me and I can tell it's bad. His smile falters and he looks at his hands. "I'm not supposed to say anything, but it seems too insane to be true. Your internship was ended early," he says softly. "Someone reported that you're having sexual relations with your boss." His dark brows creep up his face as he says it, looking at me like he can't believe it.

I can't breathe. I feel like someone hit me in the stomach with a board. I lean forward, panic flooding every inch of me. Even though Cole and I don't have a sexual relationship, it looks like we do.

"So, it's true? I'm guessing this is the guy who had your heart when I first met you, too—isn't it?" He sounds sympathetic. He places his hand on my back and pats once like a friend. "It's not going to go well if you tell them."

I sit up quickly and stare at him, "There is no sexual relationship with him. There hasn't been. It's been all work. Nothing else." My voice is soft, remorseful.

"But you wish it was," he adds, and I nod. Blinking hard, I look over at him. "Thank you. I know you'll get in trouble if they find out you told me. Did it say who made the allegation?"

He shakes his head, "No. The complaint was filed directly with your dean. The info wasn't put into your main file."

"This isn't happening," I clutch my face, horrified that I'm reacting this way in front of someone I barely know.

"Hey, if nothing happened, there's nothing to worry about." I feel desperate and lost. He leans close to my face, tucking a curl behind my ear. Our eyes lock. He wants what Cole can't. Jesse breathes, "I'll cover for you. I can tell them how we met that day on the beach. There were other people around. If you say that me and you are together, and deny your relationship with your boss, they should let it drop."

"I can't have you lie for me," I say, not looking away, not putting more space between us.

"It's not a lie," he says lifting his hand to my cheek. "I haven't stopped thinking about you. I keep checking my phone, hoping you're over him—and calling me."

I feel so lost, so alone. I need Cole, but that will just make it worse. The entire relationship with him made everything worse, including me. I want something with him that he won't give. I want his whole heart, but he won't let me in. Loneliness and fear mingle together and I can't stop looking at Jesse's lips. He pulls me to him slowly, gently pressing his mouth to mine. It's like last time. The kiss is sweet and chaste, asking me if I want him.

Indecision flashes through my mind. I could try to hold onto whatever I have with Cole, but there's nothing there. Correction, there's friendship there and nothing more. We traded sex secrets and he didn't even look at me last night. I thought I meant something to him. The way he cradled me in his arms felt like I mattered, but I went to sleep alone and woke up alone. Cole didn't see me off this morning and didn't say anything else last night. Was it cheating to continue this kiss?

There's nothing between you and Cole, so how are you cheating? The voice inside my head snaps at me like I should know better.

Jesse's breath is warm, and the feeling of his hand on the side of my face is strong and perfect. He lingers by my lips, his lashes lowered, looking—waiting for me to push him away. But I don't. I lean into the kiss, feeling a rush of emotions race by as I plummet off an emotional cliff and obliterate any chance of being with Cole.

Jesse's tongue slips past my lips and into my mouth. He strokes me slowly, like he's thought about this since the first time we met. I want to lean into him. I want to feel nothing, to let go of the weeks I've spent with Cole, but I can't. I break the kiss and look down. Jesse's hands remains splayed on my cheeks, cradling my face. I can't look at him.

"Sorry. I just can't..." my voice is shaky and trails off.

He touches his forehead to mine, "It's okay. You don't have to say anything, Anna." When he leans back, he drops his hands to his lap. He smiles at me sadly, "I wish I had better timing. I wish I found you first."

I glance up from my hands, and try to smile, but I can't. Everything is pressing down on me, making me feel like a claustrophobe trapped in a coffin. I can't stand it. I want to nod at Jesse and act like he doesn't affect me, but he does. I stand and he does the same.

"You okay?" he asks, trying to catch my eye.

I mean to look up and nod, but a sob catches in my throat. Tears fill my eyes as I nod and cry, "Yeeees."

"I think you mean no." He steps toward me and says, "Come on. Let's go grab an early dinner."

"Why are you being so nice to me?"

"I'd rather be your friend than nothing at all. Besides, it seems like you could use a friend right about now, anyway." He keeps his distance, occasionally brushing against my arm or directing me by my elbow, as we walk across campus and emerge onto the jammed streets. It's rush hour. He takes me into the first place he sees and we grab a table in the corner.

I dab my eyes with a tissue and look up at him. He's the only one who seems to want me, and I keep telling him no. What's wrong with me? Jesse is my age, my type, and I'm pushing him away because I want something I can't have—Cole Stevens.

"So, you want to talk about it?" he asks, leaning his arms on the table.

"There's nothing to talk about. Nothing happened with me and Cole. Nothing's happened the entire summer."

"But you wish it did?" he says.

I nod. "I thought there was something there, but I was wrong. When we talked about it last night, he pretty much told me no."

Jesse's face twisted with confusion. "Then where'd the complaint come from?"

I shrug. "No idea. It's a slap in the face after last night. Honestly, you got further with me than I got with him."

Jesse smiles. "Did I?"

I nod and look up at him. "If I met you a few weeks ago..."

"I know," he says. "Listen, if things fall apart, you risk not graduating. We need to focus on that. That's the main problem right now." I nod, agreeing with him. "Let's assume that they find you guilty." My spine goes rigid as my mouth falls open.

"But I didn't—"

"I know, but say things go to hell—worst case scenario. You'll need another internship. Something where you can jump in and wrack up a ton of hours fast. Did you have a fallback?" I nod. Sophia ended up being my second choice. "I'd contact that person if the shit hits the fan and the university scratches your hours, especially if that studio showed any interest in you. It's the fastest way to fix it."

I think about that for a second. I'd be back where I was in the beginning, except Sophia would know I'd chosen Cole over her. I wasn't sure how she'd do with that. I nod and look up at Jesse across the table. I wonder why I can't let Cole go for him. I wonder if I do this to myself—pick guys who are defective to prevent having a real relationship with them. It seems like a double strikeout, first with Edward and now Cole. Meanwhile there is a perfectly hot guy sitting in front of me, who seems genuinely interested in me. I sigh and lower my gaze to the table. I'm such a head-case.

"That's really the only option I have, right? Go back to Sottero and beg?" I look up at Jesse to see him nod.

"Do you have classes in the fall?"

I shake my head. "No, I finished everything early by taking short courses last year. Usually people have their internship over the summer, come back and complete their classes. The dean let me flip them around so that I could walk in graduation at the end of August."

"So that's your best bet. Go see the dean, deny the whole thing and hope it was just some jealous guy spewing crap. Maybe it won't go anywhere." Jesse waves at the waitress and she refills our glasses.

Sipping my soda, I ask, "You think someone did this to me on purpose?" Who would do that?

Jesse shrugs, "Maybe. Or maybe something just didn't look right. Is there anything that would have made someone think you were together?"

My face flames. "Ah, well that answers that question. Listen, Anna." He leans forward in the booth and pats my hand to get my attention. "Think of it as just another hurdle to jump over before graduation. No big deal. It's your boss that's going to catch hell for it, not you."

"What do you mean?"

"It's against university policy to have a sexual relationship with your intern. Period. If they think he did it, well, I'm not sure what they'll do, but since it's Cole Stevens I don't think it'll just get swept under the rug. Tabloids have been following him around for the past couple weeks. It's like they sniffed out something brewing below the surface with him."

As Jesse speaks I think about the woman in the red gown, his lawyer. Something bad was coming. Something Cole already knew about. My stomach twists and I wonder if he already knew about the accusations, if that's the reason why he won't touch me. Hope and dread flood through me, making me feel sick.

Jesse sees me pale. "Listen, you can handle this. Keep acting like it's nothing. Don't react until it hits the fan, okay?" He squeezes my hand. I look up at him and nod slowly. There isn't a doubt in my mind that it already has and I'm the last to find out.

CHAPTER 4

"Anna Lamore is here to see you," says a woman twice my age. She looks up at me with judgment in her eyes.

The intercom buzzes back, "One moment."

"Have a seat. He'll be with you shortly." She gazes at me briefly and then returns to tapping the keys on her computer. I slip into a seat and wait. Students come in and out, scheduling their appointments to make last second changes to their fall schedule.

The commercial carpet on the floor is pristine. It must be new. The walls are lined with commercial art -- if you could even call it that -- of large flowers in ugly vases. The pale mint green paint does nothing to add any warmth to the room either.

The big brown door in front of me cracks open and the dean walks out. Dr. Grillo is a vertically-challenged man, close to fifty years old with a dusting of grey scattered through his remaining hair. He wears a brown suit with a pair of loafers that have seen better days.

"Miss Lamore," he calls my name and holds the door open. He doesn't smile at me the way he usually does and my stomach drops into my shoes.

I walk past him into the office. He closes the door and clears his throat as he makes his way to his desk. "Since there is no easy way to begin this conversation, I'm just going to jump right in." He sits behind an old wooden desk piled high with papers. He shifts his work to the side, folds his hands together, and looks at me sitting across from him. "Miss Lamore, someone has brought to our attention that you may be in an inappropriate relationship with your internship supervisor. Is this true?"

My voice catches in my throat, "No," I clear my throat and say it again, louder. "No, it's not true. Whoever told you that was misinformed."

The dean's shoulders don't slump with relief when I say it. "Anna, we know you're an adult and can make your own choices when it comes to dating, however, when coupled with academia—"

I cut him off. "Nothing happened." My hands are clutching the arms on the chair so hard that my knuckles are turning white. I don't let go. This has me so angry that I can't stand it. "Cole Stevens has been an excellent supervisor. My internship is going well, which is why I can't understand who would say this."

"You haven't been sleeping with him?" He asks me pointe blank.

I don't think he means it literally, so I shake my head, "No. We do not have a sexual relationship. This is ridiculous! Graduation is too close for me to start over. You have to believe me." I'm pleading with him. It hurt that Cole rejected me, but this makes it even worse.

"I'd like to, Anna, but the person who brought this matter to our attention has proof that you did stay at Mr. Steven's residence on multiple occasions."

My skin prickles as I realize what it means—someone has been following me. All those times I felt like someone was watching me, I thought I was insane, but now I'm angry.

"So, let me get this straight, Dr. Grillo. Someone provided you with proof that we were having sex. Is that what you're saying?" I'm at the edge of my seat, ready to bounce out of it. Fury is fuming silently inside of me, threatening to explode. This is so wrong.

"Please Anna, calm down. It's enough to have your internship pulled and have Mr. Stevens reprimanded. We cannot allow even the appearance of indiscretion when it comes to academics. You know this, Anna. Do you want people questioning your grades? Do you want them to say your class rank had nothing to do with your mind? They will -- especially with regards to you. You're at the top of your class. I'm sorry Anna, but we can't let this slide. You'll have to find another internship and start over in the fall."

"But that means I won't graduate until December."

"I'm sorry," he says. "There is nothing I can do about that. The internship is a requirement for graduation."

"If I get another internship and complete the requirements in the next three weeks, can I still walk in August?" I don't breathe. I didn't want it to come to this, but this is what it came to.

The dean leans back in his hair and looks at me like he feels sorry for me. "If you can complete the requirements, then yes."

I nod slowly. I don't know what to say. It hurts that my words don't matter, that the appearance of a relationship was enough to damn me. A question crosses my mind, "Have you spoken to Mr. Stevens yet?"

Dr. Grillo nods, "Yes. He knows the repercussions for such an accusation." I wait for him to explain, to tell me more, but he doesn't. Instead he stands and says, "Go to the registrar's office, get new forms, and if you manage to talk someone into an internship now, file the papers directly with me."

CHAPTER 5

Emma isn't home yet. I move around the tiny apartment, wandering like I'm lost. I don't know what to do. Jesse was right. My internship with Cole is void and I have to start over. Nerves choke me, but I have to do it—there are no other options.

Dialing her number, I wait for Sophia to pick up. "Sottero Studios," she says, even though she has caller ID and knows exactly who it is.

"Ms. Sottero, this is Anna Lamore. We met earlier this summer at an internship interview."

"Yes, Anna. How can I help you?" Although that's what she said, her voice sounds clipped, like she doesn't want to waste more time on me.

"I need an internship. I'm willing to work every waking moment for the rest of the month."

She sighs. "What happened? Did Cole fire you? I told you to avoid that man, but you didn't listen. Why should I take you now?"

That is a good question. "You shouldn't," I say. "I should have listened to you. I'm sorry to have bothered you. You've been more than kind. Thank you for your time—" I feel dejected and embarrassed.

She cuts me off, "Oh, don't be so melodramatic, Anna. It's not the end of the world, it's an internship. Come to my office tomorrow morning. Bring the papers. We'll get you started. How many hours do you need to log before the end of August?"

"Three hundred and twenty," I say cringing.

"Not a problem," she replies. "It's wedding season. We can knock that out in a couple of weeks if you're willing to work 18-hour days."

"I am."

"Good. Be here at 8:00am." After giving me final directions on attire and locations, she hangs up.

I hold my phone in my hand looking at it. Nausea washes over me. It feels like I stabbed Cole in the back. It's necessary I tell myself. Cole will understand.

The key scrapes the lock and Emma pushes through the door. "Oh, my god. Has hell frozen over?" She glances around the room and then back at me with a grin on her face. "Are you actually going to sleep in our apartment tonight?"

Emma should have been the only one who knew where I have been sleeping. Leaning on the counter I ask, "Did anyone ever talk to you about me? Ask where I was sleeping?"

She tosses her purse on the couch and sits down like her knees broke. "No. What's going on?"

I told her everything and she listened with her mouth hanging open. "No fucking way. What did Cole say?"

"I haven't spoken to him yet."

"He's going to be pissed."

"I think he already knows," I say. "His lawyer's been around a lot lately." I press my lips together to keep from saying more. "I need to go see him." I head toward the door.

CHAPTER 6

By the time I get to Cole's apartment, it's nearly midnight. I walk through the front door and call his name. When I don't get a response, I make my way through his house and find him sitting in the blue chair in his bedroom. A glass of amber liquid is in his left hand. His dark eyes look more black than blue. He sits in the shadows with the lights off.

"Cole," I say, and he looks up at me in the doorway. I linger there for a moment, afraid of what will happen when I tell him, but from the look on his face I suspect he already knows.

"Miss Lamore."

"Anna," I correct and walk to the bed and sit on the edge across from him. "I suppose you already know."

He stares at me blankly. Nerves slither over my skin and make me shiver. Finally he says, "The University told me that you'll no longer be working for me. Is that your decision?"

"I don't have a decision, Cole. I need an internship to graduate. If I don't do one, the last four years mean nothing." My voice is higher than usual. Panic spreads through me. He doesn't want me to leave, but I have to.

"You're the one who decides, Anna. Not them." He swirls the contents of the glass and stares at me like I stabbed him in the back.

"My decision would have been to be with you. My decision would have been to have you touch me. My decision would have made the accusations true." The words pour out of my mouth and don't stop as I rise and step toward him. "But my decision doesn't seem to matter." I stand before him with my hands on my hips. Cole stares up at me.

"I apologize for depriving you, Miss Lamore."

"Anna."

The way his eyes bore into me steals my breath. "But I make decisions and stick with them. I will not touch you."

"Fine. Then don't." Turning on my heel, I mean to leave, but he grabs my wrist.

My pulse skyrockets as he speaks. "I won't," he breathes inches from my lips. The way he says it sounds sexy, like that's all he thinks about. He steps forward and I back into the bed. "Sit," he says and I comply.

The intensity of his gaze and the way his body moves, like he wants to crawl across the bed and take me, makes me shiver. I don't speak. I can't. The entire thing seems surreal.

"Touch me," I breathe.

Any restraint Cole kept in check snaps. His lips gently brush against mine and I melt. My stomach flips inside of me and I want to tangle my fingers in his hair, but he pulls away. His hands are splayed on my face. He presses his forehead to mine and sucks in a ragged breath, before stepping away from me and back into his chair. I don't know why he left, what he's doing. He relaxes a little, and grips the sides of the chair.

My body aches for his touch. I'm wound so tight that it feels like I'm coming undone. "Cole, you can't leave me like this."

"I don't think you're up to the kind of things I like to do." Cole tosses back the rest of his drink and leaves the glass on the table next to him. "And I have no intention of pressuring you. You're too young for me, Miss Lamore. There's no way this will end well."

"Anna," I say breathlessly. My eyes lock with his. "And I don't care how old we are or aren't. I know you want me. I can feel it. I can see it in your eyes, in the way you look at me." His lips part like he's going to say something, but he doesn't. He watches me as I crawl back onto his bed and lift my shirt over my head. I wiggle out of my pants and sit half-dressed on his bed. He watches me, his eyes drinking in every inch of my body. I kneel there, letting him look before saying, "Show me what you like."

Cole remains still, slouching back in the chair like he doesn't care that there's a naked woman on his bed, but his eyes say something entirely different. They are dark, and threaten to devour me.

Cole blinks slowly, like he made a decision. His voice is even, unemotional. He breathes normally, like I don't affect him. "Lean back against the headboard, and part your legs." His tone is firm, commanding. It makes me feel afraid and excited. My eyes are locked on his face. I can't look away. Pushing myself up, I lean back against the headboard and part my legs. He can see between my legs from where he's sitting. My heart slams into my ribs as my stomach swirls with anticipation.

"Slip your bra off," he commands. I reach around and unhook the bra. Cole watches carefully, taking in the sway of my breasts. When my hands are over my head, I realize how much he likes to watch. I slow my movements before tossing the bra to the floor, letting him look. "Now the panties," he says.

I lift my bottom, and slide them down my thighs. I lift my legs, pulling them out of the leg holes one at a time. I pick up the bottoms and toss them to him. Cole catches them and presses the scrap of fabric to his face and breathes in. The action shocks me so much that I gasp. Cole glances up at me and smiles that predatory grin he has sometimes. It makes me shiver, but I'm not backing down. I want him and this is what he wants. I part my legs, spreading them wide. Cole's eyes are locked on the sensitive flesh between my legs. I press myself back against the headboard, arching my body as I do it.

His eyes drift to my breasts and then my face. His eyes lock with mine.

"Take one hand and spread your lips. Take the other and run a single finger over your clit, barely touching it." His voice slides over me. His words make my face turn bright red. Cole watches me, his arms folded, his gaze hot. My left hand parts my lips and my breath hitches. I lower my gaze when my right hand is on my clit, but he says, "Watch me, Anna. Don't look away."

I stroke my clit and look into his eyes, "Yes, Cole," I purr his name and blink slowly. My hand moves between my legs stroking the sensitive skin again and again, never taking my eyes off of him. My body flares to life, the lower parts of me tingle with anticipation, wanting more. My hips lift slightly, meeting my hand.

Cole sits across the room. He leans back in his chair, his hands on the arms. He breathes deeply, and leans forward watching me, not breaking eye contact. When my hips start to buck, he says, "Only move your hand, Anna." Cole's voice is hard, commanding.

I watch him as he says it and notice his gaze darken. He watches me move my hand across my body, stroking myself slowly. I try not to move and find it difficult. If he suggested doing this, I would have been mortified, but in the moment, it feels sexy and I don't want to stop. My fingers move against my slick flesh with Cole watching, his gaze taking in every slow blink, every hitched breath as I fight to keep my senses and not come.

Cole's gaze shifts between my eyes and the place between my legs. He watches as my muscles tense, and I try to remain still. I have trouble keeping my eyes open. I want to close them and lose myself in the steady heat that's building between my legs, but Cole changes things. The onslaught of sensations flooding through my body overwhelms me. I want to do anything he says, I want to hear his voice telling me what to do. It's hard to stay still, but Cole's eyes pin me, so that only my hand moves.

"Faster," he says. "Harder."

My hand develops a quick rhythm moving between my legs. Wet heat throbs inside of me, begging for release. Every inch of my body is corded tight. My stomach twists into knots as Cole watches me. The way he sits there makes me think he doesn't care, but his eyes say something else.

The damp heat spreads as my fingers stroke the skin between my legs. My mouth parts and I'm breathing hard. I fight my body as it wants to move, and buck my hips into my hand. I've never wanted to be touched so much in my life, but Cole doesn't move.

Instead he says, "Stop." My hand stills and I'm shaking. "Pinch your clit. Hard."

My fingers grip the nub and press together. Air rushes out of my throat in a high pitched moan. I can't think. I can't talk. I want Cole to fuck me until I can't walk. I want to feel him inside of me, pushing against me. The pressure on my clit is tormenting me and I realize that I've closed my eyes. When I reopen them, Cole is standing over me.

I'm trying so hard to stay still, but I can't. My muscles are twitching on their own, making my hips move the tiniest amount. Cole grabs me by my ankles. He yanks me until my feet hang off the end of the bed. Crossing my ankles, he forces me to flip over. I lay face-down on my stomach gasping, with Cole between my legs, standing at the foot of the bed. Before I can say anything, I feel a hand across my ass. He strikes me and it stings, sending jolts of electricity through my pussy. I yelp and look back at him.

Cole says, "A little mistake gets a little spanking. Two more, Lamore."

I relax and put my face down on the cool sheets. I purr and his hand lands on my bare skin again. I gasp and my knees threaten to give out. I want him. I can't stand him teasing me like this. By the time the final strike comes, my body is ready for it. My hips buck as his hand connects making him strike me harder.

Cole pulls me until my hips are hanging off the bed. "Spread your legs." I part my ankles and feel the cool air rush between my lower lips. Before I have a chance to breathe, I feel Cole's hand on my back, pushing me into the bed. His hand slides lower, down to the small of my back. I remain like that, with my ass in the air, hoping he'll fuck me.

Cole brushes his jeans against my ass, allowing me to feel his excitement. I want his hard length inside me. I bite my lip to keep from calling out. I can't see what he's doing, but I felt his hands on me, between my legs. He strokes me gently a few times, feeling me, learning every inch of me. He grips my clit hard and I start to lift off the bed, but his hand is still on my back and holding me down. "Don't move, Lamore."

As he speaks, I feel warm breath across my soft, damp skin. I shiver. He's going to kiss me between my legs. The heat of his tongue makes me gasp, but I stay still. He licks me from my ass to my clit, his broad tongue sweeping over every inch of me, caressing every soft fold. My hands clutch the bed to keep from screaming. I want more. I can't stay still. Then his tongue is inside me, thrusting deeper, tasting me. He shifts his hands until he holds my hips and pulls me down harder on his face. Rocking me slowly, he builds a rhythm that I can't ignore. His tongue licks and sucks me, tasting every inch of me, driving me wild until my body is coiled so tight I can't last another second.

"Cole!" I cry as I shatter, coming in his mouth. His lips don't pull away. His tongue licks my tender skin, tasting me until he is finished.

When he lifts his head, Cole steps back. My arms are weak, shaking—but I manage to roll myself over. My heart feels like it exploded. I try to speak, but only huffs of air come out. When I look at Cole, his gaze isn't readable. He lifts me onto the bed, gently laying me on the pillows next to him. I am completely naked, sucking in ragged gasps, trying to stop and gain some semblance of control. But Cole just watches me. He lays on his side, bare-chested, above his jeans. His gaze lights a trail over my abdomen as he trails his finger from my navel to my neck.

"Cole," I moan his name, not wanting him to stop.

"Anna," he whispers in my ear, making me shiver. When I finally come back to myself, I gaze up at him.

"That was the sexiest thing anyone has ever done to me."

He doesn't say anything. Cole just slips his gaze over my body taking in the slight sheen of sweat and sliding his finger over my curves. Finally, he says, "I shouldn't have done it."

Taking his hand, I push myself up on my elbow and look him in the eye, "Don't say that."

"Anna, it was a mistake. I have trouble refusing you. Please forgive me." He sits up and pulls his hand out of mine. Crossing the room, he places his hands on his dresser and doesn't look back at me.

My heart is pounding hard again, reacting not to excitement but the regret that floods his voice. "There's nothing to forgive."

"But there is. There is so much." He turns and when he looks at me fear crawls up my throat like an icy hand. "I think it's best for both of us if you complete your internship and seek employment elsewhere."

"What?" It feels like I a sucker-punch. I sit there, pulling up the sheet to cover me.

"It's for the best."

Anger flashes in my eyes, but Cole doesn't look away. Grabbing my clothes, I pull them back on hastily. "Fine." My voice is flat. "I'm done with this. I'm done with you."

CHAPTER 7

I cried my eyes out for the rest of the night and it shows. Sophia Sottero looks like perfection next to me with my puffy eyes and dark circles.

She gives me a once over in my black skirt and white blouse. It was the same outfit that Cole told me was too formal for work. "Anna dear, you look like hell frozen over. If you want to work eighteen-hour days, you can't stay up doing god-knows-what the night before. For the next three weeks, you're mine. No one else. Understand? Tell this boyfriend he'll have to wait, because I won't have this." She gestures to me like I'm disgusting.

Offense flows through me. I don't look that bad, but I also don't look perfect, which Sophia obviously demands. I nod, "Yes, ma'am."

She puts her hands on her hips and says, "Good. I'm glad we understand each other. Now, go grab me a cup of coffee—two creams, no sugar—and bring it to my desk. You'll do that every morning." I nod, realizing I've been demoted to gopher.

Thoughts of Cole flood my mind as I try to adjust to working with Sophia. She's anal OCD to the max. If I think about her too much she makes my eye twitch. Later that afternoon, another intern found me in the ladies room.

"You have been in here way too long," she says zipping around the room, washing her hands and drying them before running for the door.

"What are you talking about? It's barely been three minutes."

She glances back at me, her dark eyes wide. "I know. Hurry up or she'll bite your head off."

After washing my hands, I emerge from the rest room.

"Ms. Sottero wants you in the shooting room," says another intern. She glares at me like I'm irresponsible.

I head to the shooting room and kick off my heels as I walk through the door. Sophia looks over at me, her dark eyes darting to my feet and then back to my face. "Shoes are required at all times, Anna dear." She sighs and walks toward me. "It appears that I'll be unteaching what Cole has taught you. Assuming nothing, all right?"

I slip back into my shoes and nod. I don't like the way she speaks about Cole. I sense some unspoken resentment there, but I can't put my finger on what exactly. A bride and her entourage arrive a few minutes later. I become a coat rack. Then I help dress the bride, pulling corset strings and making sure she looks perfect. I fan her train. I bring her water. I do everything that Regina does. Sophia doesn't trust me with the lights or the camera. I groan internally. This is going to suck.

Sophia snaps her fingers in my face, "Wake up, Anna. Really." She scolds. "Fan her train again and give her back her flowers."

When I hand the bride her flowers, I notice she's fidgeting - which seems to irritate Sophia. "Is something wrong?" I ask.

"Yes, the top of my foot is itchy. I think it's from the petticoat. It keeps tickling me." She moves again trying to get the itch. When she can't she looks up at me, "Could you do it?"

That sums up the rest of my first day at Sottero's: scratching feet, fetching coffee, and being all around slave labor. Sophia is kind enough to remind me before I leave that this internship position is not paid.

CHAPTER 8

It is late by the time I walk through the front door. Emma is sitting on the couch with Jesse. Surprised, I stop in my tracks and look up at him. "Hey," I say.

Emma waves at me, "He came by about an hour ago. I told him to wait for you." She pops a chip into her mouth.

Jesse stands and walks toward me. "I hope that was okay." He says, uncertainty lining his face.

"Of course. It's fine."

"I saw the papers for the new internship come through the office. Actually, I was the one to enter them into your account. I assume things with the dean didn't go well."

"Hardly," I say, taking off my heels and rubbing my feet. The idea of shoving those on again tomorrow sounds horrifying. "They scrapped my hours with Cole and made me start over."

"I'm sorry Anna. I know how much you were dreading that."

I try to sound like it's a good thing, but don't quite manage it. "It's fine. I originally wanted this internship anyway. Life has a funny way of sorting things out. I just didn't belong with Cole, I guess."

Jesse looks up at me. We gaze at each other for a beat, before I look away. "Uh, let's go back here to talk, so Em can watch whatever's on TV."

"I can leave. Damn, just say it Anna." Em says getting up.

"Sit down, grump. Eat your chocolate. You're acting like the PMS Troll again." Jesse's eyes go wide as I toss Emma a Hershey bar.

She catches it and laughs. "Sorry. And thanks."

"No problem," I say, and indicate Jesse should follow me. As he walks into my room, I say, "Now don't get the wrong idea. The apartment is really small and for some reason you know more about me and Cole than Emma does."

Jesse nods and looks around for a place to sit. He chooses the chair in front of my desk. "I didn't think it was an invitation for a booty call." He grins. "I'm not that dense."

"And that's why I like you." I peel off my jacket as I talk and put my shoes in the closet. Jesse watches me. He dangles his arm over the back of the chair.

"So," he says, looking at me shyly. It's a very different gaze than the intense looks Cole gives me.

"So," I reply and smile weakly at him. The corners of my mouth fall and my worries can be seen plainly on my face.

"It'll be all right, Anna. You can do this. Think of the time with Sottero like trying to sit through Peters' class if it was a short course."

"That's about the only thing that would be worse." Professor Peters was so boring I never even noticed Jesse sitting in front of me. I had to drink two Red Bulls to keep my head from hitting the desk. Thinking about Sottero, I say, "She's nothing like I thought she'd be. Cole let me shoot...on my own. Sophia has me getting her coffee and scratching people's feet. Feet, Jesse."

He nods sympathetically. "So, I've heard." He pauses for a second, leans toward me. His gaze falls to the floor and then back up to my face. "You know, there have been some interesting remarks about her when all the internship papers are handed in."

"Such as?"

He smiles at me, and I get the feeling he's telling me stuff I'm not supposed to know. "Nothing you can't handle, not after putting up with Stevens. Sottero can be thoughtless and pushy. The interns didn't feel they really got a hands-on learning experience. It was more like going through the motions to get to the next phase of life. But on the bright side, Sottero's name is gold. You'll get a job when you're done without a problem."

Pulling off my thigh-highs from the toe, I wad them up and toss them on my bed before sitting down hard. "I had a job. It was a great job."

Jesse asks, "It sounds like you miss it."

"A little," I glance up at him.

Jesse glances at his watch. "I should get going. I just wanted to stop by and make sure you were okay."

I nod and stand. "Better. Today was definitely better than yesterday." Yesterday, when Cole jerked my emotions around like it didn't matter. Yesterday, when I finally gave up on him even though I didn't want to.

CHAPTER 9

Sophia snaps her fingers at me, "Anna, dear, we must hasten."

Hasten? Really? Sophia Sottero is like Mary Poppins on crack. She smiles widely and makes everyone love her, well, everyone who doesn't work for her. It seems like the interns scatter when Sophia is around. She's constantly snapping her fingers and smacking people with newspapers and magazines like they're wayward puppies. It's getting on my nerves, but I made it through a week. Jesse was right. I can do this. The shorter time span meant longer hours each day, but it meant less days as well.

I jog toward her and she frowns at me, snatching the prop out of my hand, "Do not run."

I smile and nod. I want to tell her that she's friggin' crazy and then quit, but I can't. I deal with her the best I can. If I was stuck here permanently, I'd bash my brains in.

My mind drifts back to Cole. That night on his bed still floods my dreams and I can't stop thinking about it—about him. Sophia is telling the bride how stunning she is and it sounds sincere, but she sneers when she turns to take the other camera in my hands. It's clear she thinks the girl looks like a train wreck, but when she turns back around Sophia is all fake compliments. I get tired of this. Day after day, it's the same thing.

I finally ask, after a shoot one afternoon, "When will I be allowed to assist with the lights? Or a shoot? Or tag along to a wedding?"

Sophia turns slowly and looks at me like I've said something funny. When I wait for an answer, she places her hand over her heart and says, "Oh my God, you're serious. You think you'll get to shoot. How sweet."

"Of course I thought I'd get to shoot. You told me over the phone that I'd be doing all of these awesome things, and I'm not doing any of them. I'm not learning anything." Sophia has me sorting extension cords and wrapping them with zip ties. A large orange cord dangles from my wrists as I speak.

"I told you about the things you would do if you were hired here. I wasn't referring to the internship, dear." When Sophia says "dear" she really means "idiot."

Remembering the conversation, I shake my head. "No, I specifically recall you telling me to intern with you—that Cole couldn't teach me the things you could. Then you went into detail about what those things were. Bundling extension cords wasn't on the list." I sound snitty, but I don't care. I feel like this was the biggest bait and switch I've ever fallen for.

Sophia steps toward me, her stiletto heel clicking on the tiled floor. "Cole, is it? Not Mr. Stevens?" She arches a brow at me. When I say nothing, she smiles as if she knows how hard I've fallen for him. "Do yourself a favor and get over him."

I hate the way she's talking to me. I smirk, "I've never been under him and I don't plan on it, so there's nothing to get over. He was just more casual in how he conducted his business."

Folding her slender arms across her chest she says, "I see. And tell me, Anna dear—did he keep you around? No. He fired you like all the rest. Every year it's the same thing; interns calling up, crying their eyes out that Cole Stevens fired them. Please hire me, Ms. Sottero." She tilts her head at me, "I would have thought you had more sense."

I never told her that the university was the reason I didn't finish with Cole. I can't reply without making it known, so I just look away.

"Thought so," she says, and saunters away, spewing verbal vomit at the next client.

CHAPTER 10

After two weeks of non-stop Sottero I want to rip my ears off and my nerves are shot to Hell. Jesse offers to meet me at the bar on the way home. Still wearing my work clothes, I see him standing outside waiting for me. He looks good, wearing dark washed blue jeans and a black blazer. When he turns his gaze in my direction, his eyes slip over my tight skirt and sheer blouse. My jacket is over my arm. I would have thrown the shoes away on the subway, but walking barefoot in the city was a surefire way to contract cooties.

"Thank God," I say, when I get close enough. My entire body wants to fold in half.

Jesse grins and takes my jacket. "That bad?"

"Worse," I say heading for the door. "Take the worst thing you can imagine and multiple it by a hundred. Then add the word idiot to the end and that sums it up. I plan on getting completely and totally drunk. I'm afraid you'll be responsible for me for the rest of the evening."

"Sure, but won't Sophia go crazy on you if you show up with a hangover?" He holds the door for me. I look into my purse, trying to fish out my ID in the dim light. There are a few people in line in front of us.

I shake my head, "Nope. Tomorrow is Sottero-free. I have the day off. My only day off, so I plan on getting every annoying thought of her out of my head so I don't accidentally claw her face off Tuesday morning."

Jesse laughs. "Your eye is twitching again."

I feel it flutter and press them closed, listening to Jesse chuckle. His arm wraps around my shoulders and pushes me forward. When I look up, I hand my ID to the guy at the door. He nods and let us pass.

The bar is dark and fairly crowded, but there are so many people in Manhattan that, at times, I go weeks without seeing a familiar face. I don't expect to see him sitting there at the bar, hunched over a drink. When Cole looks up, his gaze makes my heart convulse.

My feet don't move. Whatever Jesse was saying is lost.

Cole's gaze slides from me to Jesse, to Jesse's arm at the small of my back pressing me toward the bar, and Cole. I stiffen and feel Jesse's gaze on my face. He follows my stare across the room as he asks, "What's wrong?"

I don't answer. Instead I watch Cole get up and toss cash on the bar. He walks toward me and I'm caught in those sapphire eyes. There's nothing else there. There's no bar. There's no Jesse. There's no Sophia making my life hell. It's the way it was last time we were together. It's all tension and tingles. It's all sweaty thoughts and scandalous surges of lust.

Cole stops in front of us. "Miss Lamore," he says.

I don't correct him. I try to steady my voice even though my heart is beating wildly. "This is Jesse."

Cole turns his gaze to Jesse. "Mr. Oden."

Jesse finally figures out who this is, "Wow, Mr. Stevens." He sounds like a star struck teenager.

Cole glances at me once more and says, "So this is what you're doing now?"

Smirking I say, "This and Sottero. Bet you wish you could watch."

When I say Sophia's name, Cole's eyes snap to mine. I have no idea what possessed me to say it, except I don't like his innuendo and I can't let it alone. Saying I know how he likes to watch seems harmless enough, but I know he does. Remembering the way his eyes moved across my body the last time I was with him is enough to make me damp just thinking about it.

"You're mistaken, Miss Lamore." His tone is flat, like he couldn't care less. "Good night." Cole walks out the door without a backward glance.

My entire body is strung so tight it feels like my head will burst. Jesse takes my hand and pulls me to the bar. He waves down the bartender and orders us shots.

"So, that was Cole, the guy who's been giving you a mind-fuck since before we met?" Jesse asks and I nod.

The drinks are placed in front of us. I'm not a heavy drinker and I know that if I swallow that I'll fall out of my chair, but I'm not thinking. I take the tiny glass and throw back the contents. It burns my throat as I swallow and I open my mouth wide.

Jesse watches me and laughs, "What was that?"

"I don't drink a lot. I like to be in control of things, and being drunk is kind of the opposite." I glance at him. "I usually drink wine."

"How many glasses 'til you fall over?"

I shrug, "Three, maybe four."

He laughs, "Well, no more shots for you. Part of this therapy is venting and you can't do that if you pass out after one shot." He orders me wine. Grateful, I take the glass and sip it. "So rant. Pick one, because now I suspect Stevens is going to be part of what's driving you crazy. If he looked at you any harder, he'd need a condom."

Grimacing at him, "He doesn't like me like that."

"Um, are you blind? Did you not see that back there?" Jesse's brows shoot up his face and he points to the spot where Cole stood. "He wants you bad."

"Well, I told him I was doing you."

"Yeah, thanks for that one, by the way. He's probably waiting for me outside so he can chop my nuts off."

I spew my wine and try to use the tiny napkin to wipe it up. "He is not. He's not like that."

"Not like what? A guy? Anna, I may be wrong about other things, but not this." He switches to beer after doing the shot. "Hell, I don't even—"

Taking his jacket lapels in my hands, I pull Jesse toward my mouth. His lips land lightly on mine. Shock silences him and I feel his lips move against mine. When he pulls back he's grinning, "You always make guys stop talking that way?"

I smile softly and down the rest of my wine. "Wait until you see what I do later." I waggle my eyebrows at him.

Jesse is too sweet for his own good. He takes my hand. "About that, I don't mind being your plaything—I mean I'm actually really excited about it—but let's keep it to one thing at a time, okay? Check off your list in order. Number one: Get drunk. Number two: Get home. Number three: Kiss Jesse good night."

Smiling at him I say, "You don't want to be the rebound guy." The softness in his voice and the way he looks at me makes me think he wants more than that, when I'm ready to give it.

He shakes his head. "Definitely not. The more I'm around you the more I can see that you're worth waiting for."

CHAPTER 11

I no longer know what I'm saying. My heart spills over my lips as Jesse alternates between walking me home and carrying me home.

"I just want to be with someone who likes me the way I am. It seems like such a major thing." I stumble and Jesse holds my elbow, righting me. I glance at him and the streetlights continue to spin. "Whoa."

He smiles at me and helps me along, occasionally saying soothing words. It finally dawns on me that I shouldn't be saying this stuff to him and I grow quiet.

I stare at the sidewalk, at my feet as we walk. I'm barefoot. My thigh highs are in my right hand. I don't really consider where I step. Jesse steers me around things that might puncture my feet.

"Penny for your thoughts?" he finally asks as we walk up my front stairs.

Leaning on the door, I turn back to him. "Why'd I let him do it? Why did I let him get to me like this? I can't get him out of my head. He's always there. His voice is always there echoing inside my mind." I glance up at him and say what I'm thinking. "I'm an idiot. Sottero is right. She calls me Anna Idiot, you know, and she's right. Only a total idiot, I mean a prime, grade A, kind of idiot would fall in love with a guy twice her age who doesn't even like her. How am I supposed to deal with this? I don't even know what to do, Jesse. There was no relationship. No breakup. There should be nothing to get over, but I feel like I've had my guts ripped out."

As I speak, I slide down the door and sit on the front stoop. It's nearly 3:00am and New York is as sleepy as it's going to get. A couple walks hand in hand down the street, their faces close as they whisper to each other.

Jesse sits next to me and runs his hands through his hair. "Anna, you had a relationship. It's normal to feel something when it's over. It doesn't matter what he says, I see it when he looks at you. He wanted you. He wants you still. I have no idea what's holding him back, but I can't say

I'm not happy about it." I lean on his shoulder and he puts his arm around me.

I sigh. "You sure you don't want to be the rebound guy? All sex, no strings attached?"

He laughs, "You don't want a rebound guy. They have herpes."

This pulls a smile to my lips and I look up at him. He's grinning at me. "Just wait a little longer. Deal with one thing at a time. Wait out Sottero, then deal with the rest." I nod, accepting his plan, because I don't know what else to do.

CHAPTER 12

The knock on my bedroom door sounds like cannon fire. I groan for Emma to go away, but she comes in anyway. Crossing the room, she quickly flicks on a light. I bury my head under my pillow.

"Go away, Em."

"Can't babe," she says and sits on the edge of my bed. "You need to get up." The tone of her voice is wrong, even with the mind-splitting headache, I can hear it.

Glancing out from beneath the covers I ask, "What's wrong?"

She hands me a newspaper, but I don't understand. I sit up slowly and grab my head. The paper slips off my lap. Emma picks it up and gives it to me again. "Look, Anna."

I force my eyes to focus and see a picture of Cole. The headline says MULTIMILLIONAIRE COLE STEVENS IS RUINED. My heart lurches as I clutch the paper and gasp. Turning to Emma, I ask, "What is this?"

She has that look on her face that parents have when they have to tell their kid that their puppy died. My stomach churns and I feel sick. She takes my hand like I'll need her support. "I don't know. It says that Cole was in a lawsuit and settled. His properties were awarded to the other party as part of the settlement. Le Femme is gone."

"Oh, my God," I can't think. I can't breathe. Wildly, I try to read the article, but my eyes won't focus. "Who's the other party? Who'd he settle with?"

"Sophia Sottero."

The name smacks into me like a frying pan. "What? Sophia? How? What does it say? I can't fucking see!" Tears sting my eyes and even the headline blurs.

"It doesn't have all the details, but it sounds like they've been in a dispute for years and Cole finally settled to keep it out of court. His assets are going to be liquidated to pay off the settlement. It looks like a rape charge that was hushed. The article claims the nature of the attack was private and Sottero didn't comment to the paper this morning."

"That's why she gave me the day off." I rub the heel of my hand into my eyes. "I can't believe this."

Emma sits next to me and says nothing. Her hand is on my shoulder, then she just looks at me with sympathy. "Did he hurt you?" The question makes something inside of me snap.

"No!" I scream in her face. "He didn't fucking touch me!"

She holds her palms up, "Sorry, I didn't know how to ask and after reading this... forgive me, but I saw the way he looks at you. I just want to make sure you are okay."

There it is again, that same phrase—the way he looks at me. I shake my head and instantly regret it. "How does he look at me, Em? Like an intern? Like a student? Like he can't stand the sight of me?"

She tilts her head and snaps back, "No, Anna. Like he wants to tie you up and fuck you. Like he can't get enough by just looking at you. Like he won't stop if you ever give him the chance." She spits out the words like they're poison. Each one makes me feel more lost than I already am.

Near sobbing, I say, "He never looked at me like that."

Em smiles and shakes her head. "He looked at you like that every day."

Her words are too much. Tears spill down my cheeks and Emma's tone softens, "Hey, I didn't mean to dump this on you first thing, but it gets worse."

Wiping the tears from my eyes I ask, "How can it possibly be worse?"

She turns to the page with the full article on Cole's ruin and there is a smaller article across from it with information about the alleged sex scandal at the university. It ends with not naming the student involved. I glance up at Em.

"They figured it out?" I ask.

"Reporters have been camped on the front steps since 4:00am. You're lucky you missed them last night."

I bury my face in my hands. Shame floods me, flushing my entire body scarlet. This can't be happening. I stumble out of bed and go to the window with Emma warning me to stay out of sight. I peek through the blinds and cringe. It's true. There's a swarm of people toting cameras outside. I suck in a sharp gasp and release the blinds.

Looking at Emma, I say, "What do I do?" My voice shakes. I need to cry or yell or something but my hangover prevents me.

Emma says, "We shove through them and get the hell out of here. We'll hang out with your parent's for a while and give them time to go away. They shouldn't smear you for not wanting to talk to them about it."

"But it makes him look guilty if I don't." I tilt my head back against the wall. My entire body aches. Why did I choose last night to drink too much? This kind of crap always happens to me. Once I decide to do something selfish, like wallow around in my own misery for a night, it blindsides me the next day.

"I just wanted to get over him," I say to Emma with my eyes pressed closed.

"I know, Anna. I know."

CHAPTER 13

I get dressed and Emma says she'll help me out the door. I don't plan on speaking to them. I'm going to make a beeline for my bike and not come back until they're gone.

"Ready?" Emma asks as she reaches for the front door knob.

I smooth my jeans and tug on my leather jacket. I look too badass to be taken advantage of -- at least I hope I do. I have no idea how I'll react to their questions, so I put on the huge sunglasses Emma wore to a 70's beach bash last year. They cover half my face.

"These are guilty glasses," I tell her. They're the kind movie stars wear when they get tossed in jail for drinking and driving or something equally stupid.

"You don't look guilty. You actually look a little intimidating with that helmet under your arm. Listen, I'll follow you to your motorcycle to make sure you get out okay. Just keep walking. Don't stop." I nod sadly. "You can do this, Anna. I know what they'll do. This is my job, remember? I'd die to be able to interview you right now. Every single one of them is standing there hoping you'll crack and say something worth reporting. They're hoping you'll say it to them, that they'll be the reporter who gets the story."

"Wait," I say as she starts to open the door. Emma stops and turns toward me. "That's not a bad idea. What if you interviewed me? What if you had the story so that they followed you when I walk out the door? You can tell them that you'll answer a few questions and a full story will be in your paper."

Emma stares blankly at me for a moment. "I can't ask you to do that. So much has happened. I don't want to make it worse for you, and a story might do that."

I point at the people parked on the porch, "Too late for that, now. Let's just try to control the carnage. Besides, I can't hide out at my parents forever and Sophia expects me in tomorrow. It's my last week."

Her eyes bug out, "You're still going?"

"I have to. What choice do I have?"

She nods slowly and crosses the room. "So, Miss Lamore," she says in a different tone, one that tells me she means business, "come sit and tell me your story."

The plan works. When I step out onto the porch an array of flashes blind me. They expect Emma to walk with me, but she stays on the steps and does as I asked.

"I'll take a few questions on Miss Lamore's behalf. The entire story will run in Newsday tomorrow." The reporters polarize. Some continue to follow me, ignoring Emma, but eventually even they stop in their tracks and look back at her, unsure of who to follow.

I hustle to the parking garage and once I'm out of sight, I take a deep breath to steady myself. I can still see them even though I'm in shadows and out of sight. They look for me, but can't tell where I went.

Turning, I walk toward my bike and will my heart to slow. I swing my leg over and quickly pull on my helmet. That's when Edward appears again. He's walking to his car, which is parked right next to me.

He rushes toward me and wraps his arms around me before I have time to blink.

"Anna! Thank God you're all right. I'll kill him for touching you. I swear," he says holding my helmeted head in his hands, "I'll make sure he never touches you again."

I'm past the point of reasonable conversation. I'm angry and hurting. I hate that he's here now, seeing me like this. I hate that he assumes I let Cole use me like that. I swat his hands away. The expression on his face changes rapidly from concern to shock. His lips part like he's going to say something else stupid or condescending.

I speak before he has the chance, "Nothing happened between us. It was lies. I didn't cheat on you. I never did anything with Cole like they implied in that article, so don't stand there feeling sorry for me because nothing happened. It's part of whatever crap is going on with my current boss—an attempt to smear Cole more than she already has. She tossed me under the bus with him. Do you understand? I'm pissed, but other than that, I'm fine."

Edwards eyes are too cool for someone so mad only seconds ago. He nods calmly. "Many victims can't accept what happened to them. It's not your fault, Anna." He reaches for my hand.

I snap. I can't stand him. I don't want to be here with him. I smack his hand and rev the engine as I kick start the bike. "Stay away from me, Edward. If I see you again, even by accident, I swear to God that I'll punch you. So just stay away." My voice is full of anger as I speak. When I finish I don't wait for him to respond. Instead I gas the bike and peel out of the parking spot, zipping into traffic.

I drive too fast, bobbing and weaving when there's no need. I do everything possible to hold myself together until I step onto my parent's doorstep. Then the tears start and don't stop.

My mom takes me in her arms and for once doesn't ask about anything. She runs her hand over the back of my head, and pulls me inside.

CHAPTER 14

"Frankie, grab us some coffees. Anna looks like she could use one." Ma says.

Daddy grabs the coffee pot and makes me a cup the way I like it. Then he grabs some cookies from a white bakery box and puts them on the plate, too. He hands it to me and I know he's thinking of me when I was little and he knew what to do. Now he stands there awkwardly, not sure if he should chase down Cole and skin him, or wait and listen to what I have to say.

"Here baby," Dad says. His voice is gruff, like his rage is barely in check. After a moment, he says, "Tell me the truth. That guy, the one you brought here—was he forcing you to...?" Dad can't finish the sentence. His face turns red, his mouth crushing into an expression of fury as he says it.

I reach out for his hand and look him in the eye. "No. They lied. The paper lied, Dad. Whoever had that article run was gunning for

Cole. I just got caught in the splatter." At least I hope that's it. Admitting that Cole somehow wronged Sottero like that, with a settlement so large, is unthinkable. Cole is always so careful, not touching, always asking the assistant to do things at shoots. I never even saw him touch a woman at the studio, well, besides me.

I backtrack and tell my parents about the dean and the internship. I tell them how I was surprised that I liked working with Cole and how horrible it was with Sottero. When I'm done they know everything. I even told them that I had a crush on Cole, and that he said no.

Dad's shoulders relax as I speak, but the tension in his arms remains the same. He still wants to break something. There's no doubt that Dad would be happy to kill someone and bury them in the backyard if they hurt me. The nervous twitch of his hands, the way his fingers move like he wants to strangle something doesn't stop, even after he knows the truth.

Ma is silent, which is unusual. She watches me as I speak and I feel foolish telling her about the crush on Cole. I don't mention the stripping, the touching right before he told me good-bye. Sadness consumes me, but I don't want it to. Clearing my throat, I push away from the table.

Ma says, "Where are you going?"

"I have to find Cole. I have to know what's going on. Whether I like it or not, I got sucked into this mess, and tomorrow I'm supposed to walk into Sottero's and act like nothing happened?" My voice is getting louder, more terse as I speak. I can't help it.

"No, of course not, but I'm not sure if talking to Cole is a good thing now or not."

Grabbing my helmet, I say, "It's a good thing. I need this. It'll tell me what I need to know. It'll give me closure." I strap my helmet on as I speak, my fingers expertly moving the strap through the metal loops. I pause for a second, thinking of Edward and glance at my parents. "Has anyone been out here looking for me?"

Dad shakes his head, but Ma looks away. I tilt my extra-large, helmeted head and put my hands on my hips. "Just tell me, Ma. Who was it? And when?"

She blinks rapidly, looking at my face. "Just a young man. He said you knew him."

My heart flutters faster. "What's his name?"

She fumbles it for a moment and shakes her head as she tries to remember. "He didn't say, but he knew so much about you that I thought you were close. Is something wrong?"

I stare at her for a minute, too afraid to ask if it was Edward, if the man at the door matched his description. I can't fathom it. I can't picture him finding my parents and driving all the way out here to do...what? A chill races up my spine.

"Is someone following you?" Dad asks, voice stern. He looks at me, still tense.

I don't want to worry them more, but I feel sick. My stomach is churning like I drank sour milk. Flashing a false smile, I shake my head. "No, Dad. I'm fine." I give him a hug from behind, careful not to hit him with my helmet. "I'll be back after dinner. Call me if you need anything."

CHAPTER 15

Dialing Cole's number, I sit on my bike and wait but he doesn't answer. I think about where he'd be, where he'd go, and I know where he is. That place outside the Le Femme studio in the Hamptons. He went there last time he got bad news.

When I get there my skin is chilled. It starts misting like the sky is going to open up. There are no cars out front. No reporters. There's a sign on the door that the studio is closed. Ignoring it I reach for the handle, but it doesn't open. I place my helmet on the porch, under the awning, so it doesn't get wet.

Unzipping my leather jacket, I walk around back looking for the path that leads to the bench down by the water. The sound of the waves fills my ears. My stomach is climbing up into my throat. I don't know what to do or what to say when I see him.

I stop a few paces back. Cole is sitting on the bench. He is leaning forward, his head in his hands. His dark hair hangs over his fingers as he stares at the ground. Everything I feel for him comes rushing back. I can't stand to see him like this. Suddenly, I don't care that he pushed me away, that he told Jesse he could have me. I step toward him slowly, carefully. When I'm a few paces behind him, I call his name.

"Cole."

He doesn't move. Instead he closes his eyes tightly and clenches his hair hard. His fingers practically pull it out by the time he sits up and looks at me. "Lamore. What are you doing here?"

I want to go to him and wrap my arms around his shoulders, but I don't. I maintain my distance. The sky opens up and the mist turns to drizzle. Beads of water cling to my bare arms and run down to my wrists. My hair finally stops frizzing under the weight of the water and drips onto my tank top. My jeans stick to my skin, making me shiver. But none of that matters. The look in Cole's eyes makes me forget everything else.

"I saw the paper. What happened with you and Sottero?" Cole watches me, his eyes giving nothing away. I step closer. "I have to know. They ran an article next to it. One about me."

Cole exhales loudly and stands. "So that's what you want? A piece of me? Well, get in line. Sottero will wipe me clean. You can take whatever you can scavenge before that." Cole turns his back to me and walks toward the water. The ocean is churning like a storm is coming. The waves crash into the shore.

"What are you talking about? I'm not here for a damn thing. Damn it, Cole! Wait!" I run up behind him and grab his elbow.

He spins around. Leaning down in front of my face, he says, "Yes, you are. Is that why you did it? Is that why you couldn't keep your pants on? Now you have something to go with your claim at the University? I would have given you anything you asked for, but doing it like this was—" he shakes his head and doesn't finish. His fingers pinch his eyes and I can tell his voice is caught in his throat. "Just leave. Tell Sottero you got what she needed. Game over."

"I swear to God, i have no idea what you're talking about." Tears stream down my face and mix with rain drops. "I went crawling back to Sottero after the school told me I couldn't intern with you. I didn't tell her anything." He doesn't turn back to look at me. "I didn't do anything!"

He turns quickly, his eyes burning like blue flames. In a low tense voice he warns, "Don't lie to me." He practically growls the words at me. My heart pounds harder in my chest. I don't step away even though I want to run. "Someone gave Sottero exactly what she needed to hang me. You're the only explanation."

Swallowing hard, I look him in the eye, "I never said anything to anyone about you. I sure as hell didn't tell Sophia Sottero!" I'm shouting in his face. He doesn't flinch. He doesn't back away. "She's a two-faced bitch. I can't stand her. That's the truth." Cole shakes his head ever so slightly, like he still thinks I'm lying. I lean closer so we're nose to nose. "I have never lied to you. Go ahead and think whatever you fucking want, but you're deluding yourself."

"You had nothing to do with Sophia? Nothing to do with the paper? Come on, Anna. How foolish do you think I am? Your roommate is a reporter. You've been planning this with Sottero from day one. You think I didn't notice the guy you sent snooping around? You think I didn't see him watching me? Watching you? Looking for whatever she needed to seal her case."

"What the hell are you talking about? I didn't send anyone to follow you!"

He continues like I didn't speak, "I didn't touch her. I never hurt her. Do you know why she did this? Do you know?" I flinch when he yells in my face. "Because she thought I lied to her when we were younger. That Tiffany's ring in the safe was hers. The night I gave it to her, she fucking ran it over with her car. Want to know why, Lamore? Want to know why your boss ripped my heart out and ran it over? Because of my name. My fucking name. She thought I still had my inheritance and I was stupid enough to think she loved me." My jaw drops as horror bubbles up into my throat. The ring box, the one that I saw, was Sophia's. She used him. She rejected him after his family disowned him. My God. The devastation from that betrayal is strewn across his face. It was too thick to hide.

"You think I helped her?" I can't breathe. Something changes as he speaks. I finally understand what he's been through, why I couldn't get close to him. Sophia broke him. His family shattered him and Sophia destroyed whatever hopes remained. Cole's been alone all this time, too afraid to get close to anyone.

"Stop acting now, Anna. I applaud your efforts. You were very convincing. I admit it, I fell for it. I fell hard for you." His eyes narrow as his voice changes. Instead of anger, it's laced with apathy. "So tell me, how much did she pay you to get close to me and stab me in the back? One mil? Two?"

I stare at him. Tears overflow from my eyes and continue to fall in a silent stream. He thinks I betrayed him. He thinks everything that's happening to him is because of me. I can't think of anything to say, any plea that would make him hear me. His eyes burn into me as they slide over my skin with scorn.

I don't answer him. I can't.

"I thought so," he says. It feels like he hit me with a bat.

His words knock my breath from my lungs, but I don't look back. The fact that he can even think that makes me sick. There's no reconciliation. Not this time. Not for us. Sophia Sottero decimated any chance we had. She fucked with his mind twenty years ago and she stole his life's work today.

I find myself walking back toward my bike, wondering how this happened. Sophia Sottero was everything I wanted to be. I said as much to Cole. Damn, he must have cringed when I said it. He knew what she was, what she was capable of, and I was sputtering like an idiot… talking about my idol like she was flawless, like she was a god. No wonder he thought I helped her. I couldn't blame him. If I were in his shoes, I wouldn't trust anyone either. I couldn't. And after this, I didn't know if I ever could. I'd been lied to and used, manipulated into being the straw that cracked the back of the famous Cole Stevens.

Turning back, I stare at a destroyed man staring at the sea. The wind whips his dark hair, his wet clothing clings to his body, but he doesn't care. I watch Cole—I see the man I love becoming a hollow shell of what he once was and I vow that I'll destroy Sophia Sottero for everything she's done to him. To us. Cole has never seen forgiveness, so neither will she.

SECRETS

Vol. 4

CHAPTER 1

Anger is coursing through me in waves. I can't control it. I feel betrayed and utterly decimated. The knot growing in my stomach forces its way up my throat and strangles me. My shirt is soaking wet, clinging to my body like a second skin. Drenched hair is plastered to both sides of my face. As I walk back to my bike, I grab the pony ring from my pocket and then wring my hair out while I walk. Water spatters on the pavement. The rain is slow and steady, barely more than mist. The sky is gray and the sea churns behind me with Cole standing, watching the waves crash into the shore.

Riding in the rain is stupid. I'm hyperaware of that, however, I have to get away from him. The words Cole said were like lashes to my soul. The way he looked at me, like I betrayed him for money, makes me sick. Quickly, I walk in long strides, slamming my boots onto the pavement, toward the front door. I grab my leather jacket from under the awning and pull it on. Cole doesn't turn. I know he won't move until he hears the motorcycle roar to life and fade into the distance.

I secure my helmet and swing my leg over my bike. I look back at Cole one last time, knowing I'll never see him again. He's too angry, too hurt to see through Sophia's web of lies. There are too many secrets between us and now there's no way to fix them. It feels like a hand reaches inside my chest, grabs onto my heart, and squeezes. It crushes me, making my chest feel like it's going to cave in. I can't stand it. I can't breathe.

Shaking my head, I ignore the water pouring down my face and start the bike. Grabbing hold of the handlebars, I flip up the kickstand with my foot, and slam the bike into gear. My life sucks. It doesn't seem to matter what I do, it's always wrong—with Sophia, with Cole, with Edward—oh, God! It never ends. Every mistake strips away a confident piece of me and replaces it with a version of Anna that is jaded and hard. She's not me. That's not who I want to be, but I can feel her calling to me through tainted scorn. I want to crush Sottero. I want to obliterate her for what she did. I blink the rain water from my eyes and lower my head. I don't want to be that person, but I no longer know what I want from life at all. Nothing is the way I thought it would be. My ideals are gone.

Pressing my lips together, I feel the lump in my throat tighten, as I turn away from Cole. I start down the driveway and turn onto the street. I don't get far. The engine revs harder than I intended and the back wheel starts to slide. I'm not going very fast, not yet, but the street is slick and the motorcycle is heavy. I try to correct and lean into the skid, but it's too late. Gravity has me in its grip and isn't going to let go. A scream rips out of my throat and blasts every other sound to oblivion. The bike comes down on top of me. My helmet strikes the pavement hard, but I don't stop. My bottom leg is caught under the bike, and my jeans are getting torn apart as I skid to a stop. I push on the bike, trying to get up, but I can't make it move. It's too heavy and I'm too small. There's no leverage.

Before I know it, the motorcycle is lifted off of my and Cole is yelling. I can't focus on him. I look at the street, at my leg. My fingers lift and touch my head. I blink. The helmet is still strapped in place. Cole's voice echoes inside my mind, like his words are a memory and not being shouted in my face. I shake my head and it clears. Panic makes my heart pound harder.

Cole is trying to lift me, but I won't let him.

Suddenly, I'm yelling back, "I don't need your help!"

Cole is irate. He's shaking. The muscles in his arms are bulging, ready to hit something. "Anna," he growls. "I can't believe you're doing this to me. You can't—" his jaw hangs open and he freezes, as I pull the bike up and get back on. "What the hell are you doing? You can't be serious." His tone changes, it shifts from angry to sensible.

I restart the bike and stare at him. "I'm not staying here. Maybe you didn't realize it before, but Sottero threw me under the bus, too. Some jackass has been stalking me, and you don't believe a damn thing I'm saying. You're not the only one who's hurting. I don't have to stay here and explain myself to you, and even if I did—from that look on your face—I don't think you'd believe me, anyway."

My leg throbs like it's on fire. I look down and see an angry red gash showing through torn jeans. Fuck. It looks bad. I start to move, pressing my boots to the ground to get the bike going again. I won't turn so sharp a second time. The street is slicker than it looks.

I have to get out of here. I can't do this. I feel my heart crumbling, turning to ash. Oh God, the way he's looking at me like I stabbed him in the back. I can't stand it. I intend to ride away without another word when Cole steps in front of the bike and puts his hands on the handlebars. "Don't be stupid Anna. It's raining! You already fell once."

"I'm nothing, but stupid, Mr. Stevens." My eyes blaze as I glare at him. The tension in my jaw is so tight that it feels like the bone will snap. I can barely part my lips to speak. "Believe what you want, believe that I did it—that I pretended to fall in love with you—and that I'd do it again. You know how much I love money, how much I want to ride the coattails of others to achieve my success. That sounds just like me, doesn't it, Mr. Stevens?

"Every inch of me was covered in lies. You don't know me at all. Everything from my whacked out parents, to my fall two seconds ago, was constructed to make you fall for me. I'm a liar and a snake." I stand on my tip toes and lean closer to his face as I speak. "I don't love you. I never have. Now, let go of my bike before I run you over."

Cole stands there shell-shocked. Since I arrived, nothing I said to him even came close to registering in his brain, but that did. What I just said makes him stare at me like he's no longer certain of anything. I twist the handlebars hard, and yank them out of his grip. Before Cole can speak, I throw the bike into gear and pull away. I feel his eyes on my back until the road twists and I'm out of sight.

CHAPTER 2

Ma pulls the door open and her delighted smile quickly fades into horror. "Oh my God! Anna, what have you done?" Ma is frantic when she sees me. I look like a drown rat that's been smacked with a sword. The gash on my leg is bright red and looks horrible.

"It's nothing, Ma." I sit down hard at the kitchen table after walking up the stairs. There's a trail of muddy puddles in my wake. I look back and say, "I'm sorry. I can clean that up." I start to push myself up, but Ma slams me back down into the chair.

"Sit," she snaps. "Frankie! Get in here! Your daughter has a hole in her leg!" Ma yells with that forceful voice of hers. She's wearing a pair of grey sweats, and white slippers. "What'd you do? I told you not to go looking for him."

Daddy walks in and looks at the floor, then up at Ma, and finally his gaze lands on me. I'm soaking wet and the hole in my jeans is damning. I did something stupid and can't hide it. "What the hell happened?" He's angry now. Daddy hates it when I get hurt and when I tell him it was from the bike, he'll want to bash the bike in with a hammer.

"It's not as bad as it looks. My jeans ripped and it's raining. There isn't that much blood." I put up my hands, trying to get them to calm down. "I know that it looks really bad, but it's just a scrape. I promise."

"I told you, Anna! That damn thing is a death trap." Daddy is more livid than I've seen him in years. That's all he manages to say before biting his lip so hard that his jaw trembles.

Ma is gnashing her teeth at me from behind Wet 'n Wild pink lipstick. Her hands are on her hips, like she means to beat me with a spoon, but she doesn't. An instant later she deflates and grabs the scissors. "Let's have a look." She cuts away the leg of my jeans and grabs a first-aid kit. She's shaking her head and muttering things as she cleans out the abrasion. I let her, gritting my teeth as she pours peroxide on the cut. When it's patted dry, it doesn't look that bad. The cut is long and thin, nowhere near as bad as it looked when I walked in the door. "Go take a shower and we'll bandage that up. You were lucky this time, Anna. Most people aren't."

After steaming myself in the shower, I emerge in a pair of dry clothes. The rain has stopped and night has fallen. I sit at the table, not saying much, pushing my food around on my plate. I can't eat. I feel lost, like I'm sinking in quicksand, but I have no desire to break free. I push a meatball with my fork. It makes a red smear across my plate.

Ma has been watching me. Finally, she asks, "So, did you find him?" I nod. "What happened?" Worry shines in her eyes. I don't want to tell her, but I feel like I should.

"He didn't believe me," I say softly. "He thought I was after his money, like Sottero." My voice is barely audible. I push the meatball back into a pile of untouched spaghetti. Ma used to make this meal when I was little and had a bad day. They had seen the train wreck coming and warned me to leave Cole alone, but I didn't listen.

Ma understands. "I remember what that felt like, finding out that someone was only there because I was rich. I found out who my real friends were when Mother disowned me. There weren't many. It's a hard lesson to learn. Cole's never had everything taken from him before. I remember how much I wanted to—"

Normally, I wouldn't tell someone else's secrets, but I cut her off, "He's had this happen before. Cole's situation was similar to yours. His Dad tossed him and didn't give Cole a dime." I find myself telling Cole's story, about Cole as a young solider, the battered Tiffany's box, the rejection and heartache I found in Cole Stevens. When I finish, no one speaks.

I put down my silverware and push away from the table. As I stand, I say, "Now it looks like I'm just like the rest of them and only after his money."

I walk outside and sit at the table where Cole and I spoke not so long ago. I stare at his empty seat, trying to push past the waves of nausea that pound into me. After a few minutes, Daddy walks down the steps and takes the seat next to me. We sit together in silence, both of us staring at Ma's gardens that are overflowing with sweet summer blooms. The rain makes everything have a thick, fresh scent.

Daddy finally sighs and leans on the table. His forearms are thick and covered with gray hair. I used to think those arms could protect me from anything. "You remember what this garden looked like when you were little?" I nod. It was barren, mostly dead grass, sand, and rocks. The previous owner did nothing to cultivate the patch of land. "There was nothing here. It was ugly, Anna. But when your Ma saw this house, she knew it was home. There are people like that, ones who see the good in something even when there's nothing to see.

"You're like her, in that way—always seeing the best in people—even if there's nothing to see but a clump of dust there from what had once been. I never had that. I couldn't look at something that was all busted up and see what it could be. But you, you're like her with that. You could see what that man was before he ever told you, didn't you?"

I stare at Daddy, wondering what he's trying to tell me. I nod again, slowly. "What are you getting at, Dad?"

He looks at the garden again. His thick fingers tangle together and he cracks his knuckles. When he looks back at me, he says, "But that's only half the ticket. You got part of me in there, too." He pauses, trying to think of what to say next. "Me and you do without. We always have, always will—money's nothing but paper to us. Yeah, we need it to pay bills and feed the family, but it's not the stuff of life. Me and you, we love with our whole hearts, and it's dangerous. It can change you, Anna. It sure changed me." He glances up at the window. Ma is standing there, drying a pot. The silver gleams in the light as she twists the cylinder in her hands. "There's a time to accept defeat and admit that you lost, and there's a time to fight for what you want. No man won a woman's heart by running away."

"Cole's not going to chase after me, Daddy." I stare at my hands as I say it, knowing it's true. The look in Cole's eyes said it all. Every wall I managed to knock down was erect and stronger than ever. Cole shut me out.

"I'm not talking about him, sweets. I'm talking about you."

Blinking, I look up at him. My brow pinches together. "What about me?"

"Life isn't filled with do-overs. How many shots you think you're gonna get at love? Most people are lucky if it comes their way once. Are you seriously telling me that you're going to let him walk away?"

I smile at Daddy, like he doesn't understand. "I don't have a choice. I went to Cole. I told him the truth, and it didn't matter. Lies are easier to believe."

Daddy smiles back like he knows better. "That's true, but you know what? Anything that's worth having is worth fighting for. Love is a strange thing. It shows up when you least expect it and defies expectation.

"Ya know, I actually dumped your Ma? I told her that she'd be happier marrying some rich guy, that he could take care of her in a way that I'd never be able to. I said I didn't want to see her anymore. Your Granny even sent me a thank you card with a bunch of cash inside to stay away." He smirks. "I sent the card back, wrote REFUSED on it in a big red marker. I didn't walk away for money. I walked away because I thought your Ma would be happy. Two days later, your Ma shows up, suitcase in hand, and that letter. I saw the red marker, and knew what she was holding.

"Money's like poison, Anna. Too much of it kills anything that's worth having. Too much dough makes you paranoid, always wondering who—if anybody—loves you, and who's just trying to get a piece of you. Truth be told, no one loved your Ma, not even Granny.

"The ones we love are worth fighting for. Me and you are fighters, Anna. We don't let things slip between our fingers, unless we want them to." He stands and looks down at me, arching a dark brow. It seems like a challenge, like he's saying I'm made of thicker stuff—that I shouldn't slink away if I want Cole—but I have no idea how to fix something that's so broken.

CHAPTER 3

Before sunrise, I'm back on the parkway, headed toward my apartment. I need to stop there, ditch the bike, and put on clothes for Sottero's. My internship only has a few days remaining. My heart pounds harder as the clock ticks closer to eight. I hate her. I don't want to see Sottero, but I feel like there's something I should do.

I walk into my room with a towel wrapped around my body and another one in my hair. As I walk to the closet I feel a line of goose bumps break out across my back. Shivering, I clutch the towel and turn around expecting to see someone behind me, but the room is empty. I glance at the window, and see people moving below. I blink a few times, wondering if someone had been watching me. If so, they're gone now. Just in case I have a peeping tom, I dress quickly, making sure the closet door blocks my naked body.

As I walk toward the front door, I see Em in the kitchen. She says, "Are you seriously going in?"

I nod, "What am I supposed to do?"

"Kick her in the balls, because she must have huge *cojones* to use you like that." Emma's eyes narrow as she shakes her head, like she's disappointed. "What are you going to do?"

"I honestly don't know. Part of me wants to confront her, but that won't change anything. And I need to graduate."

"Do you?" Em plants a seed in my mind and it takes root immediately, twisting and turning, asking questions that I don't want the answers to. She continues, "I mean, do you really need a graduate degree to run a photography studio?"

Why did I choose this path? Why did I get two degrees to do a skilled job? Why did I have plans to get a doctorate? Because that was pretty much what Sottero did, because I had idolized her and was following in her footsteps. My head turns slowly, as my eyes widen. I didn't realize it, but I based my entire future on this horrible woman.

"Oh, shit." Em mutters, "I broke your brain." She rushes out of the kitchen, dressed in a nice suit—which is weird—and wraps her arms around me. "Ignore me. I'm being stupid. I didn't mean to imply anything. Finish what you started." She smiles at me, holding my shoulders, knowing that nothing is getting through because of that dazed look on my face. "That's what you always say, 'finish what you start.' It's classic Anna. Do that."

My eyes come into focus and I look at Em's blue eyes, and a smile spills across my face. Nodding slowly, I say, "That's exactly what I'm going to do. I'll finish what I started."

Emma is calling after me as I bound down the front steps. I changed out my heels for my sparkle yellow Chucks and take off for Sottero's. I know exactly what I'm going to do.

———

My thigh highs pull at the scab on my leg as I walk in determined strides toward Sottero's shooting room. She's in there getting ready for a bride that should arrive any second. I grab her cup of coffee along the way. The light brown liquid swishes as I walk, and gets close to the brim, but it doesn't spill.

Determination floods me. I'm not letting this woman ruin my life. I'll take the rubble and rebuild from the ashes. I'll be better for it. The only way I can fail is if I don't get up again, and I have no plans of staying down. Screw that.

Sophia turns when I enter the room. Her slender arms fold across her chest and her head cocks to the side. Her gaze falls on my shoes. "I am not amused, Anna dear." Anna, idiot. "Remove those before the client arrives."

I smile at her and continue to walk towards her, like I'm going to hand her the coffee. When I stop I say, "I had an interesting day off. How about you?" Sophia remains rigid, with her arms folded. When she doesn't speak, I sip her coffee and say, "Did you know that Cole Stevens raped me? That was totally news to me, because I don't remember having sex with him or anyone else recently."

Sophia's lips part, but she hides her shock quickly, "I saw the story in the paper. Accusations can be damning, my dear, but they aren't enough to win lawsuits."

"So, why'd you tattle to the dean? Did it bother you that I was sleeping in Cole's bed?" Sophia's grip on her arm tightens. It's the only movement she makes. The motion makes her ring catch the light and for the first time, I really look at the ring. My jaw drops. Sophia's gaze drifts to the ring and slowly meets me gaze. "The woman in the paintings was you!"

That makes her move. Sophia grabs my arms and hauls me to the back of the room. We stand in front of a bank of windows by the supply closet. "You listen here, you little bitch. You have no idea who you're playing with."

I rip my arm out of her grasp. Everything clicks together in my mind. Sophia and Cole were a couple. She was his muse, his inspiration, until something went wrong. Staring at her, I know exactly what made her hate Cole, what caused her to throw the Tiffany's ring back in his face. "Likewise, Ms. Sottero. I'm not the moron you think I am. I know he proposed to you, and that you declined when he told you that he was broke. You're a money-grubbing bastard, and when you found out Cole was disowned, you turned on him like the heinous bitch you are.

"But that wasn't good enough, was it? Breaking his heart and telling him you thought he was worthless didn't make you feel better? It didn't make up for all that time you invested with him, so you concocted this rape story. Exactly when was that supposed to take place? Before or after he proposed to you?"

Sophia's eyes widen as I speak. Her ruby red lips part and I swear to God, she has a forked tongue when she replies. It slithers out of her mouth like Satan is talking. "You conniving little whore! How dare you walk in here and—"

I raise my hand and hold it in front of her mouth like a stop sign. I'm right. I know I'm right, but what I have no clue about is why Cole didn't fight the charge. Sophia's story is full of holes. "I'm done working here, and I'm done wanting to be like you." I laugh hollowly, "You know, I actually wanted to be like you? I idolized you and the way you did business. I actually believed all the shit I heard about you, about how you make each bride feel beautiful. The part everyone left out was how you talk trash when the bride's back is turned and make faces—you frickin' made faces at them, like a nine-year-old—as if they were beyond rank. Well, you're the one who's rank and if I never see you again, it'll be too soon.

"Have a nice life, Sophia. I quit." I smirk and turn on my heel.

A crowd of people have been standing behind me, including the bride who was about to have her photo shoot. Two older women stand with the young bride, flanking her. Their eyes shoot daggers at Sophia, hating everything they heard. The employees stand there slack-jawed, their eyes trained on Sophia, who doesn't move. She stands there, shell-shocked.

I'm about to walk out when I see the cup of cold coffee in my hands. I turn back to Sophia and say, "Oh, don't forget your coffee." I thrust the mug at her chest. Her hands fly up to grab the cup, but I push too hard. The contents slosh out and leak down the front of her blouse. I press my fingers to my lips before I say, "I'm so sorry that happened, dear."

I walk away with a smile on my face. Sophia doesn't talk, but I feel her eyes burning a hole into my back. I push through the front doors of the building and into the early morning air. I spin around once, laughing like a lunatic, with my arms extended. I can't help it. It was perfect. The look on her face alone was beyond awesome. I've never felt so good in my life.

However, life caught up to me when a short balding guy asks, "Anna Lamore?"

I stop spinning and look at him, nodding. "Yes?" I have no idea who he is or what he wants. The guy doesn't even look vaguely familiar. He's short, balding, with dark skin and a big fat envelope in his hands.

He looks at me sternly, and slaps the envelope into my hand. "You've been served." The man turns away as I look down at the package.

I don't know what this is, "Hey!" I shout, running after him. "What the hell is this?"

He won't look at me. He continues to walk briskly, like his main reason for doing so is to put space between us. "Read it, kid. Just show up on the date and time it says."

I stop and look at the envelope again. I break the seal and unfold the contents, watching the short man walk away as fast as he can out of the corner of my eye. People bump into me, but I'm in mental a bubble. The letters on the top of the page mean nothing. I'm staring at the court case SOTTERO vs. STEVENS. I've been summoned to appear before a committee concerning the lawsuit. Great.

It never fails. When something finally goes right, something else goes wrong.

CHAPTER 4

When I get home, the apartment is empty. Emma is at her internship/ new job at Newsday. I wonder if I'm a moron while I stand in the shower, getting pelted with insanely hot water. My mind doesn't want to think about what I just did, quitting an internship days before it's over. No, my mind wants to wander back to Cole. The crushing sensation still weighs heavily on my chest. Whenever there's a space between thoughts, Cole's face appears, his blue eyes blazing with his barbed words, *I thought so.*

Life keeps throwing things at me that I don't expect. I didn't expect to enjoy working at Le Femme. I didn't expect to fall in love with Cole Stevens. And I certainly didn't expect Sottero to be a ravenous bitch. Out of everything that's happened, I'm not sure what I could have done differently, what I could have done to prevent it. When I questioned Sottero, when I said I was sleeping in Cole's bed, she obviously had no clue. That meant she didn't snitch to the dean or contact the papers about that little story. Someone else did. I scour my arm with a loofa as I think, covering my skin in white bubbles until I'm beat red.

Who else knew that? Who else knew I was sleeping at Cole's? Emma was the only person who knew I wasn't at home. I can't think of anyone else who knew that information and would want to use it against me. Jesse knew about my feelings for Cole, but he helped me with the dean. If Jesse wanted to get me in his bed, he could have said yes when I asked him to my rebound guy. He said no. I scrub my other arm and then wash my hair. The wound on my leg is finally healing. The hot water makes it itch. I turn off the shower and dry off, wrapping my towel around me as I head out of the steamy little bathroom.

As I pad barefoot to my bedroom, I feel uneasy again. My stomach curdles and the hairs on my neck raise. I clutch the towel and shift my eyes through the room. I'm the only one here. The sensation of being watched floods me. Heart racing, I wonder if I'm overreacting or if someone is really there, looking in the window. Silently, I walk to the windowpane and stand off to the side, looking out. The street is busy like always, but no one stands at a lamppost staring at my window. I drop the mini blinds, and touch the back of my head to the wall and sigh.

I'm paranoid. When did this happen? It never spooked me to be alone before, and now I am acting like the stupid chick in a horror movie, jumping every time I walk out of the shower. Annoyed with myself for being so twitchy, I dress quickly, but I can't shake the feeling. The goose bumps won't go down and I still feel eyes on me. I pull on jeans and a tank, grab my helmet, and dart out the door. It's too damn hot for the leather jacket today. On my way out the front door, I smack into Edward.

He takes my shoulders and steadies me, "Whoa, there. Sorry, I didn't see you coming through the door."

"She's not here," I say, ignoring Edward's apology and shaking him off. I ran into him. I realize I'm acting like a bitch and turn back, practically hopping on one foot, as I fasten my helmet under my chin. "She's at work until 5:00pm. Em started that new job today."

He looks at me from under those dark eyebrows, a grin forming on his face when I smile at him. "Why are you home?" he asks, confused.

A smirk lines my lips. "I quit." That was the first time I said it, the first time that I admitted what I had done. Damn, it felt good. I couldn't stop smiling. I'm going to make my own future, become my own woman. I hid in college long enough. Those who couldn't do, teach, and those who are too chicken to try, hide out in the classroom until they need walkers. Screw that. I'm ready to try it on my own and I know exactly what I want to do. I busted my ass to get this far. I'm not wasting another day.

Edward's jaw drops open in shock. "What?" he squeaks, but I only smile broader in response.

As I skip across the street, I wave good-bye and run toward my bike without explanation. I can't wait to tell my parents what I did. There's no way in hell they'll understand, but all the same, my heart is pounding against my ribs because I know what I want and I'm finally content with that decision.

"You did what?" Ma snaps, cookie half way to her mouth. It dangles there in midair between her forefinger and thumb. Her pinky is extended—a remnant of an old life.

"I quit. Sottero held my future in her hands and there's no way in hell I was staying there, not after what she did to Cole. And, then I was thinking about why I went to grad school in the first place. You know what the answer is Ma?"

"Cause you wanted to be successful. Because you wanted to be the best in your field!" She tells me, her voice growing louder—if that's possible—as she speaks.

"No, Ma. I went because I was following in Sottero's footprints. I wanted to be like her and now I don't. She's a fraud and one of the worst people I've ever met. I don't want that life anymore, Ma. I don't want to be a wedding photographer." My words drop like little bombs, each one decimating years and years of careful articulation about my plans for the future.

From the way Ma is looking at me, I can tell she thinks I've lost my mind. Daddy is leaning against the counter, his arms folded across his chest. He's yet to say anything. He watches me and my mother, his eyes shifting between us. Frankie the dock dude is smarter than most people think.

Ma presses her fingers to her temples, trying to keep her brains from exploding and messing up the rose wallpaper she loves so much. In an even tone, she asks, "Then, what do you want to be, Anna?"

I look at Ma and then at Daddy. They aren't going to like this. I didn't really mention what I was shooting at Le Femme, but I was good at it. "A boudoir photographer."

In unison, they say, "A what?"

"A boudoir photographer. It's like a pin-up photographer."

Daddy catches on first, "Like what you were doing for Cole?"

I nod, "Yeah, I liked it and I was really good at it."

Ma shakes her head and slams her hands on the table. The entire thing shakes under the slam of her hands. "No, Anna! What about college? What about all that money you spent getting that degree? You can't honestly tell me that you're quitting college when you're so close to graduating."

"Ma," I groan like a little kid, wishing she'd understand, "I took all my classes. Those were for me. The information's already in my brain. I don't need a piece of paper to tell me that."

Ma huffs. "That piece of paper cost you twenty grand and you've got nothing to show for it."

"I will. I'll use everything I learned." I take a breath and spit it out. It's the plan I came up with on the drive out here. "I'm going to open my own studio."

Ma's lips part, but she says nothing. She looks at Daddy like I've gone crazy and urges him, "Say something."

Daddy nods his head for a moment, then tilts it to the side, asking, "Will this make you happy? Working for yourself is hard and the only person to blame when things don't work out is you. You think you're up for that Anna?"

Meeting his gaze, I nod. "Yeah. I'm good at it, Daddy. I know what I want to do.

I know how long it will take to turn a profit. I don't expect to ever be what Cole was, but I know I can support myself. All that money I saved to do post-graduate work is there as a cushion. I don't need more school, Dad. I need more guts. I've been hiding behind books for too long. It's time for me to get off my ass and start living my life. I'm not letting another day slip between my fingers."

Daddy smiles at me and my heart soars. It deafens me to my mother's voice as she screeches about how irresponsible it is for me to not finish something I started. She doesn't understand, but Daddy does. I am finishing what I started. My time with Cole changed me, for the better, and I'm ready to be that woman.

CHAPTER 5

Sitting at the counter, I shovel a spoon filled with Cheerios into my mouth. This will be the lunch of Anna Lamore until I can generate some income. From my awesome math skills, I deduced that I can live off of Ramen noodles, spaghetti, and Cheerios for seventy-three months and still manage to pay rent. If I can't manage to make my studio profitable in six years, then I'll move onto plan B. Honestly, I don't have plan B. This is it. And right now, I'm looking at the newspaper trying to find studio space, but everything is so expensive.

Jesse sits across from me and Emma is on the couch. Jesse shakes his head and says, "I can't believe you did it."

"Neither can I." I'm beaming, I can't help it. I'm so excited and terrified. I glance up at Jesse to see his big blue eyes looking at me in awe.

"I bet your mother chewed you out and threatened to throw you off the Brooklyn

Bridge," Emma says, frowning. She's trying to figure out how to use crochet hooks. It's not going well. So far, she's managed to create a lovely knot.

"Pretty much," I agree. "But, Dad understood."

"I don't understand," Emma replies with her dark eyebrows disappearing under her bangs. She loops more yarn around the needles and moves them like chopsticks. "I mean, you did a 180, like a total reversal in a couple of months. You were all wedding photography this and bridal pictures that for the past half-decade and now you're all wanting to shoot naked chicks. It's not like you."

Jesse grins. I kick him with my foot and answer Em, "It's not naked chicks, you perv."

I finally focus on Emma. She's biting her tongue and beating the crap out of the yarn, stabbing it with the needles into the couch cushions. "Die, beanie hat, die! I hate you!" She stills and looks at me. "What?"

"You have the attention span of a chimp." I smile at her, but she looks like she still wants to stab the yarn.

Jesse shakes his head, “Nah, chimps can knit. It’s more like the attention span of a fish. They seem to forget what they’re doing and blink a lot.” I laugh, which makes Jesse happy.

Emma on the other hand, slaps down the yarn and walks over to me. “Chimps can knit,” she mocks, and makes a face at Jesse. Em stops behind me and looks over my shoulder at the newspaper in my hands. “So, say I want to be supportive of this new you. What do I do?”

“Well, let’s see.” I tick the things off on my fingers as I say them. “You can keep an eye out for studio space, encourage me when I’m sick of cereal and noodles, and pretty much accept that this is what’s going to make me happy.” When I say it, my voice drops. I would have been happy with Cole. This will make me content. Happy is the wrong word. Emma sees it in my eyes.

I’m trying hard to keep moving forward and not look back. Cole hasn’t called me. He didn’t show up, crawling to me on his knees, apologizing. I don’t know where he is and I don’t want to know. He rejected me. I did nothing wrong, and he turned on me. From talking to my Dad I can understand how Cole could act that way, but I can't let it go. Maybe Cole was blindsided, but I could have turned on him when I first heard of the lawsuit and I didn't. Sottero's allegation was crap. I knew it. I didn't even ask him.

The empty place in my chest aches. I want to hear Cole's voice again, but I know I won't.

Jesse senses my mood and quickly tries to lighten it again. "There's one other thing she forgot to add to that list: Be nice to Jesse, who is the best friend I never had."

Emma's hands are on her hips; her long dark hair trails down her back. She laughs in his face and things feel normal again. I don't know what it is with me. One moment I'm fine and the next I feel like I'm made from old parchment that's turning to dust. Night time is the worst. When Jesse leaves and Em is asleep in her room, I stare at the walls waiting for sunrise. Every time I close my eyes, I see Cole. His voice echoes in my mind asking what if…

What if we didn't fight? What if he believed me?

The thoughts come unbidden and don't stop. By the time dawn creeps across the night sky, dousing the city in golden light, I'm a nervous wreck. Insomnia doesn't look good on me. There are dark circles under my eyes. No one says anything about it. They try to act like I'm fine and hope that I will be, which is what I want.

Looking at paper, I point at Jesse with my pen and say, "What he said."

"Oh my God. You two are a pair of—" Em starts to say, but I cut her off.

"A pair of what?"

She grins, "A pleasant pair of people to spend a Sunday morning with." She purses her lips and widens her eyes until she looks like a fish caught in a vacuum cleaner hose.

I laugh and shake my head. I've circled a few possibilities for studio locations. They're all small, under 1,000 square feet, but I don't want to bleed my budget on the shooting room. I have one chance at this and that's it. If I do it wrong, I'll spend all my money and have no income. That part scares the crap out of me.

"I want to see these." I slide the paper toward Jesse.

He looks it over and nods. Only a few weeks have passed since my confrontation with Cole on the beach. Jesse's been around more, trying to be supportive. "Some of these are in the hood, Anna."

"It's all I can afford." That's the problem. Starting out, I won't have much and the rent on the studio space makes up more than half of my expenses. Actually, it will take at least six sessions just to pay rent and that doesn't include any profit for me or stuff that's important, like electricity or water. It sort of limits my options.

Emma chimes in as she walks down the hall. Talking over her shoulder, she shouts, "Check the price of warehouse space on Long Island. It'll be cheaper than retail and as long as it's heated and cooled, you're in business."

My smile widens. "Want to spend the day looking at studio space with me?"

Jesse's expression brightens, "You know I do." He glances down the hall to make sure Emma is out of range. "And anything else you might want." He reaches out and places his hand over mine. Our eyes meet and my heart starts pounding harder. "I've been thinking about it and I shouldn't have told you no. If you still need me like that, I'm here for you." He means, If you still want me to be your sex toy, I'm down with that.

I didn't see this coming. I look at my hand and back at his face. I wanted a rebound guy. The nights are so horrible that I can't manage them alone. Everything reminds me of Cole. But if I have someone there, doing things to distract me—well, it sounds like a good idea. Jesse watches me carefully, like he just said something he shouldn't have.

I'm not sure how I feel about him. Jesse is more than a friend. He's sexy and has the ability to make butterflies erupt in my stomach. He can evoke a smile easily, even with me in a funk. We have so much in common. Everything about him would have dazzled me and I would have jumped at the chance to date him, but Cole found me first. Cole had become my unattainable god. Compared to Cole, Jesse was a nice guy. The contrast didn't work in Jesse's favor, but Cole isn't mine. He'll never be mine, and Jesse is sitting across from me, offering me anything that I need.

As these things rush through my mind, I look into his face. I'm silent too long, thinking about things—about him and what I want. Before he has a chance to pull his hand away, I hold it tighter. "Thank you." The words are barely a whisper. Jesse nods once and looks at me from under his brow. It's the cutest expression I've ever seen.

He stands and steps in front of me. The way he moves makes my stomach drop. I wanted this, I asked for this, but it still feels like he's the one advancing on me. It stirs something inside of me, a longing for Cole that's gone unanswered for too long. Jesse's eyes lock with mine and he lowers his face, inching slowly toward mine, until our lips gently brush together. He doesn't touch me, he doesn't force a bigger kiss. My breath catches in my throat as my body responds to him. I need to move on. When I look at him, I see that chance and don't know if I should take it.

Jesse pulls back a little bit, but remains close enough that I can feel his breath slip across my lips. He smells good, like fall and spices. When Jesse speaks, he whispers, "I won't pressure you. If you want more, you'll have to say it." My cheeks flush and he smiles, pressing his forehead to mine. "Damn, you're adorable. You blush."

I look up at him from under my lashes, "You have no idea."

CHAPTER 6

I pull into the parking garage after 8:00pm with Jesse clinging to me. When I stop the bike, he jumps off and unfastens his helmet.

Wiping his hand across his lips, he says, "I think I swallowed a bug."

I laugh, "Yeah, all part of the charm of riding a motorcycle. All sorts of stuff flies into your face, and sometimes you're lucky enough to swallow." An evil grin spreads across my face.

Before Jesse can respond, Edward appears. He's wearing jeans and a light sweater, like he's dressed for a casual night out. Good. Maybe he finally got over me and started dating again. I nod hello at him. Jesse is pleasant enough, but says nothing. Edward looks between us, and says, "Nice night for a ride, huh?"

"Yeah, it was." I look over his shoulder and don't see anyone else. Jesse steps closer to me, but doesn't touch me. It's a territorial move, which surprises me. "We went looking for studio space. Long day. Are you meeting someone or looking for Em?"

Edward nods and smiles politely. "Both. Meeting Em for dinner." Edward looks Jesse over so fast that he barely glances at the guy. "So, is this the new boyfriend?"

I start to cut him off, but Jesse steps next to me and takes my hand. "As a matter of fact, I am. Jesse," he says, holding out his other hand to Edward.

Edward raises a brow and looks at me. He looks at Jesse's hand but doesn't take it. "Well, good luck is all I'm saying."

"Edward," I scold, but he doesn't say more. Instead he gestures for us to go first. We all leave the garage together in silence and walk back to my apartment. My feet are sore, and so is my back from being hunched over on the bike, riding two-up all day. I unlock the door and we head inside. Edward veers to the couch and sits, waiting for his sister. I shout to Em to let her know he's here.

Jesse sits at the counter as I go around the half wall and into the kitchen to grab us something to eat. Trying to ignore Edward, we talk. "Which did you like the best?" We saw so many options today.

"The one out in Islip looked promising, but it bumps up against a shopping center that looked kind of sketchy." Jesse leans on his elbows, and hunches his shoulders forward.

"I liked that one too, but yeah, it kind of gave me the creeps."

"Do you need a studio? Can you shoot on location or something for a while and then get one later?" Jesse's eyes meet mine as he asks the question. It's not a bad idea and I've thought about it before.

"I could, especially if I was shooting weddings, but I'm not." I avoid saying what I intend to do because of Edward. I wish he wasn't sitting there, but Em isn't ready yet. "For this I need some place that's safe for both of us, you know what I mean? I don't want to be the icky shooter that meets people in hotels, and shooting at their house doesn't work. What if someone walks in on us? It'll look bad and I don't want my face punched in by some jealous idiot. No, I think the studio is a necessary evil. I guess I should keep looking." My hopes deflate a little bit as

I stare into the fridge, not seeing the food, just thinking about what I should do next.

Jesse makes a sound of agreement.

When Emma walks out of her room, she looks stunning. She's wearing a little black dress that makes her have that vintage bombshell figure. Em's all curves. The shoes she's wearing are too awesome. I stare at her, my jaw agape. "Holy shit! You look extra hot." I glance at Edward in confusion. "Why'd you get dressed up to go out with your brother?"

Em grins, "Guys give me their number whether I'm with another guy or not. I figured, why risk meeting the perfect guy when I'm wearing jeans and a tank top." Her eyes widen as she looks over my outfit and backtracks, "Not that there's anything wrong with that…"

I laugh. I'm always wearing jeans and a tank top. It's my go-to outfit. Besides, it's not like I can ride my bike wearing short, fluttery skirts. I glance at Jesse and his eyes are locked on my neckline. I've never noticed him checking me out before. Tilting my head, I give him a look.

Busted, he smiles sheepishly and says, “I like tank tops.”

Em snorts, “You would. You’d want to do her if she was wearing a trash bag. You’re love-struck, little boy.” She meant it to be funny, but the way Jesse looks at me, with horror seeping across his face, says Em hit the nail on the head. Before she can do more damage, she’s out the door and Jesse and I are alone.

I feel like I should say something, but I don’t know what to say. Finally, Jesse says, “It’s not like that.”

“It’s not?” I ask, relieved.

He shakes his head. “No, not really. I just know what I want and Emma sees it, that’s all.”

I nod slowly. I can think of a hundred different things to say that would make him feel better and lead us to my bedroom, but I can’t say any of them. Jesse’s gaze locks with mine. I want to move on. I want to want him, but I don’t feel it. I wonder if Cole broke me, if this is what Cole felt like around me because of Sophia. Internally, I cringe thinking about it.

After we ate and watched a movie, Jesse left and I was alone. I intended to go to bed early, but I can't sleep. I just lay there, the same way I do every night. I sit up in bed and pull the covers around my shoulders. This has never happened to me before and it kills me that it's happening now, with someone I didn't even have sex with. I shouldn't have thought of sex. As soon as I do, it lights my body like a raging fire, making me remember Cole's kisses and how they drifted below my waist. I shun the memory. I can't stand it. I have to know what happened to Cole, what he's doing. I pick up my cell phone off the nightstand and pull up his name. There's a picture and his number. I want to press it, I want to call him and hear his voice again. My thumb lingers over Cole's number, but I can't do it. Things didn't work out between us and it wasn't my fault. I tried to tell him that I had nothing to do with Sottero's spy, but it looked damning. It's a classic Anna issue: wrong place, wrong time. Part of me wishes that I knew who the snitch was, who got the information Sophia wanted, but in the end I know it doesn't matter. Cole didn't believe me. I'm not sure what I'd do if he suddenly did, if he showed up apologizing. Sometimes I'm not sure which was wounded worse, my pride or my heart. I don't know. They seem muddled together lately. I look at his name, knowing I can't dial and put the phone down. I rub my eyes with the heel of my hands. I can't stand this.

I get out of bed and throw on a black sundress and pull my hair into a pony tail, before putting on my sparkle Chucks. I look like a twelve year old, so I swipe on black liner and mascara. That's a little bit better. I head for the door. There's a bar down the street and I intend to get plastered. The sidewalks are littered with people. Most look like they're on their way home from a date or work. I shoulder past them and round the corner, not really paying attention to anything when I feel the back of my neck prickle. Stopping suddenly, I turn around. I scan the crowd. There's no one there, well no that's obviously reason for the icy dread that's crawling up my spine. I look around to dart into a shop, but they're all closed. I rush on, thinking that I'm losing my mind, but the feeling doesn't dissipate. It lingers, choking me like stale smoke. When I get to the bar, I try to hurl myself through the doors.

The bouncer stops me, and then laughs, "Holy shit, I nearly didn't recognize you, Anna." When he spoke, his voice rumbled through the room. Several heads turn to look at me, and I feel my face warm.

Damn my blushing. Why do I blush all the time? "It's okay," I say, after peeling myself off his arm. "Long day. You want this?" I hold my ID between two fingers, but the bouncer shakes his head.

"Nah, I know you're barely legal," and he lets me through.

I walk to the far end of the bar and sit with my back to the door. If I see anyone else tonight, I'll die. I hope Emma doesn't come in here. I order a shot, knowing it'll go straight to my head. It burns my mouth and throat, but I manage to swallow it and ask for another. As the alcohol warms me, I stare at the amber liquid in the tiny glass. I want Cole. I want him so badly that it feels like my chest will cave in and I won't be able to breathe if he doesn't come. I pull my phone out of my purse, but put it down on the bar.

I stare at the plastic case, at the scratches and dents, and feel lost.

I lift the second shot and down it. It doesn't burn as badly this time. The bartender gives me a third, but mutters something about slowing down. I don't care. I cradle the glass in my hand, watching the contents swirl. The door opens and closes a few times. People come and go. Their lives go on even though mine fell apart.

When I down the third drink, I slam it back down on the bar. My fingers pinch the glass. I'd been staring at my phone and the shot glass the entire time. I didn't bother to look up. When I do, I nearly choke. Those sapphire blue eyes lock with mine and steal my breath.

Cole.

CHAPTER 7

My heart crawls up my throat and into my mouth. Every hair on my body stands on end and I shiver. It's like seeing a ghost. He was mine, and now he's not. Cole doesn't move, he doesn't say anything. He just sits there in his silk shirt and watches me from across the bar. An unbidden memory flashes behind my eyes of another time Cole watched me, and my cheeks flame red.

Eyes locked with Cole, I clear my throat and tap at my empty glass. The bartender is an older guy, Charlie. His hair is graying at his temples, dark eyes, and he's really nice. Charlie pours, and steps in front of me, blocking Cole. I look up at him. "Anna," Charlie says in a whisper, "someone's going to have to scrape you off the floor if you drink that. You want me to call someone?"

I shake my head, but the room tilts. I think about something he said before about my weight and it finally make sense. I smile. "Lightweight, ah, that's what you said." I take the glass from him. My body is warm and tingly. For once, I don't have the throbbing sense of loss in the center of my chest.

Charlie looks at me and shakes his head like I disappoint him. "Let me know when you want to leave and I'll call you a cab."

I nod and regret it. The room appears to shift again. It tilts higher, like a boat stuck at the top of a wave, and then settles back to where it should be. When the room is no longer moving, it takes me longer to focus on Cole, but I do. He has stubble on his cheeks. It makes him look older than he is. There's a drink in his hand, probably scotch. His dark hair hangs over his eyes, making them seem bluer. Torment lines his face, like he hasn't slept in weeks. Cole watches me, his eyes never drifting from mine.

I hold the drink longer than I intend, but I want to be able to walk home. Right now, with the way the bar seems to be swaying beneath me, that won't be possible. I giggle to myself. I love boat rides. That's what this feels like, a boat ride. The waves roll up and down, gently swaying me, or the room, or both. I don't really care. My mind snaps back to Cole and the momentary happy thought is blasted to bits.

I roll the rim of the glass between my thumb and forefinger, watching Cole. Neither of us speaks. Words pile in my mouth of things I want to say, but I know I'll never have the chance. It makes me feel hollow and brittle. In all my life, a single man has never had such an effect on me. I feel broken without Cole, like a piece of me snapped off and will never return.

I wonder if I'm like Jesse, if Cole admires me, but that's all. The look on Cole's face says something else, but I don't know what. I lean forward on the bar, stretching my arms out to help hold me up. It forces my cleavage up, pressing hard against my neckline. I lift the glass and put it to my lips. Cole's eyes track the movement, and his lips part like he wants to say something. Our eyes lock and for some reason it feels like he's telling me not to drink it, to put the glass down. We stare at each other for a few moments and then I toss back the shot. It doesn't even burn this time. I place the glass on the bar top and look at it. It's very pretty, all short and thick. The light shines through the clear glass, making an illuminated star on the bar top. I gaze at it and all the pretty points, and when I lift my head, Cole is gone.

Anguish rushes into my chest, crushing me. I can't do this. I can't see him and not react. My arms slip down and I rest my head on the bar.

A second later I feel a hand on my back, and Cole's voice is in my ear, "Come on, Anna. I'll take you home." He slaps down some cash and it sounds way too loud.

It takes me a second to realize that Cole's trying to get me to stand up. The bartender and the bouncer both look at me like they're concerned, but neither of them says anything. Cole pushes us through the door and I'm hit with a gust of cool air. It makes me shiver. I wrap my arms around myself and look down. Sparklie yellow sneakers are on my feet. I love them! We stop walking so I can wiggle my toes and watch them glitter.

Cole's warm hand wraps around my arm, "What is it with you and those shoes?" He pulls me gently, encouraging me to walk. I look up, surprised to see him.

"I saw you in the bar," I say, smiling at his beautiful face. We stop walking and I speak to his chest, not looking at his eyes. My fingers lift and fuss with his collar. "I never thought I'd see you again, and there you are." I blink and look up at him like he's not really here. Narrowing my eyes, I try to focus harder, expecting him to vanish when I do so. When he's still there, I lift my finger and press it hard to his chest. "You are here." I want to cry. I want to weep. I want to giggle. My emotions are short circuiting and I have no idea what to do.

Cole takes my hand as my finger presses to his chest again. "I'm here. I admit, I came looking for you and lost my nerve. I didn't expect you to walk in and get plastered." He's looking at me with those sexy eyes and I feel paralyzed.

I know I need to say something. "I couldn't sleep."

"Neither could I." He looks at me with such a humble expression on his face. Cole looks lost, his eyes drink me in, as his hands linger close to my face like he wants to touch me, but he doesn't. My gaze drops to my feet. I stare at the dirty side walk and my bright yellow sneakers.

Cole lifts my chin with his finger. I gaze into his eyes, unable to look away. "I wish things could have been different." That's all he says. It's the same thought that slams around inside my skull all day long. A thousand *what ifs* keep me awake, pillaging my peace, and making me into a freaking lunatic.

"Me, too," I manage. After a moment, Cole takes my arm again to steady me, and we walk back toward my apartment.

The night air fills my lungs, but I can't feel it. I can't feel anything; not Cole's hand on my arm, not the chill in the air, not the humidity that curls my hair tighter and sticks to my skin. Numbness races through my veins. It was the only way to get through the day, and now it's the only way to tolerate having Cole so close and knowing that he doesn't want me.

We get to my door and Cole helps me up the steps. I fish through my purse looking for the key. When I lift it out, I see Cole's blue gaze and freeze. I want things to change, but I don't know how to change them. My heart beats harder, as his gaze drifts to my lips. I want him to kiss me. I want him to take me in his arms and cover me in kisses. I want him to tell me that he believes me and he'll never doubt me again. I want this rift between us to mend, but I don't know how to fix it.

Cole draws closer, like he can't manage to stand so near to me and not touch me. Before I know it, his lips are a breath from mine. His eyelashes brush my cheek as he stays there, nearly kissing me, but not. My pulse pounds in my ears. I want to reach up and take his face in my hands. I want to tell him that I love him. My body reacts to Cole, to that hot gaze, and the spot between my legs throbs. My breasts feel full, like they need to be touched. I barely breathe as Cole's lips stay there, like he's fighting the urge to kiss me.

Finally, Cole takes a breath and shudders. He pulls away, and I feel part of me ripped away with him. A shiver trails down my spine and drops into the coldness that pooled in my stomach. I can't stand it. Regret turns to tears, but I blink them away. I turn and push the key into the lock. The door won't open. I bang it with my fist, and start to cry. Cole reaches for the lock and twists the knob. The door opens and I walk through, without looking back at the man who broke my heart.

CHAPTER 8

Sunlight pours between the slats and blinds me. I roll over and pull my blanket over my head. Everything is so damn loud. The crinkling blankets sound like snapping boards. I groan and lay on my side, curled into a ball. Cole's eyes flash across my mind. Random words he said echo through my head. The sensation of his hand on my arm, how warm and strong it felt. These things flicker in my mind and are gone before I can blink. They don't connect to other thoughts. They just drift, floating on a current of regret that insists on bubbling up my throat.

Emma's voice is soft, as she speaks from the other side of the door. "Anna, are you alright?" She pushes the door open slowly, without knocking. I vaguely remember walking past her and Edward last night on the way to puking up my guts in the bathroom. "It's past noon."

Bleary eyed, I turn over and lay flat on my back, but my stomach is still queasy and protests. I push myself up on my elbows and look at her. My voice is scratchy, "I want to say that I'm fine and smile at you, but I just don't have it in me to fake it right now. I'm not fine. I'll never be fine." I breathe and feel the air fill my lungs. The words have been lodged in my mind for too long. It's something I know, but didn't have the heart to say.

Emma walks toward me slowly and sits on the edge of my bed. She pats my leg, saying, "It'll be better. Give it time."

"That's what people say when they don't know what else to do." I pull my legs into my chest and clutch my ankles under a wad of blankets. My head hurts. Emma watches me with pity in her eyes. Finally, I say, "I saw him last night."

"Who? Jesse?" Her pretty face looks confused as she tries to figure out what I mean.

I don't shake my head. It'll hurt too much. Dejected, I stare at my bedspread and say, "Cole. I was well on my way to being totally plastered when I looked up and saw him. He sat there, watching me." I find my voice doesn't want to work. It's the closest I've been to Cole in nearly a month.

"Oh, Anna. I didn't know. I'm so sorry." She scoots up next to me and puts her arm across my back and gives me a sideways hug.

"How do I get over him?" I ask, looking at her. Emma's been my best friend for years. She's been there through labs and finals, but this is the first time I've had to deal with heartbreak. I wish it would just stop.

"I don't know, Anna. I've never been that into a guy. I'm actually a little jealous about that."

"What?" I say, and glance at her, stunned. Emma always has a guy hanging around her. She seems crazy about most of them. Her answer surprises me.

She shrugs, "I might turn a lot of heads, but I still haven't found anyone that comes anywhere close to getting my heart, but you have. It makes me a little envious." She winks at me.

"My advice would be to keep doing what you're doing, because this part sucks." I rest my forehead on my knees.

Emma puts her hand on the back of my head. "So, this part isn't worth the other part?" I glance at her from under my arm. "I mean this is the down side. Every coin has two sides and the other side had you reeling. I mean, is the bad so bad that you'd toss the good, too?"

I want to say no, but right now I can't say anything. "I have to get over him."

"Anna, what if that isn't the way this works?"

"What do you mean?" That was like the worst thing she could have said.

"I mean, what if you don't get over him? What if you just learn how to get on without him? People who've been in love have that haunted look in their eyes. It's like a piece of them is unattainable, forever held back and protected at all cost."

"Like Cole's eyes."

She nods. "I don't know my ass from my elbow on this stuff, but maybe he'll always be a part of you. Maybe you don't get over him, you just learn to get on without him."

Silence fills the air. I agree with her. I need to move on. "You think I should be going out with Jesse?"

Emma pulls her knees to her chest and mirrors the way I sit. "Maybe, that's up to you. But I don't think that you'll get back to your life until you make some changes. If nothing changes, everything stays the same, right?" It was what the professor in our philosophy class said. "If you do what you've always done, you get what you've always gotten. If you want something different, then make something different."

I understand now. I just don't know if I have the guts to do it. Being a workaholic sounds more appealing, but the nights are so unbearable. I feel the shift, the change within me. I accept what I have to do, and I'm lucky that there's already a great guy there who wants me.

CHAPTER 9

I dress for dinner carefully, making sure I look like a sex kitten. My hair is smoothed and hanging loose in long waves that extend down my back. I borrowed a black dress from Em that fits me a little too snuggly, but it makes my boobs look bigger, so hey, I can deal with it. I pull on inky thigh highs with lace at the top and attach them to my garter belt. That is also black lace. It matches my favorite bra. I slip my feet into killer shoes, meaning they could kill me if I fall from this height, or that I could easily use the heel as a weapon.

When I finish, Em does my make-up and talks to me about her job. "Close your eye. Yeah, like that." A cold wet glob starts to get dabbed across my lashes, liquid liner. "Stacey is easy to work with and after you gave me that exclusive, it really helped. It also made the press disappear which was awesome, because that would have sucked if they stuck around." She's talking too much because she's nervous for me. I never dress up this much. She knows what it means, she knows what I intend to do with Jesse later to move on.

"Look up." She dabs my lower lashes with cold gook and talks as I stare at the ceiling. "He's really patient, too. They didn't teach us a bunch of stuff at college, but he said that's normal—that most of the things you use in real life are learned in real life. That's kind of like what you were saying with opening your studio. It's easier to understand when I'm doing it every day. I guess it's the difference between theory and practice."

She takes a tissue and blots my lips. I look at Emma as her eyes rove over my face, looking for imperfections in my make-up mask. After a moment she grins, and I know she's finished. Emma steps back and says, "Heeellllllo sexy."

I feel different, more confident, more certain. I thank Em and the door buzzes. She takes off to let Jesse inside as I finish up. I hook a pendant around my neck. It dangles above my cleavage and draws attention to the girls. Like they need more attention. I'm practically popping out of this dress.

I smooth the supple fabric over my hips and will myself to relax. This is a good thing. This is what's next. Since speaking with Emma, I realized that I don't have to stop loving Cole to move on. I just have to be willing to try and live my life without him.

"You can do this," I say to the mirror and turn toward the door.

Jesse is standing there with a smirk on his lips. "You always talk to the mirror?"

My cheeks burn at his teasing, but he doesn't comment. His witty retorts died in his throat when I turned around. Jesse's eyes ravage me, drinking in every detail. He steps into the room and his gaze darkens. "You look spectacular."

I smile shyly and it just makes him more taken with me. His eyes lock on my body. Jesse has a hard time keeping his gaze on my face.

"Thanks," I say. "I thought dinner, and then maybe we could come back here after?"

His eyes lift and meet mine, "Anything special you have planned for later?"

"Maybe," I grin back and lift the hem of my dress, showing off the thigh highs, and then lifting a little more so he can see the bottom of the lacy garter belt. "I thought I could show you this and a little more." I drop the skirt and it falls back into place against my thigh. Jesse looks like he's going to race across the room and throw me on the bed.

Instead, he steps toward me and takes me in his arms. He presses a gentle kiss to my lips. When he pulls away, he says, "That sounds perfect."

We go to dinner at some classy little place that Jesse picks out. We talk, but my mind keeps skipping to later. I want his hands on me. I want him to make me forget everything I lost. I wonder if I suck, if I'm a slut for forcing a relationship forward when I can't even feel anything. I hope Jesse's touch will make me feel something. I hope his kisses wake me back up and that I'll feel content in his arms.

Dinner is wonderful. After we order dessert, I excuse myself to use the ladies room. It's clear across the other side of the restaurant. As I walk, my skirt swishes above my knee, drawing male eyes. Their gazes land gently on me and I feel beautiful. Confidence surges through me as I smile. Something strange is happening to me. I'm no longer

Anna. I'm this classic sex goddess. Guys never openly ogle me, but tonight, that's all they do. One guy winks at me. I wink back and keep walking.

I spend a little too much time in the ladies room, and when I walk back to our table, I circle around the other way. I see someone—a guy—hunched over our table, blocking my view of Jesse. They're having a tense conversation. When I'm close enough, I catch the tail-end of it.

Jesse's tone is harsh, scolding, "…might be the one fucking her, but you're the one who has her heart."

"Anna doesn't—" he starts saying, but I cut him off, shocked.

"Cole. What are you doing here?" He turns and looks me over, like he disapproves of my outfit.

"That's very different than what you wore last night," Cole says coldly.

My hackles raise. I can't remember most of last night, and the innuendo will piss Jesse off. I breathe and his eyes drift to the swell of my breasts and slowly caress my neck, until Cole's gaze locks with mine. The way he does it sets off an explosion within me. I want him. I feel my body react to him, but I hide it. Cole doesn't see the desire I have for him, and he'll never see it again. "I'm on a date and having you come over and bother us isn't becoming."

Cole's brow raises, "I was just leaving, Miss Lamore. I wouldn't want to ruin your evening." He inclines his head to me and leaves. I watch him walk away, wondering how things got so bad. This is worse than when we first met.

I slide back into my seat and look at Jesse. "How could you say that to him?"

"I didn't mean to upset you. I'm sorry." Jesse looks mortified. He didn't see me walk up to the table either. His eyes won't meet mine. "I know it must have sounded horrible."

I shake my head and cover his hand with mine. He glances at me. "Don't try to explain. I know you're just trying to help me get over him."

"It's more than that, Anna." Jesse swallows hard and threads our fingers together. "I'm not sure how much of a chance I have after him. Everything I do looks weak compared to that guy. I want you,

Anna. I want you to give me a chance to make you happy." Jesse rubs my hand with his. Although his words are pleading, his voice is not. He won't beg.

I look at his hand, and then back up at his eyes. "Let's get out of here. I have some more black lace to show you." I smile at him and wink. I don't understand why Cole was at the table, but I'm not letting him affect me anymore.

We walk back to the apartment hand in hand. Periodically Jesse's shoulder brushes mine. I smile at him. Somehow we start talking about my lace. "I noticed you wear thigh highs. They're really sexy, but I had no idea you wore garters, too. That's dream territory, Anna."

My inner sex kitten is fighting to commandeer the conversation, but I keep beating her back. She sees the lust in his eyes and wants to use that to her advantage. "Actually, the bra, panties, and garters were my favorite set."

"Were?" he asks.

I wink at him. "Yes, they were my favorite set until the panties went missing."

Jesse stopped, his eyes not so subtly drifting to my hips. "You're not wearing panties?"

I don't answer. I just smile at him. He stands there panting like a cartoon character and I grab his tie. When we get to my door, I push him up against it and kiss him. I don't do the little chaste kisses he keeps giving me. I push my tongue into Jesse's mouth and slide my leg up his thigh. Jesse kisses me back and I finally feel hot. Pulse pounding, I break the kiss and turn around. Jesse leans against me, pressing me to the door. He rubs his hips against me and I can feel him, hard and ready.

He whispers in my ear. "I want you so badly. You have no idea how much."

I moan, and stay there for a second, feeling him push against me. My heart's hammering in my chest. The thought of Jesse lifting my skirt and fucking me from behind, against the door in public, races through my mind. Oh God. I fumble with my key until the door opens and we stumble inside. His arms wrap around me as his tongue finds my mouth. Jesse kisses me harder and I let him. I don't hold back.

The apartment is empty. Emma left for the night to give me time alone with Jesse. His hand grips my thigh as I slide my leg up. His fingers press into my flesh between the garters and stockings. I lean into him, kissing him harder, forcing my breasts into his chest. I keep my eyes closed, thinking about nothing except the need in my body and that Jesse is there for me. I like him. I want him. This will be good for both of us.

Jesse's hand cups my bare ass, and I moan into his mouth. My hands find his tie and loosen it from his neck. I slowly work at his buttons as we kiss and peel his shirt away, stripping him in the living room. The curtains are open, but it's dark inside. I'm confident that no one can see in unless they press their face to the window.

Jesse pushes me away. Breathless, he says, "I think we need to see the lace that started all of this."

I grin wickedly and unzip the back of the dress. It falls to the floor in a quick swoosh and I'm standing there in a sheer lacy bra, with thick lace garters where panties would be, thigh highs, and fuck-me heels. Jesse's eyes rove over my body and his hands soon follow. The lace garter belt sits right at my hips. If I part my legs, he'll see everything, and have open access to all of me.

Jesse lifts me and moves me to the couch. My legs wrap around him as he trails kisses down my neck and to my breast. I close my eyes, wanting to get lost in lust, but I see Cole's face. My eyes snap open. I won't do that. I won't have sex with one guy and pretend he's another.

Jesse feels me stiffen. "Are you okay, Anna?" His hands are behind my back, his lips gently pressing to the lace of my bra, teasing my nipples.

I nod and he continues, but I'm not okay. As Jesse's hands move over me, I notice how different they feel. I keep comparing him to Cole. It doesn't matter if my eyes are open or closed, I see Cole. In one last desperate attempt to get Cole out of my head, I lift Jesse's face to mine and press my lips to his. The kiss deepens and I hold him tightly to my body. His fingers splay on my face as he kisses me back. When Jesse rocks his hips against mine, and I feel his hard length though his pants, my façade cracks. I suck in a jagged breath and push him back. Jesse is panting. His body is covered in a thin sheen of sweat. Desire darkens his eyes, but when Jesse looks at me, he sees it.

Instead of saying something, he kisses my forehead and lies down next to me.

After a few minutes, I say, "I'm sorry. I've been leading you on and I—"

Jesse sits up and presses his fingers to his temples. His words are right—they're the words a gentleman should say—but his tone is off. He sounds scolding instead of understanding. He doesn't look at me as he speaks. "No, don't say that. Never apologize for this." Jesse releases the death grip on his head and stands, running his hands through his hair. He takes a deep breath and looks at me.

"I thought I could," I try to explain things to him. "I thought if it was going to be anyone, that it'd be you."

He turns and looks at me sadly. "So did I. You're beautiful, Anna. Everything I ever wanted—the bombshell body and the brains. I hoped that I'd be the guy who got you over him, but I see that isn't going to happen." His tone shifts from hopeful to angry. It's horrible. I don't know what to do, but it turns out that I don't have to do anything. Jesse grabs his things and leaves without a backwards glance.

CHAPTER 10

After that dreadful moment, I pull on my dress and sit on the couch, staring at the wall like it's a TV. I'm such a mess. I can't even hook-up with a guy who's nuts about me without messing it up. Why did I have to say something?

I can't stand to sit home. I pull my dress back on and walk down to the bar. This time I order a shot and just sit there, staring at it like it has the power to reveal some hidden message that I'm just too thick to understand. The door opens and I feel the cool night air travel across the room and slip over my skin. The sleeveless dress doesn't do much to keep me warm, but it does lift my ego. I've had three attempts at my number since I walked in. Mental note to self; next time I want meaningless sex, borrow Emma's dress and walk around commando. It's like the guys have X-ray vision and know I've got nothing on. Actually, this is weird for me and the no-panties-thing wasn't on purpose, either. When I went to put on the bra, the panties were missing. They weren't more than a scrap of fabric, but I didn't have anything else that would look right under the lace garter, so I went without. Those were my favorite pair of panties. They fit perfectly and showcased my ass, making it look model perfect. I asked Emma if she'd seen them, but I must have left them at Ma's house with some of my other laundry.

I cross my legs and raise the glass to my lips. Finally, I tip it back. The amber liquid slides down my throat, burning a hot wake in its path. I take a breath and order another. My process repeats. I have no intention of becoming a drunk. I won't order another drink after this shot, so I sit with it longer, allowing the buzz from the first shot to penetrate my foul mood.

I don't know what I'm upset about. So, I couldn't sleep with Jesse. That just means I'm not a slut, right? Wrong. That voice in the back of my head won't shut up tonight. I stare at the bar top. The lights gleam off the shiny surface.

I want my life to change, but I don't make changes. I keep doing the same thing. I feel eyes on the side of my face, but I don't look up. It's another guy wanting my number. I should just tell them that I'm a panty-less fraud, but he'd stop listening at panty-less. I cross my legs tighter, hooking my heel to the back of the stool. I don't look up. Instead, I trace the glow of the light on the bar top with my fingernail, while I keep my other perfectly manicured hand on the shot glass.

The guy sits next to me and it isn't until he orders that I notice who he is. His voice drips over my body like liquid seduction. He has the ability to stir something deep inside of me that makes me hot all over. I don't turn. I don't look at him. I hold my legs tighter together and try to ignore the sensations pelting my body.

Cole glances at me out of the corner of his eye, "Date didn't go well?"

"You're an ass," I reply, still not looking at him. If I turn my head, if our eyes connect, there's no way I'll be able to live through it. I'll throw my arms around his neck and beg him to take me back. I'm not a prideful person, but I can't ask him to take me back. I can't let him know how badly he's messed with my head.

"You say that to all the men." Cole sips his drink. The ice cubes clink together when he places the cup on the bar, empty. Charlie, the bartender, looks at me with questions in his eyes. I look back, willing him to understand that I want Cole to leave me alone, but Charlie doesn't get it. The bartender refills the drinks and leaves us.

"No," I say, "just to you. Did you really have to walk over and give him pointers on getting me into bed? What the hell was that about, anyway?" My skin prickles.

Cole's looking at me, his gaze is sliding over my arms and lands on my chest. Cole watches my breasts swell as I breathe, making no attempt to hide it. "Wow. Did the little guy actually say that?" After a second, Cole looks away from me. His tone shifts from condescending to serious. "That's not what happened, okay? He approached me. I didn't want to talk to him. On my way out, I went to tell him off and you walked up."

"Yeah right. Why would Jesse go talk to you? I was a sure thing, so he goes up to you and says… what?" I can't even imagine why

Jesse would do that. It makes no sense. Irritation shoots through me. I don't wait for him to answer. I do my shot and slam it on the bar, before standing, and saying, "You know what? I don't care." I turn to leave, but Cole grabs my wrist.

He holds on tight, like I'll die if he lets go. "He told me that you love me. He said he might have your body, but your heart is somewhere else, with someone else." Cole releases my arm and I freeze.

I can't move. I speak without thinking, "Why would Jesse say that? Why would he do that?"

"Because he loves you. He wants you to be happy, even if it isn't with him."

Mortified, I stare at the floor, refusing to meet Cole's gaze. This can't be happening. I feel a tremor rock through my body. I feel the cool night air against my hot skin. I feel Cole's dark gaze burning a hole in the side of my face, but I remain rigid. I can't move. Neither of us says anything. Neither of us moves. I don't know if I want the moment to end or drag on forever. Suddenly, I ask, "Are you following me?"

He nods, "Yes."

Shocked, I ask, "Why?"

"I wanted to tell you something, but I needed to know the answer to something first. I'd walk to your apartment or come in here, hoping to run into you, but I didn't get lucky until last night." I don't respond. I can't find my voice. My knees are jelly and the fuck-me heels are thinking about making me bend over a stool every time Cole's voice caresses my ears. "Tonight was different. I didn't follow you and him. I wouldn't do that to you. It was a coincidence. I was out with my lawyer going over testimonies for the hearing and your name is on the witness list for Sottero. When I saw it, I lost my mind. Then, I look up and there you are, beautiful and blindingly sexy. God, every man in the room wanted you."

"Not every man," I breathe. "Not the one I want." My words free me and I can move. I don't look at him. I step away, expecting Cole to say my name, but he lets me leave. My eyes are on the floor as I walk to the door. Suddenly someone is in front of me. When I glance up, I suck in air, startled to see Cole.

His eyes lock with mine, pinning me in place. "That's not true." My heart rate jumps, but I can't speak. Cole's blue eyes are filled with emotion. He moves to touch me and then acts like he thinks better of it. He swallows hard and says, "Every man wanted you. Every man in this room wants you." My heart is soaring, but I yank it back like a kite caught in a wild wind, fearful that it'll break apart.

"Desire isn't enough. I'm sorry." I push past him. The bouncer holds open the door. I look into his face and nod, noticing the sheen in his eyes.

I wrap my arms around my waist and walk faster. It makes my boobs climb up my throat, but I don't care. I want this night to end. I can't take another second of it. As tears streak my face, I hear footfalls race up behind me. A hand touches my shoulder, and I whirl around, ready to scream.

Cole's breathing hard, like he'd run after me. "How do you feel about me?"

"I already told you, and I'm not saying it again. No matter how demented you think I am, I have no desire for you to rip my heart out again. Leave me alone, Cole. Go fuck with some other girl's mind."

Cole presses his eyes closed, and his lips crush together. I turn away.

He doesn't move. Cole doesn't follow me. When I hear his voice, I feel it float over me and course through me like Cole is a part of me, "I love you, Anna."

CHAPTER 11

My spine goes straight as I turn slowly, my hands falling to my sides. Shock lines my face. I stare at him. "I didn't want you pulled into the crap with Sottero. I didn't want you to think I was wealthy and then find out I had nothing. It felt deceptive. I kept you at arm's length, telling myself that those were the reasons—that it was to spare you."

He's walking towards me as he speaks. Uncertainty draws his brows together. Cole looks vulnerable. I see it in his hands, in the way he holds his shoulders back, like the weight of his mistakes is crushing him. "But it was a lie. I kept you away because I thought it'd be easier to never have you, than to love you and watch you leave me when you found out that I'd lost everything."

"I'm not her—I'm not Sophia." The wind blows gently, lifting my hair in the breeze.

"I know, but the fear was there. It's always there. Everyone who—" he bites his tongue and shakes his head. "No, not everyone. Not you. I pushed you away. Everyone else left. It's hard. This is hard. I can't understand what you could possibly see in me. Once the money is gone, no one stays."

I stand there, staring at him. My mind is telling me to walk away, to say that he did this to himself. Live with it. But my heart takes control of my body. I step toward him slowly, like a battered cat, skittish and scared. My heart pounds inside my chest, but I won't release the death grip I have on my arms. Cole watches me, like he knows he lost me; like he knows these mistakes are beyond repair. I stand in front of him, nearly nose to nose thanks to my heels.

The grip on my arms loosens, and I lean in slowly and say what's been on my mind for weeks. "I don't want your money. I want your heart." I breathe the words, fearful that whatever spell he's under will crack and I'll lose him again.

Before I know what I'm doing, I lean in closer, brushing my lips across his. The sensation's so light. Heat sears my skin from being so close, from touching his lips with mine. But Cole doesn't move. The kiss slips across his lips and I nearly step away before his brain catches up with his body. Cole clutches my wrists hard, and he pulls me to his chest. He kisses my face and my cheeks, and finally my lips. My heart pounds harder. I don't know how this happened, how this night turned out this way.

Cole breaks the kiss and presses his head to mine. "You have my heart, Anna. You've had it this entire time." He grabs me, pulling me tightly to his body and kisses me harder. His kisses make my head spin. It feels like I've lost my mind, that this can't possibly be happening, but it is. We realize we're in the street and manage to get back to the apartment. Emma is still out, but will be home soon. We head to my room. Cole pushes the door shut and locks it.

I stand with my feet slightly apart in these insane heels, feeling the cool air drift between my legs. My skin is so sensitive, I can feel every bit of me. I want his hands on me, I want him in me. I keep thinking this is surreal—that I'll wake up and Cole will be gone.

He remains on the other side of the small room with his back to the door. Cole pulls out the desk chair and sits down. "Strip for me, Anna." His voice is filled with desire. I want to do what he says.

My face burns when he speaks, but Cole ignores it. Slowly, I move my hips, and arms, taking off my jewelry one piece at a time. I have no idea what I'm doing. I've never stripped before, I just move the way my body tells me, knowing how much Cole likes to watch me. After I pull off my last ring, I raise my hand over my head, while the other hand trails down my neck, through my cleavage, and to my navel.

When I reach around behind me, I unzip the dress slowly, walking toward him as I do it. I'm just out of his reach as I turn and slowly wiggle my body, making the dress slip lower and lower until it hits the floor. Cole's jaw is tense. He's straddling the chair and his arms are bulging so much that I think he might break the chair back. I'm wearing sheer black lace, and I know he can see through everything.

I look at Cole, thinking I'm done, when he says, "Keep going, Lamore. Take all of it off."

My heart pounds harder. This is so different from the teenage kisses Jesse was giving me. My heart feels like it's going to explode in my chest. Every inch of me is tingling, wanting to be touched, but Cole doesn't move. His eyes drift across my body lazily. If Cole hadn't confessed that he loves me moments ago, I wouldn't have been able to tell.

I run my hands slowly over my body, across my stomach, and over my breasts. I stretch my hands above my head and turn, sashaying my hips as I do so, and bend over to unhook my bra. I hold it out on my finger tip and let it dangle. Cole's eyes drink me in. He doesn't look at my face for a long time, and I don't want him to. I wonder what he's thinking about as he watches my breasts sway when I remove my stockings one at a time. The last thing I'm wearing is the black lace garter belt. I slip my thumbs under the edge of the fabric and sway my hips back and forth slowly, lowering the piece of fabric until it's on my ankle. I lean forward, like I'm going to kiss Cole, but I don't touch him. The muscles in his arms and chest are tense, like he can't sit there and watch for another second, but I'm not done yet.

Slowly, I bend at the waist, letting him watch from behind, as I take my impossibly high heels and slip them from my feet. When I'm done, I sigh like I'm bored and stretch, arching my back, forcing my breasts within a breath of his mouth.

Cole breathes harder. His gaze is hot, searing my body as he looks from my breasts to the place between my legs. I stand in front of him with all my weight on one foot and my hands on top of my head. I mean to sigh, again, but it turns into a moan. I want him so badly. I want him to cover my body in kisses, tie me up, and fuck me until I scream him his name, but Cole doesn't move.

I lower myself in front of him. My legs part as I go down, and I look him in the eye. My hands are next to his on the back of the chair, but neither of us touches. "Fuck me." I say the words slowly, making my lips encase each syllable.

Cole's eyes meet mine. They promise ecstasy, but he doesn't move. I do something crazy, and stay in front of him like that, knowing he can smell my need. I leave one hand on the back of the chair and dip the other below my waist. I stroke my clit a few times and push my fingers inside. I gasp as I do it, my lips parting as I sigh seductively. Cole's eyes never leave my face. He watches me as I do it and I know it's made him hard. The bulge in his jeans is all mine.

When I slip my fingers out from between my thighs, I lift them to Cole's lips and say, "Taste me." He complies and parts his lips, opening his mouth enough for me to slip my fingers inside.

Each time his mouth sucks my finger, my body reacts. My nipples become taut, and my breasts swell, aching for his touch. His lips suck on my fingers, slowly teasing each one. It makes my body throb with desire. I want those lips pulling my nipples and teasing me into ecstasy. This isn't enough. My head falls back as I pull my finger from his mouth.

Cole grins at me. It's the first confirmation he's given that he likes what I'm doing. I don't know how to have sex this way. It's not rolling around in the blankets.

It's a prolonged dance, each of us teasing the other until we are so fuck-crazy that one of us cracks. I see it in his eyes. That's what he wants. It's a battle of wills, of teasing and tasting, without touching. My God, he is so messed up, and I totally love it.

I repeat my previous movements and slip my fingers between my legs. I'm slicker this time, wetter. I close my eyes as I push one finger in at a time and pull them away covered in my damp heat. I lift my hand to Cole's mouth again and smile wickedly. "Lick my fingers one at a time."

He does as I ask. His tongue sweeps across my finger, sucking and tasting each one. His fist grabs the chair back harder, tighter with each taste. It makes me wetter and fills my body with heat. I feel the place between my legs throb as he sucks my pinky and I'm sorry it's over.

Before I can think of something else to torment him with, Cole says, "On the bed."

CHAPTER 12

I rise slowly, brushing my breast against his cheek, feeling my hard nipples sweep across his lips as he sucks in air. Cole closes his eyes for a second and I scold him, "Eyes open, Stevens. Watching is a requirement." His blue eyes are blazing when they open, like he wants to swallow me whole. My girl parts clench in response.

I climb onto the bed on all fours and crawl to the headboard. I know what he wants. I can do this for him, but when I sit down, he says, "No. Ass toward me, in the air. Stay on all fours, Lamore."

Oh my God. I blink at him, shocked, but I do as he asks. I crawl back toward him, and once I'm at the end of the bed, I turn around. I lower my head and leave my ass in the air. I'd give anything to have his hands on me, to feel his dick pressing into me right now, but I refuse to be the one to cave first.

"Rub your clit," he says from the chair. I move my hand over my sensitive flesh and instantly feel the need to have him inside me. Every inch of my body is screaming for him to pushing into me again and again. Lust races through my veins and I rub. I keep my hips still, knowing that's what he wants.

Before I know what's happened, he's behind me. I stop rubbing for a second and he slaps my ass. The sting of his hand shoots through my leg and between my thighs. I gasp. He says, "Don't stop. Don't push back, and don't come."

Grabbing the pillows around my head, I moan his name. Okay, maybe I'm ready to beg. Cole is still dressed, so whatever he's planning to do isn't going to involve fucking me senseless. I continue to rub in slow circles as Cole's hand cups my butt. Suddenly, his other hand is between my legs, pushing into me. I gasp and move, not expecting his fingers there. His other hand slaps me and I moan. I want to fall on the bed. I want to be bad so he'll do that again.

Cole pushes his finger inside me and slips in another, warning, "Don't move, Lamore." I rub my nub and keep my butt in the air.

He pushes in another finger, slowly stretching me. The sensations shooting through my body have me so close to the edge. Panting, I feel Cole moving his fingers and it feels like magic. My body wants to writhe against his hand and move with him. It takes everything I have to stay still, to let him tease me like this and not move. I whimper, clutching the sheets in my fists, but manage to stay still. When he adds his fourth finger my body responds without me telling it to and hugs his hand.

"Be still," he warns.

"I am," I breathe, with so much lust burning through me that I can't stay still for another second.

That's when Cole's fingers do something I didn't think they could. He twists his hand and suddenly it's inside of me. I scream his name, not expecting the pressure, but it fades quickly to a more tolerable level. I sigh, realizing that I'm loving it. He strokes me from within, using his entire hand. Cole moves so carefully, so gently.

My body throbs, and heat explodes from inside of me. I'm wetter than I've ever been. I don't care that this will make me blush all shades of red in the morning. I love it and I want more. My fingers move as Cole required. I keep my hand between my thighs, and my ass pushes back, making his fist slide deeper inside of me.

"Slowly, baby. I don't want to hurt you." Cole rests his other hand on my back and tries to still me. My body is so hot and wet. I tremble when he touches me, desperately wanting a release. "Gentle, slowly, Anna."

"I want more, harder. Please Cole."

"I want you to be able to walk later. I'm not done with you, yet." His voice is like liquid sex. It pours over me and I can't stay still. "Try this, sway your hips back and forth slowly."

Closing my eyes, I do as he says and sway back and forth. The rhythm builds inside of me, building hotter and hotter in my core.

Cole rocks me like that until I'm a mindless sex slave, begging for him to be with me. "Please, Cole, please be with me. I need you. I need you inside of me." I clutch the blankets harder, trying to stay still.

Cole's magic hand is still inside me. "Pinch." I do as he says, and he removes his hand, slipping one finger out of me at a time. By the time he's finished, I'm ready to hump anything. My mind has officially left my body. I fall on my stomach, facing down into the pillows. My hand slips away from my nether region. I lay there with every inch of me hypersensitive.

Cole trail kisses over my back and whispers in my ear, "I'm going to fuck you until you can't walk. You'll have a hard time sitting down tomorrow, Anna."

His words make me crazy. "I want it. Do it. I need you. I want you. Please, Cole. Please." I'm begging him for sex as he rolls me over. I look up into his dark eyes and see the man I love. He bows his head, taking my nipple between his lips and sucks. The sensation shoots warmth through my core and makes me scream his name. He's gentle at first, teasing and sucking.

When he stops, I start to beg again. "Fuck me, Cole. Please…" I arch my back and spread my legs.

He watches me, still wearing all his clothes, kneeling above me. I see the erection pressing against his pants. I have never been so jealous of a pair of jeans in my life. I want his dick on my face, in mouth, and inside me, pumping me hard. I want to wrap my legs around his waist and have him ride me until I come.

"Please," I beg again.

Cole lowers his head, his dark hair is damp, and hanging in waves. "I want to, it's just that every time you beg me, I have to make you wait longer. It's all part of the fun. If you want to be fucked senseless, stop begging me, Lamore."

I smile at him. It's one of those sex smiles that's sleepy and sensual. "You want to fuck me senseless?" There's a question in my voice.

Cole looks down at me and shakes his head. "Of course I do." His voice is deep and filled with need. I lift my hand and press it to his jeans, feeling him through the fabric.

"What happens if I strip you and jump on?"

He laughs. The sound fills my soul. I feel a connection with him. It's like we're linked, like we understand each other. And I'm glad that he likes sex this way. It's better than I imagined.

His hand slips between my legs and he pushes into me. "Oh God, you're so wet, Anna." He pushes hard one last time, forcing his finger in a far as it can go and pulls out. Raising his finger to his nose, he inhales and then wipes my damp heat across his lips.

"You smell so sweet, so perfect. Taste for yourself." He lowers his head and kisses me, allowing me to taste what he tastes. I lick his lips and swallow, kissing him deeper. I want to show him I'll do anything he wants. "That was so sexy. I had no idea you were so adventurous, Miss Vanilla."

Grinning, I say, "I lied, remember?"

"I thought you were just saying what I wanted to hear."

I shake my head gently. Cole watches my face, his blue eyes pinning me in place. "No, it's true. I'm a wanton woman, slightly slutty most of the time, insanely slutty around you." He smiles and presses a kiss to my neck, before his fingers go back to work on my bottom, pinching, pushing, and teasing me until I can't form a coherent sentence.

I pull at his shirt until it opens, ripping the buttons off the front. His chest is perfect. I pull him down on top of me and rub my naked bottom against his jeans, but he stops me. "Beg for it, Lamore."

Breathing hard, I say, "I thought you didn't want me to?"

Cole doesn't answer. Instead he slips off his jeans and boxers and tosses them on the floor. Cole straddles me, pushing his long, hard length against my stomach. He takes his hand and holds his length, rubbing it against me. He slips the tip of his long shaft along the outer edge of the sensitive flesh between my legs, moving it in slow circles, watching my face as he does it. When my hips buck, Cole pins me so I can't move.

Cole continues to torment me. I bite my lip to keep from begging him, loving the way he makes me feel. The teasing was so intense, so insane, that every inch of me wants to cry out his name.

Cole's voice pours over me when he speaks. "Come on, Anna. I know you want it. Beg me."

He presses himself into me a tiny bit, just enough so that I can feel how hard and sharp he is. When Cole pulls away, he continues to rub his thick shaft in slow circles, teasing me. He dips into me again, so shallowly that I can't stand it.

My body is corded so tight. I scream, begging him, "Please, Cole, please!"

"Please, what?"

"Please, fuck me! I need you! Please!" I keep screaming please as he slides inside of me. His fingers continue to work the hypersensitive nub and nipples, making me completely crazy.

He pushes in slowly and I gasp at his size, at how he fills me. Cole fits inside of me perfectly. Pulling out gently, Cole repeats the motion until we are clinging to each other, thrusting as hard and as fast as we can. I'm so high from lust, sex, and Cole that I don't think I'll ever come down. Every part of my body is soaring higher and higher, as he brings me closer and closer to climaxing. Cole pushes into me one last time and I shatter. Clawing his back, I scream his name and writhe against him. Cole pounds into me as I come, shattering with me, loving me completely and totally, until we are both spent. He falls breathless on top of me, his body covered in sweat, and then rolls to the side.

I blink slowly at him, like this is a dream. He's watching me with those beautiful blue eyes. "I love you, Anna Lamore."

I smile sleepily back and snuggle into his chest. "I love you, too."

CHAPTER 13

I wake the next morning in Cole's arms. His naked body is pressed to mine. I smile and slip out of bed and pad down the hall. The scent of coffee is too appealing to resist. I emerge in the kitchen wearing my old robe. Emma is at the sink and Edward is on the other side of the counter. I feel funny seeing him, but I guess I have to get used to it. He's Em's brother. He was around before we were a thing, and he'll be around after. Besides, nothing could shake this afterglow I'm rocking.

Emma hands me a cup. Her lips are curved into a devilish grin, "So, you going to tell me how you started the night with one guy and ended it screaming for a different one to fuck your brains out?"

My cheeks burn as I blush. I punch her in the arm and don't look at Edward. "Emma!" I hiss. Sheepishly, I look up at her and realize that she heard me last night. Mortified, I bury my face in my hands.

Emma shoos Edward out and the front door closes before she winks and says, "That's the way sex is supposed to be—all fireworks and begging for more."

I sip my coffee, still too shy to talk. As I wake up, the things we did last night come back to me. My cheeks are going to be stained red for the rest of my life. As if he knew I thought of him, Cole appears behind me and kisses my cheek. "Good morning, lover."

Emma watches us with an amazed expression on her face.

"What?" I ask, after laughing a girlish giggle when Cole pinches my ass. I watch him walk to the coffee pot, thinking of all the things he did to me and wondering when he can do them again.

Em shakes her head, "Nothing. It's just that I didn't see it before. You two whack-jobs are perfect for each other. Who woulda thought?" She leans her chin on her hand and stares at us like we're zoo creatures drinking coffee in her kitchen.

I swat her. "Stop it. It's not that strange."

"He's twice your age, and everything you hate. Of course it's strange. And it's wonderful, because I've never seen you so happy before. I expected you to tell me that you regretted last night, not this."

I smile and snuggle into Cole's strong arms. His chest is bare, but he has his jeans on. He looks at Anna and says, "You're the one who told her to sleep with the boy?" Cole doesn't say Jesse's name.

"Yes, and it was a good plan to get her over you." Em shrugs, "although it looks like your plan to show up and sweep her off her feet worked better." She takes a swig of coffee and puts the mug in the sink, and heads toward the shower.

When the water turns on in the bathroom, Cole pins me against the counter, holding me in place with his hips. He's dying to talk to me about last night. "Did I hurt you?"

"No," I answer, shaking my head, looking into his bottomless blue eyes. I lower my voice to a whisper, "I liked it. I think I may be a little bit of a nympho."

He grins, "That's my girl."

I spend the next hour with Cole. We talk about me and my studio, although I never get around to the fact that I quit grad school and walked away from my diploma. I don't want him to think it was because of him. I want to find the right way to tell him at the right time. We are sitting at the table and he's leaning back, one arm over the back of his chair, grinning at me. I love that smile.

"Come to my place later." He's not nervous at all. He says it like a command, like he can snap his fingers and I'll just show up. Honestly, after last night that's all it would take.

Leaning forward, I bat my eyelashes at him, "Sounds good to me." Then I straighten up in my chair as a question forms in my mind. "You still have your city apartment?"

He nods. All the witty banter deflates and is gone. "Yeah, my lawyer is trying to hold onto the studio and my home. She seems to think it's worth fighting for."

"But, you don't think it's worth fighting for?" I ask. This doesn't make sense. He worked his whole life to achieve this and for some reason he seems like he's letting Sophia win without a fight.

"It's not that easy." He leans forward. His bare chest was distracting me before, but now I can't tear my gaze from his eyes. They look haunted.

"Try me."

Cole's eyes flick up to meet mine. His lips remain pressed together, and then he decides. I see it flash across his face and his body relaxes a little bit. "If I engage Sottero in a lawsuit, it invokes my family's right to repeal use of my name." He takes a deep breath and says, "Basically, if I fight Sottero, I could lose the right to my last name."

I blink rapidly. This doesn't make sense. "I don't understand. You're basically rolling over and letting Sophia screw you so that you can keep the last name of people you can't stand? Am I missing something?"

Cole looks torn. His eyes shift from side to side and he won't look at me. His brows come together forming worry lines between his eyes. Finally, he says, "It's the only thing I have, the only thing they gave me. Cutting off my name is like losing an arm. I could do it, but it's not the kind of thing I'd volunteer for."

"So, what then, you let Sottero take everything you have so you can keep your name? Then what?"

He looks at his hands on the table. His gaze lifts to meet mine, "Then I start over. I did it before. I can do it again."

For some reason this is making me irate. He won't fight back. "You can, but you don't have to. I love you Cole, and so take this with that in mind, but why do you want to keep the last name of the man who disowned you? What's the point? It's a name. It's not who you are." His spine straightens and I know I've landed on what's holding him back. "Cole, you've forged your own path. You're not one of them. Let the name go."

"I can't. It's my past. It reminds me of who I am, what I came from, and where I'm going. I can't do it. I can't risk losing my name." Anger fills his voice. I don't know if he's trying to convince me or him.

I smile sadly at him and put my hands on top of his. "Whatever you do, I'll support you, but consider this. If things go well for us, if marriage ever becomes a path we want to go down, I would take your name without a second thought, but I'd still be Anna Lamore. I'll always been me, even when the name is gone." I smile sadly at him, wishing he could understand. "That name may have defined the first part of your life, but it doesn't have to define the second. You are who you chose to be. No piece of paper, no grouping of letters, gets to decide that part. That part is up to you."

Cole stares straight ahead and I wonder if I've said too much, if I've crossed a line, but then he reaches for my hand and pulls me around the table to sit in his lap. I'm wearing my bathrobe and he's wearing jeans. I snuggle into his chest as his hand presses my head to his shoulder. He breathes deeply and says, "Sometimes it's scary how articulate you can be. It's like you saw my past, like you were there or something."

I decide to tell him, "Remember how I told you that this stuff kinda did happen to my family?" He nods. "It happened to my mother. My Grandmother didn't like my Dad. She didn't think he was good enough. Ma ran off with him. She lost her inheritance and her name. And you know what's funny?

I never once felt sorry for Ma. Yeah, we were broke, but some things are worth more than money, ya know? And when you find them, you hold onto them no matter the cost."

Cole's silently presses a kiss to my temple. "I'm glad I have you."

"You'll always have me."

CHAPTER 14

We stay like that for a little bit. Cole has to take care of some things with his lawyer this afternoon, in preparation for the court case later this week. Before he leaves, Cole smiles at me and leans close, whispering something naughty in my ear. When he pulls back he sees my face turn bright red as I smile sheepishly.

God, I love him.

Cole leaves for his apartment after that and I have the place to myself for a few hours. I spend the day getting girlied up for later tonight. After painting my nails, I lay in a hot tub filled with bubbles, relaxing and feeling happy. Memories of last night play through my mind and I let them. The way Cole's hands felt on me, the way his eyes seared my skin, everything Cole did was exactly what I wanted. I've never had a sex dream that made me that excited. Having it happen in real life was insanely awesome. I nearly giggle thinking about what will happen later tonight.

I hope there will be more watching and teasing. And, maybe, Cole won't mind if things get a little kinky.

I smile to myself and close my eyes, leaning my head back against tub. I've never been this happy, like ever. I don't believe in fate, but that's what it seems like. Cole and I are meant to be together. Nothing can keep us apart. It scares and astounds me how much I love him. I decide that's a good thing. I relax, flicking my toes and popping bubbles occasionally, when I hear a noise. My forehead creases as I sit up a little bit and listen harder. The water dripping off my body muffles it so that I can't hear much. It's not a loud noise, so I don't know why it concerns me. It's the kind of sound a cat makes when it jumps off a couch and onto the floor. We don't have a cat though, and all the windows are shut. For a second, I think a squirrel or something got inside, but I should hear nails scraping on the floor and scampering little feet. Turning, I dangle my arms over the edge of the tub and listen. I sit so still that the only thing I can hear is my heartbeat. Maybe it's not an animal.

"Em, is that you?" I call out, but there's no answer. The feeling that I'm not alone doesn't fade. I try to ignore it, write it off as strung out nerves from the past few weeks, but when I lay back in the bubbles, I can't relax. The bathroom door is shut, but not locked. I feel a crazy urge to lock it and hide. I glance around and curse silently. I usually leave my phone on the counter, but it's in the other room. My pepper spray is in my purse, next to my bed on the floor. I don't have anything in here to protect myself with, except a curling iron and some hairspray.

Stop it, Anna! I scold myself. *There's no one here.*

On principle, I lean back and force myself to sit in the tub for another five minutes. I'm not some scared little kid who can't stay home alone. I try to close my eyes, but it creeps the hell out of me. My entire body is covered in goose bumps and I shiver like someone stepped on my grave. My throat tightens and I want to scream.

I sit up slowly, trying not to make a noise. I feel stupid for reacting this way. I locked the front door after Cole left. The windows are all locked. There's no way someone got inside. I would have heard the door split open. The sound should have been loud, but it wasn't. It was soft, like a paw striking the carpet.

Just as I decide to get up, the floorboard outside the bathroom door creaks. Instinctively, I tense. My eyes widen as my pulse jumps up into heart attack territory. I stare at the space between the bottom of the door and the floor—there's a shadow. Someone is standing there.

I don't move. I don't breathe. I sit there in the soapy water waiting for Em to knock. It has to be her. It has to be. But in my gut, I know it's not. The hairs on the back of my neck are all standing on end. Every inch of my forearms is prickled with bumps. My throat goes dry. It feels like I should scream, but I can't. I can't blink, I can't swallow. I just stare at the shadow and shiver. The sound of a hand resting on the doorknob echoes through my ears.

I'm waiting for something to make sense, waiting for Emma's voice, but it never comes.

SECRETS

Volume 5

CHAPTER 1

The metallic click of a fingernail against the doorknob sends me out of my mind. Whoever is there knows damn well that I'm in here. I force my muscles to move, to stretch, as I stand and get out of the tub. Taking the only thing that I can use as a weapon, I grab a can of hairspray, intending to spray and smack the intruder with the can, if I get that lucky.

The shadow shifts and the floorboards creak. The nails jiggle the knob once more and then are dragged down the door in one slow sweeping motion. My heart climbs into my throat as my pulse goes into heart failure territory. Every inch of my body is shivering, but it has nothing to do with being cold. I want to grab the towel and wrap it around my body, but I'm too afraid to turn away from the door. I stand there after I step out of the tub, letting the water roll off me and onto the floor. Puddles form under my feet.

My fingers clutch the can of hairspray tighter. I shake it and pull the cap off, putting it down softly on the counter. My nerves are shot to hell. I know someone is on the other side of the door and for whatever reason, they haven't opened it yet.

I reach my hand slowly toward the knob, ignoring how my fingers shake, as I lift the can of hairspray in my other hand. My breath catches in my throat. My fingers touch the cold metal knob. Every last breath of air is crushed out of me. I stare, unblinking, ready to fight whatever assailant lies on the other side.

Without warning, I yank the door open. I scream and spray, practically dancing in fear, trying to see who was waiting on the other side. After a second, I get enough of my brains back to realize that no one is at eye level. My gaze falls to the floor and I scream. A raccoon the size of a dog is hissing at me, and looks like it's ready to attack.

"Awh, what the hell, what the hell, what the hell!" I scream—almost sing—as I act without thinking and jump over it. When I leap over the thing's head, it twists to look at me. It must think I'm attacking, because it fights back. It rears up on its hind legs when I'm airborne over its body. My foot connects with the side of its head and the raccoon goes flying backwards into the bath, as I fall on the floor. It splashes in the tub, while making the most ear-piercing sounds I've ever heard. The animal clings to the side of the tub, trying to climb out, soaked. And completely pissed. I gawk at it for a second and then scramble my naked butt across the hall and go running into the living room. The insane animal runs like I'm the one attacking. It darts past me, soaking wet, and climbs our bookcases. The entire time, I'm screaming like someone is killing me.

When the knock at the door comes, I throw it open to see the eighteen-year-old high school kid that lives next door. His gaze is downcast at first and he starts to ask, "I heard yelling and wanted to make sure..." His voice cuts off as he stares at me wide-eyed.

The blast of fresh air and James' unblinking brown eyes remind me that I'm naked. I turn and snatch at a sweater that's hanging by the door and wrap it around me as quickly as possible. I slam the door shut behind James. Responding to him, I say, "No! That thing attacked me!" I'm breathing hard and can't catch my breath. My pulse won't slow and James looks like his brain melted. I blink at him as I tug the sweater tighter around my shoulders. The bottom of my ass is hanging out. I pull the sweater down, but then my boobs are hanging out. Hysterical sobs start to bubble up my throat and James seems to remember that I'm a real person.

I'm pointing at the raccoon. It's perched on top of the bookcase with its hackles raised, hissing at us. "That thing broke in. I thought….I thought," I blubber, motioning at it, "it was a—"

James finally snaps out of it. He says calmly, "It's fine, Miss Lamore. He's just spooked." James looks around and asks, "How'd he get in here?"

"I have no clue," I say, my voice shaking, my entire body billowing like a reed in a breeze. I shiver and I can't stop.

James' eyes flick between me and the massive rodent snarling on my top shelf. Its little black muzzle looks like it'll rip my face off if I step closer. James seems to decide something and steps towards it. I grab his shoulder, and scold him like he's five, "Stay away from that thing! It's crazy."

James smiles and shakes his head. "He's just spooked." Ignoring me, James steps toward the animal, making cooing sounds. The raccoon stops hissing, but still looks mortified. It doesn't move. After a moment, James turns to ask, "Do you have an apple or something?"

Nodding, I go to the kitchen to grab one and return, giving it to the kid. "Don't let it bite you. Your mother is going to kill me as it is."

James lifts the apple in the air. He uses a pocket knife to cut small pieces off. James can barely get the first few pieces to the psychotic rodent, but eventually its stomach overpowers its fear, and the giant fur ball climbs down. James opens the front door and throws the remains of the apple outside. The raccoon runs after it, and bounds down the front steps. I slam the door shut, and lean against it, splaying my fingers against the metal. I close my eyes, and tilt my head back. A major freak out is building inside of me.

James clears his throat and seems to look anywhere but at me. "It looks like he got in through the chimney." The kid points at the old fireplace and the knocked over candles that had been on the hearth. "I can tell the landlord to fix the trap, and you should board that up. I have no idea how he squeezed his way down. Usually squirrels are an issue, not raccoons."

I realize he's talking, and blink. Looking at him, I shake my head, saying, "No, I'll tell the landlord about it. You've been enough help." My face is burning. I think I was running around naked in front of this kid for way longer than I should have. I bite my bottom lip to keep it from trembling. "Thank you."

He smiles awkwardly at me and says, "It was my pleasure." James smirks and then disappears through the door. I push it shut behind him.

Then, I plaster my hands to my face and fall to the floor and cry. I cry because my emotions are so tangled that I can't tell which way is up. I thought someone was there, that the person who was following me was ready to butcher my body and hide me under the floorboards, and my only defense was a can of hairspray. I'm pathetic. No one's been following me. I let me mind runaway with brains.

CHAPTER 2

After I pull myself together, I head back to my room to change. Something feels off, but I can't tell what. I glance around and everything looks the same. *It's just the raccoon*, I think to myself. He probably got in here and moved some things. Ignoring the ice swirling in my stomach, I go to my laundry basket and heft it onto the bed. I'm still trying to find my favorite pair of panties. I dig through the basket, but they don't turn up. The dryer doesn't eat expensive panties. I'm usually so careful with them and I cannot imagine what I've done with them.

Annoyed, I suck in a gasp of air and sit down hard on the bed, letting the cold, damp, sweater I'm wearing to slouch down a little bit. The window is closed. Sunlight pours into the room through the slats in the mini blinds. I pull my hair out of the towel. I take a second to figure out what else to wear, when I look up.

Across the room is my dresser. It's old, a hand-me-down, and the top is covered in make-up, blush brushes, and lip sticks that I didn't put away. A square mirror with a chipped edge hangs above the dresser. Scrawled across the glass in bright red lipstick is a single word.

WHORE.

Every nerve in my body is already frayed. Seeing this makes me come apart. I feel myself unraveling bit by bit and I can't stop it. My heart climbs into my throat, pounding wildly. My jaw drops open as I stand and walk toward the piece of glass.

I glance around again, but no one is here. I'm alone. There is no other sign that someone has been in my room. I touch my fingers to the cold pane, touching the W with my index finger. It's written in lipstick, my favorite cherry red lipstick. It's the one that I like to wear on dates. Shaking, I yank my hand back from the mirror like I've been burned.

Someone was here. It wasn't my imagination. It wasn't a raccoon that freaked me out. Someone had stood outside my bathroom door and then come in here.

Frantic, I dress, pulling on jeans and a tank top. Fear slices me into little bits, making my mind freeze up and not work. The only thing I can think is to ask James if he saw someone leave my apartment. I walk outside, run next door, and bang on his front door too hard. His mother appears. She has bright red hair that's pulled away from her face with combs. A spattering of freckles line her pale cheeks. Her name is Gabby.

"Is James around?" I ask, breathing I little too hard.

Gabby's arms fold over her chest, "What'd he do?"

"Nothing," I shake my head. "Well, actually, he helped me get a raccoon out of my apartment earlier. I wanted to ask him if he saw something."

The square of Gabby's shoulders soften and she turns, bellowing for her son over her shoulder. "Thank God that's all you had to say. I thought you were going to tell me he knocked you up or something." She shakes her head and turns away from the door, leaving me on the porch alone.

I ignore her statement, which should have irked me, and glance up and down the street. It's filled with people. No raccoons. No one wearing a sign that says STALKER.

James appears at the door. I step back to let him out and he walks onto the porch. "What's up?" he asks, pushing his hands into his pockets. "More rodent problems?"

I shake my head. I can't look him in the eye. Something creeps down my back and suddenly, I wonder if it was him—if this kid has been the one watching me, following me. I glance up at him, and think I'm insane. James is a good kid. "I think someone was in my apartment right before you came in. Any chance you saw someone come out when I started screaming?"

James's eyes flick to the side like he's remembering. His hand touches his jaw, but he shakes his head. "No, just the scream. And your door was locked when I got there. I would have come in if it wasn't. I thought someone was hurting you."

I nod slowly, my hope sinking into my stomach. "Oh, okay." I turn to walk back. I feel the mental fog thicken. I don't know what to do.

James says, "What's the matter? Why do you think someone was inside?" I can't answer him. I don't want to admit it, because that will make it real. Right now it's an abstract idea, but if I say it… Oh God. I wrap my arms around my middle and turn off the steps. I start to walk away when James calls after me, "Hey, wait a second." He follows me back to my door, asking questions that I can't answer. Finally, he says, "Are you all right, Miss Lamore?"

No, I'm not all right, but what am I supposed to say? He's a kid. I don't want to burden him with this, and if I say another word, the tears I'm holding back will spill down my cheeks. James looks at me, waiting for an answer.

I glance at him, and force a smile. "Anna, call me Anna. I'm not that much older than you. Thanks for helping earlier." James nods slowly, like I might say something else, but I don't. He turns to walk away and I go back into my apartment.

I shut the door behind me and flip the deadbolt lock even though its daylight. My throat is so tight and dry that I can't swallow. Hysteria pushes its way through my veins. I want to get out of here and never come back.

I go back to my room, find my phone, and press in the numbers for Emma. I have to tell her even if I don't want to. If she comes back here alone and something happens to her, I'll never forgive myself. Em's voicemail picks up, since she's still at work.

I try to say it briefly, but as I'm talking, I think that I sound way too scared for what happened. So someone wrote something nasty on my mirror?

Someone was in your apartment, Anna! My mind snaps back. Shaking my head, I change the reason for the call and tell her a raccoon got in and to be careful when she gets home. I hang up and tap my phone. For some reason, I can't say it. I can't admit what happened, yet. At the same time, I don't want her walking in here at night, alone. I have to do something.

I call his number without thinking. He picks up on the second ring. "Edward?"

His voice sounds surprised, "Anna? What's going on?"

"Any chance you could come over later? I have an appointment and I don't want Em alone here."

He asks what happened. I tell him about the raccoon, and that I'm a little on edge. I don't know where it came from and the more I think about it, the less likely it seems that it came down the chimney. I wonder if the perv threw it in the apartment when he came in. I fall silent and Edward says something, but I don't respond. I blink, looking at my mirror.

"I'll head over now, okay? You sound out of sorts." I start to protest, but he's gone. I look at my phone and the screen's gone black.

I run to the kitchen and get the Windex. I scrub away the letters before anyone else can see them. I pick up my make-up and put it away, but one tube of lipstick is missing. The one that was used to write on the mirror is gone. I can't think about it. I need Cole. My mind feels like its floating in glue and doesn't want to think. My thoughts are sluggish. The shakes calm down to a small tremor. I fold my arms over my chest to hide it.

I pace the apartment, looking for signs of entry, but there is nothing. Just the hole in the old chimney. That fireplace was part of the reason why we chose this apartment. Although it doesn't work, the hearth is really cute. I stare at the busted up wood and the door buzzes.

I check to make sure it's Edward first, and then let him in. His dark hair is wet like he just took a shower. He's wearing jeans with a cream colored shirt that's tucked in neatly at his waist. He looks me over once. "What's the matter?"

His question makes me want to cry, but I can't say it. It sounds stupid. I'm crying because there was a nasty word on my mirror. I'm crying because I'm not a whore, but someone thinks I am. Biting my bottom lip, I shake my head and don't look him in the eye. "Nothing's wrong, just frazzled. That raccoon scared the hell out of me. I need to finish getting ready. Maybe you can seal up the fireplace? It looks like he came in that way." Lies, lies, lies. The pit of my stomach twists. I hate lying.

Edward nods and walks away from me, into the living room. I return to my bedroom and feel a little bit better since I'm not alone. I hear Edward moving things and then the sound of wood snapping as he cleans up.

I pull the heated flat iron through my hair, careful not to burn myself. When I finish, I look like a different person. I put on a different outfit than I originally intended. I grab a pair of black leather pants and a tight tank. I put my make-up on darker than usual, trying to hide the fear in my eyes. I don't want this to ruin my night with Cole. He already has too much on his plate, and in comparison, this seems silly.

Edward wraps his knuckles on my open door. He stands in the open doorway watching me as I apply a coat of mascara. "It's boarded up."

"Thanks," I say, trying not to stab myself in the eye. I hold the wand and glance at him, "Do you mind hanging out until Emma gets here?" I look at the mirror and carefully brush my lashes with the black goop. My hand shakes slightly. I rest it on the dresser and take a breath. Why can't I calm down?

Edward leans against the door frame and folds his arms over his chest. I can tell that he isn't going to cooperate unless he knows what's going on. "What's this about, Anna? I can tell something's bothering you. Just tell me. Maybe I can fix it." His eyes burn a hole in the side of my face. He hated it when I wore makeup when we were dating. He likes that au natural thing going on.

"I don't want to get into it now, Edward." I finish and put the make up back in my drawer. I turn to him and say, "Please, do this?"

Edward nods once, but his eyes don't leave mine. I feel a chill work its way through my body. He never had sex with me and he's watching me get dressed to have sex with someone else. The way he looks me over makes me nervous, but then again, everything makes me nervous right now. I go to brush past him, when he gently takes me by the elbow and stops me. I turn toward him.

"You'd tell me if you were in trouble, right?" he asks. "We may not be lovers anymore, but I hope you still think of me as a friend."

Breathing slowly, I feel his fingers on my arm. The contact feels wrong. I turn toward him so his fingers slip away. I want to say that we were never lovers, but I know where he wants this conversation to go, and I don't want to rehash the past. I want to get to Cole and stay with him until all my apprehension fades away.

I smile and say, "Of course, I do. Like you even need to ask that, Edward? I could have called anyone, but I called you."

I walk down the hall and grab my helmet. Strapping it under my chin quickly, I grab my keys. Edward speaks as I get ready to go. His eyes are downcast, making him look vulnerable. "You only called me because I'm Em's brother. If it was just you here, alone, we both know who you would have called." He means Cole.

"But I didn't. I called you. You're here now. And I could have called him anyway, but I didn't."

Edward looks at me funny, his head tilting slightly, "You didn't tell him?"

"Tell him what? That a rabid animal tried to take a bath with me? No. It seems more embarrassing than anything."

"What else happened, Anna? I can see it in your eyes." He steps towards me and my heart ricochets off my ribs. I can't talk about it. I squirm away from him.

"Someone got in, okay. I don't want to talk about it, but I can't let Emma come home and find a pervert in her room."

"Someone broke in?" he asks, his eyes narrowing as he shakes his head. "Anna, did you call the cops?" I shake my head. Edward looks at me, things finally clicking into place. "You didn't tell anyone, did you?"

"I told you," I bit back. It feels like I ate a can of nails. I can't stand the way he's looking at me. I can't stand the way I feel, like my heart is going to explode at any moment. Just talking about it makes everything worse. "Just watch out for Em." I turn toward the door and place my hand on the knob.

Edward shakes his head and follows me to the door. "Fine, fine," he says reassuringly. "I'll be here when Em gets home, but I've got to tell you that you're a real piece of work."

"Right back at ya."

CHAPTER 3

I pick at a tomato on my plate. We're sitting in Cole's apartment. When I arrived he greeted me with the sexiest grin I've ever seen. "I didn't think you were into that," he says, eyeing my outfit.

I smile back, but I'm still nervous. When I pulled my bike out the parking garage, I got spooked. My neck prickled and I'm to the point that I'm ready to jump out of my skin. The thing is, I don't know how to tell him. Cole is great, and it's not that he won't understand, it's more that he'll over-react. Saying what happened out loud makes the whole stalker thing real, although if I think about it at all, the lipstick letters on my mirror already did that.

We're sitting at his table, which is made from some exotic dark wood. I lean back in my chair and look up at him. "I had something weird happen today."

"Tell me about it." Cole grins at me. He expects a wild story and he's going to get one. My stomach twists as I think about telling him and a lump forms in my throat. The smile slips from his lips. Cole leans forward and takes my hand. "What's wrong?" It's a command. I can see it in his eyes.

I don't want to wriggle out of telling him, but it feels wrong to tell. Maybe I'm stupid, yes, that's it—I'm a class A, completely insane idiot. I have to tell someone. Worry pinches my throat tight. What if he doesn't believe me? What if he thinks it's nothing? *Stop it, Anna! Just tell him.* I suck in air and dive into my story starting with the bathtub and ending with James flushing the raccoon out the front door. Cole's eyes widen as I tell it, but he doesn't laugh. He hears my voice hitch and become smaller, more strained as the story goes on.

"And then what?" His blue eyes lock with mine.

I can't look away and the feeling climbing up my throat won't subdue. It's raw fear. I try to keep it out of my voice when I speak, but I can't. I lick my lips and take a breath. "When I got to my room, I noticed that someone *had* been there. They took my lipstick and wrote something on my mirror."

Cole's body tenses. Every muscle in his strong arms twitches. He's no longer eating. Cole looks at me, his lips parted slightly. His fingers ball into fists. He's fighting back the reaction he wants to have. Fury. "What was written on the mirror, Anna?" His voice is soft. It's the opposite of his body.

My lips are sealed shut. I can't speak. My voice won't come. My lips won't move. Cole comes around the table and pulls me into his arms. I start to sob into his shoulder. He pats my head and I manage to blubber out, "Whore. He wrote 'whore' on my mirror with my lipstick. The tube is gone. He took it."

Cole says soothing things that don't register. He holds me tight and the crushing fear that I felt all day cracks and falls away. He pulls me from the embrace and holds me at arms-length for a moment, trying to see my face. Looking into my eyes, he says, "You didn't see anyone? Hear anyone?"

I shake my head. "No. At first, I thought there was a person at the bathroom door, not an animal. I saw shadows and thought they were feet. Then I open the door and it's a raccoon. I was convinced that I was going nuts, that it was just an animal in the apartment, until I saw the mirror." My eyes are glassy, but I've stopped crying. "I asked James if he saw anyone leave, but he didn't."

"The apartment was locked up?"

I nod. "It's not like it's Ft. Knox, but I'm pretty sure everything was locked."

"Is there anything else missing? Or out of place?"

I nod slowly, feeling the realization creepy up my throat like bony fingers. "A pair of panties is missing."

Cole just stares at me. His nostrils flare and he blinks. "When? When did all this start?"

I pull away from him and slip off his lap. I have to stand. Nervous energy floods my body and I start to pace. His eyes trail my movements and his arms fold over his chest. I try to swallow again, but it hurts. My mouth is too dry. "I don't know. I felt like someone was following me, but there was never anyone there. And then I thought it was you—"

"Me?" he says shocked.

"Yeah, you said you were following me around, trying to talk to me. I assumed that you were following me."

"Anna, I never followed you like that." Cole runs his hands through his hair. "Shit. I can't believe someone is doing this to you. I went to places where I knew you'd be. I never stalked you. This is a fucking stalker and he's gotten into your house." Cole pauses a beat and lifts his eyes to meet mine. "Does Emma know?"

I nod. "Yes, well, sort of. I felt weird telling anyone. I mean all that stuff in the beginning was just a feeling. No one was there, and I figured that I just lost the panties, but then today..." I shake my head and my eyes sting with tears. I blink them away and rub my eyes with my hand. "I called her brother over so she wasn't there alone after dark. I left her a message on her phone. I haven't had a chance to talk to her yet."

"You told her brother?" Cole asks. "You told him that someone was in the apartment?" I nod again, trying to remember exactly what I said. The day had that white haze over it, like it was a memory from a long time ago. The part with the bathtub and the raccoon is vivid, but the rest grows fuzzy fast.

"I told him that it wasn't safe for Em there alone. I asked him to stay the night and didn't really say why. He promised he'd stay."

"You need to tell her," Cole says. His eyes lock with mine. I'm standing in front of him with my arms wrapped tightly around my middle. I hate feeling like this and talking about it makes it worse. Cole asks, "Who do you think it is?"

"I don't know," I answer, and close my eyes. I press my fingers to my temples and glance up at Cole as I speak. "For a second I thought it was James. He was there when I was screaming, but he was on the other side of the door. James doesn't have a key and the door was locked. If he got in, I don't know how.

"And that doesn't make any sense anyway. The kid's in school. He'd have to be cutting and ditching curfew to show up at the times when I've felt spooked." Goosebumps spring up on my arms. I try to rub them away. Cole steps toward me and pulls me to his chest.

"It'll be okay. You stay with me," he kisses my head and holds me.

"Cole, I can't." I look up at him, not wanting to mention it. "Sottero wants to take everything you have. If you don't fight back… you'll have no home. Besides, whoever this is will just come at me when you aren't around. I'd file a police report, but what am I supposed to say? I don't have a description or a name. I don't have anything."

Cole looks like I kicked him in the stomach when I mention the lawsuit. He turns from me and sits down at the table. He works his jaw and is quiet for a while. I walk to the kitchen and grab a bottle of wine and open it. After pouring two glasses, I return to the table and offer him one. I chug mine like it's a shot.

Cole looks at me and I know something's changed. His back straightens. Cole stands and says, "I need to make a phone call."

Cole disappears from the room. I hear his voice, but can't hear his words. I don't know what he's doing or who he's talking to. Tonight was supposed to be a night of passion, a night of sticky sex, and sultry smiles. Instead, I'm spending it recanting how my day went to hell and that some nutjob thinks I'm a whore. I down another glass of wine and lean my head on my hand. In a moment, my body feels warm as the wine works its way through me. The fear that's been coiled in my throat all day lessens.

Cole reappears and drops his phone on the table. He walks toward me and never takes his eyes off my face. Cole slips his hands around my waist and pulls me to my feet. Running his fingers through my straight hair he says, "I'll protect you. I promise. Nothing will happen to you."

I nod. He watches me for a moment and something shifts. I feel safe with him. I know I am. It doesn't make sense to be so scared and then feel so frisky, but I do. I want him. I want his hands on me. I want him to hold me. I don't care what kind of kinky stuff he had planned for tonight. I want to show him that I love him. I want things to be soft.

I thread my fingers through his hair. They graze across his cheek as I do, feeling the stubble under my skin. He leans his head toward mine, and I feel his mouth on my lips. Cole kisses me lightly, like I might break. His tongue sweeps across the seam of my lips and I part them for him. The kiss deepens. It becomes hotter and possessive. Cole's hands slip over my body, pulling me to him, claiming that I'm his.

I moan into his mouth and press my chest against him. His hands are on my back, drifting lower, feeling my curves. When he grabs on tight and pulls me up, I crash into his mouth and the kiss changes. Instead of being light, his tongue strokes my mouth like he'll die if I pull away. His lips smash down on mine. His fingers tangle in my hair and pull gently, tilting my head back and opening my mouth more. When his lips drift to my neck, I can't stand. I feel my knees give out and he catches me in his arms.

Without a word, Cole sweeps me up in his arms and carries me to his bed. He places me gently on the covers and looks down at me. "You're amazing, you know that?"

I smile softly at him. "What happens if I say that I'm not so sure?" I feel uncertain, like my life is spinning out of control. I don't know who I am any more. I don't understand why someone is stalking me or what they want, and the red letters burn behind my eyelids every time I blink. I pretend that it didn't bother me, at least I try, but there's a twisting inside my stomach that doesn't quiet. It chokes me. I tangle my fingers together as I look at him.

Cole sees the worry in my eyes. He winks at me and turns away like he's decided something. Curiosity flames through me and I sit up. Cole takes something from behind his dresser. They're large prints in a black Le Femme box. "These will change your mind." His voice is soft.

"What is that?" I cross my leather-clad legs on the bed and sit up. Cole walks back to the bed and sits across from me.

He hands me the box and says, "See for yourself."

I lift the lid and set it down on the bed next to me. Tissue paper is folded over the contents. I push the thin papers back, parting the thin sheets until I see the photographs. My hand stills as I recognize the model. I glance up at him, "These are from that day…?"

He nods. "Yes, and if there is any doubt in your mind about how incredibly seductive, alluring, or sexual you are after seeing those, well, I'll just have to take more." Cole grins wickedly.

I react wrong. I feel it coming and I know it's the wrong response, but I can't stop it. Instead of feeling better, tears well up in my eyes and spill down my cheeks. I suck in air so fast that I choke. Cole shifts so that he's sitting next to me, his gaze rapidly sweeping my face trying to figure out why I'm crying. I hold the picture in my hands, trembling. It's beautiful. The trail of crystals that draped my body, the way he posed me, the light and shadows…

I rasp in a jagged breath and try to stop acting like a lunatic. "These are beautiful."

Cole takes his hand and rubs my back as I look at the portrait. He kisses a tear from my cheek and whispers in my ear, "You're amazing, Anna. You stun me into silence, and it's not just because of any one thing. It's you. It's who you are, everything from your sharp wit, to your amazing eyes, to the way you wear those pants like they're jeans—which they're not by the way—you're the best thing that's ever happened to me." His eyes are on the side of my face as he speaks. I can't turn. I'll explode into a ball of tears. As he says these things, a smile spreads across my face.

I look at one image, and then the next. I say nothing for a while, just gazing at his creations, seeing me how he sees me. The images that were painted with light showcase every curve. The stones glitter in the darkness, giving the impression of my curves that remain unseen. A pale violet light rims my waist and hips, trailing up to my breasts, and spilling onto my neck. My face is turned toward the light source, and unlike his old work, my eyes are prominent. There's a look on my face that I wish I could conceal. It makes me feel completely naked, as if being stripped wasn't enough. I feel like he's captured my soul.

"It's perfect," I finally say.

Cole is watching me, his blue gaze never leaving my face. He drinks in the look in my eyes, the way they devour the picture and take in every tiny detail. "So are you." He leans in and kisses my cheek. It's a gentle kiss, chaste even.

I smile in response when he pulls away. Glancing at him, I say, "I'm glad we met. I'm glad you interviewed me and not someone else. I'm glad I wore that hideous outfit and insulted you. If I hadn't, none of this would have happened. I—"

Cole doesn't let me say anything else. He takes the box from my hands and sets it on the dresser before leaning in and pressing his lips to mine.

The last few times we were together, everything felt hot to the point of combustion. This time it is different. Cole's kiss is soft and perfect. He makes no attempt to watch me the way he did last time. He stays with me, kissing my mouth like he's searching for something, like I'm the one he needs, the one he wants. His hands slip over my body, feeling each curve as we lay back on his bed. I reach my arms around his neck and tangle my fingers in his hair, losing myself in the kiss. It's a good kiss. There's no other word for it. There are kisses that burn with lust and then there are others that are sweet. This one is both. It burns, but it doesn't make me crazy. Lust doesn't surge through my veins, something else does, but I'm not entirely certain what.

I let the kiss linger and Cole is no hurry. His tongue seeks mine, playing, feeling the curves of my mouth. He tastes me like he could never get enough. Cole's hand lingers at my waist as the other finds my cheek. He brushes the back of his fingers across my jaw and down my neck as the kiss continues. I can barely breathe. My body is warm, yearning for his. I want to take Cole in my arms and never let go. The world around me vanishes. Every worry that occupied my mind disappears until there is only the two of us, lost in this kiss.

Cole slowly moves on top of me, leaning all his weight on one arm. His fingers play in my hair and his other hand slips beneath my shirt. He splays his fingers on my stomach and slides his hand around to the small of my back, pulling me closer to him. I feel the heat of the kiss, the desire building between us. That attraction has always been there, but this is more.

Breathing hard, Cole breaks the kiss and looks down at me. "I love you, Anna."

His blue gaze makes me feel like I'm flying. I smile widely and say, "I love you, too." We continue kissing, maintaining a slow pace. Cole kisses me, enjoying my mouth before moving onto my neck. His teeth nip my ear, before pressing gentle kisses along the side of my neck.

I pull him to me, trying to flip him over so that I can spoil him with affection, but he won't let me. "No, Anna. I want you like this. I want to show you how much I love you." The way he says it sounds like a question, like he's asking me if it's all right.

My heart is pounding. The way Cole looks at me is wonderful and terrifying. I'm not sure what he means, but I want to find out. I tuck my hair behind my ear. "All right." I hear my voice and am surprised at how frightened I sound. This is different for us. Lust burns hot and bright, but this—whatever this is—feels like forever. It feels like love, the kind that doesn't ever fade away.

Cole's eyes follow my fingers as I move the curl. The corners of his mouth pull up. He looks down at me and asks, "You only do that when you're nervous."

"Maybe," I confess.

Pressing a kiss to my neck, he asks, "What's making you nervous, Miss Lamore?"

My eyes close as his lips press to my neck. God, his mouth is so warm. I enjoy the sensation. "Well, my boss says he wants me…" my lips twitch. I'm trying to smile, but I can't. I'm scared and unsure why. My eyes lock with his. I tell him the truth. "I can do the lust thing, Cole, but I've never done the love thing." My pulse pounds harder, until the only sound I can hear is my heart racing. I can't swallow. I can't breathe. I don't know what I expect him to do. Confessing that I've never been in love before doesn't seem that intimate, but now, at this moment, it does. I wonder if he knows what I feel. The crash of ecstasy and fear are twisting together inside my chest. My jaw locks as I press my lips together.

Cole is quiet for a moment. He looks at me, his eyes slipping over my face. Finally, he says, "At one time, I thought love was so devastating when it was over, that it wasn't worth the risk. I don't think that anymore. I think love's worth chancing the agony that things may go wrong. Besides, I don't want to live like that, always wondering what I could have had, if we would have been happy. I've done that. It's a lonely life, Anna.

"There are only a few things I'm certain of. I have here and now. I have today. I had thought that there were no promises in this life, nothing to grab hold of—I used to think that nothing was forever, Anna. But this, me and you, it's worth the risk. You're already part of me, and it's not that I can't let you go, it's that I don't want to. I love you, Anna. You're worth the risk." He caresses my cheek with the back of his hand. His gaze doesn't stray from my eyes.

"What made you change your mind?" I lean into his hand. His touch makes my stomach fall away. I feel like I'm flying or falling—or both. The moment feels surreal, like it's passing in slow motion.

Cole's eyes lower. Answering, he breathes, "You. You changed my mind. You changed my world…"

Taking Cole's face in my hands, I pull his lips down to meet mine. I kiss him. It feels like my life is in a free fall. I don't know which way is up and at that moment, I don't care. I feel *found* in Cole's arms. I feel whole. The feminazi inside my mind is screaming at me, but I ignore her. Relying on another person isn't weakness. Wanting a man doesn't mean I'm not a strong woman. It means I have a heart. It means I can love someone and for some crazy-ass reason, he loves me back.

We spend the night together in his bed, neither of us sleeping. Cole's hands study every inch of my body. His lips follow, and he touches me, kisses me, and learns my body. I lay on my back as he strips my clothes away, leaving me naked. His eyes rake my figure, but he quickly moves on to caresses and kisses so soft and adoring that I'm floating in sheer bliss. My skin grows hot as my insides twist with each gentle touch. Every kiss is like a flame licking my skin. I feel Cole slide between my legs. He touches lightly before pushing his hard length inside of me. I moan and dig my nails into his back. I feel dizzy and giddy. There's a smile on my face and no matter how hard I try, I can't hide it.

Cole's hands tangle in my hair. He whispers in my ear, kissing my neck, as he rocks into me over and over again. I wrap my legs around his waist and pull him in farther. We stay like that, in that euphoric state for hours, until Cole finally pushes me over the edge. My body shatters as I come. Every inch of me is hypersensitive. I feel him inside me and want him there. My nails claw his back as he finds his release, saying my name. He moves to pull away, but I hold him there.

Looking into his eyes, I say, "I love you, Cole."

Our sweat covered bodies are tangled together. He lays on top of me as I stroke his hair. My heart is pounding and I can't stop smiling. My messed up cave-man has a soft side.

CHAPTER 4

The night passes slowly. When I try to fall asleep, I find that I can't. The red letters are there when I close my eyes, sending my pulse into panic mode. I refuse to be thrown out of my home, but this stalker has done more than that—he's gotten into my head. Fear courses through me and I shudder. Cole lays next to me, dozing on and off. He feels me move and tightens his arms around me, hugging me to his chest.

I hear his heartbeat, slow and steady. The warmth of his body pressed to mine is perfect. We stay like that for a while. Eventually Cole kisses my brow and says, "I've been thinking about what you said, about my name."

Surprise fills me. I didn't expect him to decide anything. Actually, I realized his name is important to him. It is the only part of a life that he no longer has. I guessed that his last name is like a security blanket, that it gives him comfort in some way that I don't understand. I can't rip that away from him. It makes sense. It's also the only reason I can fathom as to why he's letting Sottero walk all over him and steal his fortune.

I don't lift my head from his chest. I lay in his arms and feel his smooth skin under my fingers. "Oh?"

"I think you might be right—that it isn't worth holding onto. Not anymore. I know who I am. I don't need a name to tell me that."

Worry trickles through me. "Cole, I just want you to be happy. I'm not sure if you should listen to me on that. I really don't know anything about it or what you went through… I just," I chose my words carefully, "didn't understand before, but I think I do now."

"You think so?" He shifts me in his arms and looks down at me. His eyebrows lift into his hair. A crooked grin lines his sleepy face. I nod. "So, tell me, then."

I squirm in his arms, but he holds me tighter, not letting me wiggle away like I want to. I relax and his grip loosens. "Maybe I don't know my ass from my elbow, but it seems like that name means a lot to you. It anchors you, gives you security about who you are and who you want to be. I get why you want to keep it. I shouldn't have said anything. I was thoughtless. You should ignore me. I haven't lived your life. I have no idea about anything. I showed up in a tutu for godsakes. I seriously doubt you should be taking advice from a life-size Skittle."

I feel Cole smile against the top of my head as I speak. He trails his finger along my arm. "I like your ass, and your elbows are lovely, Lamore. And—a secret between you and me—I actually think you know more than you let on. You see more than you let on, Anna. I love you. I want to hear what you think, and on this, you were right the other day.

"That damn name carries a ton of baggage with it. Every time someone says Mr. Stevens, I think of my father. I wonder if I'm like him, even though I've tried so hard not to be. I thought I needed the reminder. I thought it guided me and helped shape me into who I am, and maybe it did, but I was thinking and realized that I don't need it any more. I know who I am, with or without the name. And I want you, without all the crap that the Stevens name brings with it."

I turn on my side. There's a pillow under Cole's arm that is behind my head. I don't know what he's saying. I look at him and our eyes meet. "Cole?" My voice is light. The moment feels fragile. I watch Cole's face, wondering what he's thinking and can't understand why he's suddenly silent.

His eyes lower, and when he lifts them again, they are completely vulnerable. "Anna Lamore, you are the best thing that ever happened to me. I want to make you happy for the rest of your life. I want to hold you in my arms every night and see your face every morning. I want you to be mine and I want to be yours." His eyes don't leave mine. "Will you marry me, Anna?"

Shock hits me in the head like a pail of ice water. "What?" I eloquently blurt out. I push my naked body up on his bed and look down at him. Sheets cover his lower body. Cole folds his hands behind his head and smiles at me.

"Are you really that surprised, Miss Lamore? Did you really think that I only took you into my bed, but managed to keep you out of my heart?"

My jaw is hanging open. I can't breathe. I never expected a proposal. My lips press into a thin line and then lift into a smile. It's like my face can't decide if I should laugh or cry. "Are you serious?" I pull the sheet up, covering my chest.

Cole pushes up onto his side. He reaches for the sheet and gently pulls it from my fingers. His eyes drink in my curves, before his gaze meets mine. "Completely. I can't resist you, and if you say no, I'm afraid that I'll have to keep asking until you say yes." He leans over me and presses a kiss to my neck. His lips are so warm. I enjoy the sensation for a moment before my mind starts yelling at me to pay attention.

"Until I say yes?"

"Mmmmh," he says, pressing another kiss to the back of my neck.

I can't think. I don't want to think. I want to say yes, but fear won't leave me alone. I try to be light, to joke to avoid answering right then. I shudder as his kiss presses to the back of my neck, right at that lust-inducing spot. "I might need some convincing," I say in breathy voice.

"I'd be happy to." Cole doesn't press me. Instead he continues his kisses down my back. I slip face-down on the bed and turn my head so I can see him. I clutch the pillow under my head as Cole lights my body on fire. His touch is electric, his kisses drip with sensuality. I can't resist him. I know I can't, and I don't know why I feel like I have to. I give in to his caresses, to his hands. He loves me and shows me. It's more than I thought I'd ever get. I thought I'd have to settle for someone. Cole isn't settling. He's perfect, and yet, I notice that I couldn't say yes to his proposal.

The next morning Cole dresses quickly. He has a meeting with his lawyer and I have to show up for the hearing later in the afternoon. I don't want to go, but it's a necessary evil.

Cole looks beautiful in his suit. The color is so dark that it makes his eyes look like sapphires. He straightens his tie as he looks at me sitting on his blue chair, with my robe barely covering me. "You make it impossible to leave, you know that, right?"

I pull my knees to my chest and see his eyes follow the sweep of my bare hip. "I know." My heart is racing at the thought of being alone. I'm afraid of the stalker. I wonder if he's waiting for me, watching me. I don't want Cole to leave, but I try to banish the crazy thoughts before they make me nuts. I'm not living my life like this. A bolt of determination strikes me and I try to tempt Cole into staying a little longer.

A wicked grin crosses my lips. I stand and allow the robe to fall to the floor. Walking toward Cole, I wear nothing but a smile. Cole freezes. His eyes watch me move toward him. Tension lines his shoulders and spills down into his arms. God, that suit makes him look gorgeous. When I reach Cole, I thread my arms around his neck and gently kiss his lips. The feel soft and warm, completely perfect.

Cole sucks in a breath and slowly releases it after the kiss. His eyes close as he does it. I step away, loving the effect I have on him. Cole smiles for a moment and then his eyes open. He looks me over and says, "I want you wearing that exact same outfit next time I see you." Cole grins, winking at me before he starts to gather his things and move towards the front door.

I laugh, following him. "I'm sure Sottero will appreciate a buck-naked Anna at court."

"I know I would," he says, not looking back at me.

I fold my arms across my chest and lean against the doorway. "Maybe I shouldn't come today. I mean, she's just going to try and use me against you—to prove whatever whacked point she's trying to make."

Cole turns and meets my gaze. He only looks at my face, but I can tell he's fighting the urge to let his eyes dip lower. "There's no way for your testimony to support her claim since you weren't there."

"But you were, and it doesn't seem to matter what you say." I wish I could make this go away. I can't stand watching this happen to him.

"I haven't been fighting this, Anna, but now I intend to. I'm not letting it slide. I'm changing my name before my father's attorney forces me to and I'm fighting back." He looks at me for a moment. At first I think he's asking me if it's okay, and then I realize that he's telling me. There's no question in his voice. He knows what he wants. He knows what he's doing and he's informing me of his intentions.

"There are some things that are worth fighting for." He winks at me, repeating my words back to me. I nod and smile softly. I don't want him to get hurt, but I think he's made the right choice. I can't hide it. Cole smiles at me. "Don't do anything stupid. Keep the doors locked until you leave. Get in and out of your apartment as fast as possible. Stay out of alleys and abandoned buildings. I'll see you this afternoon."

"Cole," my voice catches. I step toward him, hesitant. "Do you think he can get in here?"

"No, baby," he shakes his head. "The doorman doesn't let random people in, and your bike should be fine in the garage. No one can get in there either without the guard letting them through. There are a ton of cameras down there, too. Are you going to ride your motorcycle in later?"

"I don't know. Which is better? The bike or the train? I could end up in a car alone.

With the bike, I'll end up in the parking garage alone. I can park the bike on the street when I get there." Goosebumps prickle my arms as I speak. I hate this. I'm altering my life because of this douche. I rub the bumps away, but the creeped-out feeling still lingers on my skin.

"Take your bike. I'll keep an eye out for you, and you better believe that if you're a second late, that I'll come looking for you." I smile. Cole crosses the room and pulls me to his chest. He presses a kiss firmly to the top of my head and says, "No one will hurt you."

I nod as he pulls away. I watch Cole walk out the door and my pulse ticks up a notch. It nearly explodes when I shower. The scene from Psycho keeps playing through my mind in an endless loop. I watch the suds swirl down the drain and remember the ribbons of blood on the bottom of the tub from that movie. By the time I get out of the shower, I've nearly peed myself twice.

"Stop it, Anna." I say out loud, just to prove that I'm alone. The back of my neck won't stop prickling. It feels like a ghost is breathing down my beck. I go to Cole's stereo and turn it on, hoping that the noise will help. I blow out my damp hair and clip it back to the nape of my neck. I want to dress, but there's nothing here. I'd already discussed this with Cole. Emma should be home and as long as she is, I'm going to grab my suit. If not, the backup plan is to buy another one. Maybe it's a stupid time to be cheap, but I really want my suit. It fits me right and there's no way I'm going to find another one in a few hours and make it to the courthouse on time.

I call Emma, hoping she's home. She picks up on the third ring. "Anna, are you okay?"

"Yeah, Em. I'm fine. I'm at Cole's. Are you okay?"

"God!" she spews swear words at me like a drunk gremlin and then asks, "What the hell happened? Edward said an animal got in, and then James came by to make sure you were okay. He said you asked him if he saw someone leaving the apartment? Anna, what the hell is going on?"

"Edward didn't tell you?"

"Tell me what?"

Rage shot through me. I clenched my free hand and wanted to hurl the phone at the wall. "That someone got in yesterday? He was supposed to stay with you last night. Did he—"

She cut me off, "Yeah, he stayed, but he didn't tell me crap. He just said that he wasn't leaving. The ass slept on the couch all night. He was really tense, so of course, we fought like crazy. Then, when I tried to call you, you didn't answer." Em breathes, trying to steady her tirade. "How'd you know someone got inside?"

My veins fill with ice when she asks the question. The red letters flash in my mind. I steady my voice. "Because they wrote something on my mirror with my lipstick—'whore.'" My voice is too soft. I can't hide how much this is freaking me out. Emma is silent. I expected that she'd be spewing foul words, but she says nothing. "Em?"

"Sorry, Anna. Oh my God. I didn't know." She coughs and clears her through. It sounds normal when she speaks again. "Do you think it was a fluke? Like a random break-in or something."

I want to say yes, but I know it's not. I can feel it. "No, it's not random. I've felt like I've been watched for a while now. Some nights, I would have sworn someone was following me, but I never saw anyone. Then this happened. Anyway, I wanted you to know. Our apartment isn't safe. Neither of us should be there alone."

"Edward said the same thing. He wouldn't leave. I thought he was just being an ass. Damn, Anna. I had no idea. What do we do?"

"I don't know. I told you, Cole, and Edward. I guess we just hope that the guy stops. It's not like I can get a restraining order or something. There's nothing to report."

"There was no broken glass?"

"No."

"How'd he get in?"

I shrug and shift the phone to my other ear. "I don't know. I'm assuming he got in the same way the raccoon did—through the chimney—but I don't know." That doesn't make sense, but then again, neither does anything else. "I need to run by there to grab a suit. I have to appear for Sottero later today and I don't have anything here. Any chance that you're still home?"

"Yeah. I'm still here. Come by and get what you need. I'll wait for you."

I pull on my clothes and race down to the garage to grab my bike. When I enter the parking lot, I look around longer than usual and then try my best not to run. My skin prickles again and my entire body is covered in goosebumps. No one is there. Anger rushes through me, but it's not enough to choke back the fear.

I have the key in hand and have already strapped my helmet onto my head. As I get closer, I see something on the seat. The seat is black, but there is something on top of the leather that looks like a black tissue. When I'm a foot from the bike, I recognize what it is. My spine goes straight and my heart jerks to a stop. My eyes go wide as I stare at my favorite pair of black panties that went missing. They are tucked under the seat strap. I'm so creeped-out that I don't want to sit on the bike. I glance at the guard in the booth and then back at my bike, at the panties. Someone took them. Someone found me here and put them on my bike, on the seat, where I'd be sure to find them. My heart is racing like a scared rabbit. The trembling in my hands is spilling into my stomach in icy waves. I feel sick, like I'm going to puke. Anger bubbles into the mix. I'm angry that someone is doing this to me. I'm angry that he got so close and I didn't notice. How could I be so stupid?

I refuse to let this ass get to me. I whip my head around, feeling the blood coursing through me like a bottle of shaken champagne. I feel wired. If he steps out of the shadows now, I'll rip his eyes out with my nails. My muscles tense, waiting for someone to appear, but no one materializes. No one claims the fear that ignited within me. I'm alone.

I take the panties and stuff them under the seat. I kickstart the bike and peel out, leaving skid marks behind. I speed all the way home.

CHAPTER 5

By the time I get home, I'm calm again. I shove my key into the lock, ready to twist it open when Emma throws the door open and pulls me into her arms. She bear hugs me until my ribs are breaking. I can't breathe and try to pry her off of me.

Edward is sitting on the couch. He stands and walks over. Resting a hand on Em's shoulder, he says, "She needs to breathe, Emma. Let go. She's fine."

Emma releases me and looks me over. She tucks a strand of dark hair behind her ear, and acts like she doesn't believe that I'm fine. "Let me look at you. Did something else happen?"

Damn it, Emma. How does she do that?

"No," I lie and walk into the kitchen. My brain asks, *Why are you lying*, but I don't want to think about it. I don't want any of this. I shake my head and smile lamely. "I'm just frazzled. Some ass in a truck almost ran me over."

"How can you be so calm about this?" Emma scolds. "What if it was the stalker?"

Uhm, I'm freaking out inside. Wow, did she read me wrong. "I'm not calm. I'm freaked, okay?" I turn to her and snap. I don't mean to. I shake my head and close my eyes. "I'm sorry, Em. I'm just kind of freaked. I'm going to stay at Cole's for a while, until this blows over. I just wanted to be sure that someone could stay here with you. Or maybe you should crash at your mom's for a while."

She laughs at that. "Yeah right." Okay, maybe that's a bad idea. Em and her Mom fight like rabid cats. "No, I'll stay here. Edward will stick around for a while, right?" He nods. While we're speaking, Edward crosses the room and slips himself up onto the kitchen counter. "I should be okay as long as I'm not alone. And you staying with Cole for a little while is a good idea."

I nod and look at my hands. My fingers twist together. I glance up at her. "Actually, it might be longer than a little while." I flick my eyes up to meet Em's.

"He asked you to move in with him?" she asks, mouth hanging open. A wide grin spreads across her face. I glance at Edward, not wanting to say it in front of him, but he's going to be around for a while.

I shake my head. "He asked me to marry him, Emma."

"Holy shit! What'd you say?" Emma's eyes are so big that they look like saucers. She practically bounces up and down as she grabs my hands. She thinks I said yes, but I didn't and I don't know why.

I do my best to treat Edward like a person, but I can't meet his gaze. I look back at Emma. "I didn't answer. I didn't know what to say."

Emma drops my hands. She's shocked into silence and stares at me with her mouth in an O. Two seconds later she shakes her head and looks at the clock. "I've got to get to work, but we *are* talking about this later."

"Definitely." Things feel normal for a second. Emma hugs me again, quickly this time. Her phone rings. Edward lifts it off the counter top and hands it to her.

"It's work." He says.

"Damn it," she mutters, and says, "Hello." Emma takes the phone into the other room. Her voice carries through the apartment for a moment until she closes the door.

Edward and I are alone. He sits on the counter, his spine ram-rod straight. "So, a proposal?"

I nod, "Yeah, is that too weird? I didn't know if I should mention it in front of you." *I don't want to hurt you more than I already have.*

Edward smiles at me and shakes his head. "Nah, don't be silly. You and Emma are best friends. Tell her anything you want. Besides, I'm not real keen on leaving her alone right now, not with someone breaking-in and all that."

"You're a good brother, Edward. Emma's lucky to have you." I say the words and mean them. He's a good brother.

Emma bursts through her door. She pulled on clothes, but doesn't have that polished look she's normally sporting. Em grabs an apple from the fridge. "That ass. He wants me there *now*. Thanks for telling me." Emma says to herself, muttering. She looks at me, "I'm sorry. I didn't mean to run out on you like this. I should have had another forty minutes. I can't believe Stacy thinks he can call me in like this."

"Looks like he can," Edward says, and Em shoots him a look that says *drop dead.*

"Stay with Anna until she leaves, okay? I'll be home at five. Let's have dinner, Edward. And I'll catch up with you later tonight, Anna. Call me when you have a second. I want to hear about Sottero and Cole. I can't believe he proposed!" She bites the apple and runs for the door, practically tripping over her feet. Turning back, she says, "I can't believe you said no!"

"I didn't say 'no,'" I reply, but Em is already gone.

When the door slams, I look at Edward. "Mind hanging out for a few more minutes?"

"No, that's fine." He tilts his head toward me. "There's something black on the back of your arm."

I twist my arm and try to look. There's a thin black line that runs from my upper arm to my elbow. It looks like tar. I press my finger against it and it smears. "Shit. What is that?" I look at my fingers.

Edward slips off the counter and comes over. He examines the black goo, but doesn't touch. "It looks like grease or something.

You want me to try and wipe it off with a sponge?"

"Nah, I know how much dirt freaks you out. I'll do it." But as I do it, I smear the black goo across my arm. It doesn't come off and now there are black streaks of water running down my arm and into my shirt.

Edward watches me for a second before snatching the sponge, "I swear, Anna. It's a wonder you're—" he stops before he says it. "Just stay still." He puts warm water on the sponge and uses dish soap to get the grease off my arm. When he's done, he throws the sponge in the sink and says, "Take a shower to get the rest of it washed off."

I glance at the time. I need to get to the courthouse early. Cole's lawyer is supposed to go over stuff with me. "Damn it." I look at the gray schmutz on my arm. He's right. I dart to my room.

Edward returns to the couch and flips on the TV. It's blaringly loud, like he's totally deaf, which is weird, but I'm in too much of a hurry to think about it. I strip quickly and pull on a robe. Racing to the bathroom, I turn on the water and scrub my arms until they're raw.

When I return to my room, I'm dripping wet. I leave a path of puddles on the floor. My robe clings to me because my skin is still damp. I towel off my legs and then turn my head to the side to dab the ends of my hair. My eyes drift across the room to my dresser. The top of it is exactly the way I left it with one glaring difference.

My heart stops. I drop the towel. It lands in a lump at my feet. Fear chokes me, making it impossible to swallow. I stare at the tube of lipstick and feel my heart slam into my ribs like I just got electrocuted. I step toward it, my hand shaking as I lift the tube. I stop in front of it, not wanting to touch it. This was gone. The perv took it with him and now it's back.

My panties on my bike.

The words on my mirror.

Horror washes over me in an icy wave. I lift the tube of lipstick and slip the cover off. It's the cherry red. The tip has been smashed like someone used it as chalk. Terror courses through me and I drop the stick. It falls to the floor and rolls under my dresser. My hand slaps over my mouth to muffle a noise that sounds like a cross between a cry and a sob.

Frantically, I look around the room. There are no signs of forced entry, no broken windows, no opened locks on the windows, no nothing. My body acts like it wants to run. The muscles in my legs twitch. I turn toward the closet, deciding to get dressed and get the hell out of here. I'm never coming back. I'll never leave Cole's side again. And I'm telling Emma to frickin' move.

My veins are coursing with panic. As I turn toward the closet, I catch movement out of the corner of my eye. Edward pulls the door open. He stands in the doorway, watching me in my robe. My wet hair is plastered to my face. A shiver slips down my spine like an ice cube. I stare at him for a second, wondering if he's twisted enough to do this to me. I think I'm going insane and ignore the warning flags my mind is beating me with over the head.

Edward doesn't look at me. He looks past me, at the dresser, and asks, "I heard something fall. Are you all right?" I nod, too freaked to talk. I clutch my robe tighter at the neck. Edward finally turns and looks at me. "Did you get the grease off? Are you clean?"

Am I clean? That question would have pissed me off a few months ago. Now, it just sends a jolt of panic through my throat. I can't swallow. My mouth is so dry. My neck feels thick, like a log, and words won't form. I nod again.

Edward steps into my room, his body blocking the door. I feel like I'm cornered. I glance over my shoulder at the window, wondering how much it will hurt to throw myself through it. Logic intercedes and tells me that this is Edward. I know him. He won't hurt me. He isn't the one that's been messing with me. But, memories that seemed odd, or didn't make sense before, come racing back.

Edward showing up when he didn't know where I was. Edward finding me outside of Cole's. Edward showing up at the beach. Emma knowing things she shouldn't have known, things I never told her. The missing panties. The cherry red lipstick that he hates. The way he said he'd wait for me, that we weren't over.

My chest tightens. I shrink back from him, still not wanting to believe what I'm thinking. Edward looks apologetic. I don't understand why. He presses his palms together and then parts his hands as he speaks, "Good. I knew there'd be a day that you came home and I'd be here—that you'd want me here."

"Edward," I manage to choke out his name. I lift my hand without meaning to, the universal sign for STOP but he keeps coming toward me. "I need to get dressed. I have to be at court. Can we talk later?" My voice cracks. It's a pathetic attempt to placate him, to ward him off, so that I can run and never look back.

He stops in front of me, my hand pressing into his chest. Edward presses his hands on top of mine. "Now's as good a time as any. I heard what you said before—about not accepting his proposal."

"Edward, I—" I try to pull my hand away, but his fingers wrap around my wrist. Edward lifts my hand to his lips and brushes a kiss against the back of my hand. I yank harder, but he won't let me go.

"You're still in love with me. I know." He says it with complete certainty.

"I'm not!" I jerk my wrist again and stumble backwards when he releases me. A pained expression draws his dark brows together. It's like he won't accept that I don't like him, that he intends to have me anyway.

"You are," he insists. "You told him no. You dumped Jessie. I can forgive your infidelity, Anna, but I won't tolerate your lying." Edward's eyes blaze with fury. His arm swings before I see it coming and he connects with my cheek in a loud WHACK.

Stunned, I stagger back into the corner. My back presses against the wall as my hands cradle my cheek. Pain splinters through my face, exploding behind my eye. I'm trembling. I can't help it. Something is very wrong with him and I never saw it coming. I plead, "Edward, this isn't like you. You—"

He steps toward me and lifts my chin. I can't pull away from him. I've pinned myself against the wall. There's nowhere to run. No way to escape. "I'm a forgiving person, Anna. I'll take you back. You don't even have to ask, but… Do. Not. Lie. To. Me." His hand squeezes my face hard as he bites off the last words staccato, practically spitting in my face.

My body is jacked up. Part of me wants to attack him in order to get the hell away. The other part of me is falling to pieces, ready to fall at his feet and sob, hoping to God that he isn't this monster he seems to be. I don't decide what to do. My body trumps my mind, and before I know what I'm doing, I tear my face out of his hands and jerk my knee up between his legs. Edward sucks in air as he staggers back from me. I have enough room to get by. I dart for the front door, intending to run screaming into the street.

Before I manage to make it down the hall, Edward is behind me. I hear only the heavy thumping footfalls and my clamoring heart. Although the TV is blasting, I no longer hear it. My bare feet slip on the hallway floor as I race forward. The puddles that I tracked from the bathroom are still there, gleaming, and knock me off balance.

All I can think is *too slow, I'm too slow.* My lungs burn. It feels like I can't breathe. I want to scream, but I have no voice. It's like a nightmare, where I can't run fast enough. My heel hits the floor hard and I slip. Frantically, my arms swing as I try to regain my balance. In that moment, Edward catches my elbow and rips me back. I jerk to a stop and whirl around, my robe swirling at my hips. His fingers dig into my arms and it feels like he'll crush my bones. Edward's face is twisted with rage. His eyes are narrow and dark. Without warning, Edward releases me and throws me into the wall.

My head hits the plaster hard, but I don't feel it. Adrenaline is pumping through me. I should be able to toss a dumpster like a superhero, but I can barely stand up. Terror courses through my body, consuming me whole. It makes my movements erratic, like I can't decide what to do or when. I twitch against the wall, and then try to go for the front door again. Edward blocks me. He uses his body to pin me in place, this time guarding his assets more carefully.

"When are you going to learn, Anna?" he growls at me. Edward's knee pushes between mine, parting my robe. A sob bubbles up my throat, which seems to make him smile. He grips my wrists, slamming them to the wall above my head. I can't move.

I take a few breaths to steady myself and intend to scream FIRE at the top of my lungs, hoping James is home and that he can hear me over the TV. Last time James heard me scream, he came running. But before I can exhale, Edward's massive palm covers my mouth. I scream into his hand. I use my free hand to try and pry him off of me, but he doesn't move. I don't know what to do. I writhe beneath him, trying to break free. I can't stand it. My heart is racing so hard that it's going to explode. I don't think. I act. I listen to the crazy girl inside my head that's telling me to bite down and lock my jaw. I listen to her when she says to take my nails and shove them straight into Edward's eyes.

I bite and scratch. Edward yells, and shoves me hard. I'm flung across the hall and land hard on my hip. I don't look back to see him pressing his hand to his eye. I don't want to see the blood on his palm. I taste the coppery tang in my mouth. I know I made him bleed. I round the corner on my hands and knees and go to the kitchen to look for a weapon. Backing myself into the corner, I grab a knife off the counter. I'm standing by the time Edward enters the room. He comes at me again, even though there's a knife in my hand. It's the big, sharp one that Emma uses to cut up chicken. I don't want to kill Emma's brother with her chicken knife, but I don't know what else to do. Part of me thinks he'll stop, but the more feral part of me senses that he'll never stop.

I clutch the knife harder. "I swear to God, I'll stab you. Stay the fuck away from me!" I yell at him, spitting his blood out onto the floor when it leaks into my mouth as I speak. A streak of his blood must be smeared across my face.

Edward laughs, like I'm a child and he can do whatever the hell he wants. "You really intend to cut me?"

"You really intend to rape me?"

His jaw drops. Edward manages to look insulted. He steps toward me and presses his hand to his chest. "Rape you? That's what you think this is?"

"Yes, you crazy fucking bastard," I growl, aiming the tip of the knife at his heart. I wonder if I should be aiming for his stomach, but I don't move. My elbows lock. If he comes at me… Oh God.

He talks to me like I'm a child, too naïve to understand his intentions. "Anna, darling, put down the knife and we can talk about this. You obviously can't tell, but I wouldn't let anything happen to you. You're mine. I intend to keep things that way." He steps toward me. Lifting his hand, he says, "Give it to me, now."

I press my body backwards, but hit the cabinets. The draw pulls bite into my bare legs. I'm pretty sure my robe is hanging open, but can't look. I don't move. Edward's eyes lock with mine. He moves towards me. He's too close. I jab the knife at him when he's within an inch of me.

Edward stops. He lifts his hands like he surrenders. "Anna, please. You know me. You know I wouldn't hurt you."

"Then leave." My arms are starting the shake, but my hands hold onto the knife like my life depends on it.

"I can't do that," he growls. "I can't let you continue to act this way. Give me the knife or I'll take it from you."

"You'll have to kill me first—"

Edward rolls his eyes, "You are so damn dramatic." He lunges at me.

I don't want to stab him. He's my best friend's brother. It makes my arms turn to jelly when he slams into me. I hear him scream, but I don't know why. Edward grabs my wrist, but I don't let go of the knife. The blade is streaked with crimson. I watch it as Edward slams my hand against the counter, forcing me to drop the blade. It clatters as I watch in horror. Then, Edward reaches to pick it up. My pulse is pounding in my ears. My mind is screaming at me to run, while every muscle in my body is corded tight and bursting with panic.

I press myself against the cabinets and slip past him as he twists to grab the knife. I'm almost out of the tiny kitchen, but Edward grabs me. Pulling me into his arms, he turns me to face the counter top and presses the knife to my neck. It's already slick with blood. I suck in air and go still in his arms. If I move, he'll slice my throat. I know he will. Tears roll down my cheeks and I can't stop them.

Edward hisses at me as he slams my head down on the counter. The knife resumes the position, pressed to the side of my throat. I feel his hips press against my bottom and feel how much he wants me. I sob, and beg him to stop, but he doesn't. I hear the zipper on his jeans slowly open.

I try to scream, but can't. His weight on my back makes it so I can barely breathe. I babble incoherent pleas as my eyes blur with tears. He doesn't answer me. Instead I feel my robe being torn away and my legs being forced apart. He presses himself against me, and stays like that for a moment. The feel of him against me makes me want to vomit. My mind flips on again, and I stop begging him to let me go. I sniffle as thoughts fly through my mind. I try to think of any plan to escape, but nothing is within reach. I can't hit him. The way he has me pinned is going to make me pass out. I can barely breathe. Edward's arm is crushing me facedown into the counter. His leg is between mine, holding them open and the knife is at the side of my throat.

Edward's voice fills with triumph. I feel something warm and slick from him slip onto my side. Out of the corner of my eye, I see a trail of red drip from his waist and onto mine. I must have cut him with the knife before. The wound on Edward's side is deep and a steady stream of blood flows from it, but not enough to stop him.

"This is for your own good, Anna." He sounds like he's enjoying this. I can almost see the smile on his face. He leans harder on my back and I feel the pressure increase, and all the air is forced out of my lungs.

I try to scream, but can't. Tears overflow from my eyes and soak the counter. I open my mouth and try to yell, but it's barely a whisper. I tense and close my eyes, not wanting to be here, wishing to God that this isn't happening. I tune out his voice, not wanting to hear his words. He gloats that he's won, that he knew he'd have me in the end. I'm aware of his hands on my body, touching me in ways he shouldn't, as the world goes fuzzy at the edges. Blood pools under my face and gets in my eye. I don't blink. I don't writhe. He has me and there is nothing I can do. My heart feels like it has exploded. My body starts to go numb. His hand is on the back of my head holding me to the counter, while he leans harder on my back with his elbow. My arms dangle lifelessly at my sides. If he lets go, I'll fall to the floor.

When he moves his hips, I want to cry, but can't. No breath fills my lungs. I sag under him as he gets ready to push into me. Just as Edward's about to rape me, the knife disappears. Then the arm that's crushing my ribs is gone and my head falls to the side. I hear his voice—Cole—as I slip to the floor. I lay on my side and my eyes flutter open. One is caked with blood and won't focus.

It is Cole. I blink slowly, trying to focus. Cole disarmed Edward and is beating him. Edward is on the floor in front of the refrigerator, covering his face with his hands. He doesn't fight back. The knife is lodged in the wall next to the door way. Blood drips down the wallpaper in tiny red beads.

It takes me a moment to realize what's happening. It feels like time is moving so slowly. Cole's fist connects with Edwards ribs. Blood is everywhere—on Edward, on Cole, and on me. My robe is ripped any laying next to my feet. I want to reach for it. I want to cover myself, but it looks like Cole is going to kill Edward. Every time he punches him, Edward's head slams back into the fridge. Blood is flowing from a head wound and from his side where I stabbed him.

I push myself up and feel like I'm going to hurl. Before I fall, I catch Cole's arm as he's about to swing another punch into Edward's battered body.

"Stop," I manage to choke out. The muscles in Cole's arms bulge. I try to hold Cole back, but can't. I start to fall, and lean into Cole.

When he sees me, the expression on his face is filled with fear. "Anna," he breathes, pressing his hands to my face. He pulls me to him and kisses my face. "I thought—" his voice catches. "I saw you on the counter, and him on top of you. There was so much blood. I thought he…"

Tears steak my face. I can't stand the look in his eyes. I lean against his chest as I speak. "He didn't… I'm okay. He didn't stab me." I lean all my weight against Cole. After a moment, he supports me so I don't fall over and pulls back to look at my side. Cole presses his fingers against my skin, wiping away the blood. "I'm not bleeding."

Before Cole has a chance to respond, the door flies open. Two cops come in with their weapons drawn. The whole thing looks wrong. It appears that Cole is the one who attacked, not Edward. They move between us, pulling me away. They give me a blanket and I realize that I'm shivering, even though I don't feel cold. They mutter something about shock and call for an ambulance.

They move through the apartment quickly and spot Edward laying on the floor in a puddle of blood. They sit me on the couch and one officer stays with me. He speaks to me, but I can't focus. I pull the blanket tighter. I hear Edward's voice and fear shoots through me in a cold burst.

"Miss," the officer says again. Slowly, I turn my face and look up at him. I squint, trying to focus, "Do you know what happened?"

"Yes," I rasp. Everything feels like it's happening in slow motion. Every time I hear Edward's voice from the other room, I crawl out of my skin.

The cop watches me squirm on the couch, pulling the blanket tighter to my throat. "Which one of them gave you that bruise on your cheek?"

I'm falling apart inside. I can't hold myself together much longer. My voice shakes as I speak. "Edward. He hit me. He wouldn't leave. He tried to…," I choke on the words, but can't manage to force them out. I stare unblinking at the kitchen wall. "Cole came and saved me." I look at the cop. Tears start to flow again and leak out of the corners of my eye. My voice is barely a whisper as I start to shiver uncontrollably. "I need Cole."

Cole has been standing across the room. One cop is watching both of us. They don't want us talking to each other. Cole moves toward me, but the officer shakes his head. "I'm sorry. One more minute. The medics will be here and you can tell us what happened."

I nod and sadness sticks to my insides like syrup. I feel like I can't breathe. Cole steps toward me. He's shaking, probably with rage, but he says nothing to me. Cole's face is pinched. His arms are folded across his chest. Blood streaks his shirt with tiny beads splattered on his cheek. He looks older somehow. It's his eyes. They reflect his fear and it's all I can do to sit still without shivering. Guilt slams into me. I did this. I made this happen. Edward did this because I led him on. I had to do something, didn't I? My eyes sting. I blink and look at my hands as I twist them together.

The paramedics arrive and swamp me and Edward. They poke me, ask me things that I know—like my name, when I was born, and that kind of thing. Then they ask what happened. I glance across the room, but Cole has been separated from me. He stands with the officers who arrived earlier with his back turned toward me. Cole's speaking, but his eyes keep cutting across the room to me when he looks over his shoulder. Edward's blood is on Cole's shirt. They probably think Cole stabbed Edward.

"It was me," I croak, trying to speak loudly, but I find that I can't. The officers look at me and nod. Their eyes say they've seen this before. One smiles sadly at me and says that everything will be taken care of, to let the medics do their work.

Cole speaks to me, his voice filled with something that breaks my heart. “It’s all right, Anna. Let them look at you.”

The paramedic next to me wants me to open my mouth. They check my throat and offer a rape kit, but I wasn’t raped. Edward didn’t get that far. I want them gone, but no one leaves. They ask me what happened. I tell them.

My story stays the same, but the guilt is killing me. “I must have done something,” I say to one of the medics. “But I don’t know what.”

The guy is well over six foot and looks like he could carry a walrus up a flight of stairs. Anger flashes in his eyes. His voice is firm, but gentle. “There is nothing, and I mean *nothing*, that you could have done to make this happen.” I nod, but I don’t know what I think. Cole is hurt. Edward is hurt. I’m hurt. I stabbed Emma’s brother. I’m going to lose my best friend.

My head feels hot and then cold. I shiver and the world goes fuzzy. Heat travels up my body in a wave and the world goes black.

CHAPTER 6

The first thing I notice is the hard bed under my back. My fingers bunch the waffle-weave blanket in my hands. I recognize the texture. Between that and the scent of disinfectants, I know where I am. I peel my eyes open and look around the hospital room. I hate hospitals. I blink slowly and the world comes into focus.

Cole is sitting next to my bed, his arm dangling over the rail, stroking my cheek. "Hey," he says, and offers a weak smile. His hand feels so warm. I shiver and want to pull him into the bed with me. I want his arms around me. I want to feel safe, but I'm too weak to move.

"Hey," I say back, confused. I don't know what happened. I don't remember getting here.

Cole sees the questions in my eyes and says, "You went through a lot. They wanted to check to make sure nothing was broken, and then you passed out. Nothing's broken, but you do have a sprained ankle." He watches me, his eyes holding mine. I see the remorse in his eyes. He wants to say, *I'm sorry I wasn't there. I'm sorry I couldn't protect you.*

But he did. We both feel guilt that we shouldn't feel. I wish I could take that away from him. He saved me. I press Cole's palm to my cheek and lean into his hand. "If you didn't come…" I take a deep breath, "How'd you know?"

"You were late and didn't answer your phone. Emma texted and said you were grabbing suit, and that she had to leave you. Then, when you didn't show, I thought something was wrong. I raced over there and found him—" Cole's jaw tenses, and he stops speaking. He works his jaw for a moment and finally says, "When I saw you, you weren't moving. You were hanging there, limp. There was blood everywhere. My God, Anna, I thought he killed you." Cole's voice tightens as he speaks. It's barely audible by the time he's done. He rubs his hand across my cheek and takes a breath to steady himself. His gaze locks with mine. "I love you, Anna. I thought I lost you."

"You didn't," I say, my voice still raspy. "I'm right here. I'm not going anywhere, dude." I grin at him, but my face hurts.

"Stop cracking jokes, Lamore. You've got a couple of stitches in your cheek. You're not supposed to aggravate it."

I nod. "So, I have to ask how you kept my parents away."

"There's no force on earth that could do that. They were here fretting and pacing each other into a hysterical mess. I sent them to the cafeteria to get coffee. They'll be back in a minute."

I lean back into the flat plastic pillow and smile at him. It's a doped-up dreamy kind of smile. "I love you, Cole."

He opens his mouth to say something, but there's a knock at the door. The doctor comes in. He speaks to me and explains a few things and is gone again.

Before he leaves the room, I ask, "Can I go home?" I don't want to stay here a second longer than I need to.

The doctor looks back at me and nods. "As long as you have some help, yes. Stay off your feet for a few days until the ankle mends. No strenuous activities." His eyes cut to Cole when he says it, which makes me blush like my face caught fire. The doctor smiles and says to Cole, "Take care of her."

"I will," Cole replies. His blue eyes drift to me and he says, "I'll always take care of you."

Things feel different after the attack. I stay at Cole's. He pushes back the court date a week, until I recover. I look like hell. My face has been beaten and is all shades of awesome. My entire body is sore, aching in places I didn't even know I had. Cole keeps giving me ice packs and heating pads. I can't believe he talked my parents into staying at his place, but he did.

I'm laying on his couch, with a pillow under my head, when Emma comes over. She hands Cole a huge bouquet of mums for me. They're so big that I can't see her when she walks through the door. When Cole takes the flowers from her, Em sees me for the first time and gasps. Her fingers press to her lips as she mashes them into a thin line.

"You're not supposed to tell people they look like hell, Em." I want to smile, but I can't. I pull up the blanket and twirl the fringes under my fingers. I'm worried she'll hate me. Cole assured me that she wouldn't, but I'm still worried. I can't undo any of this. I wish it never happened. Before I can say another word, Emma grabs my hands and starts talking.

"I'm so sorry, Anna. I didn't know. I swear to God that I didn't—" Emma can't stop apologizing. Grief lines her face. Cole perches behind her on a stool. He flips through a magazine like he isn't listening, but I know that he is.

I cut her off, "There was no way for you to know. I didn't know. Nobody did."

"I should have known. He's my goddamn twin," she rubs her eyes with the heel of her hand. Emma's beautiful face is pinched, lining her forehead with wrinkles. "I should have known."

I know how she feels. I feel the same way. I don't know why I didn't see it before, why I kept dismissing the warning signs. They were there, clear as glass, and I ignored them. We both ignored them.

Cole turns the page of his magazine, and doesn't look up. "His mistakes are his alone.

You didn't do this to her, Emma. Edward did." Emma turns to him, her mouth hanging open.

"But—"

Cole shakes his head, "But nothing. You had nothing to do with this. From the moment I met you, you've been nothing but a great friend to Anna."

"I told her you were creepy."

"Good," he says. "You were looking out for her. You sure as hell wouldn't have done this to her. Blame the person who actually did it. He's not the guy you thought he was. Blood is strange like that. You'd think the apple doesn't fall far from the tree, but some apples do. They roll so far away that they they're nothing like the rest of their family." Cole's tone is firm. He's speaking about himself as much as Edward. I feel the pain in his voice. I want to throw my arms around him. I hate hearing him speak about his father, but Emma needs to hear this, so he says it. "Blood or not—twin or not—he's not you."

Emma's eyes fill with tears. It's what she needs to hear. She looks back at me and says,

"You're my best friend. You always have been…"

"I always will be."

Emma and I share a snot-filled cry. Cole left the room at some point after we use an entire box of tissues. Emma dabs her dark eyes. "I'm not sure if my timing is crap or not, so I'm just going to tell you." She takes a breath and pushes her dark hair over her shoulder. "I met someone."

My brows inch up my face. "Really? Who?" Emma is never serious about anyone, but I can tell in the way her posture shifts, in the way her shoulders shrink in, that this is important to her and she's afraid of what I'll think. "Tell me, Em. Who is he?"

"You already know him." She presses her lips together for a moment. After taking a deep breath, she says his name. "Jessie. After you two broke up, I saw him. We talked about you for a while, and then… I don't know what happened. He irritates the hell out of me, but I like him. A lot. I didn't want to date him until I told you about it, but then this happened and I didn't see you for a while." She glances up at me. "Are you mad?"

I forget myself and smile. "No, that's wonderful! I felt so bad for him. He's so nice, but Cole… I wanted Cole. I'm happy for you, Em. I really am."

She talks to me for a while longer and tells me about Jessie, about why she likes him. She's so excited that it's hard not to feel excited, too. Then she starts talking about her internship and the paper. "Then we ran this story on Sottero. Did you see it?" I shake my head. Emma looks around for Cole, and leans in, whispering, "I thought not. Apparently, it's gotten around her social circles that she's a two-faced bitch thanks to a loud-mouthed intern that quit a little while back." She winks at me and smiles, like it's wonderful. "Her clients don't want to have anything to do with her. She's been an icon for years. The article was about how the mighty fall from grace. A few other names were in there too. It was a business piece on the importance of being genuine and remembering where your next paycheck is coming from. It seems that the arrogant fall faster and harder than anyone. I guess the article kind of double-damned her." She smiles at me. "I thought you'd like that."

At first, I think I do. I mean, she deserves whatever bad things come her way. The woman is vile, but…

Em's jaw drops, but she snaps it shut, "Oh my God. You're too good. How could you not be happy that she got hers?"

I shrug. "I don't know. Maybe my brain is broken, but I can't take joy in someone else's misery, even if it is Sottero's."

Cole's voice cuts through the room, "And that's why I love you." He walks up behind me and kisses the top of my head.

"Yeah," Emma protests, "but Sottero had it coming. You can't be a heinous bitch for two decades and not have it come back to bite you on the ass. Besides, she dropped the lawsuit, right?"

Cole shakes his head, "No, she didn't."

Emma's jaw drops as her eyes widen. "What? Is she insane?"

"She's playing the victim, Em." I say. "If she gets the press to portray her in that light, then it makes sense why she's been so bitter and fucked-up over the years. All will be forgiven. Kiss, kiss and all that."

"No," Em replies, looking shocked. "You think that's her goal?"

"I have no clue what her goal is," Cole mutters. "She's Sophia. This is typical Sophia."

I shake my head, "It doesn't seem like she wants money. She has plenty of that…"

Cole says, "Revenge. That's what she wants. She wants to rip out my guts, the way I ripped out hers."

"What are you talking about?" I ask.

"She thought I was loaded. She felt duped, Anna. Sophia was slightly off-balance before, but now, with the papers running stories about her—she's like a rabid dog jumping at my throat."

"Sorry," Em says and shrinks back into the couch next to me, obviously feeling somewhat responsible for the increase in Sophia's crazy levels.

Cole says, "It's not your fault. It's your job. Besides, Sophia made her decisions and I made mine." Cole shifts his weight. He looks at me for half a beat and then his eyes shift back to Em. "How would you like to run a story for me?"

Em's dark eyebrow lifts. He's caught her attention. "What'd you have in mind?"

CHAPTER 7

My parents insist on checking in with me so frequently that my eye twitches. My cell rings and I pick it up. "I'm still fine, Ma. Cole's taking good care of me."

"Thank God!" She blares into the phone. I pull it back from ear a little, so I don't go deaf. Ma is one of those people who talks louder on a cell phone. She acts like it's a tin can on a string and practically screams into the thing. "I'm having palpitations out here worrying about you. I can't stand you living so far away. Come home, Anna. Your old room is—"

I groan, "Ma, I'm fine. Really. And what happened could have happened anywhere. It's not like the whole stalker thing was random. He went to your house for Chrissakes. He seemed sane to you, too." I shouldn't have said it. Reminding her of her conversation with Edward is like a kick to the gut. Apparently his obsession with me was worse than anyone thought. When the police starting questioning my family, my Ma recognized him.

Ma's voice shrinks back to a muffle. "I didn't know, honey. I swear to God, I had no idea that he—"

I cut her off, "That's the point. Nobody knew and it could have happened anywhere. I'm safe here, Ma. I'll be at Cole's for a few more days and then I'll move back in with Emma."

I don't pull the phone back in time for the wave of tyrannical threats that spew from the tiny speaker. I open my mouth to respond, but Cole snatches the phone from my hand.

He speaks over Ma, "Anna's not going anywhere, Mrs. Lamore." He says it so calmly, so certainly. I cock my head at him and feel extra stubborn. I don't doubt for a second that he thinks I'm staying here indefinitely, but I feel like I need to get on with my life. It feels like I'm hiding here.

I can still hear Ma yelling back, "She better not!"

"I assure you, she is staying here with me, and if she insists on leaving, I will deposit her on your doorstep. She's not going anywhere alone until Edward is behind bars. You have my word on that." Edward's out on bail, which is why things are kind of hard right now. No one wants to leave me alone so that he can take another go at me.

Ma's voice lowers and I can't make out what she's saying. Cole avoids my angry gaze until he hangs up.

Cole sighs and hands me back my phone. "When were you going to tell me this marvelous plan?"

I squirm on the couch and pull my knees into my chest. "Never." I knew he wouldn't like it.

"I thought so." He sits down next to me. "You can do anything you want, but it's so far from smart that I can't let you go back there. He's out on bail. Edward could come after you again."

"He won't" I say, staring straight ahead.

"You don't know that."

"Cole," I take a breath, and look at him. "I don't want to hide for the rest of my life. I want to get on with things and that means going back to normal."

"What if normal where here, with me?" His eyes are like twin gems, deep and clear. His voice is so sincere, so loving. Cole hasn't mentioned the proposal since that night. Too many things happened.

My lips tug into a small smile. I lean my head against his shoulder. "Tell me what that would look like. Things are changing right now. I don't even know what tomorrow will be like and neither do you. It makes it hard to dream right now."

His arms wrap around me. "All I do is dream, right now. I dream about having you in my bed every night and seeing your beautiful face every morning. I dream about that lawsuit vanishing and having that part of my life over. I dream of being someone else's son, with someone else's name…" he strokes my hair as I listen to him. He breathes, "All I do is dream. I'm living in a fantasy world as long as you're next to me. I can't stand the thought of you leaving."

Silence fills the room. It's not the awkward kind, it's the peaceful kind. Cole wraps his arms around me tighter and holds me like that for a second. When he moves to release me and get up, I stop him. My fingers brush his forearms and press him against me. "Hope is important, Cole. Don't feel bad about that. As for your name, have you thought about what you want to change it to?"

He looks down at me and smiles. "Dude. You inspired me and I had to pick that one. People can call me Mr. Dude, the artist."

I laugh way too loud and smack his arm. "You can't change your last name to Dude! Besides, if I said yes, that'd make me Mrs. Dude and I am so not doing that."

Cole grins. He sits and pulls me onto his lap. I turn to face him. His face is a breath from mine. "Oh? So you've thought about that a little bit, have you?"

I nod. "A little bit." My heart is pounding.

"And that's the only conclusion you've made?"

"It's a pretty good conclusion, right? There's no way in hell people are going to call me Anna Dude." I laugh and he smiles. It makes the corners of his eyes crinkle the way I love.

"So, then what would you have me do?"

"Pick a name that suits you, one that makes sense, and that you'd be happy to have."

"I'm not sure there is a name like that, Anna."

I want to smile, but I try to hide it. Taking his face in my hands, I say, "Lamore." I swallow hard, letting the idea sink in. I take a breath. The feeling that I'm falling won't hush. My stomach is in my throat. "I don't know what tomorrow will bring, but I know I want you in my life. I like my last name and what it stands for. Lamore's think love is worth fighting for, that love is worth more than life, that—"

He cuts me off with a kiss. Cole's lips press hard against mine and he pulls away grinning. "I would love to take your name. Wedding or not." He's not certain that I've accepted his proposal.

"Oh, there'll be a wedding. I thought I had to know everything before I got married. I thought that my life was going to be laid out for me, that I'd go to college, graduate, get a job, get married, have kids—in that order—but it didn't happen like that. I don't have much, but what's mine is yours…" he's still quiet, watching me. I want to choke or run or jump out the window. I blabber on, adding, "If you still want me."

Cole's eyes remain locked on mine. Without a word he stands up, with me on his lap. I scream as he chucks me in the air and catches me. He makes a very loud, happy, sound that almost sounds like a whoop, and whirls around with me in his arms, spinning in circles. We both laugh and scream. I cling to his chest and close my eyes, but it doesn't stop the joy from bursting like fireworks inside of me. By the time he falls onto the couch, my face hurts from smiling so hard.

I giggle, "Mr. Lamore, you're going to be a handful."

"Likewise, Mrs. Lamore."

CHAPTER 8

"Are you sure that you want me to run this, Cole? It kind of sets things in stone."

He nods, his dark hair falling forward as he moves. "It's a warning shot. She needs to see it coming."

"Who?" I ask. "Sottero?"

He nods. "She thinks that I won't fight back because I never have, because I'll lose my name. She knows my past and what that fucking name cost me." He glances up at Emma. "Sorry—"

"Don't apologize to me. I swear like a sailor. Anna made me tone it down so I don't offend her virgin ears." Emma flips her dark curtain of silky hair over her shoulder. Somehow she always manages to have this sleek look that could make a Pantene model jealous.

My face flames red, "My ears are not virgins." I hiss, and then realize it sounds weird and grin rather stupidly.

Cole's eyebrow lifts, "We'll need to discuss that later, Miss Lamore." I smack his arm.

We're sitting in Emma's apartment. It's the first time that I've been back home since the day Edward attacked me. Em cleaned the place up. There's no blood, but the smells and the way the light cuts through the blinds is identical. I'm glad Cole didn't want me to stay here. I think I wanted to do it to prove a point—that Edward didn't break my brain, that I'm not afraid. The thing is, I am, but the fear has changed. I know who he is and what he was doing now. Instead of feeling the choking panic, I feel jittery and stressed. It's like a nightmare that surfaces during daylight, even though it was scary when it happened, in the light of day the cold tentacles of fear are still laced around my throat. I shiver and Cole pulls me closer to him. We are sitting at the breakfast bar and Em is across from us on the couch.

Emma ignores our banter. "Well, if you're sure. Once the article is submitted, I can't take it back. That's all I'm saying." She waits, watching Cole.

"Do it."

The article is short. It mentions that famed photographer Cole Stevens is changing his last name. While it might seem like a public interest story to everyone else, to Sophia it's a bomb. It's telling her to drop her lawsuit, that Cole is going to fight back, and that she will lose. It's a very gentle, tactful way to warn her to back down. He surprises me with that, especially since Sophia is so vicious.

The article runs the day before the rescheduled hearing. I lift the paper and am surprised at the prominent location. The article is small, but Sottero v. Stevens has been in the papers on and off for a while now. I suppose that's good, that there's no way she'll miss it.

Cole sees me sitting on the couch with the paper. He has a cup of coffee in his hand. He lifts it to his lips and sips it slowly before asking, "Well? Do you think that was worth doing?"

"I don't know. Sophia seems kind of crazy. No one else will know what this means, but she will." I twiddle the edge of the paper between my fingers and look over it at him. "What do you want her to do, exactly?"

Cole takes a deep breath and sits at the table. The open floorplan makes it feel like he's not that far away. The living room bumps up against the dining room, and the couch where I'm sitting is positioned in between. "I want her to drop the lawsuit, but I don't think that'll happen." He looks at the black liquid in his mug. "Ya know, I can't help but notice that you didn't accept my proposal until *after* it was confirmed that I'd lose everything." He looks up at me. "I wasn't going to fight back, they seized my assets, and I lost many of my clients, and then you decided to stick around." He sounds like he can't believe it. He looks at me from under his brow, the steaming cup in his hand.

His tone worries me. It makes my stomach clench and twist. "Money doesn't matter to me, Cole. You have to know that by now. All my life, it's been this poison hanging over my head. I take what I need and nothing more." I shrug away the defensive feeling that's coming over me. "I just don't want it."

"You're afraid of it."

"Maybe," I say honestly. "There's a duality with money, like you can chose to have money or love, but you can't have both. They negate each other, or at least it seems that way to me. So yeah, maybe your money terrifies me a little bit." I look up at him. The expression in his dark eyes is difficult to read. I can't tell if I offended or amazed him. Funny how those look so similar sometimes.

Cole's eyes lower. He looks at his mug as he speaks. "That's part of the reason why I didn't fight back with Sottero. I really didn't want to. I thought I was being like my father, crushing a woman I already shattered. I never told Sophia that I was disinherited before I proposed to her. I couldn't, and she had no idea. It hit her like a train. The ring wasn't even taken out of the box. She slapped it from my hand, put it under her car, and ran it over. The look she gave me, Anna—damn—for the longest time I thought I deserved whatever she threw my way. My fortune, all of it was made because she inspired me in the first place."

A string of images form in my mind. A young Cole returning from the army, wearing that uniform. The Tiffany's box that was battered and locked in his safe. I blink these things away. They're his ghosts and I wish they didn't haunt him, but they do. I'm quiet for a moment and then something he'd said to me clicks into place. He owes her. He said it. He thinks that he's indebted to her in a way he can't repay. My mouth hangs open for a second and I think I understand. "She gave you your camera?"

He nods. "After I came back from the military, I was listless. I had nothing to do and nowhere to live. Sophia thought that I was on an international vacation for four years. I didn't correct her. I couldn't. She thought that I had no job because of my status, that I was a playboy like the papers made me out to be." His eyes flick up to me. "Maybe I shouldn't be talking about this, but I wanted you to know how I felt about it. I deserved what I got from Sophia, as far as I was concerned. I did fuck her over, in a manner of speaking. And the gag on speaking about the agreement to use my name and my disownment made it so I couldn't respond. I deserve this Anna." The way he says it makes my heart ache. I slip off the couch and hobble over to him. Cole's eyes seek mine, looking for answers that he can't find.

I sit in the chair next to him and take his hands in mine. "Listen, I don't pretend to know what's right and what's wrong here. I hear the guilt in your voice when you talk about her, but Cole, I just don't see it. Even if you led her on to think you were still the heir—which I don't think you did—it's been twenty years. She should have let it go by now. Even if she was burned, it's unthinkable to stay mad this long."

"I thought she loved me, Anna," he says, but I can hear it. He means, *Will you leave me, too? Have I deceived you so gravely that you'll crush me as well?*

The thread of insecurity is just that, a tiny string that tugs at Cole's past and connects to his present. I want to snap it. I want to cut that thread and let things fall where they may. "There's nowhere I'd rather be right now, than here with you. I'm not going anywhere. And if there's ever a time that we have too much money, that it's getting between us, we'll fix it."

"How?"

"We'll give it away. Cole, this is about us, now. I'm not Sophia. I want you for you—all of your kinky, sophisticated, sexy self—I want you. Nothing will ever change my mind. You think I'd share my name with just anyone?" I grin at him.

"You're too good for me."

I laugh. "I'd say the same thing about you. Apparently we both make each other better. Isn't that what love is all about? It seems we stumbled on the fairytale without even trying."

Cole smiles at me and something changes. I hear it in his voice when he speaks, "So, how far do you want to push this lawsuit? You want to just get her to back off or what?"

"Sophia's reputation is hanging by a thread. I think that'll do the most damage, if you want to do damage." I think about Sophia and how horrible she is, how incredible arrogant and bitchy she acts. Her clients are leaving her. They can't get away fast enough. One spark will ruin what she has left.

"Let's see where we stand tomorrow and decide from there." Cole puts his coffee down and pulls me onto his lap. He kisses the side of my face, and then holds me tight. I love every second of it.

CHAPTER 9

"Miss Lamore, you mean to tell me that you have never seen any photographs or negatives of my client, Ms. Sottero, wearing this ring?" The lawyer is as nasty as Sophia. She's a middle-aged lady with her dark blonde hair tied in a tight chignon at the base of her neck. Her gray suit fits her bean-pole body like a glove.

I shake my head and repeat myself, "No. I told you already." Cole's lawyer told me not to lie on the stand and I'm not. I didn't see Sophia in any recognizable state, on a photograph or negative wearing that ring. I saw a naked chick on canvas wearing that ring.

The lawyer is exasperated. She comes at me again, her perfect face cracking with lines of fury. She presses her palms together. I look at the judge for a second, but he seems bored. The old guy is looking at something in front of him. I wonder what it is before I look back at Blondie. "Miss Lamore. May I remind you that you are under oath?"

"You already have."

"Then, I must ask you to tell the truth. For the last time, did you or did you not see this ring in a photograph or negative of Sophia Sottero while you were in Cole Steven's apartment?" Blondie presses her pointer fingers to her lips and stares at me. If her eyes had lasers, I'd be dead.

"No," I say fervently, "I did not." I look to my lawyer who squashes Blondie's next needling of me since my answer is still no.

"Very well, Miss Lamore. Do you care to tell me how or why you recognized the ring my client was wearing the day you quit your internship at Sottero?"

"Why does this matter?" I blurt out.

Blondie opens her mouth to speak, but Cole's lawyer is on her feet. They quibble back and forth and eventually Cole's lawyer wins. I glance at Sophia. She looks mortified. I assume that Cole doesn't let his lawyer off the leash, ever.

"Enough," the judge utters. "If you have no further questions of this witness, that pertain to this case, she may be excused."

Blondie bites her lip and returns to her seat. The judge hurries me off. I leave the stand and exit the courtroom. Reporters aren't allowed near the courtroom, but they are close enough to snap pictures of me as I walk out. Ignoring them, I turn and walk the other way.

My heart is thumping. I'm lucky she didn't ask the questions differently. Sottero must have thought I saw something else. Maybe she doesn't know her photographs are paintings? I think about things as I stroll through the halls. I don't know how much time has passed, but I'm aware that I lapped the building as I approach the ladies room. I don't know how much longer Cole will be in there today. I walk into the ladies room to check my make-up. My eyes itch like crazy. The building has that old musty scent that makes my eyes water. I stand in front of the mirror trying to rub my eyes without messing up my eyeliner and mascara. I give up and rub like crazy, smearing one eye. After it stops tearing, I take a few things from my purse, intending on fixing it when I hear Sophia's voice behind me.

"I can't believe you perjured yourself for him." Her voice is flat, but I know she's livid. Sophia isn't supposed to talk to me, but she doesn't seem to care. "I know you saw that ring in those portraits."

I turn to her, half my face rubbed clean of make-up. "Why do you even care? It's not like…" *those pictures matter anymore.* I pause. It is like that. She wants those pictures. "Is that what this is about? Is that why you're trying to seize all of his property, for those pictures?"

Her dark eyes meet mine and don't stray. "I'll hang you for this. Every single person of importance in Manhattan will believe whatever I tell them about you. It was bad enough when your hysterical boyfriend came to me about your relationship with Cole and I called the dean. I thought he was using you. I didn't realize you were so devious, Anna dear."

Rage shots through me. She did that? Sophia called the dean and cost me my internship. I want to slap Edward. He completely fucked up my life. Was there someone he didn't talk to? Furious, I hiss,

"Devious? What is it that I was trying to do? Bed a man you broke?"

She laughs, "As if anyone could break that man's heart. He doesn't have one, Anna. Why do you think I'm standing here?"

"Because you're a money grubbing bitch."

She snarls, "He took everything from me. He'll do the same to you."

"If you think that I'm listening to you again, you're mistaken. I only do stupid once per person. Sorry, you used your turn already."

Sophia's eyes burn a hole in my face. "What will it take? A cut? You want his money? Fine. Consider it done. I've spent the past twenty years trying to erase that man and he won't surrender the only thing I want."

I stare at her. "Cole's changing his name. There's nothing stopping him from crushing you. He's not going to let you win. Not this time." I toss my make-up back into my purse, and turn for the door. Sophia grabs my elbow. I jerk to a stop. When I turn back to look at her, she's in my face.

"Those pictures will destroy me. I built my name around being opposed to trash like that. I can't be seen modeling in one of Cole's risqué pieces. Find it, give it to me, and this is over."

I yank my arm back. "Being a two-faced bitch is your own damn fault. If people find out, good for them."

CHAPTER 10

I'm sitting with Cole. We are at his favorite restaurant for dinner. It's quiet tonight. There are a scattering of people at the tables around us. They lean in close and speak softly. The candlelight flickers between us, highlighting his beautiful face. I'm wearing a little black dress with my glittering Chucks. It earned us strange looks when we walked in, but my foot is still swollen. When I hobbled, holding onto Cole's arm, to our table, the waiter made that ah-ha face. No one appreciates juxtaposition in attire, except hobos and artists. Cole smiles at me.

After we're seated, I look at my hands and then back up at his face. "I know we said we wouldn't talk about court tonight, but I need to tell you something." I haven't seen Cole since this afternoon. I didn't get to tell him what transpired between me and Sophia. "It's the paintings. She wants them."

He has a wine glass in his hand. He stops, mid-sip, and his mouth falls open. He chokes out the words, "What? Why would she…?" he falls quiet and then nods, placing his glass back on the table. He shakes his head. "I can't believe this. All this time, she wanted those pictures. Is that what she's been after?"

"Cole, I don't understand why she even wants them. It's not like anyone would know it was her. They were taken twenty years ago. Not to be mean, but she doesn't look the same anymore and with her anti-smut campaign, no one would think it was her anyway."

Cole smiles softly, shaking his head. His dark hair moves like it's caught in a breeze. I want to run my fingers through his hair and tug. However, I manage to remain in my seat and keep my hands to myself. He explains, "The original images showed her face. When I processed them and put them onto canvas, I altered the pictures to what you saw. They were supposed to be a wedding gift." He smiles sheepishly. "Yeah, I stopped planning ahead after that. Anyway, Sophia never saw the images, but she knows what we shot.

What you saw, well, those weren't the original crop lines. Sophia doesn't know what I have or what I don't—she's guessing—and after you mentioned that ring, she thinks you saw the portraits and assumed the worst."

An idea bumps around in my mind like a ping pong ball. It jumps back and forth, forming a cohesive plan. It pulls a smile across my lips. I lean forward and rub my palms together like an evil villain. "You want to freak her out and shut her up at the same time?"

"You're eyes are glittering in a savage, blood-thirsty way, Lamore. You're a little bit scary right now." Cole smirks as he says it. His foot gently brushes my good ankle and he winks at me. I smile back.

"What if you did a gallery show with those portraits—the version you showed me—as the center pieces? The unseen, early work of Cole Stevens. It could be the last show you do before you change your name. We could hype the hell out of it. People would swamp to it, including the media. Sottero would wet herself, until she shows up and sees what you did, which is spectacular by the way." I grin at him and tap my fingertips together. Maybe it's not diabolical, but it would get rid of her. Plus, it gives the world a glimpse of the Cole that I think is utterly fantastic. "Maybe she'll buy them all. It's the only way to make sure no one sees them again."

Cole stares at me. I can't tell what he thinks. Sometimes I wonder if he was made without a revenge bone. I think I have two. They're both pretty small and weak, but when put together, they can be kick ass. Besides, Sophia needs to get over herself. She needs to see that she's a hypocritical idiot. I know she'll love those paintings, as much as I know she never saw them.

"When?" he finally asks. The waiter comes by with our order. The food smells heavenly.

After the waiter leaves, I say, "This weekend. It gives us a few days to pull things together. I can alert Em and she can tell the rest of the news people. I'm not sure about the gallery…"

"I can handle that," he says cutting into a huge steak.

"And I want to design the invitations," I'm giddy, bouncing up and down in my seat.

I know exactly what I'll do. I'll use the left side of the purple painting that shows the curves of her waist and chest, but nothing else. They'll be elegant, black and white, with a touch of purple. The invitation will be written on sheer rice paper, and attached on top of the gallery image with a purple ribbon. Sophia will recognize it, but no one else will.

"Remind me never to cross you," Cole mutters, looking up at me.

"Dude, it's been twenty years. It's time for Sophia to learn her lesson already."

CHAPTER 11

The gallery is chic. That's the only way to describe it. The walls stretch up into a dark copper ceiling. The foyer walls are done in midnight blue with thick, flocked wallpaper that makes me want to reach out and touch the velvet. The color combination makes the place feel warm and posh. The way the light bounces softly on the ceiling gives the illusion of candlelight, but without the flicker. Once inside, there is a myriad of walls with different pieces of Cole's work hanging on each one. A single spotlight accents his art.

The series of works of Sottero line the center of the room. They stand out against gray walls, drawing the eye around the room. The entire show is breathtaking. As Cole leads me through the rooms, we enter the back wing. I stop short. There is a portrait of me—an image that was not in the LeFemme box. It's a painting of me with angel wings made from paint and seemingly random objects. The exposure is perfect. My skin has a silky glow and is perfectly smooth. A piece of silk covers part of my chest, while crystals cover the rest of my naked self. My hair is blowing and I look completely and totally awesome. If someone thought I'm a goddess, that's what it would look like. It is standing in a back corner, set apart from the rest. The entire show has a somber feel, like the artist feels lost. Looking at the rest of the pieces has a calming effect, but this one is different than the rest. It screams of hope and happiness. It doesn't belong.

"Cole, this shouldn't be here." I say, turning to him with my heart racing a mile a minute.

"I should have asked you. I understand if you don't want anyone else to see it—"

I take his arm, stopping him midsentence, and turn him toward me. Cole thinks I'm too prude to let him show it. "That's not it, Cole. You can leave it up if you want, but it doesn't blend with the rest of the show. Those works out there are all melancholy and pensive. This one…"

I don't know how to compare it. There is no comparison. The front of the show is all *tortured artist*, and this is *happy dude*. The only speck of black on the canvas is a crow that's in the tippie top of one of my wings. There are other things too, objects that mean something to me or us; a yellow sneaker, a tutu, a red ribbon. I can't help but smile when I look at it, and I want his last show to be amazing. This is so different that I don't know people will say.

Cole pulls me to him, wrapping his arms around my waist. "It's perfect. It's everything I was missing, everything that's important to me, now." He kisses my cheek lightly, searing my skin. My knees feel like jelly for a second and I lock them so I don't fall over. I smile at him shyly.

He says, "I have something for you." Cole releases me and pulls a black box out of his pocket. My eyes grow wide and I glance between his face and the ring box—that is totally a ring box. "You're the only woman who would accept a proposal without a ring." He grins and cracks open the lid.

Inside is the most beautiful ring that I've ever seen. It's not a traditional engagement ring. There's no single diamond set on prongs. Instead it's a glittering blue stone the color of Cole's eyes, set in white gold. It's so simple and sophisticated at the same time. My hands cover my mouth as I gasp. I don't know why I'm shocked, but I am.

I'm shaking too much to move. Cole reaches for my left hand. He pulls the ring from the box and slips it on my finger. It fits perfectly. I smile, stunned into silence before throwing my arms around his neck and kissing his face over and over again.

"It's beautiful." I breathe after we part.

"It's a diamond. I saw the color and that setting, and knew it was perfect for you, my beautiful bride." Cole leans close to my ear and presses his lips to my neck.

Someone says, "Ah-hem," and Cole pulls away from me with a wicked smile on his face. "This is the infamous Anna, I assume?"

Cole nods. "Frederick, may I introduce my bride-to-be, Anna Lamore." Fredrick extends a dainty hand toward me. He's five foot nothing with wavy black hair and tanned skin. His dark eyes glitter like he's stealing a cookie. I smile at him as we shake. “Anna, this is Frederick Supoe, the gallery owner.”

“It’s nice to meet you,” I say. “Thank you for arranging this show so quickly for Cole.”

“Cole and I go way back. There’s nothing that pleases me more. He never shows certain works and I can tell from looking around that this is indeed the lost works of a lost man.” Frederick folds his arms over his narrow chest and moves towards the painting of me. He taps his front tooth and then points to the bright painting, “Except this one. This one is the most brilliant.” Frederick stares at it like he’s awestruck.

I don’t understand. I step next to Frederick. We’re nearly the same height. I glance at him. “Why?”

He doesn’t look at me. Instead he continues to gaze at the canvas. “Any man can be lost. Any man can capture that emotion in film or paint, but it takes a much more to pull up from the ashes and start again. That’s what this says to me. It says we have a new Cole. The piece is symbolic of his new name, of his new life. The front rooms are filled with the secrets of his past, but this—this is his future." Frederick turns and looks at me. "You're an impressive woman, Miss Lamore. I hope you'll consider putting on a show here."

I'm flabbergasted. I open my mouth, but nothing comes out. Supoe's Gallery is the finest in the city.

When I make a squawking sound, Cole answers for me, "She would love to."

"I'll be expecting it." He winks at me before walking to the front of the gallery. It's nearly time to open.

I want to jump up and down. Glee spreads across my face. Cole takes me in his arms and swings me around. Cole and I laugh as we whirl in a circle. I've never seen him so happy.

CHAPTER 12

Emma arrives about half way through the show. The gallery is packed with people. She moves through, asking them questions and smiling. Periodically, the guy from the paper with the camera snaps a picture and they move on to the next person. I remain in the front, away from my canvas. I want the limelight on Cole. Besides, Sottero has yet to show her face. I would have thought that she'd arrive before anyone and snatch the pieces of her up.

I sit on a black bench in the center of the room. People move around me. I can hear them whispering about Cole's work, about how he's one of the most talented artists in New York. I'm happy for him. I can't stop smiling.

I don't notice her until she's standing next to me. "Anna, dear." Her voice is curt. Sophia Sottero stands rigidly at my side. She's dressed in her normal pristine suit. There isn't a wrinkle on the entire thing.

I don't stand up. "Sophia."

She doesn't look at me. Her gaze is on the wall. Sophia's eyes rake the paintings. Her body twitches with tension. "This was your doing."

"Maybe," I confess, and stare straight ahead as I cross my ankles.

"Is this because I helped the man who tried to rape you?"

My eyes cut to the side. I glance up at her face. A million emotions rage through my body. She mentioned that during her rant the other day. "No, but thanks for that. Getting raped is every girl's dream. You basically pushed me straight into him."

Her spine straightens more, if that's possible. "I didn't know."

"That's a pretty lame apology." I don't expect her to stay here chatting me up. She looks like she wants to slash the paintings and break every piece of glass in the place.

Sophia swallows hard, still keeping her chin high. "I'm sorry." Sophia doesn't blink. Her voice retains that hard tone she always has, but I can tell she means it. I say nothing because there's nothing to say, so I nod. She stands next to me for a few moments longer before saying, "You knew these weren't full nudes."

"And you didn't." Sophia doesn't respond. I add, "Nice way to try and get them—accusing a guy of molesting you and then trying to take all of his stuff when you notice he won't fight back—that he can't fight back. If you asked, I'm fairly certain that Cole would have given them to you."

She takes a breath, but doesn't look at me. "Things didn't work like that, then. These pictures would have ruined me…"

"If they were dirty like you thought, if Cole was the sleaze you made him out to be, but he's not and these are most definitely art. The only thing I find objectionable is the model. I heard she's a real bitch."

Sophia looks down at me. "Well spoken."

I stand and step in front of her. Sophia's dark eyes meet mine. "What are you going to do now? I heard you lost half your client base and the ones you retained hate your guts, but didn't want to lose their retainer fees." My brow lifts as I speak. I tilt my head to the side and fold my arms over my chest. “Incidentally, most of your staff showed up tonight and asked Cole for employment—the interns, too. It seems that you’ve shot your studio in the head.”

“Perhaps I did.” She doesn’t fight. It irritates me. Sophia has vinegar running through her veins. She’s as nasty as they come. This attitude is like her, but the comments are not. She turns and looks at the blue painting and says, “Where is Cole?”

Cole must have been watching us, because he steps up behind her and says, “I’m right here, Ms. Sottero.”

Sophia turns. She looks at Cole with fear in her eyes. “This is all that remains of that shoot, isn’t it?”

“It is.”

“I never believed you were capable of something like this. I thought everything with you would be panties and bare skin.” She looks at him for a second. “Apparently I was wrong and you have a very fearsome way of demonstrating that.”

“You forced my hand, Sophia. I would have left them unseen. I would have let things go, but you held onto the past so damn hard. It wasn't good enough to part ways. You had to destroy everything you touched."

"And yet, I didn't destroy you." She sniffles a sad laugh, "It's quite the opposite, really. My studio is in shambles and I'm financially drained from pursuing a lawsuit that's fallen apart. And your little intern here—"

"My fiancé," Cole corrects.

Sophia smiles slowly, "Ah, well, your fiancé tells me that my staff has left me as well." Cole nods, but doesn't say anything else. Sophia sucks in a ragged breath and puts on a fake smile. She looks at me and then Cole. "I'm terminating the lawsuit." Neither of us answer.

Everything she made crumbled in her hands. Sophia built her own empire and destroyed it, single handedly. Without another word, Sophia turns and cuts through the crowd, heading towards the front door.

When she leaves, I turn to Cole. Every muscle in his body is taught, like he's ready to fight. "Are you all right?"

He pulls me into a hug, "As long as I have you, I am." He kisses my temple and smiles before disappearing back into the crowd of people.

I smile at him and sink back down onto the bench again. The rest of the night passes in a blur. Several paintings sell for astronomical amounts of money, including the angelic portrait of me. The critics will write up their reviews tomorrow, but I already know what they are going to say. I heard the words fall from their lips. The show was adequate, but the piece that defined it was the last work of an earthly angel. There are pieces that an artist is known for, a piece that defines him and that piece is Cole's.

CHAPTER 13

Sottero makes good on her claim. The lawsuit ends as quickly as it started. Suddenly, there is nothing pulling at us, demanding our attention. We spend hours at the Long Island studio, sitting on the beach and watching the surf. Cole's fingers weave together with mine.

The breeze blows his hair into his eyes and he pushes it back. The sky is gray, like it might rain and the air is nippy, like some artic air came this way early. We're both wearing sweatshirts and jeans. The ocean roars, pounding waves into the sand. I wiggle my bare toes in the sand and look at his beautiful eyes.

"Have you given any thought to the wedding?" Cole asks me.

I grin at him and nod. "Maybe."

"When did you become so allusive?" He smiles at me and bumps my shoulder with his.

"When I figured out that it drives you crazy." I smirk at him in response and bump him back.

"Don't make the mistake of thinking that I won't pin you on the sand and tickle you until you scream. I will get a date out of you one way or another."

I laugh, not believing him, which is stupid. "Yeah, right," I mutter.

Cole launches himself on me and within seconds he has me pinned. I squirm, trying to pull my arms or legs, but I can't move. When Cole goes to tickle me, I say, "Don't you dare!"

Cole's fingers find my sides under the thick sweatshirt and wiggle against my skin. I laugh hysterically and try to get away. I manage to get an arm free and tickle him back, but the bastard isn't ticklish.

"Pick a date, Miss Lamore." The sky opens up and it starts to rain. The drops fall to the ground in big globs. The water is freezing.

"It's raining!" I manage to say, but Cole doesn't stop.

"So, pick a date." Cole tickles me more and I squirm in the sand. Rain pelts my face and feels like ice. I'm the worst tickle ninja ever. I can't get away from Cole and he seems impervious to tickles. So, I curl into a ball to attempt a lame defense.

Cole rolls me around on the shore like a cat with a ball of yarn. "Next summer?" he asks.

"No!" I laugh hysterically, tears filling my eyes. My clothes are soaking wet, as are Cole's. Water pours off his face and splatters on mine. "Winter." I'm breathing hard, but he hears me.

Cole's fingers stop. He climbs on top of me and tangles his fingers in my wet hair. "Winter?" he sounds surprised. It's fall. Winter is really soon.

"Yeah. I don't want to wait." I feel uncertain. The expression on his face is hard to read. "Is that all right? Did you want daffodils or something?"

Cole laughs, "I just want you, Anna." He presses his lips to mine and I melt into his arms.

DON'T MISS IT

To ensure you don't miss H.M. Ward's next book, text AWESOMEBOOKS (one word) to 22828 and you will get an email reminder on release day.

*****

THE FERRO BROTHER MOVIE

Vote now to make it happen!

http://www.ipetitions.com/petition/ferro/

*****

This is a fan driven series-when fans ask for more, there's more.

Go to Facebook.com/AuthorHMWard and join the discussion!

*****

FREE SAMPLE OF STRIPPED

Turn the page to read a free sample of Jonathan Ferro's story.

CHAPTER 1

CASSIE

Bruce claps his big beefy hands at us like we're misbehaving dogs. "Come on ladies! Hustle! The bachelor party isn't going to be much fun if we never get there. Damn, Gretchen, you aren't even dressed, yet?"

She laughs like he's funny, even though Bruce is as far from funny as a person could get. He's the bouncer at the club and on nights like tonight, he comes with us to keep the guys from getting handsy. Some rich brat out on Long Island rented us for the night. There are seven of us going to perform on stage, plus the stripping wait staff, and dear, sweet, Bruce.

Gretchen is piling her long golden hair onto the top of her head and securing it with a long bobby pin. She's strutting around half naked, as if we like looking at her. She smiles sweetly at Bruce and waves a hand, bending it at the wrist like he's silly. "Please, I'll be ready before Cassie even finishes lacing up her corset."

She tilts her head in my direction as I fumble with my corset hooks. Every time I manage to hook one, another comes undone. Whoever invented the corset should be burned at the stake. The stupid thing might look cool once it's on, but getting into it is a whole other matter. Add in the fact that mine is a real corset—meaning it has steel boning—and breathing isn't something I can do either. I got this thing because it was authentic. I thought that meant it had period fabric or grommets or something cool. It turns out that authentic means metal rods built into the bodice, guaranteed to bruise my ribs. Fuck, I hate this thing, but I refuse to throw it away—it cost me three weeks' pay at my old job. Plus, it's not like I wear it every night. We only pull out the good stuff on holidays and for special events like this.

Bruce turns his head my way and looks like he wants to pull out his hair. I'm nearly dressed, except for this contraption. My ensemble includes the candy apple colored corset, lace-topped thigh highs, and a delicate little G-string, coupled with heels that could be used as weapons. If I ever get mugged wearing these shoes, you can bet your ass that I won't run, not that I could. These are the things I think about when I make my purchases. Can this purse do some damage? Maybe I should skip the leather Dooney and grab me that metal no-name bag with the sharp corners. My roommate and I live across the street from a drug den. Don't even get me started on that. I know we need to move, but knowing it and affording it are two different things. In the meantime, I buy accessories that can be used as weapons.

Glaring at her, I reply, "Gee, thanks, Gretch." My fingers push the next bit of metal through the grommet. This one stays put.

She bats her glittering lashes at me. "No problem." Gretchen is tall and lanky with a larger-than-life super model thing going on. I hate her. She's a bitch with a capital B. It's all good, though. She hates me, too. It's difficult to be hostile toward someone that likes you. Gretchen makes it easy to hate her guts.

Me, I'm not a supermodel. I'm nothing to look at—my mom drilled that into my head a million times. I'm completely average with sub-par confidence, but I can act. I can fake it so that once I hit that stage, I'm as good as the rest of the strippers.

No, I didn't dream of being a pole dancer when I was a little kid, but my life took some wicked turns and here I am, dealing with it. There are worse things I suppose, although I won't be able to think of a single one when I'm letting a bunch of pervs rake their lusty eyes over my naked body. The truth is, I hate this. I'd rather be anywhere else, doing anything else. The gynecologist's office, sign me up. Root canal, no problem. I'll be there early and with a smile on my face. Anything is better than this.

Bruce lingers in the dressing room for too long, staring at his watch. His thick arms are folded over his broad chest as he watches the second hand tick off the passing time. He ignores Gretch's gibe at me. I may be newer, but I pull in a lot more cash and that's what the boss likes—lots of money. As long as I keep doing it, I have a job.

I finally get my corset hooked up when Beth walks by. She's already wearing some frilly satin thing. "Hey, Cassie. Do you want me to lace you up?"

Tucking a piece of hair behind my ear, I nod. "Yeah, thanks." She laces me in, pulling each X tightly, cinching me up until I can barely breathe. "Tight enough?"

I try to inhale deeply, and can't because the metal bars inside the fabric won't permit it. I nod and press my hands to the bodice, feeling the supple satin under my hands. "Yeah, tighter than that and I'll pass out—or pop a boob."

She laughs, "You're the only one who worries about stuff like that. You're so cute." She ties off the strings and tucks them in before swatting my back when she's finished. My boobs are hiked up so high that I can't see my toes when I look down. I grab my robe and wrap it around me as we head to the cars. It's going to be a long night.

The ride to the party is short. We're on the north shore of Long Island, not too far from the coast. There are tons of old homes with huge lawns and even bigger estate houses nestled out of sight between towering oaks and pines. The place hosting the party looks like a castle. We pass through the gates and drive around to the side of the house. The van stops and we're told the usual—go wait in the servants' wing until it's time.

Beth and I walk inside, shoulder to shoulder, whispering about the garish wealth that's practically dripping from the walls as we walk inside. Gretchen and a few other girls trail behind us, chattering about what kind of tips they'll make tonight. A party like this can line a girl's pockets for a month if it goes well, but for me it'll do more than that. You see, I'm the main event, the mystery girl in the pink room—the bachelor's private-party dancer. While my coworkers are off in the main hall, I'll be earning the big bucks. That's the main reason why Gretchen hates my guts. Before

I came along, she was the top stripper around here.

It's getting late, which means the party is well under way. Beth picks up a tiny sandwich off a tray as she walks to the back of the bustling room. "You think this guy knows what's coming?"

I shrug. "Like it matters, anyway? When's the last time we were sent away?"

"Uh, never." She pops the food in her mouth and chews it up.

I'm leaning against a counter top with my elbows behind me, supporting my weight. "My point exactly. Guys are dicks. They commit to marrying a woman, but this kind of crap the night before the wedding is okay." I roll my eyes as I make a disgusted sound, and straighten up. All of a sudden I'm talking with my hands and they're flying all over the place, "Tell me, why would a guy want a lap dance if he's in love? You'd think he'd only want his bride, but that never happens. He's always happy to have an ass in his face."

"Well, your ass is pretty awesome, or so I've heard." Beth smirks at me and glances around the kitchen. We're in the way, but there isn't anywhere else for us to go yet.

"Guys suck, that's all I'm saying."

"I know. You've said it a million times." She makes a *roaring* sound and shakes her fist in the air before turning to me and grunting, "Men. Evil."

"You're an idiot." I smile at her, trying not to laugh.

She points at me and clicks her tongue. "Right back at you, Cassie."

Bruce waves us over to the other side of the kitchen. "Cassie, Beth—follow me." We duck out behind him and follow the guy down the hall and slip into a little room. It's been done up in pale pinks with silver curtains, similar to the room I work in at the club. Since this is a party, Bruce added another dancer and I got to choose. While I work the stage at the front of the room, Beth will work the floor.

Bruce points a beefy finger at the stage and says to us, "Take your places, and remember that this client is the shit. Pull out all the stops, say 'no' to nothing. You got it?"

We nod in unison. The stage is elevated off the floor, with a few steps up at either end. It looks like the stage is new, built just for me. People usually rent those gray, make-shift stages that wobble when walked on, but not this guy. They spared no expense. The walls are lined with pale pink silks and illuminated from the floor. Clear tables flicker around the room with pink flames dancing within. It's seductive. The colors blend together, reminding me of pale flesh and kissable pink lips. As I climb the steps up the side of the stage and head to the silvery tinsel curtain, I call back to Beth. "Who is this party for again? And why is he the shit? I must have missed the memo."

She laughs as she's examining one of the lights within the glass table. It looks like fire, but it can't be since it's pink. She looks up at me. "Dr. Peter Granz, and he's the shit because he's a Ferro. Hence the swank party." Beth looks up when I don't answer.

I rush at Beth, nearly knocking her over. My jaw is hanging open as worry darts across my face faster than I can contain it. "Ferro?"

"Yeah, why?"

I'm in melt down mode. "I can't be here." I glance around the room and look at the door longingly. Before I make up my mind to run, I hear male voices approaching. Fuck! My heart pounds faster in my chest. If he's here, if Jonathan sees me—the thought cuts off before it finishes.

I'm ready to bounce out the window when Beth grabs my wrist and hauls me to the front of the room. She shoves me behind the curtain and hisses in my ear, "If you freak out now, Gretchen will steal your job. Snap out of it. Whoever this guy is, he isn't worth it."

The tinsel curtain in front of me flutters, but it conceals both of us for the moment. The male voices grow louder until the door is yanked open. The curtain rustles and I'm in full freak-out mode. He can't be here. He can't see me like this. At the same time, Beth's right. I can't skip out. Bruce will run me over with the van and there's no way in hell they'll ever give me another cent.

I stand there, frozen, unable to think. Every muscle in my body is strained, ready to run, but I don't move. My bare feet remain glued to the floor as I smash my lips together.

Then, I hear it—that voice. It floats through the air like a familiar old song. Oh God, someone shoot me. I can't do this. "You don't know what you're talking about. What guy wouldn't want a party like this?" Jonathan is talking to someone in that light, charming, tone of his.

"Uh, your brother, Peter. Do you know the guy at all? He's going to act like he loves it and get the hell out before you can blink." Glancing through the curtains, I can see the second man. He has dark hair and bright blue eyes like Jonathan. The only difference is their posture. Jonathan has all his weight thrown onto one hip with his arms folded across his chest. The other guy's spine is ramrod straight, like he's never slouched in his life.

Peering at Jonathan through the tinsel, I see a perfect smile lace his lips. "Sean, I know him better than that. Pete is going to love this. It's exactly the kind of party I'd want if I was getting hitched."

"Yes, I know." Sean's voice is flat. He glances around the room with disgust, and slips his hands into his pockets. "Don't say I didn't warn you."

"Oh come on! It's Peter. What's he going to do?"

Sean laughs, like he knows something that Jonathan doesn't. "Don't let that English teacher façade fool you, Jonny. He's as hot headed as I am. No one fucks with him. He's going to consider this a slap in the face, an insult to Sidney. Cancel the strippers before he gets here." Sean leaves the room without another word.

Jonathan Ferro lets out a rush of air and runs his fingers through his thick, dark, hair. The aggravated sound that comes out of his mouth kills me. I've heard it before, I know him too well to not be affected by it. That's the sound he makes when he knows he's screwed up, when he sees that he isn't the man he wants to be. There's always been this wall between Jonathan and his family. I guess he still hasn't gotten past it. Jon paces in a circle a few times and then darts out of the room.

"Holy shit." Beth looks at me and hisses, "What happened between you and him?"

It feels like icy fingers have wrapped around my heart and squeezed. I stare after him and utter, "Nothing, absolutely nothing."

CHAPTER 2

JONATHAN

Why does everyone think they know my brothers better than I do? I'm taking advice from Sean. How the hell did that happen? I'm walking swiftly down the long hallway, chin tucked, not watching where I'm going. The golden wallpaper appears to be glowing in the dim light. I run my hands through my hair and down my neck, and smack into someone.

When I look up, I'm ready to snap. "What the— Oh, it's you."

My closest friend, Trystan Scott, is standing in front of me. The guy is the brother I never had. He's not blood, but he might as well be called a Ferro because he's that loyal.

Trystan's wearing ripped jeans, a button down shirt with the top three buttons undone, and has way too much shit in his hair. "What the hell's going on? I thought the waitresses were supposed to be strippers. That was the coolest idea you've ever had. Imagine my disappointment when I rush out of rehearsal—away from the sexiest woman you've ever seen—and get here to find a bunch of chicks still wearing clothes." Trystan smirks and shoves his hands in his pockets.

I don't bother to answer him before resuming full speed down the hall. I have to find the guy from the club and cancel my awesome plan. Damn it, why does Peter have to be so difficult. Who doesn't want strippers at a bachelor party?

Trystan follows behind. "So, how's it going?" His voice has that teasing tone, which means he knows how well it's going.

"Nice hair," I throw back, and glance at him out of the corner of my eyes. Trystan makes a face and tries to smooth it down, but it doesn't move. "What'd they use, glue?"

His dark hair is sticking up all over the place. It looks like a porcupine toupee. "Something like that. I look like a fucking idiot."

"Yeah, but it's not the hair that does it—it's the make-up."

"Awh, fuck." Trystan swipes his hand across his eyes, trying to rub it off. "I forgot. I had somewhere to be—somewhere with strippers—so I ran over here as fast as I could." He smacks my arm with the back of his hand. "So, come on Jon, what's going on?"

"Apparently this isn't Pete's MO. I'm canceling the girls before Peter gets here. Sean said he'd bolt, that titties aren't his thing."

"Titties are his thing, but he prefers a certain pair." Trystan grins and looks over at me, pressing his hand to his chest. "The ways of the heart are—"

"And what would you know about that? You're a goddamn legend. You've nailed every chick from coast to coast."

Trystan's smile brightens, but it's like there's something he's not telling me. Ever since I met him a few years ago, he's been like that. He doesn't talk about his past much, but I don't blame him. From the papers, I know Trystan's dad beat the shit out of him when he was a kid, but that's about it. The guy keeps to himself, but somehow manages to get pussy whenever he wants. A shy rock star is a fucking oxymoron, but the women fall at his feet. What do I know? Maybe I've been doing everything wrong this whole time. I shake the thoughts away and enter the main room.

The music pounds through the air, vibrating through me. The dim lights make it difficult to see the guy I'm looking for. He should be back in the kitchen right about now. I lean into Trystan. "I'll catch you later."

"Whatever you need, man." Trystan grabs my arm and squeezes. He's saying he's got my back, even if no one else does. The guy might be a train wreck, but he's good people under all that shit.

I slap his back, "Thanks. Catch you in a few. We can hit the bar after Pete gets here, because I'm not walking around sober if there's only guys here." Trystan laughs and agrees to get smashed with me later. You got to love the guy.

I weave through the crowd. There are already some strippers posing as wait staff. A woman with a tray and way too much make-up on her face brushes my side and turns toward me. "Champagne?" Her cleavage is up to her neck and the thin white shirt she's wearing does nothing to hide the black bra underneath. Fuck, she's hot. I almost stop and flirt with her—almost—but I keep walking, because I'm not a total dick. This was supposed to be for Pete. I need to fix this before he gets here.

Sean falls in step beside me. "Tell me that I didn't see Scott at the bar?" Sean hates anyone who wasn't born with the name Ferro.

"Fuck off, Sean. He's my friend."

"He's using you." Sean's jaw is locked tight as he scans the crowd. "You're too naïve."

"You're an asshole." I'm not defending my friendship with Trystan or with anyone else. Sean acts like he knows everything, and he might be right most of the time, but he's wrong about Trystan. "The guy has his own millions. He doesn't need mine."

"He's unstable."

"You're unstable." I flick my eyes over to him.

Sean smirks. "Possibly."

"I can't chat about your mental health right now. I need to find the guy before all these girls rip their clothes off. Where's Pete?"

Sean laughs and points across the room. "He just got here."

"Fuck." I take off through the crowd, cutting through the guys, shoving some aside.

When I push through the kitchen doors, I see him. "Bruce! My man—change of plans."

Bruce is a huge guy and doesn't look pleased to see me. There are half dressed girls everywhere, slipping into their tear off waitressing outfits. Damn, this would have been so cool. Bruce has his thigh-thick arms folded over his chest. He glares at me. "No refunds."

"I'm not asking for one." I stand in front of the guy and feel like a toothpick, even though I'm not. Reaching into my pocket, I feel around for a hundred dollar bill. "I need them to keep their clothes *on*."

He gives me a weird look. "They're not supposed to be waitresses, Mr. Ferro.

They're strippers and are expecting the tips that accompany the occupation."

Okay, I grab a fist full of bills and slip them into his hand. Bruce takes it and sees how much I've given him. I ask, "Maybe they could be waitresses for a couple of hours and then head out?"

"Maybe, but this isn't going to help the girls you hired for the private room. They're expecting tips, and if you cancel them out, they'll have left the club for nothing. You have to make good over there." The guy's voice is dangerously deep.

"Done. I'll go take care of it." I reach out and shake his hand.

As I turn to leave he clears his throat. "And if you'd like this kept quiet…"

I reach into my pocket and slap more cash into his fist. Bastard. The large man grins. "My lips are sealed, Mr. Ferro. A suggestion?" he asks, and I nod as my gaze cuts across the room to the clock. "Keep at least one girl in that private room for your guests. This is a party that people will talk about. You don't want them to think you're a pussy. You've got a reputation that people know about. They expect a little something extra at one of your parties."

"And you know this because…?"

"Because I've got ears, Mr. Ferro. Every man here is wondering what your big surprise will be this evening. You need to keep something for them, don't you?"

I don't answer him, because I know he's right. "Fine, I'll go speak to them. You keep the girls out here clothed."

Bruce laughs and leans back in his chair. "Done."

When I get back to the private room, I push through the doors without really paying attention until I hear a voice—that voice. It's like being hit in the face with a wall of cold water. Whatever thought I had in my head is gone. Wide eyed, I look up and scan the room. Two women are tangled together on the floor, fighting. Well, no they're not fighting, not really. I'm not sure what they're doing, and they have no idea I'm watching.

My heart pounds harder as her voice fills my head and I try to see her face. My body responds the way it used to—that hollow spot in the center of my chest aches, along with my cock. I stare in disbelief, watching two strippers wrestling on the floor, and stand in shock because one of them is Cassie Hale.

STRIPPED IS AVAILABLE NOW

COMING SOON

BROKEN PROMISES

A Trystan Scott Novel

Read more about the characters in the **FERRO FAMILY:**

BRYAN FERRO

~THE PROPOSITION~

*****

SEAN FERRO

~THE ARRANGEMENT~

******

PETER FERRO GRANZ

~DAMAGED~

******

JONATHAN FERRO

~STRIPPED~

******

TRYSTAN SCOTT

~COLLIDE~

MORE ROMANCE BOOKS BY H.M. WARD

DAMAGED

DAMAGED 2

STRIPPED

SCANDALOUS

SCANDALOUS 2

SECRETS

THE SECRET LIFE OF TRYSTAN SCOTT

And more.

To see a full book list, please visit:

www.SexyAwesomeBooks.com/books.htm

CAN'T WAIT FOR H.M WARD'S NEXT STEAMY BOOK?

★★★★★

Let her know by leaving stars and telling her what you liked about SECRETS OMNIBUS in a review!

Made in the USA
Lexington, KY
07 May 2014